THE QUEEN OF THE ROAD

ALSO BY CHRIS TULLBANE

<u>The Murder of Crows</u>
See These Bones
Red Right Hand
One Tin Soldier
[Free online: Only the Dead Remain / 3 Ghosts]

<u>Stories from a Post-Break World</u>
The Stars That Sing
The Storm in Her Smile
A Sure Thing

<u>The Storm Who Rides</u>
The Queen of Smiles
The Queen of the Road *

<u>The Many Travails of John Smith</u>
Investigation, Mediation, Vindication
Blood is Thicker Than Lots of Stuff
Ghost of a Chance
The Italian Screwjob
A Dead Man's Favor *
Godswar *
John Smith Doesn't Work Here Anymore *
[Free online: SANTA WILL BURN!]

*Forthcoming

THE QUEEN OF THE ROAD

CHRIS TULLBANE

GHOST FALLS PRESS

NEVADA

GHOST FALLS PRESS

Publisher's Cataloging-in-Publication Data
provided by Five Rainbows Cataloging Services

Names: Tullbane, Chris, author.
Title: The queen of the road : a post-apocalyptic superhero novel / Chris Tullbane.
Description: Henderson, NV : Ghost Falls Press, 2025. | Series: The storm who rides, bk. 2.
Identifiers: ISBN 978-1-955081-19-1 (paperback) | ISBN 978-1-955081-17-7 (ebook) | Also available in audiobook format.
Subjects: LCSH: Life change events--Fiction. | Quests (Expeditions)--Fiction. | Self-perception--Fiction. | Fantasy fiction. | Road fiction. | War stories. | BISAC: FICTION / Fantasy / Dark Fantasy. | FICTION / Dystopian. | FICTION / Science Fiction / Apocalyptic & Post-Apocalyptic. | FICTION / Superheroes. | GSAFD: Fantasy fiction. | Dystopias. | Science fiction. | Road fiction.
Classification: LCC PS3620.U45 Q44 2025 (print) | LCC PS3620.U45 (ebook) | DDC 813/.6--dc23.

Book cover design by ebooklaunch.com

FIRST EDITION

*For Nami,
the reason for everything*

ACKNOWLEDGMENTS

This is my eleventh full-length novel, and I think the surest sign that I am blessed is that there are *always* more people to thank:

My angel-wife, Nami, the reason for everything.

Johanna, my dearest friend, who first coined the name Queenie for a very different character.

Jamie, who reliable sources have suggested may also be some kind of superhero.

Claudia, Denise, Kat, Kerri D., Mark E., Sam, Sarah, and Scotty B, who are all fabulous authors and even better friends.

Aaron, Cory, Mitch, Montie, Tom, and Ziggy, the best beta readers Her Majesty could ask for.

Anthony, Charity, Deanna, Joe, Kerri K., Kevin, Lara, Lynn, Mike, Nicholas, and Reid, for all the support they've given over the years.

Keith and Shawn, who remain perpetually trapped in a chat-channel hellscape of their own making and seem to be making a home of it.

And always last but never least, my parents.

Eleven books down, and so many more to go!

WHAT CAME BEFORE

Long decades after the Break reshaped the world and rewrote so many of its rules, the ageless mercenary known as the Queen of Smiles finished her life quest. In the City of the Sun, she confronted her creator, the dreamer who had caused the Break, and found not a god but a mortal.

Dr. Nowhere was just a man, one who'd been living with guilt and fear for all the decades since. He hadn't had a master plan or even a plan at all. Nor did he have any explanation for what he'd done or how. For why the Queen of Smiles had been born out of the Break or what she'd been created to do.

Minutes later, he was dead at the hands of a young necromancer, and any remaining answers died with him. When the Queen of Smiles rode away, she left her mission and sense of purpose behind. She went into seclusion, turning her back on the world.

Several years passed before an entirely different queen's armies annihilated the small town of Eclipse, killing everyone and burning the place to the ground. What the Crimson Queen's troops didn't know—what nobody knew—was that the Queen of Smiles had made that town her home and refuge. When the mercenary returned from an errand to find Eclipse a smoldering ruin, she hired herself for one final job: revenge.

She was joined on that mission by an enigmatic nomad named Two-Feathers, who left his clan to guard her back… by an old man living under the weight of his own guilt for the lives he'd taken as the Free States Cape, Evan Earthquake… and by an old ally and former lover, Jules, whose band of criminals came along for the ride.

The job took them to the city of New Memphis, the capital of the Crimson Queen's burgeoning empire. There, *honor among criminals* proved a myth as multiple members of Jules' squad turned traitor. Most died for their deeds, but one, a Crow named Selene who was possessed by the ghost of the Free States' worst serial killer, survived to disappear in the resulting chaos.

When all seemed lost, Evan's sacrifice gave the Queen of Smiles, Jules, and Two-Feathers the path they needed into their enemy's stronghold. There, a battle royale ensued. It ended with the Crimson Queen dead, along with a lot of other people. The Queen of Smiles became a ruler in more than just name, having claimed her revenge and earned a throne in the process. Two-Feathers assumed the role of ambassador to his own people, and Jules graduated from a life of petty crime to bend the law on a larger scale as a politician.

And then, months later, the Queen of Smiles left with Two-Feathers, and only Jules and her general, Cyrus, knew where she had gone and why. *Queen business*, they told the rest of the ruling council. *A diplomatic mission to introduce herself to our neighboring nations. She'll be back.*

And if Jules could sometimes be found looking westward from the balcony of his new mansion in District 1, an expensive glass of cheap alcohol in hand and a pensive look on his weathered face?

That's because he knew her *ultimate* destination.

1

The thing about the road is it's always out there. Always beckoning, always whispering sweet words, promises of fresh sights, sounds, and stories. It's simultaneously a retreat and a path forward, the jagged edge between what was and what may be. Dirty poetry written in asphalt, gravel, and soil.

A sect in what's left of Ohio believes there's only one true road, that all those other pathways are just tributaries snaking out from its body to carve their way through this broken land. I've lived long enough to know that's bullshit. It's always been bullshit. Ours is a continent of roads, the fading scars of the nations that laid them, but each of those routes has its own beginning and end.

Because that's the ugly truth behind the journey. None of us travel forever. We're watching the scenery blur past. We're counting the miles behind us and those left to go. We're hurtling towards our inevitable, inescapable demise.

Even me. Even though I can't see that end—when it's coming, where, or how—I know it's out there. I know it's waiting. I know this bike of mine will one day take me down a road where even the eternal storm can no longer rage.

But first, there's a man I have to see.

○○○

Bullets tore through the air, aimed at enemies that were either invisible or non-existent. One embedded itself in a tree nearby, spraying my shell with wooden fragments. The hoots and drunken cheers that followed from downhill suggested the shooters had either run out of ammo or chosen to proceed to the next stage of their celebration.

I traded glances with Two-Feathers, crouched a few feet further up the hill in a more defensible position. Before I could say a word, the nomad set his spear aside, drew the small knife at his belt and slid into the shadows.

I let the storm within me swallow my sigh. As a Stalwart, Two-Feathers was faster and stronger than most humans. And as a nomad scout, he was sneakier than I would ever be. The men and women camped below would never see him coming.

Which was problematic because I was pretty sure they worked for me.

I abandoned the shelter of the woods and marched down to them, eleven people in my army's gray camo uniforms. The fire they stood around was burning low, badly in need of fresh fuel, its flames barely sufficient to reveal the corpses that had been piled to one side.

Along with those corpses, the wagon that stood a dozen feet away, leaning precariously to one side thanks to a broken axle, told the tale. It was the kind of wagon merchants favored, and last I knew, trade hadn't been outlawed in my freshly won empire. Not when so much of our fucked-up economy depended on that trade and the merchants who kept it running.

Any question as to the drunkenness of my soldiers was answered swiftly enough; nobody took notice of the six-two woman in leathers and a motorcycle helmet until I was standing in their midst. Even then, one of them, scrawny and as dirty as the underside of my bike after a day's journey through muddy plains, actually tried to pass me a canteen. It was full of something that smelled even worse than the corpses just a few feet away. I accepted the offering and underhanded it into the campfire, where what looked like alcohol and smelled like black mold went up in an eruption of flame and heat.

As the soldiers fell back from the fire, I cleared my throat, the sound like a rusty saw being dragged across concrete. "Now that I have your attention," I announced, "I have some questions."

"You!" It wasn't the man who'd provided me the IED. This one stood further away, his face hidden beneath a helmet and more facial hair than any non-Beast Shifter should have felt comfortable having.

"Me," I agreed, letting my true face, the smiley-face decal on my visor, sweep the gathered soldiers. "I believe this is the part where you salute your queen."

"You're no more royalty than the woman you killed. We're done with all that nonsense, and we're done with you."

I took a step toward the loudmouth leader. "So, you're what now? Independent operators?"

His smile was slick and greasy. "Something like that, yeah."

"And the merchant?" I let the storm fill my voice, nothing but jagged steel and perpetual hunger.

"He and his family had themselves a real bad day." At least two of the other soldiers laughed, but most were busy spreading out to encircle me, focused if not quite sober. "If you hand over that motorcycle you're supposed to ride, maybe you won't have to join them."

Anyone who says stupid people have no place in an empire doesn't know a damn thing about empires... or people, really. Fact is, empires *depend* on stupid people. They're the lifeblood of society. It's only when they somehow find their ways into positions of authority that they become a problem.

And I wasn't in any position to bitch about traitors either. Not when the only reason the empire was mine was because of the individuals who'd turned coat after Delia Laine's death to offer me their support and their allegiance.

Stupidity was okay. Sometimes, betrayal just made sense.

But put the two together?

I wasn't much of a ruler, but even I had *some* standards.

And I'd heard enough.

As the first of the unit attacked—a woman who thought herself clever as she crept up on me from behind—I let my shell fall away, giving voice to the storm of steel and shrapnel that lived at my core. None of these morons were Powers, let alone the trained warriors my predecessor had dubbed her Immortals. Even if they'd been sober, disciplined, and halfway prepared, they wouldn't have stood a chance.

Blood sprayed as limbs were severed. Bodies fell to the earth like cuts of meat from an overly enthusiastic amateur butcher. Here and there, an attacker got off a shot, but those bullets either missed the storm entirely or added to its fury. When I reformed my shell, moments later, ten soldiers-turned-bandits had joined the merchants' family in death.

As for the eleventh? He was sprinting for the trees when a shadow rose out of the darkness, gleaming knife in hand. Two-Feathers wasn't half as good with a blade as he was with a spear... but then, he was *magic* with a spear, so that wasn't saying much. The last of my traitorous, murderous, and downright stupid army unit died in the darkness.

The nomad wiped his knife clean on the grass and joined me in the fire's swiftly shrinking circle of light.

"I'm starting to think," I told him, "that the former army of a warmongering teenager with delusions of grandeur isn't quite as dependable as General Cyrus would have us believe."

Cyrus being the Immortal who'd led the Crimson Queen's armies before bending his knee to me and mine in New Memphis. I didn't much care for the man, but I'd also given him the impossible task of restructuring a military originally built on conquest and expansion. A fuck up here or there was probably to be expected.

Two-Feathers sheathed his knife and sent his hands through a bewildering sequence of gestures that I'd have struggled to interpret even in the brightness of high noon.

"I'm not a speed reader," I reminded him. Most of my time in New Memphis had been dealing with the hideous bureaucracy that came with inheriting the third-largest empire in the continent, but there'd been good times too. And some of those times had been the mute nomad trying to teach me the signs he'd used to communicate with his own clan, recently augmented by a book of American Sign Language we'd recovered from one of my dead councilor's libraries.

Two-Feathers had picked up ASL with disgusting speed. I, on the other hand, still had a long way to go, even when restricting myself to only the reading part of the equation.

He went through the sequence again, this time at a pace that would make a snail seem lightning quick, and I didn't need the firelight to detect the glimmer of mischief in the nomad's dark eyes.

I knew mockery when I saw it, but hell if I was going to complain. Especially when the reduced speed really *did* help.

"More defectors?" I translated. I was pretty sure he'd had a lot more to say the first time around but nodded anyway. "Yeah. Rats fleeing a perfectly seaworthy ship."

He pointed to the wagon and the corpses that had already been stacked and set aside before our arrival and gave me another look.

"Merchants," I told him. "Did you see where their horses went? They would have needed at least one beast to pull the wagon." Either the storm had scared it off, it had fled sometime *before* our arrival, or… or my former soldiers had wanted an extra ration of meat.

Two-Feathers held up one finger, then pointed out into the darkness. I took that to mean that there'd only been one horse and it was somewhere out in the forest.

"Can you find it? The forest can have these bodies, but I'm not leaving supplies behind. We'll repair the wagon, and then we're going to need the merchant's horse to pull it. Unless your mount wants to volunteer for the job?"

The deadpan expression he sent me said more than any finger waggling ever could. The nomad disappeared into the trees.

ooo

A few hours after dawn, we had the wagon serviceable again, if far from peak condition. The merchants hadn't had much… just some simple textiles from villages on their route and a few finished products that suggested they'd been to New Memphis as well. We tossed in the few weapons that had survived the storm's fury, put the merchants' horse back into harness, and were ready to depart. But first…

The nomads didn't believe in burial, and it wasn't the sort of thing I ever bothered with, but it didn't seem right to leave the family there with those who had killed them either. So, I carried the three bodies—an old man, an old woman, and a mostly-grown boy—over to the remnants of the campfire and stirred the embers back into a blaze. Cloth swiftly caught fire and the smell of burning flesh filled the clearing.

Two-Feathers' strong nose wrinkled, and both horses shifted uneasily, but all three remained, as if paying tribute to the dead.

When there was nothing left but bone, I dumped dirt on the fire and reformed my shell. Stained leathers and a visor so dirty I shouldn't have even been able to see through it gave way again to pristine black and shiny chrome, the smile across my true face bright and far too wide.

Two-Feathers climbed up onto the wagon's seat and had it underway with a flick of the reins. His normal mount trailed docilely behind, and I mounted my bike to fall in at the rear, where neither that bike nor my presence would spook the new horse.

Behind us, the other eleven bodies lay where they'd fallen, in pieces more often than not, a gift to the scavengers already on their way.

○○○

It rained blood for the next three days. A more superstitious sort might have taken that as an omen, but I'd been around long enough to see it happen before, and multiple times at that. Society wasn't the only thing that had gone pear-shaped with the Break. The world as a whole was off-kilter and I'd yet to meet an egghead who could explain exactly why.

Two-Feathers was a quarter my age, at best, but he bore the meteorological shitshow with his usual stoicism, dark braided hair matted to his head, equally dark eyes squinted against the ongoing downpour. The horses—both his and the one pulling the wagon—were far less composed, but that described the flighty creatures in a nutshell. I'd never much cared for horses, and the feeling was mutual.

My real concern was, as ever, what the rain would do to the roads ahead of us, especially as we moved beyond my empire's inner territory. As much as it pained me to admit, muddy pathways were a lot tougher to traverse for motorcycles like mine than for mounts of the equine variety.

Over the course of those rainy days, we encountered two additional armed patrols. Each time, the storm rumbled inside of me, eager to add to the blood falling from the heavens. Each time, I had maintained my shell, ignoring the impulse for chaos and carnage.

These patrols were mine. *Actually* mine, in that they still considered themselves part of both my army and empire. Empire, because *queendom* sounded wrong, even to someone whose ears were mere nubs of flesh, unseen beneath the helmet that was my true face to the world. The soldiers had made way before me with haste and admirable discipline. One sergeant had even been brave enough to trade words and ask for news from the capital.

In some ways, the unit of traitorous assholes had been easier to deal with. I'd been the Queen of Smiles all my life but having actual subjects—even in an empire currently being reshaped into a fusion of democracy and monarchy—was a whole new experience.

Two-Feathers, on the other hand, took the whole thing in stride. He'd even spared a nod for the saluting soldiers, his trailing horse prancing like it was on parade instead of slogging through the blood-soaked mud with the rest of us.

On the third day, the rain finally stopped. Soon after, we reached the nearby fort and dropped off our recovered wagon. My nomad secured some hot food for himself, some additional grain for his mount, and a fresh charge for my bike while I met with the captain in charge. The buttoned-down man seemed to think *personality* was a sin against God and country both. And maybe he was right. I didn't know much about the military, especially the mundane soldiers serving in it, but their primary advantage against monsters and Powers both came from discipline and cohesion.

After verifying both the captain's name and the fort's, I fished the relevant packet of orders out of my saddlebags and handed them over. I'd made the mistake of telling Jules, who had turned his back on the honorable career of liar, thief, and bandit to become a politician, about my trip well in advance, and he'd promptly repaid me by spreading that information to Cyrus and the rest of the council. What had begun as a journey to Fallen Mexico to find the Lord of the Dead—the boy-turned-man-turned-monster I called Bakersfield—had instead become a full-fledged diplomatic pilgrimage with far too many stops along the way.

I had sets of orders for the handful of companies we would encounter on our journey, as well as scheduled meetings with the cartels of Kansas City *and* the patriarch of Wichita. Throw in Two-Feathers' request that we stop by his clan's territory, which had become an opportunity to strike some sort of treaty with the nomads as well, and this trip felt more like work than an escape.

Heavy is the head that wears the crown Jules had told me when I complained, and he'd rolled his eyes when saying it.

I still didn't know why I hadn't killed his aging ass yet.

○○○

We departed the fort the next morning and had several weeks of comparative peace and silence traveling northwest along the trails of what had once been Missouri. Without the wagon and second horse, we made better time, and the worst thing we encountered in that stretch was a sounder of wild swine, their hooves leaving burn scars on the earth and their eyes shining like pale-blue candle flames.

The pigs left us alone, which made them smarter than most of the people I'd met in my long life, Jules very much included.

Nights were spent out under the moon and pinpricked sky. Two-Feathers had a tent in his saddlebags, but the weather was mild, and he was young enough to be comfortable just about anywhere. I let him sleep by the fire and found my own space away from horse and nomad both. There, I shed my shell and let the storm loose from its confines. If anything thought to stalk us in the night, it heard the terrible rasp of metal on metal, the hungry clash of iron and steel, and wisely moved on.

For those brief weeks, it felt like we were all there was in the world. Just a queen, her nomad, and the road, the silent, ever-raging stars stretching above us into eternity. But like all dreams, this one had to end.

A few days later, we reached the town of Eastwood.

2

Despite its name, Eastwood wasn't part of any forest. It wasn't situated particularly far east either. Clearly, neither its founder nor its current residents gave a damn about truth in advertising. The town sat at the top of a rocky promontory, accessible via a series of switchbacks that led up to the main gate. Behind and below Eastwood was farmland, a wooden lift allowing the townsfolk access to those fields.

It was, as I had said several times to Two-Feathers and anyone else who would listen, a nothing little town, neither picturesque nor particularly memorable. On the other hand, it *was* relatively defensible. That was why it was still around, while places like Eclipse, the town I'd once called home, were little more than memories. There were things in the post-Break world that could just roll over anything in their path—high-ranking Powers or natural disasters like the horrors of Texas among them—but for everything else?

Security mattered.

Eastwood had it.

Eclipse hadn't.

And that was the way things went.

I tried not to hold it against the town as we began our ascent.

We were neither subtle nor stealthy, and by the time we'd made it to the tall wall and its equally tall gate, a small crowd had gathered above us. I recognized a bunch of faces from my last visit, although the past year had weighed heavily on them. That was humans for you; here, there, and gone forever in the twitch of a butterfly's wings.

Two-Feathers shifted in his saddle, as if he could feel my thoughts turn his way.

"Name and business?" called down one of the few faces I hadn't seen before, his features and eyes equally sharp.

"My business is my own, as always," I yelled back. "As for my name? Ask the greying bastard to your left. I've been told I'm pretty damn memorable."

The man who'd challenged me received a nod from the man I'd called out but then turned to Two-Feathers.

"And the nomad?"

"Is with me. And could clear your whole wall without even touching the spear at his side," I added, suddenly irritated. "Now, open the damn gate before I huff and puff and blow it down."

The grey-haired guard took over. "I didn't know you were a Weather Witch too… err, ma'am."

The smile across my visor lost a little of its shine. *The Three Little Pigs* was a story that had died out soon after the Break, long decades before any of these people had been born. It was one more useless piece of trivia that dear old Dad had baked into my brain when creating me.

"You can call me Your Majesty," I said, sidestepping the issue. "And you are?"

"Brockington. Keith Brockington."

I didn't particularly care—he'd probably be dead of old age before I ever made it back this way—but my ruling council had done its best to impress upon me that I represented more than just myself now. My actions as an individual reflected on my empire, our allies, and a whole bunch of other groups whose names they had harped upon at length and which I'd forgotten again almost immediately.

"The mayor was at home with his daughter," added Brockington, "but he's on his way now, if you don't mind coming inside and waiting."

At my nod, the gates creaked open. I walked my bike forward, trailed by Two-Feathers and his horse. I didn't remember Mayor Grawley having a daughter, but then, I didn't remember much about the man except that he'd been bald, sweaty, and kind of shifty. Now that I knew what it felt like to have others depending on me, I was willing to cut him some slack for his behavior during the town's last crisis. Still, he'd had a smile like day-old dishwater, grease just floating on the surface.

Which ended up being totally irrelevant, because the man who made his way to us, led by another guard, *wasn't* Mayor Grawley. Instead, it was a moderately tall Asian with soft eyes, a hard face, and black hair that had crept down past his ears. He offered us a small bow.

"Jae-Sung? You're mayor now? What happened to Grawley?"

He looked away. "He died several months ago. Lift accident."

"Tragic. And Cho-Hee?" I asked, speaking of the daughter Jae-Sung had had with Vo Binh Raya, his estranged wife and the now-deceased spymaster of one of Kansas City's cartels. The last time I'd been here, the only time I'd ever met Jae-Sung or Cho-Hee, I'd been delivering them a letter from Raya.

"She is well when she is not terrorizing the neighbor's boys." He eyed Two-Feathers but didn't ask the obvious question. "What can the people of Eastwood do for the Queen of Smiles?"

"I came to see *you*, not your town."

"Ah." He nodded. "Another letter?"

"Not this time."

I didn't have features for him to read, not unless the smile across my visor was even more expressive than I'd been told, but he stiffened anyway. "I see. We should speak in private then."

Two-Feathers led his horse to a hitching post just inside the gate, but I just dropped my bike's kickstand and yanked its battery, stuffing the latter into the saddlebags I'd carry with me. Garages weren't a thing out here, and Eastwood didn't get enough traffic to bother with stables. My bike would keep just fine on its own.

We made our way down the town's dirt-packed streets in silence. Even with his promotion to public office, Jae-Sung still lived in the same house, the faded paint a contrast to the bright flowers in its window boxes. As Jae-Sung led us inside, I could hear sound from deeper within, the sound of a little girl playing. The new mayor motioned us to the living room's badly worn couch and took a seat in the overstuffed chair next to it.

"How did it happen?" he asked me, once we were settled.

I didn't pretend not to know what he was asking about. "A Body Shifter, sent to replace her and help subvert the leadership of her cartel in Kansas City."

"Politics." He dropped the word between us like a curse.

"Politics," I agreed.

"And where is this Shifter now?"

"Ash." I let the storm fill my voice. "I cut it into a thousand pieces and set those pieces on fire."

"Raya would be pleased."

"You think?"

Jae-Sung shook his head. "No. I think she'd be too busy being angry that she slipped up and got killed in the first place."

That better matched my recollection, although the other woman's emotions had grown cold and barbed over the years.

For a few moments, we sat in silence, Two-Feathers all but forgotten on the couch beside me.

"Who sent the Shifter to Kansas City?" Jae-Sung finally asked.

"Why? Are you going to seek revenge?"

"I don't—" He looked away, unable to bear whatever he saw reflected in my visor. "No. That was Raya's world, not mine. I have a daughter. She is what matters. Even so, I want to know."

"Delia Laine. She called herself the Crimson Queen."

"I've heard of her. Mayor Grawley was convinced we would one day join her empire." He cocked his head, looking from Two-Feathers to me. "*Called?*"

"Turns out two queens was one too many. Call it justice or revenge, as you like. Either way, she's worm food and I'm not."

"And her armies?"

I shrugged, my leathers loud in the small room. "I'm a queen in more than just name now. Conquest's off the table for the time being. We've got a lot of things to get sorted out first."

There was a thump from the neighboring bedroom, followed by a sharp, shrill cry as strident as any noise the storm could ever make. Jae-Sung rose to his feet, knees cracking. "One moment," he said.

Two-Feathers watched him go and then turned to me, fingers flashing. It took a few tries, but I got the gist of his question.

"Yeah," I told him. "That's the ex-lover of Raya. You remember the cartel spymaster killed in Kansas City?"

His fingers flashed. I caught roughly two words of ten and made my best guess. "I think he's been expecting her death for a long time. There aren't a lot of people who grow old in that place."

He frowned, waved at the other room and then pantomimed a person walking away.

"Oh. There aren't a lot of people who grow up right in that place either. He got Cho-Hee out and Raya… well, she let them go."

Two-Feathers grunted, the only audible noise he'd made since we reached Eastwood. Even now, I had no idea what he thought of the whole situation.

A few minutes later, Jae-Sung came back. A better person might have asked him if Cho-Hee was okay, but I could hear the little girl playing; I simply waited in silence.

"Thank you for giving me the news," he said, and if his voice was rougher than before he left, I wasn't going to mention it. "Is there anything I or Eastwood can do in return?"

"News wasn't the reason we came," I said, sidestepping the question as I turned to the saddlebags on the couch next to me. The metal box Two-Feathers and I had dug up months earlier was on top. I pulled it out, opened the lid, and passed it to the town's new mayor.

I'd removed the unintelligible blueprints from the hidden drawer, as well as the pouch of gems and one stack of coins from the main compartment, but even so, he looked down on enough gold to buy Eastwood a dozen times over.

"What is this?" he whispered.

"The treasure Raya mentioned in her letter to you."

"I gave you that treasure in exchange for your services against the raiders who threatened our town."

I looked at the gold in his lap and then up again. "It was too much," I said, voice flat.

"Ah. The balance."

I didn't say anything. I didn't know Jae-Sung, not really, and he didn't need to know that *balance* was no longer the law of my life, that the rules Dr. Nowhere had once established for me had died with him.

Jae-Sung turned to Two-Feathers for further explanation, but the nomad's poker face was almost as good as mine. Eventually, the older man removed a half-stack of coins and then passed the container back over.

"The gold is yours," I pointed out. "*All* of it. If you don't want it, use it to buy Cho-Hee something nice. Like a small country or a hundred ponies."

"Or a future."

"Right. Or that."

"That is what I'm doing," he said.

It was my turn to trade looks with Two-Feathers. The nomad remained singularly unhelpful. "I don't follow."

"These coins," he said, holding up the half-stack in his hand, "will keep us fed and clothed and prosperous for the rest of our lives. I am hoping the rest can do the same for Eastwood and my daughter."

"Then why give them to me?" I didn't remember the man being quite so enigmatic before he'd become mayor. Politics really *were* a sickness.

"Taxes for the foreseeable future, in exchange for our town's admission into your empire."

"I'm sorry?"

"Eastwood is vulnerable. The bandits you killed last year weren't the first and they won't be the last. Nothing matters more for my daughter's future than security and opportunity. You and your armies can offer that."

I wasn't sure what to say. Under Delia, most towns had been forcibly conquered, their populations taken and sent through processing camps where they became provisional citizens of the empire. If there was an existing protocol for peaceful annexation, I didn't know what it was.

Thankfully, I had people to figure that shit out for me.

"Agreed," I said, visor trained on the man sitting across from me. "But only if you tell me what *actually* happened to Mayor Grawley."

The long pause that followed was telling.

"Does it matter?"

"It does if the new mayor wants his town to join my empire."

"It's like I told you. He fell," he said, looking anywhere but at me. "Off the lift. Sometime during the night. The farmers found his body at the base of the cliffs in the morning."

"And?" Inside my shell, the storm shifted and raged.

"Jonas, his second, disappeared too. The assumption is that he might have had something to do with the mayor's accident. An argument that went bad, perhaps."

"That's the assumption. What's the truth?"

For the first time in a long while, Jae-Sung's eyes met mine, and they were anything but gentle. Next to me, Two-Feathers went still, a hair's breadth from violence.

Eventually, the new mayor relented. "Grawley was obsessed with this very treasure. He had one of his men steal Raya's letter from my home and then sent a posse down south to find whatever she had left buried. They ran into some kind of trouble along the way. Only one made it back, and he returned empty-handed, but that wasn't the end of the matter. One night, I overheard them talking about sending a messenger to Kansas City. They were planning to use Cho-Hee as leverage to get the money they felt they deserved."

"Raya would have skinned them alive."

"Yes. And then she would have come and taken my daughter away. Our daughter. I couldn't let that happen. I'm not a part of Raya's world or yours, but—"

"You killed two men," I said as gently as I could, all the metal gone from my voice. "You did it for your daughter, yeah, but don't kid yourself. That world you're talking about? Blood is the *only* price of admission."

"I did what I had to," he said, the unsteadiness in his voice a counterpoint to those words. "I don't regret it."

"Surprisingly few people do." I didn't mention that Raya had been dead long before Grawley's men would have made it back from their failed treasure hunt. I wasn't sure if that knowledge would change his thoughts on committing cold-blooded murder. "So, after Grawley died and his man *disappeared*, the town just put you in charge? Nobody suspected anything?"

"I'm sure some did—and still do—but the mayor's popularity had been fading for a long while. That may be why he became so fixated on the idea of treasure in the first place. I offered to fill the vacancy, shared some of my ideas for improving our town, and the people voted me into office. But as much good as I've tried to do for Eastwood, none of it compares to the benefits we would gain from joining your empire. Roads, security, access to medicine and technology…"

I hadn't been sure what to think of Jae-Sung the first time we met, and I remained unsure. He'd left Raya and Kansas City's criminal government behind to raise their daughter in peace… and then killed two men to protect that peace. Still, I couldn't find it in myself to blame him for either action. And what I thought of him was largely irrelevant. Fact was, the empire could do with another outpost of civilization between it and Kansas City.

"Keep the gold for now," I said, setting the box aside. "Give it to the people I send to discuss the particulars."

"What people?"

"I have a council to handle running my empire, and *they* have a whole company of bean counters. I don't have the foggiest what our taxation system looks like, assuming one exists, but whoever gets sent to speak with you will be able to hammer out a deal." And then, because he *was* the father of Raya's only child, "I'll make sure that deal is favorable."

"And what about my actions? What about Grawley and Jonas?"

"They're dead. The world moves on."

"That's it?"

"I'm not a priest or a sheriff, Jae-Sung. I won't arrest you and I can't offer absolution. I just wanted you to be honest with me." I stood with another creak of leather. "And now, we should be going."

"Are you sure? I'll be starting dinner soon, and you and your… friend… are welcome. It's not much, but I suspect it will be better than anything you might eat on the road."

I *didn't* eat, on the road or otherwise, but his offer gave me pause. I wasn't traveling alone anymore; hadn't been since a nomad I'd known only by face had inexplicably left his clan to follow me through hell. And Two-Feathers *did* eat, sometimes enough for three people.

I swiveled in time to catch the hopeful light in my nomad's eyes before he reclaimed his usual deadpan expression.

"I promise I won't poison either of you," added Jae-Sung.

And if the joke was particularly dark given his recent confession, well, he'd found the right company for that kind of humor.

3

Dinner was simple but plentiful enough to satisfy my young nomad. Cho-Hee vaguely remembered me from my previous visit but spent most of the dinner making big eyes at Two-Feathers. Not that I was going to blame her for that; I found him a damn pleasant sight to look at too.

Through unspoken agreement, neither Jae-Sung nor I mentioned Raya. I didn't know what the little girl knew of her mother, if anything, but I wasn't going to be the one who told her she was dead.

I watched as the three of them ate together in the kitchen and then, when dinner was winding down, excused myself to head outside. I didn't need to breathe, not really, but I took a deep breath anyway when I hit the street. The house was cozy enough, and clearly well-loved, but just a few hours inside and I'd already felt like the walls were closing in.

The street wasn't much better. From inside Eastwood, I couldn't *see* the road, but I could feel it. Could almost hear it calling. Cool air and unseen vistas. Silence, save for the hum of an electric motor and tires on dirt, gravel, or the occasional stone. Danger and bloodshed and possibility lurking over every hill.

I'd missed all that during the long winter months in New Memphis. Jules could have his mansion, his comfortable life, and his impossible dreams of a harem, but the road would always be my home. That too was hardwired into me and unlike everything else, it showed no signs of fading.

But I had responsibilities now.

Haloed by light from the lantern at the door, I dropped my saddlebags into the dirt and dug through them to find a stack of leather-like hides, strangely warm to the touch. I peeled the top one off and placed it before me on the ground. It looked innocuous enough, strange patterns inscribed into a thick, roughly scraped hide.

I pulled off one of my riding gloves and let it fade from existence, a piece of my shell that was momentarily unnecessary. Then, I unsheathed the knife I kept in my packs for when things needed to be cut not shredded, and cut a line across my bare palm, blood welling to the surface. Slicing your own palm is a really stupid fucking idea, whatever the Free States vids might say, but when your body is just a construct that you can reform at will, such concerns fade away. The only impediment is pain, and there's no avoiding pain.

Not in this life or any other.

As I held my palm out, blood dripped down to splash onto the rough hide. Each drop was absorbed by the leather on impact, the material greedily drinking down the nutrients I provided. A few seconds later, cracks formed in the leather, and then it split apart entirely to reveal a metal-and-flesh insect-like creature with over a dozen sets of paper-thin leather wings. Seven of the thing's eight legs were metal, but the last was a twisted, nailless, human finger. An array of cameras, clustered together like an insect's eyes, whirred as they focused in on my visor.

I reformed my shell, healing the cut and replacing the missing glove at the same time, then spoke to the cameras.

"Cyrus, Jules… I need a diplomatic envoy sent to the town of Eastwood. It's a few days northeast of Kansas City. They've asked to join our empire in exchange for protection and want to pay their taxes up front. Someone needs to figure out how that works. Also, their mayor, Jae-Sung, is an… acquaintance. Make damn sure the soldiers accompanying the envoy are on their best behavior and that you give him a fair deal."

I had barely gotten my words out before the creature took to the air. Its many wings created an audible buzz as it streaked off into the night sky, headed to where its bonded pair was stored in New Memphis.

Communication remained a problem in the post-Break world, especially outside the confines of both my empire and the Free States. *This* had been my solution for the past dozen or so years, but I wouldn't hate finding a more modern solution. Like Wichita's enormous radio tower, maybe. The only thing more disturbing than Legion's techno-organic creations was the man himself. His city, Old Baltimore, had long since been transformed into a giant petri dish for the Technomancer's experiments. I'd been there once and would never go again, and not *just* because I'd robbed the man of a whole bunch of his tech on my way out.

That had been back when Dr. Nowhere was still alive. Legion had stiffed me on a job and *balance* demanded I find appropriate compensation.

There were four devices left in my saddlebags, their receiver pairs waiting in New Memphis. Each was single use unless one of our engineers figured out how to crack the things open and recharge them without killing the organic bits, and that made them damn near priceless. I hadn't planned to use one already, but that was the road for you. You rolled with what it gave you and kept moving.

Two-Feathers was as quiet as the wind, but I sensed him emerge behind me anyway, standing in the doorway.

"I'll head back in soon," I told him.

It was too dark to read subtle finger signs, but he patted his chest, pointed at me, and made the gesture I now took to mean *go*. His expression made it clear it was a question, not a request.

"It's fine," I told him. "It's too dark now to make it down. And I didn't want to deprive Cho-Hee the evident pleasure of meeting you… or deprive you of a homecooked meal. Can't have you wasting away to nothing, after all."

He made another face and left the doorway to scoop up my saddlebags and hand them over. For a while, we stood there in the dim circle of light and let the sounds of a town settling down to sleep wash over us. The storm rumbled inside of me, anxious to be free, but I maintained my shell, the nomad's silent presence a momentary shield against the road's call.

"Tomorrow, we'll start for Kansas City," I told him, though he'd been as much a part of the route planning as me. "I'll make my scheduled appearance with the cartels. Are you still okay with heading to your clan after that?"

Two-Feathers nodded, but for just a moment, he looked uncomfortable. He hadn't been back to his clan's territory since leaving it to follow me across the Badlands. What little communication we'd had with the clan since had made him the ambassador to my empire, but that seemed more a matter of expedience than anything else. I didn't think either of us knew exactly what sort of reception he would get.

"You helped dethrone the greatest threat to the clans since the Break," I reminded him. "*All* of the clans, not just yours. I don't know how they'll feel about an official treaty, but if they don't at least welcome you like a damn hero, they're fools."

He nodded, but even I could tell his thoughts were elsewhere.

ooo

Jae-Sung's house only had two bedrooms. Rather than displace the man like I had on my last visit, I chose to sleep in the living room with Two-Feathers. After a lengthy, if one-sided, argument, the nomad agreed to take the couch. I found a comfortable seat in the easy chair, moving aside the stuffed rabbit Cho Hee had left behind.

I don't sleep, not really, and I wasn't going to let the storm free in someone's home either, so I spent most of the night alone with my thoughts, gazing into the darkness, sensing the people around me more than seeing them. Two-Feathers' deep, even breaths were a comforting background noise that almost drowned out the rumbles and grumbles of the metal within me.

I hadn't been sure how the nomad would react to Jae-Sung's confession. Two-Feathers had a strong sense of right and wrong that made him a poor fit for my business—or my old business, anyway— but he also had a heart as big as his chest. After a night breaking bread with the other man, it looked like the latter had won out, no doubt helped considerably by the bright-eyed little hellion who Jae-Sung had killed to protect.

I didn't know how young Cho-Hee was—in my limited experience, *childhood* was just one big grey area, accompanied by too much noise and almost as much mess—but if she had anything of Raya in her, then her peers in Eastwood were going to be put on notice once she had grown up.

I fished a pouch of gems out of my saddlebags and looked through the pretty rocks until I found one that gleamed blood-red in the moonlight streaming through the windows. It was the size of a fingernail and fit perfectly into the stuffed rabbit's plush paws.

May she have a better life than you did, Raya.

I knew for a fact that ghosts existed. Whether Raya's was still out there was more of a question. Wasn't sure I believed in anything beyond spirits when it came to the afterlife either. But some of the nomad clans left offerings for their ancestors; I could do the same for the few people I'd held onto, the handful of dead whose names stayed with me, even as time blurred the lines of their faces and stole the sound from their voices.

Living forever wasn't all it was cracked up to be.

My gaze strayed back to Two-Feathers' sleeping form. There were too many questions he had yet to answer. I didn't know why he'd left his clan to join my suicide mission against the Crimson Queen. Didn't know why he'd stood by me through so much, despite our differences… his heart bright and pure as only the young could manage, mine the endless spiral of a tornado touching down in destruction. I didn't know much about my nomad, and the limited communication his signing had made possible hadn't done a thing to unlock the man's secrets.

I wasn't sure I cared anymore though either. He was with me. He was true, dependable in a way that not even Jules had been. And he was decades away from the slow, lingering death so few humans survived to face. We still hadn't so much as petted, something my all-too-human-feeling shell reminded me of almost nightly, but this was his road as well as mine. We'd travel it as slowly as needed.

To a point, anyway. I was patient, not a fucking saint.

Deeper in the house, Cho-Hee tossed and turned in her bed while Jae-Sung's quiet snores filled the air of the other room. A wind briefly shook the wooden walls of their small home, but no one was awake to hear it but me.

I couldn't set the storm loose in someone's home and didn't want to interrupt Two-Feathers' sleep by trying and failing to sneak out, so I stayed in the chair as the hours passed. I let my consciousness float from one subject to another, less thinking than simply being, my mind wandering even as my shell held shape.

I'd had worse nights.

Better ones too.

ooo

When dawn broke, I was up before anyone else, and if my leathers made getting out of that chair a noisier proposition than it would have otherwise been… well, I'd already let Two-Feathers sleep the whole damn night away.

A tired Jae-Sung joined us soon after to show Two-Feathers to the outhouse. I was waiting on their return when Cho-Hee padded into the living room, her old footed pajamas now replaced with a marginally more grown-up set of hand-me-downs. She wiped the sleep from her eyes and yawned, barely even looking at me as she climbed into the chair beside me to cuddle her stuffed rabbit.

"What's his name?" I asked her, trying to keep the metal from my voice as I looked down into eyes so much like a young girl I'd once known. "Your rabbit?"

"Bunny." Her voice was sweet in a way Raya's had never been, innocent in a way that Raya's mother, Bian, had trained out of her daughter by the time she could speak. Looking into those eyes, I found myself wishing my dead friend could see her child… even as I also recognized she'd been right to let her go.

"I gave Bunny a present to hold onto," I said, tapping the ruby in the toy's grasp. "I want you to keep it until you're older, okay?"

"Is it *magic*?"

I shook my head, but she was entirely focused on her rabbit and his gem. "It's just a pretty ruby, but it's yours. A gift for a special little girl."

"And for Bunny."

"Yes. And for Bunny."

I wasn't sure what I was trying to accomplish, any more than I was sure that the girl was old enough to remember this conversation. Most likely, the ruby would end up lost beneath her bed, abandoned along with whatever other toys Jae-Sung had made for her before or after Bunny. And yet…

Thankfully, footsteps on the front porch derailed that thought before it could fully form. The men had returned.

Two-Feathers was first through the door and he stopped dead at the sight of us, me in the chair with Cho-Hee practically in my lap, murmuring nonsense words to her badly worn rabbit. The look on the nomad's face…

Something twisted inside me, and I wasn't sure why.

"Cho-Hee," said Jae-Sung, stepping past the other man's still form. "Let's get you some breakfast. Our guests have to go."

"Tea?" asked the little girl, directing her question to both Two-Feathers and her father.

Jae-Sung looked my way, but I was already shaking my head. "We need to be on the road."

"I'll pack some bread for you to take then."

I would have said no, but I'd seen how much Two-Feathers enjoyed that bread the night before. And besides, I'd just given Jae-Sung more money than I had ever encountered in a very long lifetime on the road.

It had been the right thing to do—or at least what *I* decided was the right thing—but a bit of bread in return didn't seem unwarranted.

4

Several days later, Kansas City spread before us like a festering boil on the Earth's skin. The shanty town that encircled the more established districts was as chaotic as ever; fights and parties and shakedowns happening under both the late afternoon sun and the watchful eyes of the cartel that was supposed to be enforcing the peace.

The city hadn't always been like that. At the beginning of the Break, it had been a pleasant enough place—good food, good people, and things to see and do even as the world fell apart. The loss of multiple cities, first to the Dream, and then to the Break that followed, changed all that.

Suddenly, Kansas City was a prize, and prizes exist to be won. The six cartels that controlled the city were just the latest victors in that contest.

I killed my motor before we began our approach and looked to Two-Feathers. "Have you ever been *in* Kansas City before?"

He shook his head, dark eyes never leaving the chaotic sprawl.

"Normally, I'd suggest you avoid it at all costs. There's not a lot of love for the clans here. But you're with me, and I'm expected. Just…" I sighed, blowing out air I didn't technically need to breathe.

"Chances are, you're going to see some things during our visit here. Things you won't agree with. This is not a nice place and the people who run it *like* it that way. Try not to start a war, okay?"

He sent me a look and slowly went through a sequence of signs.

"That wasn't a *war*," I told him. "It was just a job. A job that happened to end with me ruling an empire."

The nomad didn't seem impressed with the distinction.

"Regardless, Kansas City is useful as it is. It's a shithole, yeah, but it's *everyone's* shithole. Neutral ground for multiple nations, as long as nobody pisses off the cartels. And I want it to *stay* neutral."

And by *I*, I really meant my councilors. Not that I disagreed with them, this once. The cartels were a menace, and their city was even worse, but it was *contained* chaos and *contained* excess. Las Vegas before the Break, before the desert had come to life and reclaimed its streets.

Two-Feathers pantomimed zipping his mouth shut.

If I'd had eyes of my own, I'd have rolled them. My nomad was a regular comedian. I didn't think he was truly ready for Kansas City, but then few people ever were. I didn't want to leave him behind this time, not when the talks with the cartels were scheduled to take multiple days.

"Just… stay behind me and look pretty, okay?"

He grinned.

I swallowed a growl and turned my attention back to the shanty town ringing the city, to the tents, the people, and the makeshift grills where meat of unknown origin was being charred to within an inch of becoming pure carbon. It was a madhouse as always, but I quickly spotted a cartel patrol, working its way through the bedlam. That was to be expected… there was money to be made out there.

The problem? Their colors were green and silver, not the orange and black I'd been expecting.

"The Diablos are supposed to be in charge of the east gate," I said slowly. "This week and next. The merchants' wagon and our night in Eastwood has us behind schedule, but not by *that* much. So, why is the Horde out there today instead?"

I didn't expect Two-Feathers to have an answer, and he didn't try to offer one. The truth was, I was planning to meet with all the cartel leaders, not just one, so it didn't matter too much who I ran into first. But it was a change from the expected, and my long life had taught me to be cautious of moments like that. Whatever had changed—and why—bore investigation, and *that* meant getting to someone in the know.

A year ago, that would've been Raya. Now, I had other options. Not *better* options… just other ones.

I turned my bike away from the city and rode north into the woods, a silent Two-Feathers and his less-silent horse following along.

"We'll leave my bike and your horse here," I said once we'd found an empty space a good two to three minute's ride into the forest. "Send someone to get them later and bring them in after us. It'll be easier to sneak in on foot."

He showed some signs, then repeated them at a pace regular people had a chance in hell of following.

"Yeah," I replied. "I'm not sure what's going on, but I don't trust it. Better to link up with one of our observation posts inside the city than to push forward blindly."

Delia Laine, the Crimson Queen, had once had a significant presence in Kansas City… a military base, even before her forces started trying to buy the city out from under the cartel leadership. Something had gone very wrong, years before I'd gotten involved, and that complex had been destroyed, but there were other units still sprinkled throughout the city's districts, and Cyrus had given me the information needed to contact them. If we could reach the nearest safehouse, we'd have the information we needed.

Of course, the only thing more recognizable these days than my bike was the shell that sat atop it, especially the black leather and the fiberglass and chrome helmet that served as my face to the world. So, even as Two-Feathers was dismounting, I went to his larger saddlebags and pulled out a bundle of cloth.

As much as I hated to admit it, Jules had given me this idea, back when he'd snuck me into New Memphis in the sunshine yellow dress and bonnet he'd decided would make a fitting bride gift for his non-existent future wife. Hell if I was wearing a dress again, now or ever, but my usual clothes were a layer of my shell and could be dismissed just as easily. I let the black leather fade away, the dappled sunlight kissing my nude form, and then went a step further, removing my helmet and watching it disappear like smoke on the breeze.

My face was a horror show, like a candle left out too long in the summer heat, courtesy of a creator who'd moved on too early to new flights of fancy in the dream that destroyed the world. Even the half-shadowed sun was overly bright on eyes that didn't see, on lips that wiggled and wriggled of their own uncertain accord. Around my face, I wrapped a long spool of black fabric—some sort of silk blend straight from the tailors of New Memphis. I covered those eyes, the uneven cheekbones, the unfinished nose, and the mouth that drooped beneath like rotting meat.

By the time Two-Feathers had turned my way, I was covered again, from the neck up anyway. I could hear his breath catch at the sight of my form, could feel the weight of his regard, but for the hundredth time in the past year, the nomad didn't take the initiative.

We were going to work on that if I had anything to say about it. I wasn't exactly responsible for the body I'd been given, but I'd still enjoyed the appreciation of the men I'd chosen over my long life.

I took my sweet time pulling on the rest of my outfit: a long-sleeved hoodie in rough dark grey cloth, a pair of pants in the same color—specially commissioned because women my height just weren't an everyday thing, even in New Memphis—and a black leather belt that brought it all together.

I didn't know a thing about fashion, and cared even less, but the tailor had sworn this outfit hit the sweet spot between flattering and nondescript. And given that I had practically been able to smell her fear throughout the whole fitting, I didn't *think* she'd been lying.

On my feet, I kept my riding boots, as comfortable as if they were a part of me… because, of course, they were.

When the show was over, Two-Feathers pulled more clothing from his saddlebags, this time a tunic-length shirt in deep green that did almost obscene things to his shoulders while hiding his more traditional nomad garb beneath. The new shirt looked a hell of a lot better than the monstrosity he'd been gifted by a sweet-eyed mayor's daughter a year earlier in a town named Greenburg.

There wasn't anything we could do about his long, braided hair or the color of his skin, but Kansas City was a melting pot. Hopefully, he'd fit in well enough.

"We'll wait for dark," I told him, leaning back against my parked motorcycle. "Sneak in through the shanty town, make our way to the safehouse, and find out what's going on. Sound good?"

He nodded and pulled out a branch piece he'd stripped of its bark a day earlier. His namesake spear was set aside, but he unsheathed the knife at his belt and started carving. Within minutes, he was lost in his whittling, focused on bringing out whatever shape it was he saw in the branch's lines.

"Good talk," I murmured, knowing he'd hear.

I resigned myself to a long, quiet wait. We had hours until sunset, but I didn't feel like reviewing any of the information packets

Cyrus and Jules had sent with me. And I was dressed in actual clothes, which precluded me unleashing the storm. That left wandering the woods and increasing our chances of being discovered… or just standing here in silence, watching my nomad carve wood while wearing the shirt I'd had made for him.

For the first time in my very long existence, I wondered if I should find a hobby.

ooo

Sneaking into Kansas City on foot was a lot easier than sneaking into New Memphis had been. No gates. No real walls. Nothing that would pass as an organized checkpoint in any other bastion of civilization. The tents of the shanty town gradually gave way to more established, if run-down, buildings, precarious pathways replaced by streets and dark, trash-filled alleys.

Kansas City's security wasn't found in fortifications or structure, but in the formless chaos itself. It lurked in the push and pull of the many-limbed mob that made up its population, in the predators who charted courses through that milieu, closing in on the easy marks who'd never return from their 'night out in the city', and most of all, in the fact that the cartels' forces were as unpredictable as the city they patrolled. Without routines or true discipline, those well-armed patrols relied upon manpower and the knowledge that every step deeper into the city made it that much more likely visitors would find themselves caught in their net.

To wander freely through a district required a piece of rope in the ruling cartel's chosen color. They called them colors or bandanas, because I guess *bracelets* wasn't quite macho enough for such hard-bitten people. Each was good for only the specific week, and traversing the entire city meant buying six bandanas, one for each of the cartels.

Of course, even with my disguise, I wasn't going to risk an encounter with the Horde… not until I knew why they were in control of the east gate this week instead of the Diablos. As Kansas City's newest cartel, the Horde had a reputation for bloodthirst that was only partly seeded in what they'd done to their predecessors, the Aztecs. It wouldn't take much to set them off.

Thankfully, our targeted safehouse was only a few blocks inside the city proper. We got some looks as we made our way there—Two-Feathers as much as me, for once—but managed to avoid any encounters of the cartel persuasion.

The safehouse was as run down as the rest of the buildings on its block. More, maybe. While Raya had lived to the north, across the river, in a neighborhood that at least gave a polite pretense of peacefulness, most of the east gate had been beat to shit over the years, patched up by talentless amateurs, and then beat to shit some more. A sign over the battered door advertised the building as a general store— Shaky's Sundries—but the windows were boarded up and only a little bit of light leaked from within.

It was late, but not *that* late, so I tried the handle. It was unlocked, and the door opened inward to reveal a claustrophobic storefront, a narrow aisle leading between metal shelves that had clearly been cut down and repurposed from wherever they'd originated. A guard stood just inside the door, hairy enough to be a Beast Shifter stuck in mid-transformation, while a smaller man stood behind the counter at the end of the lone aisle.

I left Two-Feathers to trade grunts and measuring looks with the guard and headed for the man in charge.

"Shaky?" I asked, keeping my voice pitched low to hide the metal that so often filled each syllable. The storekeeper was maybe five-foot-four at best, gaunt like he'd spent the last forty nights crawling through the desert. The neatly cut grey hair atop his head was counterbalanced by eyebrows that hung over his eyes like untrimmed planters. He had the guts of a clock spread across the countertop in front of him.

"What gave it away?" he asked, his voice far smoother than the rest of him. As his gaze traveled up the length of my disguise and landed on my carefully wrapped head and face, the left side of his face twitched spasmodically.

"Lucky guess," I said.

"Right. So what can I do for you and your man? Maps? Food? We've had a pretty good run on rat these past few days, so that's on special."

"We're tired of rat." I made a show of looking around, despite the coverings on my face. "I was hoping you'd have a snipe or two instead."

Twitch notwithstanding, Shaky was smooth and didn't miss a beat. "Yellow-breasted or red?"

"Anything but red," I said, completing the passcode.

He nodded and leaned in over the counter, voice dropping to a low murmur. "You were marked coming in here, so I'm gonna need you to be just as visible leaving. Once you're out, make your way down the block, left, and then another left, and come back behind us via that side street. Someone will get you inside."

"Things are that bad?"

His grin was missing half its teeth. "This is Kansas City. Things are *always* that bad. But you've picked a hell of a week to come on behalf of our mutual employer." He nodded to the nearest shelf. "Take some rat meat with you so the watchers don't start to wonder."

Fifteen minutes later, we were back inside the building, this time through a side entrance that opened onto a dimly lit alleyway. As far as Two-Feathers and I could tell, we hadn't been followed, which suggested the watchers Shaky had mentioned were simply staking out the store.

I added that to the list of things I needed to find out about.

Kansas City was a place that loved its basements, and we were ushered into the safehouse's by a younger woman whose eyes were sleepy even as her hands strayed constantly to the knife on her hip. She sat us down at an old card table, poured some water into clay cups, and retreated without ever saying a word, closing the door behind her as she left.

They hadn't tried to take our bags or Two-Feathers' weapons, which was a good sign, but this was still a far cry from our reception at the fort on the way to Eastwood.

Within my shell, the storm rumbled.

Two-Feathers leaned his head back and closed his eyes. Within seconds, he appeared fast asleep.

Appeared, because I was pretty sure he was faking. If any danger appeared, he'd still react faster than anything or anyone but the storm.

Minutes later, as his long, slow breaths reached a metronomic quality, I was forced to accept that the man had just decided to take an actual nap. I shook my head, feeling curiously out of proportion without my shell's usual head and face, and passed the time by counting the spiders that had made the basement their home.

Regular spiders, thankfully. Anything larger would have almost definitely eaten the safehouse's residents by now.

It was roughly twenty-nine spiders later that the door opened again. I tapped Two-Feathers' foot with my boot but the nomad was already looking up, once again making me question if he'd been sleeping at all. We turned to watch Shaky limp into the basement, trailed by the quiet woman who'd escorted us down before.

Both were holding guns, and those guns were pointed at us.

"That's not a good idea," I told the storekeeper.

"I guess we'll find out." Despite his facial twitch and what was clearly a bum leg, the revolver in his hands was rock steady. Between

Eastwood and *Shaky*, I was starting to believe nobody cared about truth in advertising anymore. The armed pair spread out but didn't come any closer, maintaining what I'm guessing they thought was a safe field of fire.

"Now then," continued Shaky, "there's another second phrase that people who come in with your particular pass code are supposed to know. I'm going to give—"

"*Her smile is just skin deep.*"

"Oh." He coughed, cleared his throat, and sheepishly holstered his gun, motioning at the other woman to do the same. "Alright then. You have to understand... we mostly just get the occasional messenger. When someone shows up with a top-level code that nobody's ever used before, it makes a man get himself a case of caution."

"And that was your solution? A pair of .38s? What if we'd been Immortals?"

He snorted and dropped into a chair next to Two-Feathers, the woman coming to stand behind him. "Like Immortals would bother with a shop like mine. That sort just blow in and back out like damn tornadoes, and the rest of us are left to pick up the pieces. Now then, I go by Shaky, as you already know. My sister back there is Esmelda."

I eyed the other woman. She was blonde, plain, and still sleepy-eyed. Even ignoring the vast gulf of age between them, the two looked nothing alike. "Does Esmelda talk?"

"Not so much. But believe me, piss her off and she'll let you know in no uncertain terms."

Esmelda rolled her eyes and slapped Shaky lightly on the back of his head.

"God help us," I told Two-Feathers. "There's two of you."

The nomad grinned.

I turned back to a slightly confused Shaky. "I feel like you got the short end of the stick on the name front."

"It's served me well enough so far. Now, what can I do for you both? Fresh orders from our new queen all the way out there in Memphis?"

"In a way. We're trying to find out why the Horde is in charge of the east gate this week. It was supposed to be the Diablos."

"Yeah, well, like I said upstairs, you picked a hell of a time to come to Kansas City. Diablos aren't guarding the gate because they're hunkering down and marshaling their troops. Plug Uglies and the Dead Rabbits are doing the same."

The last name was the cartel Raya had worked for, which didn't make a whole lot of sense. The Dead Rabbits had been one of the strongest of the city's cartels for practically forever. It had been a very, very long time since they were challenged.

"Why? What happened?"

"Their leaders are all missing. Just vanished, and nobody knows where or how. Plug Uglies are blaming the Horde, like they usually do, Dead Rabbits are blaming the Skulls, and the Diablos are blaming damn near everyone. Whole city's a powder keg. Normal folks are walking on eggshells, but all it's gonna take is one wrong word to send this place sky high."

"Dead Rabbits aside, the cartels are *always* skirmishing."

"This is different. This will be blood like the city hasn't seen since they took over. I'm talking all-out war." He ran a hand through his cropped hair. "So, that's the mess y'all just walked into. Another day or two, and Esmelda and I will be closing shop and riding this mess out down here in the cellar. I advise you and your man to complete your mission and get out of the city while you can."

"That's going to be tough," I admitted.

"How so?"

"I'm supposed to be meeting with the cartel heads."

Shaky frowned. "*All* of them?"

"Yeah. Sort of a meet cute with the bloodthirsty criminal bastards living next door to my new empire." I shrugged. "Blame Jules and Cyrus for the idea. I sure as hell do."

Esmelda put two and two together a lot faster than Shaky, her eyes widening as she looked me over head-to-toe. She squeezed the other man's shoulder urgently.

"I left my crown with my other set of clothes," I told her and her 'brother', "but you can *still* call me Your Majesty."

Shaky's face went as grey as his hair.

"Now then," I added, letting the storm fill my voice as I leaned over the table, "let's figure a way out of this mess."

5

Truthfully, I could've just let Kansas City tear itself apart. The city didn't mean a damn thing to me, and it already felt like days since I'd been out on the open road. We *could* have just taken Shaky's advice and moved on to the clan reunion Two-Feathers was being so weird about. One less piece of bullshit diplomacy theater on my plate, and one step closer to tracking down Bakersfield, the boy who became a nightmare.

I didn't do that, and not *just* because Two-Feathers would've given me puppy-dog eyes and the world's worst guilt trip the whole way west. Like it or not, I had people in the city: five safehouses spread across the districts. And Kansas City itself was both a trading partner to my empire and our primary gateway to the west. If I let the perpetually shaky status quo here be disrupted entirely, it would mean bad things for our economy, and *that* would trigger problems at home with a population still coming to terms with my rule.

Even worse, it would probably necessitate a whole bunch of incredibly tedious meetings with the council and their designated experts of the week.

So yeah, I wasn't going to take the easy route.

Which meant we had work to do.

Step one was proving my identity, but a quick trip to the bathroom to remove my disguise and reform my shell handled that, especially when both Shaky and Esmelda saw me walk into the room with nothing but the clothes on my back and emerge with those clothes in one hand while wearing my usual leathers and helmet.

Step two was coming up with a plan. My go-to strategy of just letting the storm loose wasn't going to be of much value here, not unless I wanted to kill my way through all the cartels of Kansas City. Which I didn't... mostly because that would just cause even more problems and put both my people and my nomad at risk. It wouldn't be a cake walk either, even for me. The cartels had a few Powers of their own and some of those would be of the variety even the storm had to look out for.

So, *shock, awe, and butchery* was off the table, for now. Which left the more annoying but ultimately safer option: find and retrieve the missing leaders, if they were still alive. Find out who was responsible for their deaths if not. Make this whole looming catastrophe about justice and not just blood vengeance. Which was ironic, given that I'd killed literally hundreds of people *and* deposed a queen in retaliation for the massacre at Eclipse.

Still, if I'd learned anything from Jules' recent foray into politics it was that sometimes hypocrisy came with the job.

"We need more information," I said. "It sounds like you and Esmelda have a reasonable handle on what goes down in your district. Does the same hold true for the other safehouses?"

"There are other safehouses?"

I tried not to sigh. *Of course* they wouldn't know each other. That would compromise security, exposing all of them if any single safehouse was found.

It would also make my life entirely too easy.

"Let's put that aside for now," I said, answering Shaky's question without answering it. "What more do you know about the leaders' disappearances?"

Shaky shrugged. "Besides the fact that they all seemed to happen on the same day, sometime in the past week? Not a whole lot."

"And how did the rival cartels even find out? A few days isn't a lot of time."

He cocked his head, as if the thought had never occurred to him… and then his next words confirmed it hadn't.

"You know, that *is* strange. Huh. No idea, really."

"Think. There's got to be something more."

"I wish I knew anything. But—"

He cut off as Esmelda tapped his shoulder. She leaned forward, putting her lips next to Shaky's ear and murmured something too quietly for me to catch.

So, *not* like Two-Feathers after all. That was a shame. I was hoping she'd have come up with a better way to communicate than a thousand different finger signs flashing by at the speed of an amped-up Flyboy.

"Esmelda says she heard about the Dead Rabbits sending a few groups into the Zoo recently," relayed Shaky. "Now, maybe that's just the usual nonsense, but—"

"It could be where they think it went down." Whatever *it* was. "Right."

My empire didn't have a safehouse in the Zoo, because long-term residence there was a death sentence for anyone. *Including* the junkies and half-feral humanoids who made the district their home. That said, we had safehouses and observation posts in neighboring districts. It was good business to keep *some* kind of an eye on the most volatile district in an already volatile city.

The problem was reaching them, and the bigger problem was that I didn't know how the already on-edge cartels would react to my sudden appearance. Only a few of their leaders had known I was even coming, and both of them were now apparently missing.

My sudden presence on the city streets could very well be the match that lit Shaky's not-so-metaphorical powder keg.

I looked down at my saddlebags and the clothes I'd just stuffed back inside them. "Looks like I'll need that disguise again after all."

"What can we do to help?" asked Shaky.

"We'll need this week's bandanas, if you have them. All of them. With the usual rotation fucked beyond belief, I don't know which cartels we'll be encountering."

Which was bullshit, honestly... only the two gate districts, called the Outskirts by some, were on rotation. The rest were permanent homes to their given cartels. Still, the less Shaky knew about our destination, the better. For him and for us.

"We've got colors for this district already, of course, but I can send Jonas and Omar out to purchase the rest."

"Jonas is the slab of beef upstairs?"

"Yep. He's not on the *unofficial* payroll, but he's worked as a guard for our store for some time now."

"And you trust him?" I pressed.

"Not with anything that would get me killed, mind you. But with a task like this? Yeah. And Omar's salt of the earth. Solid, dependable, and blessedly unimaginative." Shaky shifted in his chair. "It'll take the two of 'em several days to cover the whole city though."

I'd done a few jobs to recover kidnapped people, and I knew *several days* was too long, especially given it had already *been* several days since the cartel leaders went missing. Likelihood was it had already been too long before my nomad and I even arrived in the city, but if not, then time was of the essence.

"Just have them start with Sugar Creek, the Gardens, and Raytown," I said, naming the three districts to the north, west, and southwest of the Outskirts. "They can collect the colors for the other districts while we're away pursuing our investigation."

"Fair enough." The shopkeeper and spy licked his cracked lips. "There is the slight question of funds."

For a long moment, I let the smile across my visor do the talking and watched a bead of sweat work its way down the man's temple.

"Shop not doing all that well, Shaky?"

"We keep the lanterns lit, but that's about it." He was sweating even more now. "Especially since we just had to replenish our inventory. We could *probably* cover the cost of the passes, but then we'd have nothing to live on. And people might find it strange if our funds just dried up all sudden-like."

"*All sudden-like*, huh?"

"I swear, boss! You can look at the books yourself if you want!"

I did *not* want, and not just because Shaky almost definitely cooked his 'books' the way a pyromaniac cooked beef. Truth was, I'd had to sit through a three-hour presentation from one of New Memphis' accountants not all that long ago, and that had filled my quota on budget discussions for at least the next human lifetime.

"Fair enough," I finally said. At the bottom of my saddlebags was a coin purse; I counted out a handful of coins from within and passed them over.

They weren't solid gold like the ones I'd left with Jae-Sung and Cho-Hee, of course. What I hadn't given to Raya's husband had been spent on the long journey to end her killer. I still had the gems, but even the smallest of those was too much for a few passes. *These* coins were thin, made from a mix of metals, and minted just a few miles to the northwest near Riverside, the same district Raya had once called home.

Given that we'd planned stops in Kansas City and Wichita both, it had made sense for Two-Feathers and me to bring some of the two cities' minted currencies with us. And while I'd done so without signing all the necessary forms for accessing the royal treasury, I knew the council would get over it. After all, I was the only royal left in New Memphis. That treasury was mine to do with as I chose.

"This'll get you what you need," confirmed Shaky, and if there was a certain undercurrent of greed with the way he said it…. well, he *was* a merchant. "Anything else?"

"Yeah," I said, giving my nomad a once-over. The shirt was perfect, of course—better than perfect, really—but his dark braids and bronzed skin still stood out. I couldn't do anything about the second one, but the first? "Do you have a hat?"

ooo

The Zoo was located two districts southwest of the east gate, the sole space in Kansas City that wasn't claimed by one of the cartels. They'd tried, of course, and more than once. Some had even succeeded, only to lose control again, almost as swiftly, as even trusted captains turned on their bosses, and once-reliable men proved inexplicably shifty. Some people thought there was something in the Zoo's water. Others looked back at the pre-Break times when there'd been an actual zoo there and said the ghosts of those long-dead animals infected anyone who overstayed their welcome.

I didn't know what the answer was, and I didn't really care much either. Humans didn't need to search for reasons to betray and kill one another, not when life was always so willing to provide.

By morning, Jonas and Omar had returned with the passes we'd need, all of them good for another four days before the week expired. An hour or so after that, Two-Feathers and I were on our way.

After a long one-sided discussion with the nomad, I'd given Shaky the location of my bike and his horse. The shopkeeper said he and Esmelda had a means to bring both to the safehouse. I didn't ask for details, and they didn't give them; I was just glad someone would be caring for Two-Feathers' treasured mount and that my motorcycle would be in out of the weather. We'd pick both up again once the mess with the cartels was resolved.

Assuming it *got* resolved and didn't take the whole city down with it instead.

I'd halfway expected Two-Feathers to object to the hat idea, especially when Esmelda emerged from one of their storerooms with a maroon, wide-brimmed hat probably best suited for long-dead heiresses on island vacations. Instead, the nomad seemed pleased as punch. And it *did* keep the sun out of his eyes, I guess.

We made our way from the Outskirts into the Gardens, where the growing crowds and narrow streets both made walking side by side a challenge. We got fewer looks than I'd expected between the hat, his spear, and my ensemble. I wasn't sure if that was because we were just blending in *that* well or if the common people of Kansas City had learned better than to gawk at the unusual. Either way, it worked.

But if the average resident and the sub-average criminal avoided us, the cartels were a whole lot less discriminating. We were stopped five times on our passage through the eastern portion of the city. Once by a patrol from the Horde before we made it out of the Outskirts and three times by Skulls patrols in the vastly more controlled Gardens district. The fifth time came as we crossed the border into Raytown, only to be met by the Plug Uglies in their mottled grey and black parkas.

Raytown, it should be mentioned, wasn't a town. Nor was it particularly sunny, even just an hour after high noon. But then, I hadn't seen a single green or growing thing in the Gardens either, unless you counted the fungi creeping up from the city's long-defunct sewers. I'd been through Kansas City a time or two during the Break, but most of the names had been different back then, and the rest had changed so much as to be unrecognizable. Still. It would be nice if *anything* matched its label.

In the end, I had no choice but to just let it go. Trying to find logic in dear old dead Dad's reality-changing dream was a waste of time and energy. I was living proof of that.

Each time we were stopped, we showed the correct colors—white for the Skulls, green for the Horde, and grey for the Plug Uglies—and were let through with only a moderate amount of hassling and heckling from fools who didn't know any better. That was civilized by city standards, and I gave our disguises most of the credit for it. Without its belt, my shapeless hoodie went a long way to hiding my form and the black wrap around my face strongly suggested *some* sort of gruesome disfigurement. Meanwhile, Two-Feathers gave off just the right aura of danger and competence to make us seem like more trouble than we were worth.

Even *with* the awful hat.

I'd been prepared to fight from the very first inspection, but even though I could sense the tension Shaky had talked about, could read it in the lines of the cartel members' bodies and the way they held tight to their weapons, it seemed like the rule of law was holding. How long that would last, especially if the three bosses stayed missing, was anyone's guess.

The Zoo was the next district over, due west from Raytown, but we'd been walking for several hours by that point and were due for a break. Or at least that's what I hoped prying eyes would assume when I led Two-Feathers into a virtually empty tavern just a block or two over from Raytown's center square.

A handful of taverns in Kansas City had waiters, mostly those north of the river. The Sunken Ship wasn't one of them. It was barely a tavern at all, to be honest, with a grand total of four tables, a handful of bottles on shelves behind the bar, and worn wooden floors that had been stained with blood, alcohol, and at least one other liquid I didn't want to identify.

Two-Feathers took his seat at a table in the corner, and I headed for the bar. The bartender was cleaning glasses that would have been better served being crushed, melted, and molded back into something that *wouldn't* give the drinker a half-dozen strains of disease. He looked up as I approached, and if he found my outfit unusual, he was at least professional enough to not say so.

"What can I get you?" His drawl made the simple question a journey all on its own.

"Whiskey. Crown Royal," I told him.

He snorted. "Haven't had that in this city since twenty years after the Break from what I hear. We've got the local shit or nothing."

"I'll take the local, hold the shit."

I was starting to think the person in New Memphis responsible for these code phrases and counter phrases was either pranking all of us or was just plain psychotic. Felt like a coin flip to me at this point.

"Fair enough. What about for your man in the fancy hat?"

That was *not* part of the official exchange, but it would look weird to have Two-Feathers sitting there not drinking. "Ale," I said. "The darker the better. Maybe put it in a mug that's been cleaned sometime since the Break? And by cleaned, I mean with water, not spit."

He frowned and gave me a price that explained why the tavern was practically empty. Once I'd handed over more of my currency, he poured out a mug of something frosty and then filled a tumbler glass with what looked suspiciously like dirt-colored syrup.

"Cheers," he added, in a tone best suited for a funeral or a murder.

I carried both drinks to our table. Two-Feathers took the mug, eyed the other glass, and gave me a look that needed no interpretation.

"It's supposed to be whiskey," I told him. "Or the local equivalent. I wouldn't recommend drinking it. And if it crawls out of the glass on its own, you've got my permission to stab it until it stops moving."

We waited at the table for almost twenty minutes, long enough for the bartender to disappear into the back and then re-emerge again. Two-Feathers sipped his ale without comment or expression, dark eyes distant as we sat there in silence.

More than his shoulders, more even than his undeniable competence, I loved the nomad's silence. It didn't press, and it didn't strain. It just was. Maybe he hadn't had much choice when it came to staying quiet, but he'd made the silence his own, and even the storm could find peace in that.

Finally, the tavern's only other customer wandered out with a drunken belch and an odor that might just keep him safe from muggers and other predators on the way home. With the tavern empty, I waited for the barkeeper to make his move.

Instead, a woman emerged from the back room. She was *kind of wide* the way I was *kind of tall*, but moved delicately for all her size, making her way across the room like a dancer. When she reached our table, she pulled a chair out with one hand and dropped into it.

"So," she said. "Here we are."

Two-Feathers frowned. I didn't see any motion from him, but I was betting he'd dropped a hand to the knife on his belt. Meanwhile, I kept my focus on the newcomer. There was steel in her voice that matched the steel in her eyes, and a cold confidence that wouldn't have been out of place in the upper districts of New Memphis.

"Here we are," I agreed. "Who are you?"

"The owner of this establishment. Name's Dorothea. When Colton over there told me someone had come in asking for a brand of alcohol lost in the Break, I figured I should make myself available." She picked up the still-full glass of what they were calling whiskey and tossed it down in one go. "Didn't realize we were hosting royalty though."

My bandage mask should have hid any reaction my malformed human face might have made, but she caught it and explained.

"That very nice shirt and that horrible hat don't do a whole lot to hide that your man over there's a nomad. And a tall woman dressed up like some kind of burn victim paired with a nomad with a spear? Even without the shiny motorcycle outfit, it didn't take a whole lot of thought to figure that one out."

"Plus you knew we were coming," I guessed.

"There is that," she admitted. "My handler wanted me to be ready to assist you when and if you needed it during your visit. Not that I expected you to just openly walk through my door."

"Will that be a problem?"

Her smile came and went, cold and mean and hard. "Not anymore. There were eyes on you from outside, but Raytown's dangerous even in the daytime, and the Plug Uglies are way too busy to concern themselves with the occasional mugging and murder."

Two-Feathers stiffened, but I let it go. Another death on my conscience would only be a problem if I had one.

Dorothea had an attitude and face like curdled milk, but I already kind of liked her.

"Which explains why we're meeting here instead of in the basement?"

"Sort of. The basement's where our still is located." She twitched, just a little bit, momentarily reminding me of Shaky. "Not the safest place to meet, if I'm being honest. But in the interest of expedience, why don't you tell me what brings you here tonight?"

"You don't already know?"

"Handler just said you'd be in the city. The whys and the what-fors weren't part of the information package."

I was pleasantly surprised by that. One thing I'd learned from my time with spies is that they were surprisingly shit at keeping other people's secrets.

"I came to Kansas City to meet with the cartel heads."

"That's going to be difficult."

"So I hear. I was hoping you'd know where they are or at least what happened to them."

"They went into the Zoo three days ago. Never came out."

"All three of them?"

"Yep. One pilgrimage after the next."

"Do you have any proof of that?"

"Eyewitnesses. Two of them. Both on our payroll, neither with any relation or knowledge of the other. Watched the cartel heads arrive, one by one by one."

I couldn't frown, but I felt my lips twitch in their best estimation of the gesture. "Three days and the other cartels already found out they're gone?"

"They've all got their own spy networks, but yeah, I found that surprising too. It's not the first time a boss has disappeared for a bit, but it *is* the first time their rival cartels knew about it right off."

Which made her smarter than Shaky and not just better informed. Something was off about this whole thing, and not just because these disappearances had happened right before my arrival.

"What were three different cartel bosses doing in the Zoo? Especially at the same time?"

"It's a closely guarded secret that the Plug Uglies and the Dead Rabbits have been working together behind the scenes. I'm guessing the Diablos found out somehow and figured out a way to get a share of that pie." Dorothea shrugged. "As for the Zoo? I don't know. Maybe they picked it because it's the closest thing to neutral territory around here? At least it hates everyone equally."

"So, three people enter the Zoo, each representing their respective cartels, and none of them leave again?"

"Seven people, actually. Each boss brought their head enforcer with them."

"That makes six. Unless one of those enforcers has a clone?"

Her smile flickered back into existence, the sequel every bit as bad as the initial showing. "Funnily enough, the Horde *used* to have a pair of twin enforcers. Sadly, one of them got himself in trouble with the boss, and they were *both* killed, just to be sure. No, the seventh person was the Devil's sidepiece, a little slip of a woman with dark hair and dreamy eyes. She went in with him and his enforcer."

The Devil being the unimaginative title given to the head of the Diablos, just as *Hell* was the name for their HQ up in the Woods district. I didn't know why the Devil would bring his woman with him to a meetup, but gun molls were as old as gangs themselves. Hell, the concept dated at least back to Bonnie and Clyde, two names that dear old Dad had made sure I'd been born knowing. Maybe the Diablos' leader was just in that odd honeymoon stage humans talked about.

"Did you tell any of the cartels this? The Plug Uglies, maybe?"

"And expose myself as more than just an anonymous tavern owner? Hell no. I'm here to observe, not get myself killed."

I couldn't fault her for that, but before I could move on, Two-Feathers touched my arm. With his other hand, he gestured to his eyes and cocked his head.

"The witnesses?" I asked him.

He shook his head and made a few signs I did recognize, *woman* among them.

Hell if I knew what he was getting at, but I backed his play and turned to Dorothea. "When you say the Devil's woman had *dreamy eyes*, what did you mean?"

"Half the time she doesn't seem to be looking at anything at all. Strangest thing is she was originally with the *Horde* a few months back. After that mess went down with the twins, I guess she started looking for safer pastures and had the misfortune to wind up in Hell instead."

The description she'd given aptly fit a thousand waifs in the Badlands, but the underlying *pattern* felt familiar. *Too* familiar. A lone woman shows up, then makes her way from group to group, leaving a trail of dead behind her.

The storm rumbled inside of me, metal clashing on metal audibly within the confines of the small tavern. For the first time, Dorothea's composure cracked, just a hair.

"Is… uh… something wrong?" I didn't blame the spy for the poorly masked fear in her voice, but it did make me like her just a little bit less.

"I need you to tell me everything you know about this woman. A full description, when she showed up in Kansas City, what name she's operating under… *everything*."

Dorothea swallowed and nodded. "I can do that. Or at least I know someone who can." She called the bartender over and he came running like a trained pet. "Colton. What can you tell us about that dark-haired little bit that moved from the Horde to the Diablos and ended up on the Devil's arm?"

Colton frowned. I could practically see the wheels turning in his brain as he organized whatever he knew.

"She's about 5'5" I guess? Dark hair always in her face. Pale-skinned and borderline pretty, but it's a hard kind of pretty, you know? Like she's seen some things?"

"We've *all* seen some things," said Dorothea.

"Yeah, but even so… ah hell, I don't know. Cartel soldiers seem drawn to her like ants to honey, even with her occasional weird spells. Frankly, I think there are safer ways to get your rocks off."

"*Weird spells?*" I asked.

"They say she sometimes talks in tongues or something. Before the Devil took her for his, there were a few people whispering that she might even be a witch. Those whispers died quick, and the whisperers did too, but still…"

"Does this *witch* have a name?" I was increasingly certain that Two-Feathers' instincts had been correct. Trust a hunter to recognize a dangerous predator.

"The Devil calls her Skirt, on account of that being what she mostly wears, but she went by something else when she showed up this past winter. Sarah maybe? Or Stella?"

"How about Selene?" My voice was flat. Nothing but metal, more metal, and the storm's unending rage.

"Nah, that's not it either." Colton frowned for a second then slapped the table. "Sally! That was it. Seemed like such an old-fashioned name. Hell, even Skirt's an improvement."

I traded glances with Two-Feathers. I'd eventually told him the identity of the ghost riding our traitorous former companion, Selene. To now go openly by Sally was a special kind of fuck you to the world. It was also *exactly* the kind of gesture I could see the Free States' greatest serial killer making.

"Has *Sally* been spotted leaving the Zoo?"

It was Dorothea's turn to answer, shaking her head slowly. "Without the Devil or the other bosses? I don't think so, but one girl stands out a lot less than the rest." The spy frowned. "Why do I get the feeling that this bit's location is suddenly more important to you than the fate of the heads of Kansas City's three largest cartels?"

"It's personal."

I signaled to Two-Feathers, and he rose in a fluid motion that had Dorothea visibly adjusting her estimation of the nomad. Normal people just didn't move like that, and in the heavy woman's eyes, that made him every bit as dangerous as me, if not quite as fancy.

The nomad hefted his spear and turned to me, handsome face asking a question he couldn't voice.

"Yeah," I replied. "We're going to the Zoo."

6

Before we could leave, Dorothea leaned back in her chair, fingers dancing along the table's edge. "This Sally person. What did she do, if you don't mind me asking?"

"She turned traitor." Technically, she'd been one of *three* people on Jules' former crew to do so, but the others were already dead. Selene, or Sally, or whatever she wanted to call herself, had made it out of New Memphis in one piece, despite the riots that ravaged the city. "Killed someone she shouldn't have and left us out to dry."

"I take it she's a Power?"

I waved Two-Feathers back to his seat and fixed the spy with a look she could feel if not see. "How do you figure?"

She shrugged. "She's still alive after crossing you."

Dorothea wasn't dumb. I didn't hate that in an employee.

"She's a Crow," I admitted.

The other woman shivered. "Another fucking Crow in the Zoo. That's just what this city needs."

"*Another* Crow?"

"The last one happened way before you took over. Was a time when your predecessor kept a secret processing station in the district.

Technicians, cages, company of soldiers, the whole deal. Not sure how you feel about all that—"

"The soldiers I'm fine with." I remembered the squad of deserters I'd wiped out on the way to Eastwood. "Mostly. But the technician program has been shut down. There are enough nightmares in the world without us making new ones."

"Music to my ears. Visited the station once when I was new in my post. Never been so glad to be a spy instead of one of the rank and file guarding that madhouse, I'll tell you that much.

"Anyway," she continued, "the bright souls at this processing station managed to 'kidnap' a visiting Crow a few years ago. Bet they were proud of themselves for it too… right until he wiped them and the whole facility off the face of the planet with a wave of the walking dead." She waved my empty tumbler at Colton and waited for the man to refill it. "Walkers in the streets of Kansas City? As you can imagine, the cartels were none too happy. Might be the last time any of us saw them all working together."

"What did they do?" I'd read that the empire had lost its primary base in Kansas City but had never dug deeper into the story. I'd personally experienced the results of the horror show that was the Crimson Queen's re-education program; its loss had been good fucking riddance, as far as I was concerned.

"The *official* story was that they leveraged the situation to get favors from the Free States, seeing as how said Crow was one of their citizens. Of course, after that same monster went south and conquered all of Mexico, even the average moron on the street knew that story was bullshit. Can you imagine the fucking Bloods or Skulls trying to tell the *Lord of the Dead* what to do?"

Bakersfield. Sometimes, it seemed like I couldn't take a step without tripping over one of the disasters Damian had left in his wake.

"And now a second Crow is running amok." Dorothea hawked up some phlegm and spat on the floor, drawing an aggrieved look from her bartender. "Any idea what this one wants with the cartels?"

"She could be looking for a new hideout, a new target, or both. The fact that she fell in with the Devil tells me he has something she needs or can at least give her access to it."

"Maybe something in the Zoo?"

Guessing at the motivations of a madwoman was a fool's errand, especially when that madwoman was herself being ridden and controlled by the ghost of another madwoman. Still, I couldn't see it. "With that place being neutral territory, I'd think she'd have just gone there on her own."

"That's a real good way to get dead, even for a Power."

"The Zoo's not that bad in short spells," I told her. "I've walked those streets. Sounds like you have too."

"Have you walked them lately?"

"It's been a while." More than a decade, really, but nobody needed to know that. Half my council members were busy playing the long game, waiting for me to die of old age when their heirs would be well positioned for the inevitable power grab that followed. If they realized I was *never* going to die of old age?

Well, I didn't need another civil war.

Dorothea responded to my words, ignorant of the thoughts that accompanied them. "That's what I thought. After the Lord of the Dead's visit, the district changed."

"How so?"

"It got wilder. Darker, even. More alive than not. Like maybe *he* stirred up the ghosts that make that place their home. It used to just be dangerous. Now? I wouldn't give this Sally much chance of survival, not unless she's on the same level *he* is…?"

"She's not. Not even close." At least the body Sally was in wasn't. Selene was just a woman with a knife and a surprising capability for punching beyond her weight class.

"Then she'd have needed help to get where she was going."

"Safety in numbers."

"Yeah. You know, if I were going to spend more than a day in the Zoo, *I'd* have brought an army. Can't imagine the cartel bosses are any less safety conscious. Which means they weren't planning to be there that long."

"Something went wrong."

"Or right, maybe. But what?"

"Or who."

"You think your Sally is responsible somehow?"

"I plan to find out."

Dorothea tossed back another two fingers of pseudo whisky, her expression never changing. "I'd heard stories about you, long before you became our boss. If even half of them are true, I'm guessing you've got what it takes to survive the Zoo just fine. As for tall, dark, and quiet over there? Only a Power moves like him. Provided he's tough enough, he might make it through too. But *surviving* the Zoo is one thing. Finding your way through streets that shift and change all on their own is something else entirely."

I studied the other woman. "Is that an offer?"

"That's up to you."

Which meant she wanted something in return. "You aren't going to volunteer in service of queen and country?"

"To hunt down six people and a Crow in the Zoo?" She shuddered, but this time there was a touch of theatricality to it. "Like I said earlier, I'm a spy not a soldier."

I gave a moment's thought to enlisting the cartels for the search. It was their leaders who were missing, after all. The problem was, dealing with whoever had found themselves thrust into command amid a city-spanning crisis would take time, and I didn't have any to spare. If Sally was still in the Zoo… if Dorothea could get us there before she fled again…

"What do you want in return?"

"Just a house."

"Where, exactly? Riverside or the Woods?" They were the only two neighborhoods in Kansas City that made sense.

"New Memphis. District Three." She tilted the empty glass back and forth, refracted light spilling across the table. "White fence. Couple of bedrooms. Maybe a dog that's not gone so feral I'll have to worry about it creeping in at night to eat me or Colton."

Colton stirred from his place in front of the bar. His eyes lingered on the heavyset woman in a way that would have made their relationship clear if her words hadn't just done so.

"A house." I didn't know much about real estate in my capital city, but vast swaths of District Three had been destroyed in the riots that preceded my ascension. Reconstruction was ongoing, and that meant an opportunity for whoever got tasked with fulfilling Dorothea's request. Jules, most likely. "We can do that. Shall we go?"

"I wasn't done quite yet."

The storm stirred again inside of me and my voice went flat and cold. "Royalty or not, there *are* limits to my generosity."

"This is the last request. Promise." She'd gone pale again but rallied. "I want a promotion. Something on the administrative side of your spy network."

That wasn't as big an ask as she thought it was. If she was moving to New Memphis to live in her fancy house, she clearly wouldn't be able to maintain her role as a spy in Kansas City. As far as I was concerned, it would be better to leverage her skills in some way than to lose them entirely.

Maybe all those endless meetings with my council were starting to pay off. I was even thinking like a ruler now.

"I don't tell our spymasters how to do their job, but I can make sure you're introduced. Given the casualties that accompanied my claiming the throne, someone of your experience will probably be able to write her own ticket."

"Then you've got yourself a guide."

"And a guard," said Colton, retrieving a shotgun from behind the bar.

Dorothea started to say something, saw the bartender's face, and sighed. "Right. If we're going in force, you'd better check if the Sparrows are available to come too, Colton. And put up the sign out front saying we're closed."

The bartender nodded and headed for the door.

"Sparrows?" I asked.

"Eli and Nika Sparrow. They're siblings. We think. Muscle-for-hire that spend a few hours a week on my payroll. And yours, technically. They're the ones who handled your watchers earlier. Both Normals, like me and Colton, but they're survivors and good in a scrap."

"Fair enough." I wasn't sure what two more Normals could really offer, but the extra bodies would at least reduce the odds of Two-Feathers getting shot. "How long do you think it'll take to get them?"

"We can leave for the Zoo now. Colton and the Sparrows will meet us at the Raytown exit."

My favorite kind of waiting was the kind that didn't happen. I pushed back my chair and rose to my feet in a weak imitation of my nomad's supernatural grace. "Alright then. Let's go."

Two-Feathers grabbed his hat.

ooo

True to Dorothea's word, Colton was waiting with two others just shy of the heavily marked boundary line between Raytown and the Zoo. The Sparrows were small and slim, each dressed in head-to-toe leather that reminded me of my own riding gear, if far less clean. In lieu of motorcycle helmets, they had on battered goggles over face masks, not a shred of skin showing anywhere.

"Huh," said Dorothea. "It never occurred to me before, but the three of you could almost shop at the same store."

I didn't reply because I'd been thinking much the same thing. Except for the height difference, they looked a lot like a blend of my usual appearance and my current disguise.

"Nika's the one with the sword and other blades," continued the spy. "Eli's got the hand cannon and hatchets."

I assumed she knew that from experience, given that both were of a similar size, utterly androgynous, and impossible to tell apart. "We should head on in then. The clock is ticking. You're up front with me, Dorothea. The rest of you, keep an eye out."

Despite all the signs warning pedestrians away, the Zoo felt a lot like any other district at first. It was only when you were fifty feet in that you realized the already narrow streets had narrowed even further, that the previously straight lines of the city roads had developed a bit of a wiggle, twisting and turning in a way that created blind corners all around. Just that quickly, a neighborhood became a warren of winding, uncertain pathways.

Several blocks in and those changes magnified. There was a thickness to the air that even I could sense, a feeling of being observed that far exceeded the rightful paranoia that flooded the rest of the city.

The scavengers of the district watched us from their shadows, the occasional mad giggle escaping from uncaring mouths, but there were six of us and my five companions were all clearly armed. So, even as those scavengers stared and laughed and loped through trash-strewn side streets in our wake, none seemed willing to pick a fight.

Not yet anyway.

"Do you know where we're headed, *guide*?" I asked an increasingly nervous Dorothea.

"Fingers, the Plug Uglies' boss, entered from Raytown," she answered, "and then headed west."

"Makes sense since Raytown is their district."

"Right. But the other two entered from the north and headed southeast. I figure wherever they were meeting is the intersection between those two paths."

"And?"

"And that narrows the search down to a handful of blocks instead of the whole district."

It took an effort not to stop then and there. "I'm not sure we really needed a guide just to search a handful of blocks."

"Maybe, maybe not," she admitted. "But if they're *not* there? If they simply met up and went elsewhere? That's what you've got me for."

I was starting to second-guess my positive thoughts regarding smart employees.

○○○

We'd been in the Zoo for almost twenty minutes when things finally went sideways. There was no signal, no carefully arranged ambush, no semblance of a plan at all, really. Just a flood of unwashed humanity rushing at us from the alleys, armed with everything from knives to clubs to decomposing limbs.

I was ready, but Two-Feathers was even faster, meeting the stream of attackers from our left, his spear in one hand, his long-bladed knife in the other. The first scavenger died in mid-leap, the second moments later, the third while still blinking away the blood of her predecessors. The Stalwart waded through the attacking Normals like a farmer taking the harvest.

There were times I worried about my nomad. There was a softness to him that was as intriguing as it was potentially fatal. But once the blood was flying?

That man was a killer, just like me.

To our right, Nika and Eli were slower, as all Normals must be, but between the woman's sword and the other man's gun, they seemed to be stemming the tide. Behind us, Colton's shotgun boomed twice, momentarily drowning out the rest of the noise.

In front of us though?

Nothing but open space.

Dorothea was headed toward freedom and safety when I grabbed her by the shoulder and pulled her back.

"Go guard your man's back," I told her.

"We need to push forward!"

I shook my head. The people of the Zoo were feral, but that didn't mean they were dumb. Like animals, they'd have a certain level of cunning, and that meant they'd left the way forward open for a reason.

They were trying to drive us *toward* something. Or someone.

And I refused to be herded.

"Go," I said again. Maybe it was the lack of fresh shots from Colton's shotgun that convinced her, or maybe she heard something in my voice. Either way, she pulled the revolver from her belt with a curse and headed back to help.

I didn't spare a glance for Two-Feathers, who was the next best thing to a god of war in the narrow confines of his alleyway. Didn't spare a glance for the Sparrows either, even as they slowly gave way to the unending tide of savagery coming their way.

Instead, I unwound the scarf from my misshapen head and tucked it into my saddlebags. I pulled the bulky clothes from my body and added them in too. For a moment, I was more naked than the day I'd been born, wearing only my riding boots and surrounded by the squalor of a shitty city's worst neighborhood.

And then, as whoever it was the scavengers had been trying to drive us toward finally abandoned their position and came forward, I banished my shell entirely and unleashed the storm.

○○○

They called this district the Zoo because there'd once been an actual zoo here; a series of caged enclosures where people could come and see what lurked out in the wilds of the world. The Break had reshaped both city and terrain, and those animals were long dead, gone and forgotten beyond vague rumors of ghosts and feral influence, but what came towards the storm came charging in on four feet, claws or hands and feet digging into the dirt roads, propelling their bodies forward at speeds even Two-Feathers might not have been able to match.

They weren't people, not anymore.

They weren't Powers either, though that was probably how they had started.

They were things now, creatures as much bestial as humanoid. Beast Shifters locked into one shape because they'd all but forgotten the other. Heads like bears or mountain lions. Bodies a strange mix of fur or scales and skin. Some limbs still human, others ending in great, flesh-rending claws, talons, or tails.

Behind me, I sensed Dorothea stumble away, caught between helping her man and gawking at the death hurtling in my direction. She might have shouted something, even, but that noise was lost beneath the sounds of the storm, beneath the steel and metal and twisting loops of barbed wire that surged forward of their own accord.

The former Shifters didn't slow. Momentum and thousands of pounds carried them deep into the storm's embrace, and then through it and back out into the open air. But what emerged on the other side, still a dozen feet away from my saddlebags and the clothes I'd carefully tucked inside, was just meat and tissue. Once-coherent form now reconfigured, rendered into shredded pieces of flesh and artfully described arcs of blood.

Four Shifters, taken by the Zoo and warped into something else, now changed a final time by the ever-hungry storm.

I reformed my shell in the midst of the carnage and turned my helmet—my true face, showing at last—back to the rest of our group. Two-Feathers had more than stalled his wave of attackers; he'd broken it entirely and was now joining the hard-pressed Dorothea and Colton. On the other side, Nika was locked in combat with two scavengers, another dozen or more trying to claw their way toward her. Eli had dropped to one knee, reloading his hand cannon.

A part of me wanted to join my nomad, but he was the one person in our party who didn't need help. I headed for the Sparrows instead.

Nika sensed me stepping up beside her, somehow, and reacted… poorly. A strike that severed the grasping hands of her closest assailant at the wrists turned just as quickly into a lightning-swift slash at the person on her flank: me. I watched the eyes behind her blood-spattered goggles widen as she realized I wasn't another scavenger, but it was too late to pull the blow.

It was also way too late for me to dodge it. Razor-sharp steel tore through leather and then the flesh of my shell. Strength that suggested that Nika was a little more than Normal carried her sword all the way through my body and out the other side. The shock in Nika's eyes turned to horror as she bisected her employer's employer—

—and then I freed the storm again, for just a micro-second, and reformed my shell, hale and hearty again on the other side of her strike. Only the splatter on the walls showed that there'd been any damage done at all.

"Stand back," I told Nika, my voice a metal version of the Beast Shifters' snarls. She did so in mute astonishment, glancing at the sword in her hands as if to verify the blood on its blade. "And stay out of my way."

I didn't wait to see if she obeyed, because while my shell is just a container, human more in aesthetic than function, it *does* feel pain… and there's nothing like a yard of steel cutting you in half to trigger some serious emotion.

I dropped my shell once more, and the storm gave that emotion voice.

7

It took over an hour to reach the area Dorothea had identified as our search zone, and by the time we did, the spy and I were the only two who *hadn't* taken some damage. Eli had a nasty gash across his chest from a shiv that had begun life as some sort of glassware, but most of the other wounds were superficial: scrapes, bruises, and at least one bite that had thankfully not quite broken skin. Even so, each open wound got a baptism in alcohol from the bottle Colton had in his pack, because infection was otherwise all but guaranteed.

When Dorothea announced that we had arrived, I gave her a look that didn't need interpretation through the smiley-face on my visor. I was the only of us who wasn't filthy by that point, and only because reforming my shell did the same thing for bloodstains that it did for physical damage.

"I think you undersold just how much the Zoo has changed," I told her, in a voice dry as days-old bone. "This is insanity."

"It's way worse than it should be." Her dark hair was matted to a shiny face and scalp, and her eyes were in constant motion, trying to spot the next attack before it came. "If it had been even close to this a week ago, the bosses would have brought more than just their top enforcers with them. I don't know what's stirred the district up."

"Huh. I think I might."

Sweaty and terrified, Dorothea still wasn't dumb. "The other Crow? Sally?"

"If there's any truth beyond all those rumors about ghosts in this district… maybe? I could definitely see *her* agitating the afterlife."

"Then the sooner we get to her and the others, the better."

I wasn't going to argue with that.

The problem was, a search of the nearby blocks turned up a whole lot of nothing: boarded-up houses, burnt-out husks, and more garbage than any mostly empty neighborhood should ever have. But cartel bosses or backstabbing bits in a skirt?

Nope.

What we did find was one building that had had some of its boards removed, allowing access. There were a few half-smoked, hand-rolled cigarettes out front, and a boatload more inside, where a table and six chairs had been set up. It was clear that someone had stood and waited outside for a while, and then several someones had met within. But after that? Hell if I knew. They were gone now, and that was all I could say for sure.

Then again, I'd never been much of a tracker, even in the comparatively less chaotic environments of the great outdoors. Two-Feathers was a different story.

I looked to the nomad, but he was way ahead of me, crouched low as he examined the interior. That ridiculous hat was somehow still in one piece on his head despite the series of attacks we'd weathered. A still-bleeding Eli dropped to one knee next to Two-Feathers, who pointed out a series of impressions in the room's dirt-covered floor that apparently meant something to them both. The pair retreated outside and the rest of us followed, doing our best not to step in anything gross or important.

After a good fifteen to twenty minutes, the nomad turned to me and made a series of signs at half-speed so I could actually understand them.

"Three people waited out here," I translated for the others. "And then were met by four more."

"It looks like our targets," added Eli, in an accented voice as neutrally androgynous as the rest of him. "They spent a day or two talking inside, judging by the cigarette butts and trash, and then left again."

"That would have been what... two days ago? Why didn't they make it back to their respective districts?"

Eli indicated a trail I could barely see let alone interpret. "It looks like they went deeper into the district. All seven of them."

"Can you follow them?" I asked, including both my nomad and the Sparrow brother in the question.

"For now," said Eli, supported by Two-Feathers' nod. "But if we encounter any areas of higher traffic..."

"We should get moving." Colton was nervous, head on a swivel as he watched our rear. "We only have four or so hours until sundown."

"Two-Feathers and I will take point this time," I said. "Eli, you follow behind and make sure we're not missing any trail signs as we go. Then, Dorothea, Nika, and Colton."

"Putting our two Powers at the front leaves us thin on the flanks," pointed out Dorothea.

"If we get attacked, I'll handle the front and Two-Feathers will drop back to help you all," I said, letting her misconceptions of what the storm and I were slide. "But we haven't seen anything living in almost ten minutes. Maybe we've burned through the Zoo's surplus of scavengers and monsters for the day?"

A chorus of discordant yipping howls, the kind that might come from coyotes on pharmaceutical-grade narcotics, split the air in answer.

"Well now you've done it." A spark of humor filled Colton's slow drawl, almost lost beneath Dorothea's sigh. "You've gone and made it a challenge."

○○○

As we moved deeper into the Zoo, the attacks never slowed, but the makeup of our attackers slowly shifted. Fewer half-naked scavengers. More feral humanoid creatures. After a point, I was forced to accept that they weren't Shifters at all, not unless the Badland's entire population of Beast Shifters had somehow gathered in not just Kansas City, but a single one of its districts. No, these were regular people who had been warped physically as well as mentally, though the how and the why of it escaped me.

That was actually *good* news… for us, if not the city. Shifters healed. It made them a pain in the ass to fight, especially for those whose weapons were a little bit less *comprehensive* than the storm. But insane animal-human hybrids? They fought with agility and strength well beyond what Normals should have, but they bled and died almost as easily.

We'd traveled another ten blocks before Two-Feathers finally lost the trail, whatever fragments of footprints he'd been following swallowed up by a day-old battle scene and the greater traffic of the men and creatures we'd been killing our way through. There weren't any corpses, which didn't mean much considering at least some of the inhabitants of the Zoo were cannibals.

While the trackers widened their search radius, the rest of us explored the nearby buildings, but it was clear the cartel bosses had kept going. *Where*, exactly, remained the question of the day.

First, Eli and then Two-Feathers returned to us, each shaking their heads. They'd gone out at least two more blocks, but that traffic the Sparrow brother had warned us all about had erased whatever trail there was to follow.

I was starting to develop a distaste for the Zoo.

"Thoughts?" I asked the others.

Nika said nothing, fully absorbed in cleaning the array of edged weaponry she carried with her. Colton stayed quiet too, frowning as he counted the handful of slugs he had left for his shotgun. But Dorothea…

The spy was frowning too, but there was more to her expression than just glum dissatisfaction.

"What is it?" I asked, stepping closer.

"We've been traveling mostly in a straight line since the meeting spot, right?"

With the way the warped streets twisted and turned, I wasn't sure, but Two-Feathers nodded.

"Given how much the district has changed, I could be wrong, but… I think I know where they might have been headed." She turned back to me, voice firming. "I know you said this Sally wasn't a patch on the Lord of the Dead, but… does she have any kind of a connection to him? Beyond them both being Crows?"

"Less her than the ghost riding her, but yeah. Why?"

"Because if we kept going straight in the direction they'd been going until now, I'm pretty sure we'd hit the processing station where he let himself get captured."

"You said that station was destroyed."

"It was. Burned to the ground with a whole bunch of walkers and dead soldiers inside. Probably a mess of prisoners too, since I'm guessing *he* didn't care about freeing them."

"You'd be surprised," I murmured in a voice of serrated steel.

"If the whole place was destroyed, why would three cartel bosses, their head enforcers, and an apparently dangerous person of interest all head over there?" asked Colton. "Especially when they'd already probably overstayed their welcome in the Zoo?"

I shook my head, the wan sunlight reflecting off my true face.

"There's only one way to find out."

Another hour of travel, but twenty minutes into it, Two-Feathers found signs that we were on the right path. There were still seven people in our target group, although one appeared to be walking more heavily than before. We found another battle scene, but again, it looked like the district's inhabitants had gotten the worst of it. The good news was we were maybe only a day behind them. That was also the bad news. A day was a hell of a lot of time.

I could sense as much as hear the creatures of the Zoo prowling the alleys around us, but the last dozen or so failed ambushes had taught even these wild things some semblance of caution. We were only attacked twice more before we reached our destination. By then, Colton was out of ammo, and Nika had picked up a limp after being bowled over by someone who thought he was a wolf, but we were all still alive.

Just like our targets.

We stood for a moment in silence, taking in the first open space that the Zoo had provided us since entry. It wasn't a park or a town square; it was a wide swath of destruction. Old destruction, by the looks of it… a few metal posts protruding up from ash and scorched foundations.

Say this for Bakersfield… he did nothing small. Whatever fire he had started when destroying my empire's processing station had leaped to neighboring buildings where it had consumed their purely wood framed structures entirely. Given the tight confines of the Zoo, it was a miracle the whole district hadn't burned down. As it was, almost three full city blocks were simply gone, yet another deathly monument to the Crow's passage.

I'd played a part in Bakersfield's survival. In his growth, even. I'd sown some of the seeds that led to my deadbeat dad's destruction. Hell if I knew how I felt about that, even now. Something told me that would depend a lot on what we found down in Mexico, on what Bakersfield would have to say when we finally met.

But in the meantime? There was a very different Crow who deserved every bit of what she had coming for her.

We just… had to find her first. Because the other reason I'd stopped was that there wasn't a damn person in sight.

I pointed to the free-standing metal posts. "If anything screams former military base, it's those. Let's see if we can figure out what they came for and where they went next."

Five minutes later, that first question remained a mystery, but the answer to the second was clear, even to me. The creatures of the Zoo seemed to avoid this place, and that had made our targets' trail easy to follow. It led deeper into the wreckage of what had once been a facility, a few leftover posts sketching out the layout of halls or maybe rooms as we went. That trail ended near what would have been the rear of the building. There, rubble had been laboriously cleared aside to expose two metal doors, set into the earth. The doors themselves were rusted, but the hinges had been recently cleaned, and damage to the doors' exterior showed where someone with superhuman strength had torn out the lock.

"You didn't say this place had a basement," I told Dorothea.

"I didn't know it did." The spy frowned again. "So whatever brought Sally and the others here might be something from—" She spared a glance at the Sparrow siblings. "—*your* empire?"

"The ghost riding her may have seen it back when she was still hanging around Bakersfield," I concluded.

"That was years ago. Why come for it now?"

"She's a Crow," I pointed out. "Things don't always have to make sense."

Although… I was pretty sure it had taken Sally quite a while to find the woman we'd known as Selene—a Crow who was both strong enough to handle being ridden by the dead serial killer and too weak to keep her at bay. At the time, Selene had been down in Texas, working with the rest of Jules' crew.

But now? Well, she'd killed her intended victim in New Memphis and come straight to Kansas City. Whatever she was after here, whatever she'd sold the cartel bosses on, it was almost definitely nothing good. For the cartels or the rest of us.

It had taken some time for our targets to find and then clear the door, meaning we were hours behind now, not days. A *lot* of hours, granted, but according to Two-Feathers, the trail we'd followed led down into that basement and there was no matching trail coming back up. And that meant that there was either another way out or our prey were still down below.

Either way, our next steps were obvious.

I took hold of one door, while Two-Feathers grabbed the other. We pulled at the same time, metal groaning as doors that had opened only once in the past few years were opened yet again. The hinges, at least, operated silently, if not smoothly. The doors didn't open a full one hundred and eighty degrees but got stuck about two-thirds of the way in each direction, protruding outward like the mandibles of something vaguely insectile. Beneath, stairs led into the earth.

"We're going to need torches," muttered Colton, "which means finding some wood that *hasn't* already been burned to ash."

Two-Feathers shook his head and tapped the bartender on the shoulder, gesturing toward the base of the stairwell. As deep as it was, it shouldn't have even been visible. In fact, most of the stairs down weren't… but dim light illuminated the final few steps.

"There's light already down there," I said, stating the obvious.

"That doesn't look like torchlight," said Dorothea, her voice now a whisper. "Gas lantern either. Don't tell me this place still has a functional generator even after this?"

I knew better. I'd seen lights like that before. In fact, they decorated almost every street corner in the high-tiered districts of my capital city where the rich people lived.

"Those are glowtorches." Everyone but Two-Feathers just looked at me, and I sighed. "They're a type of light source originally created by Legion back east."

Dorothea shivered at the mention of Baltimore's twisted Technomancer ruler. Smart woman.

"I didn't know there were any in Kansas City," I added.

"You think the bosses brought them along?" asked Eli.

I started to say no but stopped. My predecessor *had* sent a few gifts to the Dead Rabbits as part of her campaign to conquer the city by something other than force. Those gifts had even included an honest-to-God car. A few glowtorches barely even rated by comparison.

"Could be," I admitted. "Or they could have been part of this underground bunker from the beginning. Either way, it looks like we'll be able to see where we're going. Keep the same formation; we don't know what we'll encounter down there."

"The doors weren't exactly quiet," said Colton. "Got to think they know someone's coming."

"It depends on what's down there," said Dorothea. "A few turns, a few rooms, a couple of doors… sound doesn't carry as far as you might be used to."

I nodded, partly agreeing with the spy and partly just eager to move. Time was wasting, and we'd already burned enough of it already.

I went first, Two-Feathers several steps behind. He knew better than to crowd the storm when a fight was all but certain. Even so, we reached the base of the stairs without issue and found the remnants of another metal door, this one solid steel and significantly less weathered than the one above. It was thicker too, thick enough that the quantity of conventional explosives necessary to gain entry would have brought the whole place down too.

That hadn't stopped our targets. There were plasma marks etched deep into the steel that suggested a Pyromancer or Lightbringer, and a hole had been punched through the security door where those scars would have at one point intersected. The edges of the hole had then been peeled back to create an entryway we could all easily fit through. A small pile of additional cigarette butts suggested they'd been stuck here a while… and that at least one of our targets had himself a bit of an addiction.

"The burn marks are from the Dead Rabbits' enforcer, Endless," said Dorothea, voice hushed. "Emits cutting light from his fingers. Range isn't more than a few feet, but that's usually plenty."

"And the strongman?"

"That's the Plug Uglies' enforcer. Goes by Beef Stew."

"*Beef Stew?*" I didn't try to keep the incredulity out of my voice.

"Eh. I didn't name him."

I looked at what was left of a door that would have given the storm fits and revised my estimate of our targets' abilities upwards. Hopefully, they'd surrender Sally without a fight. If not, Endless would have to go first. Lightbringers were one of the few types of Powers the storm didn't do well against.

Past the remnants of the security door, the hall led straight ahead for roughly thirty feet before making a sharp turn to the right. Tracks led down through the hall, obvious even to me, thanks to the dust that coated everything else. A single door was set in each wall, and the place was lit by glowtorches to the left of each door. The lights were mounted in sconces, suggesting they'd been here for some time.

I kept my voice low, more metal than melody. "Two-Feathers and I will clear one room at a time. The rest of you, stay here while we do so. Someone needs to keep an eye on anything that might come down the stairs, while the rest of you should be prepared to stop any runners."

"You're not planning to… kill them all, are you?" asked Dorothea.

"Just the Crow. Kansas City's current status quo works for me, considering they're willing to work with my empire. Who knows what would happen if we removed the bosses?"

"You could always annex it," suggested Colton. "Doubt the city could get much worse."

I felt the smile across my visor go flat, though I wasn't sure if it was because he was suggesting I would be a lateral move from six vicious cartels… or if I was just horrified by the idea of trying to rule this shithole on top of my own empire. Either way, I didn't favor the man with a response.

"Anyone runs your way, shoot them in the leg," I said instead. "Unless it's the woman calling herself Sally. Her you should straight-up murder."

Two-Feathers and I made our way down the hall to the first door. It was made from thick wood, and its seal in the frame wasn't perfect, but the only lights were those in the hall with us. Like the gates above, the hinges for this door and the one across the hall had recently been cleaned.

I didn't sense anything within but looked to Two-Feathers anyway. He shook his head, meaning his Stalwart hearing hadn't picked up anything either. That didn't make the room *safe*... there were any number of things that might evade both of our senses, but it *did* lessen the chance that any of our targets were within.

Two-Feathers crouched on the door's other side with spear in hand, his dark eyes fixed on the closed door. Given that I was more or less immortal, we'd both agreed I'd be the one opening the damned thing.

I squeezed the handle and pushed inward. Whoever had cleaned and oiled the hinges had done their job well; as heavy as the door was, it moved easily, the only sound coming from the air it displaced.

Inside were the remnants of a bedroom, drawers pulled from a dresser to lie on the floor and a large table turned on its side. Even the mattress was off the bed, and the long, vertical slashes in its underside told me the people who had tossed the room had been looking for something and not just making a mess.

I doubted there'd be anything to find, given the thoroughness of the search that had already occurred, but I'd have our resident spy case the place anyway. First, we needed to clear the second room.

Rinse. Repeat. Reflect. I spent a few extra seconds this time, just to make the crouching Two-Feathers send me a mildly exasperated look, and then I was pushing my way into a second bedroom, the twin to the first in size, furniture, and condition.

I didn't know why this processing station had had a basement, let alone bedrooms in that basement, when there'd reportedly been an entire barracks up above. I wasn't sure how Sally—meaning the ghost riding the woman we'd known as Selene—knew about this place either.

But what mattered was that they'd come here for a reason. And every door they had to break down, every room they spent time searching, meant we were closing the gap.

I ordered Dorothea and Colton to glance through the trashed bedrooms, leaving the Sparrows to guard the stairs. Meanwhile, Two-Feathers and I headed further into the facility.

A ninety-degree turn took us to a different stretch of hallway, this one with three doors instead of just two. All three were open, and the rooms within were dark and quiet. My nomad and I worked our way through them, one after the other, finding a bathroom, two storerooms, and absolutely zero answers.

At the far end of the hall?

More stairs, descending ever deeper into the earth.

8

We lacked the manpower to keep leaving two-thirds of the group behind, so I sent Two-Feathers back to retrieve the others. So far, we'd been lucky to not encounter any intersections or splits, and that meant the second stairwell could serve as a chokepoint just as well as the first.

And it would put the Sparrows closer to us if they were needed to help protect the more fragile members of our team. Eli didn't seem to be a Power at all, and Nika would almost definitely test out as a One or a Two in the Free States, but they were armed and a hell of a lot more dangerous than Dorothea and her boytoy.

"I don't know what this place is, but if this floor held living quarters and storage, I'm guessing the important stuff is below," I told them all, as we prepared to push downstairs. "Same plan when we get down there."

"Hold the stairs and watch for squirters," acknowledged Eli.

"Search any rooms that you've cleared," added Dorothea.

I let the smile on my visor wash over them. As far as teams went, they were a far cry from some of the heavy-hitters I'd rolled with in the past, starting with the Old Man himself and ending with the crew that helped me take New Memphis… but they were professional enough, and that went a long way.

Also? None of them had tried to betray me yet.

That had to count for something.

There was another security door below, and the pile of cigarettes here was significantly larger, suggesting either growing nerves or a longer delay. Or both. Through the hole that Endless and… *Beef Stew*… had made, we could see more glowtorches. A lot more. The hallway was significantly longer than the last, though it still only had two doorways set in the middle of that hallway, suggesting the rooms themselves must be larger too. Two glowtorches flanked those doors, but there were additional sconces before and after, each holding one of Legion's creations.

Or at least the New Memphis version of such—all the organic material that typified the lord of Baltimore's insane inventions was missing, leaving just the underlying machine pieces. If the bastard had been here, instead of sequestered away in the castle he'd built in the middle of his city-sized petri dish, he'd have no doubt complained about the loss of efficiency brought about by such a change. Shockingly, not everyone was comfortable with—let alone capable of— using people parts in their manufacturing process.

These doors were all similarly open, but whereas the left one appeared to still be intact, the right-hand door appeared to have exploded from within, wood fragments strewn across the hallway and into the other doorway.

Given the thickness of those doors, and the thoroughness of this one's destruction, I was guessing it had been hit by some kind of explosive. Either that or a high-end Power. I was pretty sure Two-Feathers could put a hole through the solid wood, if not tear the door off its hinges, but even he would be hard pressed to smash the whole thing to kindling.

Once again, I had him hang back. I didn't sense anything in either room, but whether it was a trap or a living creature, *something* had destroyed that door, and it had done so from the inside. Even a Stalwart was too fragile to risk.

I went into the room with no door first, as quietly as I could—which was not very. Unlike the floor above, this room had glowtorches inside as well as out. I took in a few details as I scanned the area for any signs of life or movement—polished cement floors, workbenches dominating one side of the enormous space, mechanic bays dominating the other. Finding nothing of interest, I moved just as quickly to the other room.

Another workroom, by the looks of it, although this one had more tables and no bays. A series of shelves along the far wall had been swept free of contents, but otherwise, this room was as clean and clinically spotless as the last.

As long as you ignored the two bodies a half-dozen feet inside the door.

One of them was human, dressed in cartel chic. In life, he would have been at least half a foot taller than my own 6'2", and significantly wider, speaking to either absurd genetics or someone with a Titan's powerset. In death, he looked small and broken, dwarfed by the humanoid machinery that lay in pieces next to and atop his body.

Even before the Break, robots had been more the domain of science fiction than reality. Post-Break, the problems with power scarcity had made that field a dead end for everyone but people like Legion… but apparently nobody had told that to this android or its creators. The thing was large enough that it must have barely fit through the door, and I no longer wondered what the mechanical bays in the previous room had been for. Metal plating had been dented in some places and torn away in others, exposing the wiring beneath that had allowed the cartel bosses and their enforcers to finally bring the thing down.

That spoke to another reason robotics weren't a focus for most current governments: even with the best of materials, it was hard to develop anything that could withstand the more offensive-minded Powers. Maybe if power sources and the necessary materials had been available in abundance, androids would have made sense as a force that could scale, but as one-offs, they simply weren't worth the expense.

Two-Feathers joined me without me having to summon him. The nomad's dark eyes scanned the interior before he relaxed, just a bit.

"One dead body leaves six living ones still to find," I told him. I kicked the dead Titan over and nodded at the bandana tied around his bicep. It was grey and black. "Looks like the Plug Uglies' enforcer. Not quite stiff either, so this happened only a few hours ago. They stripped him of his gear but left the body behind."

"They'll be back to collect him," said Dorothea, joining us from the hallway. "Plug Uglies have a thing about gathering their dead. Think it adds to their rep to never have a corpse wearing their colors lying about."

"Do you know this one?"

"That's Beef Stew, sure enough." She scanned the holes in the former Titan's body. "That thing must have packed some serious power to get through his skin. I once saw him take a bullet to the face and laugh it off."

"At least we know for sure we're on the right track," said Colton, trailing in after his boss and lover. "If not exactly what they were looking—"

We all stopped as a sound reached us from the hallway. It was distant and muffled, but even so…

"That was a scream," said Dorothea, going pale. "The ugly kind."

"Which means someone's still here and, for the moment at least, alive." I ducked back out inro the hall and motioned to the Sparrows, telling them to hold their position. "New plan. The four of us head for whatever made that scream. We'll search the other rooms after."

"You're the boss," said Dorothea.

"Are you going to be able to keep up?"

She flushed then scowled. "Colton and I will be right behind you both."

I doubted that, but it didn't matter, really. I wasn't sure how well the storm would fare against a robot like the one we'd found, but two Normals and one empty shotgun weren't going to turn that tide anyway. Two-Feathers and I would just have to make do.

Riding boots weren't made for running, but I managed anyway, my nomad loping easily beside me. He sent me another look that I had no trouble interpreting, but I waved him off. Yeah, he could reach the screamer a lot faster if he went on ahead, but that would leave him facing Sally and whoever else had survived this strange scavenger hunt.

Two-Feathers was good—he was really, really good—but he was also mortal. And hell if I was going to let him get himself killed before we hashed out what we were to each other.

Two more halls, each a sharp right from the previous one, until I was pretty sure we were back below the burned-out husk of the above-ground facility. All the doors we passed were open, but we didn't even slow, relying on the nomad's senses to sweep the rooms as we ran past.

Another scream came from up ahead, this time a lot closer, and even more anguished than the last. As we approached, a slight figure in red skirts and an ill-fitting bodice darted out from the furthest room. Even sixty feet away, I recognized the woman we'd called Selene, dark hair and pale blue eyes that didn't at all seem surprised to see us. In her hands, she held… something. She turned and scampered for the door at the end of the hall.

Two-Feathers kicked into a sprint, but it would've taken a Speedster to catch her in time. Instead, he took four long strides and launched his namesake spear. The weapon cut through the air, almost as swift as any bullet, and with far greater power behind it. It reached the Crow as she pulled open the door, but she ducked forward with inhuman grace, and the spear caught her in the shoulder instead of piercing her straight through.

That was still enough to toss her forward, but she rose again a moment later, her movements jerky and exhibiting none of the previous grace. She slammed the door behind her moments before Two-Feathers arrived, and the nomad's charge ended with a thud against a door that shook in its frame but refused to give way.

"Check on the screamer," I called to him, still two dozen feet back. "I'll handle the door."

With a nod, he was past me, knife in hand now that his spear was lost behind the locked door. I kept running and dismissed my shell, sending the storm howling the last few feet to vent its fury on the door. Hardwood gave way but it was slower than I'd have liked. First slivers, then strips, then entire chunks ground down into fragments and sawdust. I didn't try to take the door down; I just used the storm to tear a hole and then sent the storm through into the room beyond.

It was small, it was dark, and it was empty.

I reformed my shell in the room and stumbled, realizing what the storm had missed. There was a trapdoor in the floor, now open, with a ladder leading down into the depths. I ignored the ladder and simply jumped, landing with a splash in something vile. It was too dark to see, but I didn't use eyes to see anyway, not really. I could sense that I stood at an intersection. Six tunnels led away from it and what felt like a mix of water and sewage lapped at the narrow walkways along each tunnel's side.

There was no sign of our fugitive Crow. Wherever she'd gone, the door had given her enough of a head start to get her out of the range of my senses. I'd need a tracker, some actual light, and a fucking prayer to find her in all this mess.

Especially with the same ghosts who'd no doubt alerted her to our presence now guiding her through the darkness.

I was starting to understand just why the Free States hated and feared Crows so much.

With nothing left to do, I waded back through the filth to the ladder I'd ignored on my way down. The sewage didn't seem to want to let me go, but I pulled myself up onto the ledge anyway, reformed my shell again so that the leathers were pristine, and started the climb back up to the facility.

Above, I took the five seconds needed to search the sewer access room more thoroughly but found it as empty as it had seemed. Which meant Two-Feathers' spear was somewhere down below, either with the Crow or lost in the rivers of sewage.

This day kept getting worse. The only thing Two-Feathers treasured more than his spear was his horse, and we'd left *that* outside the city.

I removed the bar from the door and pulled what was left of it open before entering the hallway and making my way to the room I'd sent Two-Feathers to investigate. Dorothea and Colton were only now making their way around the far corner. Judging by the way they stumbled to an uncertain halt, the yellow face across my visor had lost its smile entirely.

I ignored the two and pushed into a room that had seemingly begun its life as some sort of storage vault but was now serving a second career as the set of a horror vid. There were two bloody bodies on the floor, both in the colors of the Dead Rabbits. The first had been stabbed at least a half-dozen times from behind, the second had a gaping smile where his throat should have been. A third body was strapped down to a table, limbs hanging over the side and bound to each of that table's legs.

I didn't know a lot of the cartel leadership on sight, but I recognized the Devil in his flamboyant best: red shirt, black leather pants, and knee-high boots like he was some sort of pre-Break aristocracy. That shirt was now in tatters, as were his pants, testament to the many, many cuts that had been made by a small-bladed knife and a woman with entirely too much experience in agonizing death.

Sally had wanted this death as slow and painful as possible.

Only… the Devil wasn't quite there. Not yet, even if it was just a matter of time.

Two-Feathers was trying to stop the bleeding, but it was like trying to hold back the ocean with his hands. I didn't bother. Instead, I stepped past the nomad and leaned over the Devil, letting my visor fill the only eye Sally had left him, an eye that was almost all pupil and broken blood vessels.

"Help…" the Devil begged, for likely the first time in his life.

"There's no helping you," I said, my voice more metal than sound. "Not without the kind of Healer who hasn't walked this earth in decades. But tell us what we need, and we'll at least end it quick."

He didn't nod—I wasn't sure he *could* nod anymore—but I took his silence for acquiescence.

"What were you and the other cartels here for? How did Sally get you to come to the Zoo?"

"Weapons," he breathed, every word paining a man who'd made his living from causing the same. "The kind this city hasn't ever seen. Enough to take over. Three cartels instead of six. A stronger position to negotiate with…" He blinked once, blood leaking out of his mouth as it quirked into some grotesque rendition of a smile.

"With me," I finished. "Weapons? Is that what she took?"

He tried and failed to shake his head; eye fluttering closed again. "No weapons. All lies. Just death."

"Then what did she take? Why was she really here?"

The Devil coughed once, tried to form some final word, and went still.

Fucking humans. Even the bad ones died too soon.

οοο

Colton lost his lunch on entering the room, adding to the ambiance. Dorothea was able to hold it down; she identified the other two bodies as Endless, the Dead Rabbits' Lightbringer, and Smith, that same cartel's former boss. We found the missing two back in the rooms we'd sprinted past. Both were dead, although it looked like one of those deaths had come through traps and a second automaton, and the last had been perpetrated by Endless himself.

"Near as I can tell," said Dorothea, emerging from the last such room, "after the first two enforcers went down, Smith and the Devil made a plan to cut the Plug Uglies out of their new government. Ol' Fingers never saw it coming."

Fingers being the now-former boss of the Plug Uglies. By that point, he'd been alone, and that was a bad place to be among your criminal peers.

"And then Sally did for the others," I concluded.

"I guess she had a special hate for the Devil." Despite herself, Dorothea was looking a bit green. Given that most of the man's fluids had been decorating the table, floor, and walls of the storage room we'd found him in, I didn't hold it against her.

I nodded. "Another name on her endless list."

"Are you *sure* Sally's just a low-ranking Crow?" That was Colton, wiping his mouth and trying not to focus on anything around him. "I saw Endless fight once. He took five men down like they were standing still. And Smith was a Power too, even if he kept that fact on the downlow." He frowned. "A woman with a knife whose only power is that she talks to ghosts? I just don't see it."

I didn't either, which irritated me to no end. We'd spent months with the Crow back when she was going by Selene, and she'd been spooky as shit, of course, but the most she'd done was kill a handful of armed soldiers. Had she really been capable of slaughtering Powers all along?

I didn't know and I didn't like not knowing.

We sent Colton back to update the Sparrows, while Two-Feathers went down into the sewers with a glowtorch he'd ripped from its sconce. The nomad emerged soon after, empty-handed except for that glowtorch, and followed by a stench that had Dorothea gagging. No spear, and while he *had* found a trail for Sally, he'd lost that trail again almost as swiftly.

My nomad didn't emote a whole hell of a lot, but I could read the frustration in his eyes.

Absent other leads, we returned to our search of the facility. Other than the vault where the Devil had been tortured and killed, the rest of the rooms were split between science labs and workrooms. It was in one of the former that we finally found a clue.

"You're going to want to read this," said Dorothea, bringing over a leather-wrapped journal.

"Just summarize it for me."

"This lab was put in place by your predecessor to handle experiments considered too dangerous for New Memphis or even the processing station above us."

"The robots?"

"As far as I can tell, they were just a side project. Armed security that they didn't have to pay or feed."

"What were they working on, then?"

"A lot of things." She read the lack of patience in my body language with a diplomat's precision and hurried on. "But as far as I can tell, most of those things never came to fruition. Last entry in this journal is from right around the time your *other* Crow objected to being kidnapped. They must have gone up into the main facility when the alarm sounded, leaving all of this behind. It was probably their ghosts that told Sally something of value was down here in the first place."

I let my silence fill the spacious room. Sooner or later, the spy would get to the point.

It didn't take long; again, Dorothea *did* have a brain.

"As for *what* that was, I'm not a scientist, and a lot of this guy's technobabble is completely beyond me, but… it sounds like it was supposed to be a new kind of dampener."

"What?" Dampeners had been the invention of a Free States Technomancer named Cornell who had attempted to mimic the active abilities of those Powers known as Nulls. Cornell had died not long after his invention went public; turned out a lot of Powers hadn't taken well to one of their own giving the government a way to even temporarily strip them of abilities. But by that point, it had been too late; dampeners were being built and installed in the handful of places that both needed that sort of security and could afford it.

Because that was the thing that *didn't* make any sense about what Dorothea was saying. Dampeners involved massive amounts of machinery and even more power to impact comparatively small spaces. The supernatural prison known as the Hole occupied almost forty acres underground, and most of that was dedicated to its dampeners.

Meanwhile, whatever Sally had run away with had been small enough and light enough to fit in her hands.

"He referred to it as a PNPD," she continued. "Meaning Portable Nullification Pulse Device." She turned to another page and scanned through its handwritten contents. "At the time of the last journal entry, he'd just finished a working prototype… I guess that's what she took? It does have to be recharged after every use."

"So less a dampener than a disruptor." It didn't make things much better, and I was betting *that* was how Sally had killed the three people in the vault. Surprise could make all the difference when accompanied by a sharp knife, especially if the victims found themselves unexpectedly without their powers.

That left us with two problems. The first was Sally herself… on the run, presumably bleeding but very much alive, and now in possession of something that made her even more dangerous. Assuming she would be able to recharge it, the PNPD would dramatically widen the scope of available targets for her never-ending mission of murder.

The second problem was the journal in Dorothea's hands. We hadn't found a ton of paperwork in our search, owing to there only being a single working paper mill outside of Wichita, but any or all of it could contain more clues on what exactly the unnamed Technomancer—and I was convinced that was exactly what he'd been—had done to create his device.

If these things were able to be made without a Technomancer's skills? Not to mention mass-produced?

It would change the world all over again.

And I honestly had no idea what I wanted to do about that.

"I'll take the journal," I finally decided. "We'll put together a larger group to come move both the bodies and retrieve the lab work. But first, we need to deal with the cartels. We've found their missing bosses; we need to get that word back to whoever's next in each gang's chain of command before someone dumb does something even dumber and the whole city burns down around us."

There wasn't much more to say about that. This had been a colossal failure, but at least what we'd found might keep the city in one piece. We gathered the Sparrows and Colton on our way out, hurrying through the hallways and up both flights of stairs. I wasn't sure how much time we'd lost down below, but if we could avoid spending the night in the Zoo, I wanted to do so. The district had been dangerous enough to my team in daylight.

Unfortunately, when we emerged into the remnants of Bakersfield's devastation, the sun was long gone, replaced by stars that were only occasionally visible through a thick cloud cover.

That was the bad news.

The worse news?

The cityscape wasn't entirely dark.

Flickers of crimson and orange dotted the horizon to our east and north, revealing that some of what I'd initially taken for clouds was instead smoke. The fires were distant enough that they had to be occurring in other districts. And even over the dull, wordless murmur that filled the Zoo's streets, we could hear another sound.

Gunfire.

The sound was too sporadic to be a single large-scale battle and too widespread to be just a single skirmish.

Shaky's prediction had come true: war had broken out in Kansas City between the cartels.

This diplomatic mission of mine was going great.

9

Part of me wanted to retrieve my bike, ride off, and let the districts tear themselves apart. I wasn't responsible for the cartels, and I wasn't responsible for Kansas City either. People would die, yeah, but people *always* died. That was the way of the world, and there was nothing I or the storm could do about that.

Maybe if I'd been alone, I'd have done just that. Hell, even a year earlier and I *definitely* would have. But Two-Feathers had put two and two together just like I had, and even in the darkness I could picture the look on his face. My nomad could kill—and had, many times over—but he wasn't a killer down to his bones. He had a moral compass completely at odds with most people I knew, and he wasn't the sort to sit back and watch innocents pay the price for someone else's ambitions.

Even if it *was* happening in a city he didn't like.

So instead of heading for the hills like a sane person, I pulled our crew back into the bunker where there was light to see by and we could all hear something beyond the sounds of a city descending into true chaos. Nika and Eli were looking squirrely and Colton was just plain scared, but it was Dorothea I turned to.

"What's the plan, boss?" she asked, voice tight in a way her studied nonchalance couldn't quite mask.

"A cartel war was always a possibility, right?"

"Of course." She swallowed. "This is kind of a worst-case situation though."

"Still, you must have given some thought to how such a war would go down."

"Maybe on quieter nights, sure."

"Care to share with the rest of the class?"

The spy blew out a long breath. "Honestly, I don't—"

"You're not being graded on this," I told her, as if schools were a thing anywhere outside the Free States and New Memphis. "I just need a better idea of what might be happening."

She took a deep breath, swallowed again, and nodded. "Well, with the Diablos, Plug Uglies, and Dead Rabbits all missing their leaders, they're probably the most vulnerable. The Horde were down a bit after they lost their enforcers a month or so ago, but that's only made them more aggressive… and their numbers have been growing steadily."

"Which is why they took over the eastern Outskirts so quickly when the Diablos didn't show up."

"Right. Now, because the Dead Rabbits are up in Riverside, they're probably the most secure of the gangs, unless the Diablos join up with another cartel to make a play. Which… *probably* won't happen, given the rhetoric being thrown around by the Devil's captains lately. But it's the Plug Uglies that are in a *really* bad spot, seeing as how they're sandwiched between the Zoo, the Skulls, and the Horde. The two cartels will almost definitely be headed to Raytown to see who can take out the Plug Uglies first."

"You said earlier that the Uglies and the Rabbits had a secret alliance?"

"Yeah, although I'm guessing that went out the window when Smith and Endless conspired with the Devil to kill Fingers a few hours ago."

"Which is something their respective cartels don't know about."

"True. Why?"

I let the variables roll around in my head, like the dice Jules used to throw before he started cheating at cards instead. There was a lot we didn't know, and a lot less we could do about it, but districts were burning as we spoke, and while nobody would mourn a thousand or so dead cartel members, inter-gang violence would swallow the city whole.

Maybe… maybe what this city needed was a little bit of well-applied benevolent authoritarianism.

"Because," I finally replied, letting my gaze sweep across the five people in my temporary crew, "we're taking Kansas City."

"We are?" asked Colton.

"With what army?" Eli wanted to know.

"The one you're all going to help put together."

For the first time, Nika spoke, her voice an eerie match for her brother's. "You're not paying us to fight a war."

"No," I agreed, the storm audible in my voice. "But I'll pay triple for you to help me win one."

ooo

We burned even more time standing there in the bunker, as Dorothea did her best to download all the relevant information in her head. Names I vaguely recognized from a briefing I hadn't paid much attention to. Old grudges and rivalries that hadn't been important enough to make it into that same briefing. Quirks and habits and known flaws for the people who mattered.

All in all, it took almost an hour to put a plan together and gather everything we needed. It took several more hours to make our way north out of the Zoo, and the journey was only that quick because the district seemed content to let us leave.

Once we neared the river, we split into pairs, each heading to our respective assignments. I went east, skirting the edge of the Zoo until I reached Raytown again, walking through streets that even the rats had been wise enough to abandon.

"This is bad," said Dorothea, for at least the fourth time.

"That's the world for you." She was the guide, but I was walking fast enough that she had to occasionally jog to keep up. "Welcome to being an active participant, and not just an observer."

"I'm not—"

"A soldier. Yeah, I got that much the first three times. But you signed up to do more yesterday. Welcome to all that entails."

She was silent for a bit, then spat again. "That house better be worth it."

"A house, a fence, and a dog," I confirmed. "Although I'd suggest a cat instead."

"Why a cat?"

"They're survivors."

"Once I'm in New Memphis, I won't *need* a survivor. I want blind, unwavering loyalty and affection."

Which explained Colton. To each their own.

There was another chorus of gunfire, this one not quite so distant, and I picked up my pace. The plan, such as it was, required the Plug Uglies to be in dire straits… but still operational enough to be of use.

"How many more blocks?" I asked.

She eyeballed the houses we were walking past. A few had light leaking out through shuttered windows or from under closed doors, but the rest were nothing but dark shadows. Silhouetted against the fire-lit skyline, they looked like unmarked tombstones. "The Uglies' base should be twenty minutes or so away… but those guns sounded a lot closer than that."

That left me in a bit of a quandary. We could try to circumvent whatever skirmish was happening now and head straight for the base where Fingers' remaining captains were likely holed up. *Or* we could make our presence known here and now by helping out. The second option would leave the Plug Uglies in better shape overall and probably worsen our negotiating position, but it would also give us a better in with the cartel.

The storm clashed inside of me, ever-hungry, ever-eager, and I couldn't find it in me to disagree. Saving a handful of Plug Uglies wouldn't change their dire straits or the fact that they had two full cartels gunning for them, but it *would* paint me in a positive light. And considering I didn't want to wipe out Raytown's ruling gang—that the whole point of this plan was to harness them instead—good impressions mattered.

I headed for the action.

We were a half-block away from the gunfight when I remembered I wasn't by myself, and that Dorothea was a lot less durable than Two-Feathers. Barely slowing, I turned to the closest house and kicked in its plywood door. My shell wasn't as strong as a Stalwart, let alone a Titan, but it wasn't weak either. Wood exploded inward to reveal three people huddled inside the house's main living space: a man, a woman, and a child. Two scrambled for safety, while the third came at me with a length of old rebar that could have been part of the storm.

I took the weapon away from him, and put him down, doing my best to avoid any real damage to someone just defending his family. The storm's noise filled the room, barely constrained by my shell, and drowning out even the nearby gunfire.

"I'm going to finish the nearby fight," I told the family. "This woman will stay here with you until it's safe."

"Miss Dorothea?" asked the woman, her voice tight with fear and shock. She stood between us and her daughter, blocking the path to the house's only bedroom.

"Hi, Casey. Sorry about the door. When this is done, I promise I'll send Colton over to repair it."

The other woman nodded, straightening slightly.

"You two know each other?"

Dorothea gave me a look. "I'm a businesswoman in the district. Casey and Carl both occasionally take their meals at the Sunken Ship."

"Fair enough. Keep your head down. I'll be back to collect you when the bullets stop flying."

I left as the man—Carl—was still finding his way back to his feet. The door was a lost cause, hanging from a single hinge and splintered where my size-twelve boots had caved it in, but I pulled it shut behind me anyway. In the darkness, you could barely tell it was broken.

If you ignored the light streaming through its cracks and holes.

And the way the whole thing swayed in the breeze.

...I probably should have just knocked.

ooo

When I reached the intersection, the skirmish was almost over. There were a dozen bodies in the street, and the light leaking out from nearby houses told me most of them were wearing grey and black. The armed men and women moving through the corpses, on the other hand, were in green and silver.

It had been a coin flip whether we'd be facing the Horde or the Skulls, but it looked like the Horde had been first to the fight. That was good. According to Dorothea, the cartel was already down two enforcers, and that would make my job a little bit easier.

Even better? They were the new kids on the block, and they'd ruffled quite a few feathers on their path to power.

There were still a couple of Plug Uglies alive, but they'd taken shelter in a shallow doorway, and some of the Horde were moving to flank them, operating more like a military unit than the ragtag bunch of hoodlums they were supposed to be.

With the darkness as cover, I wasn't spotted by the rest of the small force until I emerged from my side street. The first few shots were either meant to be warnings or a direct rebuttal to my thoughts about their level of training… bullets ricocheted off building walls around me, not a one coming even with a half-dozen feet.

The next salvo didn't have that problem. My shell staggered as three rounds tore through my chest and a fourth left a hole in my visor and a larger hole in my face and the back of my head. That last bullet didn't make it through the back of my helmet but instead ricocheted around inside, doing further damage.

And that *fucking hurt*.

I didn't dismiss my shell so much as the storm just tore its way free of its own volition, leaving behind flesh and blood and frailty to fall upon the nearest gang members. More shots rang out—a lot of them, this time—but it was music the storm couldn't hear, tiny bits of metal madness dismissed or even absorbed by the greater chaos.

Bodies fell in wet chunks. A few of my would-be attackers fled the slaughter only to find themselves slipping in their own victims' remains, helpless and unable to escape the steel and shrapnel that came surging down the dark street.

I reformed my shell, whole again, and turned to the rest of the Horde's kill squad. These were the ones who had been flanking the Plug Uglies; they now found themselves caught between their prey and a predator they had no answer for.

"We don't want no trouble," stammered one, holding his hands and rifle above his head. "We ain't got beef with the Queen of Smiles."

"And yet here we all are." I took a step closer, then another, and the five of them retreated in uneasy silence. "If it were up to me, I'd let you leave," I lied, "but a plan is a plan. You can understand that, I'm sure."

"Plan? What plan?"

"The plan where the two Plug Uglies in the doorway get off their asses and shoot you from behind," I said, letting impatience and annoyance join the steel in my voice.

It took a second—long enough for me to *really* question the greater strategy I'd established with Two-Feathers and the others—but even as the Horde started to wheel about, shots rang from the doorway in question. Two targets went down, including the one trying to bargain for his freedom, and by the time the remaining three returned fire, the storm was dancing among them, ripping, rending, and generally adding to the bloody artwork already painted across the street and walls.

I reformed my shell again, shiny black almost invisible in a sea of crimson, bone, and green and silver scraps. A half-dozen steps brought me to the two surviving Plug Uglies and under the light of the house they'd tried to find refuge within, I saw exactly why they'd been so slow to respond.

One had her legs splayed out in front of her, barely propped up by the door as blood gushed from at least three places in her chest and abdomen. I didn't have to check those wounds to know she was a goner. It was some kind of minor miracle that she'd survived this long, let alone shot a gun and hit anything.

The second Plug Ugly was in better shape.

Sort of.

He'd only taken two hits. The first had burned a line through the hair at his temple, missing both his ear and anything vital by an inch in divergent directions. It bled profusely, as most head wounds did, but otherwise looked superficial. It was the other wound that was problematic. A bullet had shattered his elbow and what remained below, dangling by threads of tendon and muscle, was never going to be right again. A tourniquet, applied just above that elbow, was the only reason he hadn't bled out yet. Still, his other hand clutched a rifle, and the eyes that wandered up my long form were aware, if flooded with pain.

"Well, shit," I said, looking down at him. I hoped the other skirmishes were going better than this. The plan required the Plug Uglies to be battered but not yet broken. If the Horde was close to finishing off their rivals… well, I'd have to figure something else out. "I'm guessing you're not up to walking?"

"I know you," he murmured, wincing as he tried to stand. He couldn't have been more than twenty or twenty-one, younger even than Two-Feathers, and a hell of a lot less dangerous.

"Most people do, kid."

"Tried to shake… you down… once…"

He slumped back against the wall and would have tipped over entirely if I hadn't gotten an arm under his. His non-fucked-up arm, not that you could tell from the strangled scream he made when I halted his fall.

I bit back a sigh, ducked down, and slid my other arm under his legs, straightening up again until I had him in a princess carry. A live Plug Ugly should serve as my ticket to see whoever was heading up the defense, and if this skirmish told me anything, it was that I needed to see them ASAP.

But first, I needed my guide.

"Lot of people have tried to shake me down over the years," I told the barely conscious man in my arms as we headed back down the street. "The fact that you survived your stupidity means I must have liked you."

Hell if I could remember him though. I'd have blamed the darkness, but the truth was both faces and voices had a way of blurring over time, like footprints in the rain.

His eyes were scrunched shut, tiny whimpers escaping with every step I took, but he was still coherent enough to shake his head. "Lily saved me," he managed.

Okay, that *did* ring a bell.

"Last year? Western outskirts?" I didn't have to see his nod to know I was right. There *had* been a mouthy shit on the patrol that stopped me, the patrol Lily had been leading. But what was his name? "Were you… Keith?"

"Kev."

"Right." I didn't bother saying that Kev had seen better days; he was already living that truth. Instead, I used my foot to knock on a door barely hanging from its upper hinge. Moments later, Dorothea answered, sharp eyes taking note of the body in my arms.

"We need to go," I said. "Now."

"Is he going to make it?"

I shrugged, eliciting another moan. "I guess we'll find out."

The spy turned back to the family. "Carl, make sure everyone stays inside and in the back room. Keep your heads down at least until morning. I've got to take this woman to the district bosses. Once things are safe again, Colton will be here to fix things up."

If she got a reply, I didn't hear it. She did her best to pull the ruined door shut and then gave me a look every bit as eloquent as Two-Feathers'.

"I didn't know you had friends in the district," I said, ignoring that look as she led us down a different side street.

"Friends are a luxury for people in my business. They're just customers. That's about as much as you can hope for."

That sounded depressing.

And honestly? Kind of familiar.

ooo

It was another twelve blocks to the nondescript series of rowhouses that the Plug Uglies had transformed into their headquarters. Along the way, we ran across the remnants of three battles, one which the Horde had clearly won, and two where the bodies littering the streets were a mix of both green and silver and grey and black.

The headquarters, at least, were still in one piece. Barricades had been erected, and men and women manned the battlements, torches lighting the surrounding intersection. Bodies below those barricades were evidence of at least one unsuccessful assault by the Horde.

Battered but not yet broken.

Thankfully, that still seemed to be the case.

10

I took the lead as we approached, given that I was a hell of a lot less vulnerable to errant bullets than Dorothea. Kev was still in my arms, but he had passed out again. If it came to it, he'd never know if he got killed by friendly fire.

Thankfully, someone up on the barricade had a brain, and even as rifles were swinging to point in our direction, that person was shouting at the would-be marksmen to stand down. I entered the halo of light and then reached the makeshift gate—two wagons pushed together—without a single bullet being fired.

"What do you want?" called down a different voice.

"I need to talk to whoever's in charge with Fingers gone."

"They're uh… busy."

"Is that Kev you've got?" asked someone else. "Where's the rest of his crew?"

"Dead," I said. And then, before anyone could get weird on me. "I came too late to save the others, but he's still alive. So far."

I waited for the gate to open, but nobody took the hint. Behind me, Dorothea shifted nervously.

"Are you here on a… uh… job?" asked another gang member, this one barely visible atop the barricade.

"Not yet. I was just in the neighborhood. Think of me as a concerned citizen."

"But—"

"Look… you can open the gate, or you can sit here waiting for the other cartels to kill you," I interrupted. Arguments with the gate guards weren't going to get me anywhere, and time was wasting. "Either way, make a fucking choice."

"We can't let you—" started the first guard.

"Fine." I lowered Kev's unconscious body to the street, straightened up, and turned to go.

"Wait! Where are you going?"

From the look on Dorothea's face, she was wondering the same.

"Away," I said, nothing but metal in my voice. "The way I see it, the rest of the Horde will be here by daybreak, and even if you do somehow fight them off? The Skulls will be right behind. If you idiots don't want me to stop that, I might as well find somewhere with a view and enjoy the show."

That stymied the two gate guards long enough for a third man to reach them, this one older, smaller, and trimly dressed in the cartel's colors. "What's going on?" he growled, low voice a dead ringer for the one I'd heard shouting a minute or so earlier. "And why is that *vato* bleeding all over the street when he should be in the infirmary?"

"That's Kev," I called up. "He needs a doctor."

"I can see that, given that I still have both of the eyes my *madre* gave me. But what about you? What can the Plug Uglies do for the Queen of Smiles herself?"

"Like I told your men, I need to speak with whoever's in charge. And to be honest, I'd rather not have to kill a bunch of you to do so. Considering I'm here to save your cartel, that would be… counterproductive."

"Save us? How are you planning to accomplish that?"

I fixed him with a look he could feel if not see. "I can tell you one thing for sure… it *won't* be by standing out here waiting for the other cartels to crawl up your collective asses."

"None of the stories ever said you were funny." He shook his head and called down below. "Open it up."

One of the wagons was slowly rolled far enough to the side to clear a path for entry. I passed through, met on the other side by the three men I'd been speaking with.

"I'll take the queen and her friend to Ezekiel," said the newcomer. "One of you *putos* can see to our injured man. We're going to need every gun we have if this miracle plan turns out to be nothing but shit in a can."

"None of the stories ever said *you* were a poet," I told the older cartel member, following him through an oversized door into the conjoined buildings. Dorothea remained on my heels, quiet as a mouse.

"Makes you wonder," he replied. "Anyway, I hope you're on the up and up, because shit's gone sideways. No Fingers, no Stew, and now you show up in the middle of the night looking like the Grim Reaper herself." He paused to give Dorothea another look. "And you're traveling with… the woman who owns the Sunken Ship?"

"I needed a guide through your district," I said.

"Sure." He led us down a narrow corridor and past a tripod-mounted machine gun operated by three men at the far end. Two turns later, we passed through an internal courtyard with balconies on the second and third floors looming over us, and then back into another, slightly nicer, hallway. "Anyway, Ezekiel's the underboss. When Fingers didn't come back, we started preparing for war, but the fucking Horde were on our patrols tonight before we even knew they were here."

"And now?"

"Now, when they come to finish us off, they'll at least find themselves in a fight." His smile was half gold and half ivory. "Unless they hired you to cut the head off the snake, in which case we're just plain fucked, I suppose."

"Some people might think twice about taking a potential assassin right to her supposed target."

"You said it yourself. We turn you away, we die anyway. We try to stop you… well, I've heard the stories. Same shit, same day. Better to trust you're on the level and maybe get out of this in one piece."

That was a whole lot more rational than I'd have expected from the cartel's rank and file. Dorothea had gone over the upper ranks of each cartel, and given this man's demeanor and intelligence, I was betting he'd been part of that briefing. But putting a name to his unassuming face…

"You're not *Crazy Carlo*, are you?" I asked, citing the name of one of the Plug Uglies' older captains.

"I guess you actually *have* heard of me."

"I thought you'd be… well… crazier."

"That's the thing you'll learn when you get to my age," Carlo said, conveniently ignoring the fact that there'd been stories of me since before he was born. "People grow up, but the names and titles they earn along the way? That shit just sticks, know what I'm saying?"

I tapped my visor and the smiley-face decal splashed across its surface. "I really do."

"I guess you would. Zeke and the other captains have been trying to work out some sort of plan that won't get us all skinned and worn like coats." Two guards flanked a closed door, and angry voices were audible from within. "Sounds like it's going just as well as expected. There's a reason I was out on the wall instead."

I kind of liked this non-crazy version of Crazy Carlo.

I really hoped I wouldn't have to kill him.

The two guards weren't happy about stepping aside for me, especially with Kev's blood still all over my leathers, but they weren't dumb enough to ignore a captain's orders either. As they scooted out of our way, I turned to Dorothea.

"Stay here," I said, collecting the small bundle that she handed me. And then, to the guards. "This woman's a business owner, a resident of your district, and someone I hired as a guide. Keep her safe."

"We're not your—"

"Just do it, *vato*," said Carlo, cutting off the protest before it could fully form. He didn't wait for acknowledgment but pushed the door open.

I followed the cartel captain inside.

There wasn't much to recommend the main meeting room of the Plug Uglies' leadership. It was half the size of my council room back in New Memphis, and while the furniture was nice for Kansas City, it was also a hodgepodge of styles and designs. Maybe the few months in my capital had made me a snob, but I recognized when someone's interior decorating style boiled down to *steal whatever looks even sort of nice from neighboring houses.*

Hanging lanterns lit the center of the room with a warm, ruddy glow but deep shadows cloaked the room's corners. A large table dominated the room with an oversized easy chair at that table's head. The chair's upholstery had probably started life as some shade of white but was now every bit as grey as the cartel's dominant color. It was one of six chairs at the table, only three of which were occupied. Against the left wall, an additional five people lurked, their demeanors screaming *enforcer.*

If *my* gang was being attacked, I'd have had those enforcers out on the street doing damage. As far as I was concerned, that was strike one against the cartel's new leadership.

Seated in the oversized chair, Ezekiel looked like he'd have been more comfortable standing with the other barely civilized killers. He wore a grey vest instead of the cartel's usual jackets, and his bare arms were every bit as big as the now-dead Beef Stew's. Burn scars covered one side of his face and most of his scalp.

To his left was a woman I'd known long before Dorothea's briefing. Lily had a face only a mother could love, and a level head that had kept her breathing in a traditionally male-dominated cartel. A year ago, she'd been stuck on patrol duty; she'd come a seriously long way in the time since to have a seat at the table.

The final captain had long hair that reminded me of Two-Feathers and scrawny shoulders that immediately put that comparison to bed. He went by Bones for reasons that had nothing to do with powers and everything to do with his lack of physique. I didn't think much of the nickname, but it still beat the hell out of *Beef Stew*.

Bones and Ezekiel were arguing when we entered and kept on going, neither one taking any notice of our arrival.

Eventually, Carlo cleared his throat.

"Carlo? What are you—" Ezekiel's voice trailed off as he realized the captain wasn't alone. He surged to his feet, not quite Titan-sized, but still large enough to respectably loom. "What is this?"

"Your lucky day," I told him. "I'm here to offer the Uglies a deal."

"The queen herself has come to bargain?" Beady eyes scanned my form head to toe in a fashion I'd become all too accustomed to since my creation. Ezekiel's smile was every bit as mean and as ugly as Dorothea's... but that was fine. It was his aura of unearned, smug superiority that I took issue with.

That was strike two.

He waved a massive arm. "By all means, take a seat, and fill us in. If I like the sound of this deal, maybe I'll even pass it up the chain to Fingers when he returns."

"Fingers isn't coming back. Beef Stew either." My voice was flat, empty of anything but metal. Ignoring the offered chair, I underhanded the object Dorothea had given me. It hit the center of the table with an audible thump, rolling a few times.

Bones had leaped away from the table, as if a few feet would have protected him from any bomb I'd smuggled inside, but Lily remained seated. She reached over and peeled the fabric away to reveal a gaudy monstrosity of a ring.

"Where did you get that?" demanded Ezekiel.

"I found Fingers and his enforcer dead in the Zoo," I said, speaking to all nine people in the room instead of just the underboss. "Figured the Plug Uglies would want to know."

"You just *found* them?" Zeke sneered. "How do we know you didn't kill them?"

"Why would I come here if I had?" I held back a sigh. Fingers, by all accounts, had been a clever man. His underboss was a disappointment.

Ezekiel didn't have an answer, but he didn't let that slow him down. Instead, he took the ring and slid it onto his right pinky. Made for a far smaller man, it got stuck at the first knuckle.

"We'll get back to Fingers' death," he warned, "as well as whatever part you did or didn't play in it. But if he's gone, that means I'm the boss now. Whatever deal you've brought us, you'll have to sell me on it. So, what are you offering?"

"I'm offering the Plug Uglies' continued existence, the Horde's complete destruction, and backing for you and two other cartels to run this city."

That set the three captains—Carlo included—muttering among themselves, but Ezekiel didn't seem impressed.

"And what do you want in return?"

"Control."

"Yeah, fuck that."

"What do you mean *control*," asked Lily, speaking for the first time.

"That's not your question to ask—"

"Just that," I answered, talking over Ezekiel's protests. "Publicly, everything continues as usual. Privately, the Plug Uglies work for me."

"You want Kansas City," murmured Carlo, shocked realization coloring his words.

"I don't *want* it, but I'm not going to sit here and watch it burn either. Not when that would fuck up trade and create all sorts of problems on my empire's borders." I turned my smile on the room. "You boys had your chance and dropped the ball."

"Sounds more like a collar than a deal," said Ezekiel.

I didn't say anything, instead borrowing a page from Two-Feathers and letting silence speak for me. The city had seen more than its share of collars. The Plug Uglies were as much a part of that as anyone.

"What if we say no?" asked Bones, in a voice as insubstantial as the rest of him. "Will you kill us?"

"No need. I'll just stand back and let the Horde do it for me. Maybe their leadership will be more reasonable when the killing's done."

"The Horde? Reasonable?" Carlo's voice was low, pitched only to carry to me. "You really *do* have jokes."

"The Skulls then. Word is they'll be here soon too."

"Take your deal and get out," growled Ezekiel. "One boss to another, I'm gonna let you walk free despite this disrespect, but fuck if I'll ever be your slave."

Any other day, and that was a stance I could almost appreciate, but in the face of certain destruction? As far as I was concerned, that was strike three. Nobody outside of the Free States even knew what baseball was anymore, but Ezekiel was well and truly *out*.

"Boss…" Bones turned back to the bigger man. "We're on our back foot already. The Horde outnumber us and they're coming. Add in the Skulls…"

"We live on our feet and we'll die on them too! If any of you have a problem with that, you can fuck right—"

Ezekiel's words cut off with a gasp as thunder erupted in the meeting room and a bright crimson flower unfurled in the underboss' chest.

To my right, smoke drifted lazily from the barrel of the revolver now in Crazy Carlo's hand. The giant took two steps towards the older captain and the gun barked again, once, then twice.

For all his size, Ezekiel wasn't a Titan. Three bullets, two to the chest and one through the center of his snarling face, sent him crashing to the floor.

The enforcers had made it halfway across the room, but slowed with Ezekiel's death, uncertain what to do about the sudden change in their power structure.

"I take it you're the new boss?" Lily's voice was dry, doing a bang-up job of masking the fear underneath.

"After killing our leader?" Carlo shook his head. "What sort of precedent would that set for the street rats? One of you two will have to take over. Exile me for my actions and I promise that'll be the end of it. If you choose to execute me instead… we might have to continue this conversation."

Given that he was the only person with a weapon out and at the ready, it seemed suicidal for the other captains to take him up on the second option. The enforcers had already demonstrated they weren't fast enough to stop bullets.

Lily and Bones looked at each other. The slender man shrugged as he returned to his seat. "Captain's as far as I ever wanted to go, to be honest. Got myself two women, a nice place, and more than enough responsibility as it is."

"You'll back my play then?" Lily asked him, receiving a nod. "Well, shit." She sighed and made her way over to Ezekiel's body to retrieve the ring from his pinky finger. It fit easily on her pointer instead. As she took her place on the closest thing the cartel had to a throne, bloody though it was, she turned to Carlo. "I want to hear more about the queen's deal, but we've got you to deal with first."

"I lived outside the city when I was just a *niño*," said the other man. "I can manage again."

"Maybe, but you and I both know the Plug Uglies have a rule. Once you're in, you're in. Nobody leaves the family alive. Besides," she added, ignoring the way Carlo's grip tightened on his gun, "we're already low on manpower and brain trust both. I can't afford to lose my new underboss."

"Your new…" Carlo tilted his head for a moment, then holstered his weapon, taking a seat at the table. "I guess you're right, boss. The Plug Uglies need to stick together if we're going to get through this."

"Damn right." She looked to Bones, received another nod, and then turned to the still-silent enforcers. "Anyone have any issues with that decision *or* my ascension, now's the time to have your say."

The room stayed quiet.

"Good," said Lily. "Which brings us back to the queen's deal."

"Ezekiel was a raging asshole with a micro-penis," said one of the enforcers, a woman with a deep southern drawl and every inch of her skin covered in tattoos, "but that don't mean he was wrong neither, boss. I ain't gonna be a slave. Not again."

"I'm not interested in slaves," I told her. "Now or ever. What I want are vassals."

The proclamation didn't get quite the reception I'd hoped for, a bunch of people turning about and muttering to each other. Finally, Carlo spoke for the rest of their crew.

"What the fuck's a vassal?"

11

It took a while to explain what a vassal meant to people who'd never even heard of public education, let alone the feudal system. It took even longer to elaborate on the plan that dead Ezekiel had rejected out of hand. In the end, the Plug Uglies' three remaining leaders accepted my deal, and they and the enforcers swore themselves to secrecy. As far as the rest of the city would know, they would remain independent, having simply hired me to help defend the district.

I wasn't worried about any of them breaking that silence either. If word got out that the Plug Uglies were working for a foreign warlord, their lives collectively wouldn't be worth a damn. Having made the deal, they were now stuck with honoring it.

Or with waiting until the time was right and then trying to double-cross me, which would get them dead *almost* as quickly. Lily already knew I didn't play; the rest of her people could either take her word for it or find out for themselves.

As for why I was bothering to save one of Kansas City's cartels? As much as I hated to admit it, I'd realized that my predecessor's original tactics made sense. As good as *taking Kansas City* had sounded when I said it, it would be almost impossible to manage without destroying the place… and that would rob it of its value as both a buffer zone and free trade hub. The cartels were undeniably shitty, but they were what passed for current government. It would be better and more efficient to suborn that government from within than to rebuild the whole thing from the ground up.

For once, I was pretty sure my councilors would agree with me, whenever word got back to them. After all, wars were expensive. And that was money that could be used to rebuild their palatial estates instead. But now, I had to make sure my new pet cartel survived the coming day.

"This plan doesn't feel all that different from what we were already doing," said Lily, leaning against the backside of the overturned honest-to-God piano that formed the upper part of our section of the outer barricade. Even from our raised vantage point, the sun was barely visible on the eastern horizon; it looked particularly bloody behind the haze of smoke. "I thought we'd be taking the fight to the Horde."

"You lost half your patrols before I even got here," I reminded her, "and would have lost even more overnight. If I thought you had the manpower left to meet the Horde in the streets, we'd be out there. As it is, it's better to pull everyone back to a defensible position. And at least your enforcers are out helping with the defense instead of spending their time being wallflowers inside."

"Even so, the Horde's got more Powers than we do, and more people besides. And the Skulls…"

"Missed their chance to be first to the party. They'll hold back now and see who survives the battle and what condition they're in. And by then, the opportunity will have passed." I clapped the smaller woman on the back, staggering her. "You need to unclench, Lily. Boss of the Plug Uglies can't be seen as some sort of worrywart."

"You'll take out the Horde's Powers?" she asked for at least the third time since we'd left the confines of the base.

"That's what you're paying me for," I said, my voice now pitched loud enough to carry to the rank and file nearby. Better they all see this as just another hired job for the Queen of Smiles. That way, there was no risk of them spilling secrets they didn't know.

It took another hour or so for the Horde to realize there were no free roaming targets left in the district streets, and during that time, at least two more fires were started in the district, judging by the smoke plumes. I watched that smoke, hoping the fires didn't spread. The Plug Uglies had a Weather Witch, but he would have been classified in the Free States as a Category One or Two at best; he couldn't generate much more than a raincloud and even then only within line of sight. We'd have to hope the fires burned out by themselves or stayed contained until the battle was over.

Eventually, the first enemy squad appeared, loping into sight like animals rather than the near-professional unit I'd encountered the previous night. By then, our preparations were in place. The side streets had been blocked off with debris and the rubble of at least two hastily abandoned houses, leaving only one path to the base. Our barricades were packed with defenders, and another few dozen Uglies waited below on the safe side of the wagons, serving as both our gate defense team and our mobile reserves.

I watched and waited as the Horde gathered, numbers swelling until the cartel's name was as much a description as anything else. Finally, I turned to a white-faced Dorothea, standing to my left. "You're up."

"There's literally hundreds of them." She didn't look like she'd gotten a ton of sleep. I honestly wasn't sure how much of that was the upcoming battle or worry about Colton. We hadn't heard from any of the crew since parting ways.

"I don't care about the unwashed masses out there," I reminded her. "They're inconsequential. Just point out the Powers among them."

The spy swallowed and nodded, dark eyes scanning the teeming crowd. She began to identify individuals, rattling off their names and powersets as she went.

Lily leaned in toward me, her voice quiet. "*I* don't even know all the Horde's Powers and they're one of our main rivals. How does a *tavern owner* recognize them on sight?"

"Let's just say the Sunken Ship will need a new owner after this is all said and done," I replied, my voice equally quiet despite the storm's metal. "Dorothea's got a new job waiting for her back at the capital."

I watched Lily put the pieces together. "Shit. She's been here as long as *I* have."

"She's good at her job."

"Which just proves you're not talking about the tavern. I've tasted their hooch."

"I'm shocked you can still speak, let alone see."

"It was touch and go for a while," she snarked. The banter seemed to be doing more to restore her spirits than all our defensive preparations combined.

"I don't see the boss or underboss," said Dorothea, finally winding down. "Just a couple captains, a few enforcers, and the handful of unranked Powers still working their way through the loyalty trials."

It wasn't as bad as I'd feared, but it wasn't great either. Even with the twins dead, the Horde still had well over a dozen Powers. And ten of them were out in the field, marshalled against the Plug Uglies' five. Worse, while most of the enemy Powers Dorothea had pointed out were Stalwarts, Titans, or Shifters, there was one Speedster—what the Free States called a Jitterbug—as well as a Wind Dancer, a Pyromancer, and a Lightbringer.

I doubted any were strong enough to qualify to be an Immortal, let alone serve as one of the Free States' Capes, but those last three might give the storm difficulty. Even steel had its melting point, after all, and a strong enough wind could stop the storm in its tracks.

I'd have to kill them quick.

Once the intersection ahead of us reached max capacity, the Horde started to howl, their noise a disquieting callback to the sounds the Zoo's feral inhabitants had made. Plug Uglies nervously shifted back and forth on the wall, but the storm gnashed its metal teeth inside my shell, anxious to be free, anxious to bring its own brand of chaos to a city that thrived on such things.

"Come and get it," whispered Lily.

As if in answer, the first wave of the Horde's assault finally advanced. They didn't charge, but stalked forward instead, savoring the carnage that was to come.

Nobody ever accused gangbangers of being smart.

A few shots rang out from our wall as the enemy moved into range, but most of the Uglies' response came from below. Two of Lily's enforcers—one a Titan who seemed to be suffering from malnutrition, the other a Body Shifter who could only add mass to two limbs at a time—pulled the wagon gate open, revealing the tripod-mounted, belt-fed machine gun we'd moved outside. Muzzle fire unlike anything I'd seen since my assault on the Crimson Queen's army erupted, and death swept the front ranks of the oncoming attackers, mowing humans down like wheat on a farm.

In a perfect world, we'd have wiped the Horde out then and there. But there hadn't been space on the hastily made barricades for the tripod, and that meant the machine gun's field of fire was limited by the aperture of the gate. And while the gun was spitting out rounds faster than I or anyone else could count, it was running through the Plug Uglies' small supply of linked ammunition just as fast.

Still, at least a hundred enemy died in less than a minute, with another few dozen strewn across the intersection and screaming in pain.

There was a reason my empire still employed a standing army despite also having Immortals to call on.

Sometimes, the old ways worked best.

By the time the gun ran dry, the remainder of the Horde's initial assault wave had adjusted, finding safer lines to advance and moving from a slow march into something more befitting their cartel's reputation. Our two enforcers hurriedly closed the gate again, and the sound of the heavy machine gun was replaced by bolt-action rifles from the Plug Uglies up on the walls.

A few of the Horde stopped to return fire, while others just charged the barricades, leaping over their own dead in desperate bids to reach the low walls. Here and there, a few attackers were already up amongst the defenders, but they were cut down just as quickly. I stepped away from the fragile humans surrounding me, and dismissed my shell, joining in the carnage.

Ten minutes later, and that first wave had failed, leaving a couple hundred corpses and almost half as many live casualties. We'd taken our own lumps, but the trump card of the heavy machine gun had made the outcome of that assault obvious from the start.

Unfortunately, that card had now been played, and the numbers of the Horde barely seemed diminished.

Even if they'd brought the entire cartel with them—and judging by the absence of their leadership and several enforcers, they hadn't—both Lily and Dorothea had *drastically* underestimated how large the Horde had grown. I was starting to wish the Skulls had been the first to the party instead. It would have been out of character for the Horde and also fucked up the rest of my plan, but I was no longer confident the Uglies would survive long enough for that plan to matter.

"Shit," said Lily, breathing heavily as she looked out across the sea of waiting enemy. "They must have emptied the entire Outskirts too. Shit shit shit." It seemed to have become her favorite word since taking command.

"That's one wave taken care of," I said. "Looks like it'll be a race to see whether we run out of ammo before they run out of bodies."

An hour later, we were losing that race, and our lines were sagging. Lily had been forced to call on the last dregs of her reserves, sending them to fill in the gaps now appearing like magic in the cartel's defenses. When the latest wave finally broke, they left as many of our dead on the walls as theirs. Still, Lily's enforcers had helped make the difference against the mundane troops the Horde had continued to throw at us.

Finally, the enemy captains got impatient.

Hundreds more of the aptly named Horde waited in the intersection and the streets beyond, but they held back now as two handfuls of people emerged. Three of them were enormous and all of them had been pointed out earlier by the spy now standing at Lily's side.

If I'd known the Horde's Powers would make it *this* easy to identify them, I'd have let Dorothea stay inside.

The man in the lead had, for some reason, opted to add a cape to his ensemble. His eyes glowed a brilliant white and energy streaked across the open space to strike the gates. That impact, powerful as it felt to those up on the wall, firmly placed the Lightbringer in the lower echelons of Powers. One of *my* Immortals would have carved right through both wagons; *his* strike barely rocked them.

The next wave of Normals charged forward. Most of the Powers stayed together out in the intersection, guarding their less durable companions as the Pyromancer and Lightbringer unleashed their abilities on our increasingly flimsy barricades. Here and there, a few joined in the melee instead.

I made a judgment call. Rather than leaping over the wall like I'd originally planned, I ran along it. One of those enemy Powers had already reached the top and was tearing through a half-dozen Plug Uglies with casual ease, moving with the kind of grace I recognized from Two-Feathers.

There was an ongoing debate about whether Stalwarts or Titans made for tougher combatants. A perfect blend of strength, speed, and agility vs. a slower, less agile individual with greater strength, mass, and durability? For most, it really depended on the Power in question and what sort of defense, if any, you could mount against them.

For the storm though? The answer was clear.

That section of the wall was clear of our troops by the time I reached the enemy Stalwart, so I dismissed my shell in mid-stride, loosing the chaos of my soul onto the world. A cloud of steel and sharp, jagged edges engulfed the perfect warrior and all that agility and martial prowess simply bought him an extra second of screaming, as his last-second, impossible dodge resulted in the upper half of his torso plummeting off the barricade while everything else was rendered into bloody meat.

I reformed my shell and turned my smile on the rest of the Horde's Powers.

One down.

Nine to go.

○○○

It wasn't all as easy as that.

Nothing about dealing with humans ever is.

After the Stalwart's obliteration, I went back to my initial plan and jumped down to the street outside the barricade, heading straight for the cluster of Powers. I killed Normals by the handful as I went, each new corpse another meaningless moment in my hunt.

The problem with the storm is that it's mighty but not particularly fast. I devoured everything in my path, but that just let those other Powers see me coming.

A few showed they had more balls than sense and made their plays: a Titan trusting in skin that could barely stop bullets, a Pyromancer overestimating the strength of his own fire, two Stalwarts and a Body Shifter who thought attacking the storm from multiple angles would reveal a weakness.

The others saw just what the storm did to their companions and scattered. This was the part where they were *supposed* to pull back or outright flee, but there was a pre-Break quote about plans and first contact, and apparently, it remained appropriate.

A space cleared around the storm and then around my shell when I reformed it, but the Horde's attack continued unabated, cartel members charging the walls in waves that had were now blurring together into a single chaotic charge. Some of the Powers I'd hunted retreated into the vastly smaller crowds of attackers still choking the streets, but the rest joined the assault on the barricade.

They couldn't kill me, so they'd chosen to ignore me instead.

As tactics went, it was maddeningly effective. After all, the Uglies were their target, not me, and as indomitable as the storm was, it couldn't be in multiple places.

I headed back toward the barricades, cutting down anyone I could along the way. The walls had been breached at multiple points, defenders gathering in clusters instead of neat lines, as the advantages of defensive positions gave way to the dominance of vastly superior numbers. Of Lily's enforcers, only two were still upright, and even Dorothea now had a gun, firing into the enemy throngs like the soldier she claimed not to be.

At the base of the barricades, the Horde had started to bunch up, some waiting to climb their way up onto the wall and others milling about behind the crowd trying to push through wagons that had been overturned so they would no longer roll.

The only reason the gates were still shut was because I'd killed every Titan that had taken the field. Even so, there was one Stalwart at the front and at least fifty people who were hacking away or even throwing their own bodies at wood that had already been battered and scorched by the enemy Pyromancer and Lightbringer.

I could help hold the walls, but the gates would fall.

I could defend the gates, only to have the Horde go right up and over the walls.

I was really starting to regret *not* bringing the honor guard Cyrus had suggested. It turned out even a general knew a little bit more about diplomacy than I did.

I stayed at the gates, both because I was already there, and because they made for a smaller area to attack or defend. I couldn't hear the screams as the storm tore its way through the Horde, couldn't see the faces as some of the less rabid attackers turned and saw jagged edges chewing their way toward them, but people died and died and died.

I reformed my shell atop the corpse of the last Stalwart, pieces of me missing from where something large caliber enough had knocked shards of the storm away and watched the handful of attackers left at the gate finally break and flee. Two were cut down by fragments of the storm winging their way back to me, filling the empty spaces inside and plugging the gaps in my torso and one arm. The rest just kept going, and it was a long moment before I realized I was *able* to watch them go, that they weren't just being replaced by the next wave upon wave upon wave.

Above me, the battle on the barricades continued, but the intersection had bodies piled atop each other where they'd fallen, and in the streets beyond…

The remnants of the Horde were in turmoil, smoke signifying more gunfire even as the battle above drowned out the distant sounds. Casualties dragging themselves back to the presumed safety of the Horde's lines soon found themselves under fresh assault.

Two-Feathers and Colton had come through.

Reinforcements had arrived.

Still, it would be a while before they could reach us, and the situation on the barricades was still perilous. I couldn't see my nomad, but I waved to him anyway, then turned back to the wall and began to climb one of the uneven, ever-shifting ramps the enemy had made of their own corpses.

I reached Lily as the last of her enforcers went down, incapacitated if not quite dead, and I threw his opponent off the wall without even dismissing my shell. Both the cartel boss and the empire spy had swapped their guns for weapons—Lily a dagger as long as her forearm, Dorothea a truncheon that had probably begun its life as a table leg. They were liberally spattered in blood, but they were alive, and fell in behind me. I fought to the next pocket of survivors and then on down the wall, gathering survivors and killing the enemy as I went.

It took twenty minutes to clear the walls, and by the time we did, the battle out in the streets was over, though all the gun smoke reduced visibility to almost nothing.

"What happened?" asked Lily, finally able to catch her breath. Around us, a line of Uglies were working to get their more badly injured brothers and sisters down and into the infirmary, leaving only a few dozen able bodies to man the wall.

"They were attacked from behind," I told her.

"Another cartel?" Lily went pale under all the blood. "Shit. We don't have the manpower left to fight the Skulls." She scanned the meager number of troops left on their feet, all of them wielding melee weapons now instead of guns. "Hell, we don't have the manpower left to fight *anyone*."

"Then it's a good thing these ones are friends."

At least I hoped so. I *still* hadn't seen Two-Feathers, let alone the colors of the newly arrived cartel. I was going to feel really dumb if the Skulls had shown up after all.

Thankfully, the Uglies' otherwise useless Weather Witch soon got a breeze going. Smoke cycled up into the sky, swiftly emptying out of the intersection and nearby streets to reveal armed men and women picking their way through the bodies. My eyes went to the nomad among them, armed with a rifle and missing his hat, but Lily focused on the colors on display: blue and grey.

"The Dead Rabbits?" she breathed, turning to me. "How?"

"Old alliances," I told her, keeping the truth ambiguous. "And new ones."

The *actual* truth was that I'd empowered Two-Feathers and Colton to make a deal on my empire's behalf. The Uglies would be our secret vassals, and the Dead Rabbits would be our less-secret favored trade partners. Meanwhile, if the Sparrow siblings had reached the Diablos...

A distant boom shook the city, and we all looked to the east, where a thick, black tower of smoke was rising into the air, the volcanic eruption to Raytown's minor fires.

"That's..."

"The Springs District," I finished for her. "I'm pretty sure the rest of the Horde just ceased to be a problem."

"The Rabbits again?"

"Diablos. I might have sent them word that we'd also found the Devil's body, and that the cartel responsible would leave their back door unguarded when they came for the Uglies."

The Diablos weren't getting trade deals, but they *were* increasing their territory like they'd wanted to for ages. That made three of the now-five cartels in the city that either owed my empire or at least had a solid working relationship with it. It wasn't *military* conquest, but it was a solid start on the sneaky variety.

"The Horde killed the Devil? *And* Fingers?" Lily tore her eyes away from the funeral pyre for her cartel's rivals to send me a questioning look. "Smith too?"

"Would you believe me if I said yes?"

"I'd say it would be pretty convenient, especially now that the Horde has been wiped off the map."

"And?" I asked, keeping my tone level.

"Convenient is good. The Uglies need to heal up and recruit heavily before anyone realizes how weak we are. We don't have the luxury for vendettas."

"Glad to hear it."

"Besides," she said, turning back to watch the Dead Rabbits finish off the fallen, "I'm sure you'll tell me the real story sometime."

I definitely wouldn't.

12

Even with surprise on their side, the Dead Rabbits lost dozens of fighters in the bitter street fighting to clear Raytown of the Horde. The Diablos lost even more in their attack on the Horde's base. And as for the Uglies… well, I wasn't sure they had enough active bodies to throw a block party, let alone run a district. Meanwhile, the two cartels who had sat back and done nothing—the Skulls and the Blood—came out of the whole affair untouched. I'd formed alliances or agreements with three of Kansas City's five remaining gangs, yet those three were now all far weaker than they had once been.

In the short term, anyway. In the long term, our trade agreement would dramatically boost the Rabbits' prospects, just as the acquisition of more territory would juice the Diablos' recruitment numbers. The Uglies were a bigger concern, even with whatever my empire might do to prop them up, but that was life in Kansas City. The weak worked their asses off to not become victims and sometimes, even that wasn't enough.

Three days after the short-lived war, the five remaining cartels gathered for the summit I'd originally come to attend. With the loss of some of their legendary names and quite a few minor monsters whose stories would now never spread, the men and women who met in Riverside seemed diminished. Mortal in a way their predecessors had at least pretended not to be.

Maybe some of that was the war, whose effects would be felt for years to come, but I chalked the rest of it up to the summit itself. Few things sucked the mystique and menace out of humans faster than hours spent sitting behind scavenged tables, debating diplomacy and politics.

A few buildings down from the city's one and only working mint, I listened as each cartel spoke their piece. I even added a word or two myself when the moment arose, which wasn't often. In truth, it was hard to hear the plights of my rivals and would-be allies over the song of the road, the tapping of Two-Feathers' foot against the floor behind me, and the storm's call… not to *action*, not after the war, but to *activity* at least.

I'd spent months in New Memphis, with its too-soft comforts, and now a week in Kansas City where blood was as much of a business as trade. The deals being hammered out mattered—and my ability to influence those deals through the three cartels I had my hooks in mattered even more—but sometimes, words were just wind given shape and too much significance. I wanted that wind streaming past me instead, the road beneath my wheels, the horizon eyeing my steady pursuit.

Since I'd been born, my life had been about a quest for answers and about the balance I was forced to observe. That quest was long over, balance had become more an ideal than a rule, and… well, I had other fucking places to be.

The summit lasted four full days before the words had all been said, agreements made, and alliances or treaties reaffirmed. When it was done, I hired the Sparrow siblings to take Dorothea and Colston east to the nearest fort with a letter of introduction, an information packet for the council, and orders to see the former spy and her beau safely to New Memphis. I paid Shaky and his supposed sister an extra coin each for retrieving my bike and Two-Feathers' prized horse and keeping them in one piece even after the Horde abandoned the Outskirts. I left Lily with the keys to the Sunken Ship and a few words of my own that she would either listen to or not while she took advantage of the promised peace to rebuild the Plug Uglies into something new. Something better, maybe.

Lastly, I made damn sure that the face of the woman I'd known as Selene was spread far and wide among the cartels, accompanied by a bounty big enough to buy a mansion if she was returned very, very dead. Chances were, she was long gone, seeking her next target in some other town in the Badlands, but every door I could close to that woman would make it easier to hunt her down. And the ghost riding her could either finally leave in search of an afterlife or spend eternity back in Bakersfield's orbit.

Hell, maybe the baby Crow would have a way to banish her, even. He was a Full-Five, after all. That had to be useful for something more than just zombie apocalypses.

With my business done, I tore west through the city on rubber tires and a battery-powered engine, Two-Feathers close behind on his horse. We skirted the Zoo and its unquiet ghosts and half-feral inhabitants. We cut through the Park, where the Bloods' soldiers walked eerily quiet streets in crimson parkas and black face-masks. We wove in and around the shanty town that made up the outer edges of the western Outskirts and then finally—finally!—as if by magic, the tents and buildings fell away and all that remained in front of us was open sky and the unknowable expanse of wilderness.

The Badlands' most infamous city slowly receded in my mirrors. Maybe the deals we'd made would bear fruit, ushering in a new era for a place that somehow always managed to endure. Maybe both new and old alliances alike would hold, and fresh trade would flourish, adding civility to mere civilization. Maybe the lives spent so freely for nebulous city regions and garishly colored bandanas would finally be given some meaning.

Or maybe the whole fucking thing would fall apart within weeks of our departure. Maybe words would just be wind after all, and humans would return to doing what they did best in times like this and places like these. Maybe savagery wasn't just the order of the day, but of the century and the era.

If I were a betting woman—and I wasn't—I'd have put my money on the latter. Because while life was often brutally brief, the blood and the hatred it sparked endured, much like the city itself. It pooled in the alleys, waiting to stain the next generation, to seep into babes born gasping and wailing in shadowed corners and too-cold homes. If there was another way for the world to live, I didn't know it, and I'd certainly never seen it. Maybe someday, someone would be born to change all that. Maybe they'd even live long enough to see that change take hold.

But as for me? I'd been created from chaos and born to the road… and I had places yet to go.

"Let's skip Kansas City on the return trip," I said, and though my voice was barely audible over the tires, hoofbeats, and hum of my motor, the nomad at my side was quick to agree.

We rode for hours, and my mood lifted with every mile put behind us. The problem with living forever was that you couldn't help but see people come and go, some cut down before their time, others laid low by age and time. That was also the positive. *This too shall pass* was less an adage than a life lesson. The older a human got, the more *they* had to either acknowledge reality or flee it. I'd been born without that choice.

The world is a toilet.
Life is what it is.
This too shall pass.

The trick was to find your purpose, your *what's next*. The goal that would occupy your time, your energy, and your attention when you might otherwise fixate on things beyond your control, on the lives that came and went in the endless night, on the distant stars that raged and inevitably fell silent.

I had this trip to find Bakersfield.

I had an empire I needed to learn to rule.

I had the man riding ever-silently in my shadow.

Everything else was just a question of time or travel.

○○○

The boundary of Two-Feathers' clan territory was two days' ride by bike from Kansas City, and almost four days' ride when there was a horse involved. We stopped when night fell, the weather seasonable enough that the nomad once again did without his tent. Just a campfire, a bike, a horse, and two people, adrift in the Badlands. While the storm made its noise, it was a muted grumble, ever-hungry, yes, but halfway satiated by the chaos of the city's two-day war.

I waited for Two-Feathers to scrub his pan clean with a splash of water from our stores and a handful of dry sand, and then I joined him on that side of the fire.

"We need to talk," I said.

He gave me a look more eloquent than words. If I'd had eyes, I'd have rolled them.

"You know what I mean."

Teeth flashed in the orange light of the campfire, the first grin I'd seen from my nomad in days. Still kneeling beside the fire, he sketched out a credible pantomime of a bow, grin widening.

"Sarcasm doesn't become you," I lied, but he could hear the laughter in my voice as well as I could. He patted my knee and sat back on his haunches, waiting.

And waiting.

I was not, by nature, a reticent person. While I wasn't given to speeches or soliloquies, I said my mind whenever and wherever I wanted, as Jules could attest. I wasn't the sort to gladhand a client or talk my way out of a battle—the reason my crews had always had someone else to serve as our face—but shooting the shit in a bar or on the road or after getting sweaty with a townie who found the helmet exotic rather than a turn-off?

That had always come easily to me.

Which was why it made no sense that I sometimes struggled talking to Two-Feathers. The silence between us was usually comfortable; it was when words got involved that things sometimes went to shit. Part of that was him not speaking—not verbally, anyway—but a greater part of it was just who we were. For all his skill, bravery, and competence, he came from a different life and a different mindset. For all *my* accomplishments, I'd ultimately been a hired killer for longer than even his clan's elders had breathed. Silence, mutual respect, and… whatever *this* was… had helped build a bridge between us, but it was woven from thread and spanned a miles-wide chasm. Too often, it felt like the wrong word could tear it to shreds.

So I sat there for a few minutes in that comfortable silence, letting the voice in my head run amok with its worries and its fears. Giving in to the uncertainties that plagued even someone like me.

Then, I reminded myself that I wasn't a child, that I'd *never* been one, and got on with business.

"I'm sorry you lost your spear," I told him. "I asked the head of the sewer maintenance guild to have her workers keep an eye out for it when they're below, but even if they do find it, I don't know what shape it will be in."

Two-Feathers held his hands before him until he was certain I was watching them. Slowly, he moved through a sequence of signs. I only recognized about two-thirds of them, but that was enough to string his meaning together.

"You'll make another one?"

He nodded.

I waved at the campsite. It was mostly rolling hills west of Kansas City for at least another day, but there were a few groves of trees dotting the landscape and we'd made our camp in one of the larger ones.

"Did you want to get started tonight? I don't know where your old feathers came from, but these are hickory trees. I'm pretty sure that's a hard wood."

How I knew that was anyone's guess. Either someone I'd ridden with in the past had mentioned it or it was yet another piece of minutiae dear old Dad had baked into my brain.

Two-Feathers answered with another set of signs. I had him repeat a few before I got it.

"You'll need a spearhead?"

He nodded and pointed in a direction that the stars told me was northwest.

Toward the clan territories.

"Right," I agreed. "Guess we'll take care of it when we get there."

From his expression, it wasn't *quite* what he had been saying, but I guess it was close enough that he didn't see a need to correct it. Which was just as well… my sign reading was improving—slowly— but the darkness and the fire's unsteady light made everything that much more difficult.

"In the meantime, if we encounter something problematic, let me handle it," I told him.

He reacted pretty much like I expected, but the disadvantage of sign language is that it's all too easy to speak over. I ignored whatever he was trying to say and kept going.

"I'm not doubting your skill, but all you have is the rifle you took from Kansas City and your knife. The first won't be good against anything dangerous enough to be a real problem, and the second puts you in arm's reach of that same threat. One of us can die. The other one, not so much. Your clan's not going to be happy if I get you killed before they get to see you again."

He frowned, presumably frustrated by my flawless logic.

I waited a beat. "Spear aside, how are you doing?"

Two-Feathers gave me another look and cocked his head.

"You said this was your first time in Kansas City, right?" I elaborated, waiting for his confirmation. "Even on a good week, the city's a bit of a shock, and this was not a good week."

The nomad nodded, both his fingers and his face still.

"I just want to make sure you're okay," I finally said. "You know… with everything that happened."

Instead of answering, he pointed at me.

"Am I okay?" I translated. At his nod, I shrugged. "It's nothing I haven't seen before." Truth was, I'd seen worse and done worse too, but a part of me didn't want to mention that. "You're a stranger to this life though, and I know you and I sometimes see things differently."

He cracked half a smile at the understatement of the century and showed me his hands. In the flickering light of the fire, he made a few more signs.

"Did we make things better?" I wasn't sure how to answer that. Assuming some of the agreements held, I'd at least improved my empire's position in Kansas City, but that wasn't what Two-Feathers cared about, and it certainly wasn't what he was asking. "I think so? War was inevitable, thanks to Selene. If we hadn't gotten involved, that war could have been a lot worse. Multiple cartels battling each other over the span of weeks or even months instead of a handful of days. More of the city's general population would have gotten caught in the crossfire."

The fire popped and crackled.

"Long-term though," honesty compelled me to add, "I don't think it will matter. A lot of people have tried to change Kansas City since the Break and each time, it reverts back to something barely recognizable as human."

The nomad held up a fist, index finger wrapped around the thumb, and then signed an L with the same hand, before making a gesture like he was throwing both signs in my direction.

"That's life?" My odd biology made swallowing unnecessary, but I did so anyway. "Yeah. I guess it is."

He gripped my shoulder, strong fingers squeezing, as if to give me the comfort I'd been trying to offer him, and we just sat together, silence falling like a blanket over the campsite, cozy and soft.

I could've remained there all night, but my nomad was human and needed his sleep, and the storm was chaos and chaos wanted to be in motion. Eventually, I reached up and patted the hand still on my leather-clad shoulder.

"One of these days, I'm going to figure you out," I told him.

Two-Feathers grinned and headed for his bedroll.

I stayed up for a while longer, letting the fire's light reflect off my true face. When my soul became too chaotic to contain, I walked away from our camp into the darkness and gave the storm its freedom under the distant stars.

oooo

The next few days passed in similar fashion. Most of the traffic out of Kansas City headed southwest to Wichita or east to my empire, so we had the western road mostly to ourselves. On the second day, we crossed paths with two wagon trains, hours apart from each other. The first had fifteen armed guards, the second only two, but it was the latter that would be truly bad news for anyone dumb enough to attack it. I traded wary nods with the pair of guards, a man who'd gone past gray to flat-out grizzled, and a woman at least ten years his junior with eyes that could cut at a hundred paces. They kept their wagon train moving, but I could feel their gazes on me long after we'd passed.

Two-Feathers, being a sentient being with working eyes, caught the whole exchange. When we were alone again, he rode up beside me.

"Dusk and Twinfall," I told him, naming the man and woman, respectively. "Years ago, they led a crew of heavies that was the equal of anything the Old Man ever put together. Had some epic battles with Peace and his cult up by the Great Lakes too. Pretty much controlled swaths of the Badlands all by themselves. Until something happened."

The nomad made a gesture I had no difficulty interpreting.

"I don't know, and they haven't said. I'm guessing they encountered something even worse than they were. Only thing we do know is that the Mission came across a pile of bodies in what was once North Dakota. Whole crew had been done in, except for Dusk, Twinfall, and Twin's brother, Savant."

I shook my head. "The Mission, being the Mission, took the survivors to a nearby town for healing, even knowing who they were and what they'd done. Savant didn't survive that journey, and Dusk and Twin were touch and go for months."

It had been Mammoth who told me that story. Mammoth, who'd been the leader of the Mission before becoming just another body in Bakersfield's wake. Mammoth had always seen the best in everyone, his heart the only thing bigger than his giant frame. With him gone, it was hard to imagine the Mission still being, and all too easy to imagine what would happen to the towns dependent on that group's charity work.

"Anyway," I finally continued, "when Dusk and Twin made their reappearance, they weren't running a crew anymore but hiring out as security and protection instead. Working to defend the kind of people they used to prey on. Took a few years and even more bodies before people realized it wasn't some sort of scheme. Since then, they've been left the fuck alone."

It always made waves when criminals found religion, especially names as big as those two had been. Mostly because it just didn't happen very often. Even for the handful of predators who *weren't* rotten to the core, the only certainty in the outlaw life was violence. Death tended to come calling long before remorse or redemption became more than random words starting with *r*.

I wasn't sure what Dusk and Twin had seen out in the dark steppes of the Badlands—what had ravaged a crew that made even holy terrors like the Old Man and Peace wary—but it had changed the two of them to the core. Like the new cartel leaders we'd met with in Kansas City, the pair were diminished now. Shadows of what they had been. Reminders of what no longer was.

Lesser… but still breathing.

There was probably a lesson of some sort in all that.

Two-Feathers said nothing, of course, thoughts hidden behind the bronze skin of his strong, expressionless face. Still, he turned back as he rode, looking at the clouds of dust that were the only evidence of the wagon train that had ridden out of sight.

"There aren't a lot of us left," I said. "People who rode in the Badlands' heyday, I mean. Hell, Jules was a young buck who only came along at the end of that era, and even he's aged out into retirement. Peace ran afoul of the Singer. The Old Man died in his chair. Nemo was hung from Wichita's great wall. Soon, it'll just be me, staying the same while the world spins around me."

He pantomimed a crown atop his head.

"I was *always* a queen," I reminded him. "It's only the empire part that's new. Nothing else has changed or ever will."

His horse snorted, spraying snot all over the road.

And that, I supposed, was that.

13

We ignored the trail that led to the ruined remnants of a nothing town once known as Eclipse, and the separate road that led slightly southward to the fort that served as a tomb for Eclipse's killers. It had been over a year since I'd seen either and nature would already be doing its part to reclaim them both. That was the way of things, and hell if I was going to let a little thing like memory or sentiment stand in its path.

Instead, we turned north. While I'd ridden through almost every clan's territory at least a dozen times without issue, I let Two-Feathers take the lead. My ties with the nomads were solid—had been so for ages—but I was and would always be an outsider. Having one of the clan's sons lead the way, especially after I'd made him ambassador to my empire, seemed like something Jules would call *properly diplomatic*.

Hours later, we journeyed right past the place I usually stopped, nomads materializing out of the night to lope easily beside us. They ignored me entirely, but the lead guard—taller than Two-Feathers, if not quite so broad-shouldered—spoke with my nomad in the language of their clan. Two-Feathers responded, falling back into the older, less detailed signs he'd used before we found the book in New Memphis.

Whatever they said to each other, the other nomad gave a low whistle that sent our second escort peeling off back into the darkness.

If there was one thing I'd learned in my decades traveling the Badlands, it was that there were *always* eyes watching a clan's borders. People who ignored those silent watchers did so at their own peril. The clans weren't technically a nation, let alone an empire, but when they all came together, they were a force to give anyone pause.

We traveled for more than an hour and the only sign that we were nearing the camp was the increasing number of guards we passed on the way in. Two-Feathers' clan wasn't one of the larger ones, but they could still fill a good-sized town on their own, with people left over.

When the Break had mostly run its course, when cities had risen or fallen or disappeared all on their own, taking their respective populations with them, the people of the former central and mid-western United States of America had found themselves in the Badlands, isolated and hunted by things far worse than just Powers. Some had responded by turning their towns or villages into armed camps, leaning heavily on whatever safety walls and a few firearms could offer. Others had looked to the one group seeming to flourish in the new reality: the natives who had originally populated that same land.

Long before the Free States would become a beacon for those seeking civilization, the natives had represented a different kind of shelter in the Badlands. And so, villagers who left their walled encampments sought refuge with the local tribes. Some were more welcoming than others, of course, but over the decades, the tribes had grown until they became clans instead. Native and non-native blood mingled as the newcomers adopted a lost way of life that had been given new meaning and value in the post-Break world.

Which was to say that, even in the darkness, the guards who met us on our journey to the clan's current campsite didn't all look like Two-Feathers. Braided hair was blond or brown as often as black, and while most faces had been painted varying shades of bronze by the ever-present sun, their features spoke to a dozen different ethnicities or—even more often—a blend of such.

I received my share of looks from our growing escort. Some were wary, some were dismissive, and some were just plain male. I couldn't help the form Dr. Nowhere had created me with—and there'd been plenty of times I was happy to use it to my advantage—but still… there were appropriate and inappropriate times and ways to eye-fuck a woman. I'd found, more often than not, that it fell to the storm to teach people that lesson.

Two-Feathers, being Two-Feathers, said nothing, but he fell back again until we were riding together, his mount fighting to keep its distance, even as its rider did the opposite. Dark eyes sought out the overeager admirers on our crowd and stared them down, one after the other.

Hell if I needed someone to protect me, even a Stalwart, but that didn't stop it from being all kinds of adorable. The smile of my true face widened to stretch across the visor, causing at least a few of my few remaining would-be admirers to shudder and drop their eyes.

By the time we spotted the light from the nomads' fires, we were practically on top of the camp itself, tents appearing out of the darkness in careful arrangements that meant everything to the inhabitants and nothing at all to me. Most of our escort veered away again, headed for their own tents, or returning to their posts surrounding the camp, but the rest directed us to the single figure waiting at the nearest fire.

An elder. I recognized the old man from almost a year ago, when I'd come seeking word of Eclipse's destroyers, and he'd asked for news of Bakersfield in exchange. The firelight made deep canyons out of his wrinkles, but his back remained as straight as any twenty-year-old's.

I killed my engine, dropped the kickstand, and dismounted. At my side, Two-Feathers handed the reins of his horse to one of our guards and hopped down.

"We greet the Storm Who Rides," said the elder, his voice thin like leaves long after they had fallen, "and the empire she now leads. Leave all past grievances behind with your bike and be welcome at our fires."

Recent history notwithstanding, there weren't a lot of places I'd willingly walk away from my bike, but the nomads had strong feelings about theft, and even stronger feelings about guest rights. The motorcycle would be safe and untouched during my stay.

While I was here as a diplomatic envoy, not a supplicant, some old habits die hard. For me, balance was one of them. "I have seeds and coin to offer for my stay," I said, slinging my saddlebags over one shoulder.

"There is an order to all things," he replied simply. "In two days, we will have a feast to celebrate your arrival. And," he added, looking to the nomad at my side, "to welcome back one of our own. When the ceremonies are complete, there will be time to discuss matters of commerce and politics."

I didn't make an issue out of the delay. Travel in the Badlands was anything but certain, which made schedules dependent on that travel even less so. Two days was quite possibly the shortest amount of time the clan could take to put together a feast… and even if I wouldn't be able to enjoy the food, I was willing to wait things out for Two-Feathers' benefit.

Besides, we'd already been gone from New Memphis for more than a month and had literally thousands of miles left to go. What were two days in the face of all that?

"That will do," I said, and for once the storm stayed quiet. "Thank you for your hospitality."

"The land gives freely and we would be fools to hoard its bounty for ourselves." He raised one gnarled hand, and a young man stepped out of the darkness beside him. "We have prepared a tent for you and your possessions; Aidan will take you there."

I took two steps toward my guide, then paused. My nomad hadn't budged, his eyes locked with the elder's.

"Two-Feathers?" I asked. "Are you coming?"

"Our clan's son has a tent to call his own," said the elder.

I ignored him and kept my gaze fixed on Two-Feathers, who looked as uncomfortable as I could ever remember seeing him. Finally, the nomad turned toward me and gave a single, stiff nod.

"If there's a problem…" I began, and this time, the storm filled my voice with all its chaotic fury.

Two-Feathers shook his head, making the sign I recognized for *no* even in the dim light, but the storm wasn't satisfied, and neither was I. We were here as much for him as for my empire, and I was more than happy to skip straight to Wichita if he asked for it.

"Two-Feathers' tent sits at his family's fire, where only those of his blood may venture unless invited," the elder said, soft voice clashing with the metallic rumble of the chaos I carried inside me. "They wait for him, as they have every night since his departure last year."

Oh.

For some reason, it had never occurred to me that Two-Feathers had family. Part of that was because *I* never had, unless you counted Dr. Nowhere, who had dreamed me into reality and then forgotten I even existed.

A larger part was that few of those I'd ridden with over the long years had had family. For those who turned to a life on the road, parents were often either the reason for that life or simply not a concern anymore. Hell, even Bakersfield had been an orphan; mom dead, dad locked away for the crime. Raya's mother and then Raya herself had each had a daughter, of course, but they'd been the exceptions to the rule. Despite Two-Feathers' young age, I'd never spared a thought for the parents that were almost definitely still alive.

"Of course," I said, metal fading from my voice. I didn't know a damn thing about family except that it could drive people to acts of heroism and villainy both, and that I would always be best served by staying out of its way. I turned to Two-Feathers, whose face was a dark mask on the edges of the fire's light. "I'll see you tomorrow. We'll talk then."

He made a sign that I couldn't quite read and then turned away, slipping into the shadows of the camp as easily as someone who'd been born to it. Because, of course, he had been.

When he was gone, I went to join my guide and then stopped yet again, meeting the elder's rheumy-eyed gaze with the smile across my visor.

"Is there a story there?"

"There is, but it is Two-Feathers' to share."

"He's not great about that sort of thing."

"No," came the quiet reply. "I can't imagine that he is."

I bit back my sigh as the elder departed, not quite trailing Two-Feathers but heading in a similar direction. My assigned guide—Aidan—offered a salute, hand to a chest with more bone than muscle and which was entirely bare despite the chill.

"I can take you to your tent," he said in a squeaky voice.

"Your name is Aidan?"

"Until I earn another, yes." Aidan was blond and blue-eyed, with a beak of a nose better suited for a buzzard than a young teenager. He puffed out his chest in a display that didn't have the effect he was probably hoping for. "I'll earn mine before the end of the season. Listens-to-Wind is certain of that much."

Listens-to-Wind, I was guessing, was their shaman. Each clan had different words for the role, according to their heritage, but its function remained largely the same… an advisor to the chief in times of war or to the circle of elders in times of peace, and one who professed to speak on behalf of their ancestral ghosts.

I had as much use for religion as anyone else who'd been created whole cloth from nothingness in the middle of the apocalypse, which was to say none at all, but I didn't discount the shamans' powers either. There was no rule that said Crows had to be the only people with a pipeline to the afterlife.

What that had to do with predicting the future remained an open question though, and I suspected Aidan wanted some sort of reassurance from me about earning his traditional name. Unfortunately, we'd just met, and I didn't know what the process entailed in the nomad culture.

My ensuing silence spoke for itself.

To his credit, he didn't deflate *too* much but instead turned to lead me deeper into camp. There were well over a dozen fires still burning, despite the hour, and Aidan skirted around most of them before arriving at a single tent. Its flap was thrown open, but the dying embers of the nearby fire did little to illuminate its interior. Two other tents sat on the opposite side of the fire, dark silhouettes against a sky stricken with stars.

We weren't *quite* in the center of the camp, as far as I could tell, but we weren't far off either. It was an overt show of trust, putting me in the heart of the camp and therefore close to the elders' own tents, but it was also a problem. I didn't sleep, which made a tent more about privacy than anything else, and while I liked my own space as much as the next person, I needed more of it than that tent could provide. The storm would want to be set free from its shell, and the center of a camp of civilians seemed a lousy place for doing so.

But Aidan wasn't in charge of the camp's sleeping arrangements, and I doubted he'd have the authority to change mine. It would be one more thing to raise with the elders. For one night, I'd make do.

"We hear stories about you," said Aidan, reminding me that he was still there. "The Storm Who Rides and the Queen of Smiles both."

I nodded. "A lot of people have."

"Are the stories true?"

I sighed and took a seat by the fire. "You're going to have to be more specific."

"They say you've lived forever."

"Not forever, but long enough."

"And you can't die?"

My voice went flat as I thought of the Old Man, of Raya, of Evan, and all the other people—assholes and friends, both—who had become just faces in my memory, doomed to fade away with the grinding of the years. "Everyone dies. Some of us just die harder than others."

Aidan was young, but not so young that he couldn't pick up social signals. He swallowed the rest of his questions, and I'd been around enough teenagers over the years to know how hard that must have been. "I've been assigned to you for the next few days," he said, pointing at one of the other tents. "I'll be sharing your fire and sleeping over there. I've filled the waterskin in your tent and there's some dried jerky in a pouch by the bedroll, but if you need anything more, I'm here to provide."

He gave me another chest-thumping salute and headed for his tent. My voice, low but pitched to carry on the night breeze, caught him halfway.

"Why did Two-Feathers seem less than thrilled about reuniting with his family?"

Aidan shrugged. "I don't know for sure, but I'm guessing it's because he's been gone a year?"

"And?"

"The note he left said it would only be a matter of days."

"Note?"

"Yes. He left his post and the scout who came to replace him found only words, carved in the mud. As a blooded hunter, he can make his decisions, of course, but Elder Snow-Falls says our first duty should be to clan and family. Maybe Two-Feathers regrets his departure?"

That didn't ring true to me, but maybe I was biased. The way I saw it, Two-Feathers had left the clan to seek me out and had saved my motorcycle in the process. Months later, he'd been instrumental in bringing the Crimson Queen to her much-deserved end, gasping for breath in her own throne room as her subjects looked on impassively. By leaving his clan, he had helped save *all* the clans.

I didn't understand clan dynamics any more than I did family ones, but I'd have to remind my nomad of that when I saw him again.

ooo

The next day came in like an avalanche and went out almost as quickly. Most of the clan was busy preparing for the feast, but Aidan stuck by my side throughout. It was still morning when I addressed the matter of my sleeping arrangements. The elders didn't even ask for an explanation, which was the first minor victory my new status had won me with the clan. I watched as a gaggle of young men and women broke down both Aidan's tent and my own, and then we followed them to the encampment's western edge where both tents were reassembled again. Even as the others left, Aidan was down on his hands and knees, digging out a firepit with what looked like a hand trowel.

"Why did you want to move our tents?" asked the young nomad, clearly opting not to follow his elders' examples.

At first, I wasn't sure if I wanted to answer or not, but standing there in silence watching a kid at least ten years Two-Feathers' junior do hard labor didn't hold much appeal either.

"What do the stories you've heard say about the storm?" I asked him instead.

"They say you *are* the storm." He used the excavated dirt to make a ring of earth around the pit. "Isn't that true?"

"It is and it isn't." I thumped my chest with one fist. "The storm is chaos and cold steel. Motion and disarray. It's a part of me but also separate." I didn't expect him to get it—and by the expression on his face, he was living down to my expectations—but I waved off the still-forming questions. "It's not important. All you need to know is that the storm needs to be set loose now and then and can be indiscriminate when free. A tent can't contain it, and the countryside is better suited than the center of your camp where anyone might wander through and find themselves turned to meat."

Aidan swallowed, looking at his tent, sitting on the other side of the fire from mine. "So, uh…"

"If you hear a rocking, don't come a-knocking."

"What?!"

"I…" I hesitated, the noon-time sun reflecting off my helmet and true face. Where had *that* come from? It sounded like another bit of pre-Break wisdom that dear old *Dad* had baked into my brain. "I have no idea. Just… don't follow me when I leave camp at night. If you *have* to, then keeping your hands and feet to yourself is your best bet at keeping them at all."

I was being a little bit dishonest, of course. I did have control over the storm, most of the time. But in lieu of sleep, there were long moments when I let my mind drift away, when the storm and I could pretend we were separate thoughts and not flesh and blood married to the endless spiral of a tornado touching down. And if someone wandered through when I was lost in those moments…?

Well, Tommy Two-Fingers hadn't been born with that name, and he hadn't had it when he first started riding with me either.

I waited as Aidan went to his family's fire to pick up lunch and then followed the young teen as he gave me the penny tour of the camp. The clan elders were set up in the center, not far from where we'd been initially sleeping, their tents distinguished from the rest not by size or even decoration but wear. There was easily space for eight tents around their fire, but only six to presently fill that space. An elder I didn't know was sitting outside, smoking a pipe as long as his forearm, while another had just hung her teapot over that same fire. Both wore the simple clothing that typified nomad lifestyle—vests, jackets, and pants made from the animals they hunted for sustenance— along with beaded necklaces and other jewelry made by local craftsmen.

The clans traded with a handful of thoroughly vetted merchants from the greater world, but most were big on self-sustainability. Given how quickly and drastically things could change in the Badlands, I found it hard to blame them.

Neither elder looked up at us as we moved past, but Aidan saluted them anyway, and he waited until we were a good distance away before resuming his tour guide narration. To the north of the camp, we came across a large group of nomads who *weren't* helping with the feast. Men and women, from Aidan's age all the way past Lily's, were waging mock combat against each other, both sun and firelight glistening on sweat-covered bodies. Here and there, a nomad interposed themselves between combatants to correct whatever they were seeing, their voices lost to us beneath the clatter of spear against spear or knife against knife. Even further away, a dozen nomads armed with bows and the occasional rifle took aim at distant targets.

The nomad lifestyle was very much in the name… they followed the herds that were their clan's lifeblood, growing only whatever crops they could in the months where a more permanent camp like this one could be established. They were hunters first, gatherers second, and farmers a very distant third… but they were all tough as hell, as more than one bandit group had discovered far too late.

I picked out a few obvious Powers among them: a Titan around Two-Feathers' age wielding an honest-to-God claymore like it was a toothpick; a much younger spearman and the knife-wielder facing off with him, both of whom moved with a Stalwart's grace; even an archer whose hands blurred at a speed no Normal could match, sending arrows at her target as swiftly as her bow allowed.

A few of the younger trainees waved to Aidan, and he waved back before glancing my way and resuming his attempts at dignity.

"If I hadn't come, would you be out there today," I asked him, "or at your family's fire helping prepare the feast?"

"A little bit of both. The first hunt of the season leaves soon—we'd be feasting to celebrate that even if you and Two-Feathers hadn't come. Anyone who wants to join the hunt must prove to the blooded hunters that they won't be dead weight."

"And it's on the hunt that you'll earn your name?"

He nodded, eyes never straying from the combatants before us. "Yes. I mean… I hope so. There are other ways to become an adult in the eyes of the clan, but this is my path."

His words were soft but uttered with an implacable certainty found only in the young or criminally insane.

"Are your duties to me going to cause you to miss your opportunity to join?"

He grinned and shook his head. "I was chosen as your guide because I'm the best of my peers. Well, aside from Vinit or Lachesis," he allowed, nodding to the olive-skinned Stalwart wielding a spear and the woman stalking him down with a knife. "And even against them, I can take one bout in five. Falling-Rock says that's as good as can be hoped for against the Blessed."

Blessed being their name for Powers. Falling-Rock, I was guessing, was the claymore wielding Titan.

"He's not wrong." Stalwarts weren't bulletproof, at least at the lower rankings, but they were a nightmare for almost any Normal to deal with. Both Vinit and Lachesis looked to be less skilled *and* less gifted than Two-Feathers, but the difference between them and their peers was evident. Aidan must have some skills of his own.

We stayed and watched the training for an hour or two. I didn't have anywhere to be, and Elder Snow-Falls had made it clear that any political discussions would happen after the feast, not before. It cost me nothing to give Aidan time to hopefully glean something as an observer instead of a participant.

When Falling-Rock called the training to a close, the afternoon sun was just starting to head for the horizon. We moved on. First, we went to the larger space where the feast would be held and a handful of women were decorating poles that had been erected that morning. Then, we headed east, to the open field where the clan's mounts grazed. I spotted Two-Feathers' horse out among the rest, the bulk of them running freely to and fro like children playing games. A few younger colts trotted shakily after their older peers, evidence that the herd continued to grow.

There was no corral or fence, nothing to keep the horses from running off toward the distant horizon, but the handful of nomads squatting on the hillside didn't seem concerned, their eyes turned not toward their prized mounts but outward, looking for any predators foolish enough to think the herd easy prey.

I didn't understand the nomad lifestyle any more than I understood city folks', but traveling with Two-Feathers had taught me that he prized his horse above everything else, with his spear—now lost thanks to Sally—a close second. Where I figured in all of that remained an open question, but given how I felt about my bike, I could accept coming in third.

Maybe.

Of my nomad, we didn't see any sign. When I asked Aidan where he might be, the answers were almost obnoxiously vague. Something about *returning to the clan* and *probably with his family or the elders*. I just nodded and let it go. Maybe I'd meet Two-Feathers' parents and maybe I wouldn't. I knew humans attached some value to that sort of thing, even now, but the nomad had his shit to do, and I'd let him do it.

Still… for all his enthusiasm, Aidan was a poor substitute. And so damn chatty that even Jules in his prime might have struggled to keep up.

When night fell, I left Aidan by our shared fire and walked into the darkness until I found a small hill that had been stripped bare of trees by the wind. I climbed to the summit where the stars spread above me like an audience of long-dead celestial beings, wan light the last vestige of their existence, and there, I finally exhaled. Air followed by sound followed by metal as the storm shook loose from its shell and resumed its rightful place, wild and free beneath the night sky.

I'd had worse nights.

Better ones too.

14

The feast was, as promised, an event. The whole damn clan participated, with even the scouts rotating in to spend some time with their families or simply partake of the food available. According to Aidan, the celebration was more about the official advent of spring than it was our arrival, but the elders weren't above multi-tasking.

I was seated with those elders on a row of blankets close enough to the fire that even the least hearty septuagenarian wouldn't feel a chill. The only elder I'd met prior to this visit—Elder Snow-Falls—was on my left, and the woman I'd seen making tea—Elder Moon-Over-the-Trees—sat to my right. There were six elders in total, as I'd gathered from the number of tents, and if half of them looked at me like something dangerous that had crawled in out of the plains uninvited, they at least kept their opinions to themselves.

Or… voiced them in a language I didn't understand. There was a lot of that, both as the elders greeted the members of their clan and as they spoke to each other, often using names that bore little to no resemblance to the monikers I'd been provided. I wasn't a diplomat and had no real desire to become one, but it was easy enough to let those foreign words wash over me. If they wanted me to know what they were saying, they'd translate. My seat among them said more than any words could.

Whatever the results of our impending negotiations might be, Two-Feathers' clan was treating me like the visiting head of state I technically was.

The eating went on for a very long time. Despite her size, Moon-Over-the-Trees could pack away food at a pace that would have stunned most of the hot-blooded young men I'd known over the decades. What she didn't eat made it into the mouth of the calico cat in her lap, its dainty bites a contrast to its owner's. Snow-Falls was a lot like the cat in his approach, picking slowly through the food on his dented metal plate as if every bite was both an experience to savor and an opponent to conquer.

As for me? I had been given a plate of my own, but the fact that it only contained a few token pieces of food told me that either the stories were more comprehensive than I'd realized… or Aidan had reported back to the elders that their guest didn't eat at all.

My guide had peeled off to join his family upon our arrival— the father blond just like his son, the mother small and dark—but I caught the occasional glimpse of him in the throng of clan members that formed an ever-shifting ocean around the feast's central fire, people coming and going in waves and then returning again just as suddenly.

Two-Feathers was present too, though we'd been limited so far to exchanging glances from a distance, like stars in one of the Free States' sappy romance vids. He stood with an older woman who shared his features if none of his size, and a younger woman with night-black hair and dark eyes that seemed drawn to my nomad like a magnet to iron.

His mother and sister, no doubt. I couldn't find anyone who seemed to fill the role of father, but that too was life in the Badlands, even for the nomads.

I was studying the trio when Snow-Falls turned to me. "Am I correct in believing that this is your first time attending a clan feast?"

I looked down at the plate of food in front of me and back at the elder. "Yes."

"We thank you for honoring our ways, even if you yourself cannot partake." He made a gesture, and moments later, a boy even younger than Aidan was there to take my plate away. Given the nomads' aversion to waste, it was a certainty that someone would be getting an extra serving. "Now that we have shared in the earth's bounty—even symbolically—we will be proceeding to the next stages of the spring feast. First, there will be a recitation of deeds performed over the prior year. Then, some of my fellow elders will share tales from the clan's past."

"The *elders* will?" I didn't know a lot about nomads, and Two-Feathers' clan less than most, but I *had* been traveling these lands for decades, and I'd picked up a few things. "Isn't that last part usually a task for your clan's shaman?"

Snow-Falls was silent for a moment, Finally, he nodded. "It is. However, Listens-to-Wind and his apprentices have left us for the time being."

"I didn't realize they ever did that."

"It is rare, admittedly. Still, there are times when the spirits call, and those who hear them must answer. And this time, it was not just our clan but every clan that was so affected."

Meaning dozens of spirit guides, or whatever the hell nomad shamans really were, and probably three times that number of apprentices, all leaving their clans. But why, to where, and for what?

"The Mother of Webs fights a war to the north," Snow-Falls said, once I asked.

"And your shamans went to battle her *without* warriors? Because that's not a fight they're going to win, I promise you." Frankly, it wasn't a fight they'd win even *with* the warriors, but I wasn't going to say that aloud. *The Mother of Webs* was the nomads' name for the Weaver, a Spider Shifter even older than I was, whose thousands of children had made western Canada her empire.

"You misunderstand," said the elder, his voice somehow gentle and bleak at the same time. "The Mother of Webs is *losing* her war. Listens-to-Wind and the others were sent by the spirits to offer aid. Whatever the nature of the enemy, our warriors would be as powerless as hers."

I wasn't sure what to say to that. The idea of the nomads helping the Weaver was almost as insane as anyone or anything waging a war against that creature, let alone *winning* it. With Dominion, Tyrant, and my so-called dad all pushing up daisies, I'd have placed the Weaver in the upper echelon of Powers on our continent, along with Grannypocalypse, the Singer, Legion, and possibly Bakersfield himself. What could drive *her* to the breaking point, let alone convince the clans' shamans to head north to offer aid?

I didn't know… but I needed to. Or at least my empire did. Because anything that could threaten the Weaver and mobilize the clans was sure as shit a threat to my own people. And if clan warriors couldn't help, I wasn't sure that my army would fare much better.

I made a mental note to send another winged message back to New Memphis once the feast was done. Cyrus had scouts that could be dispatched to find out the truth. By the time we made it back from Mexico, there would be answers waiting for me, and if I knew the square-jawed Immortal, at least a half-dozen tactical responses too.

As I was still struggling to muster a response to Snow-Falls, one of the other elders—delicate and fine-boned, like a bird stripped of his feathers—rose to his feet. His reedy voice somehow carried above the crackle of the fire to reach the clan members assembled about us, and even further to those sitting at other fires. He spoke in the clan's native tongue, meaning I understood none of it. Snow-Falls offered to translate, but I didn't miss his hastily buried relief when I declined.

The man was as tough as boot leather, but *elder* wasn't just a title and I couldn't imagine talking at length after a meal like this one would rank high on his list of fun activities.

As if to prove that point, the other elder kept his speech short. When he'd sat down again, wrapping a brightly colored blanket around himself like it was a cape or funeral shroud, the crowd shifted, letting someone through from one of the other gatherings. Moments later, a young nomad woman stepped into the fire's nimbus of light.

She, too, spoke in words I didn't understand, but I'd been riding the earth for longer than most people had been alive, and body language, at least, remained the same. Given her stance, the strong timbre of her voice, and even the proud gaze she swept across fellow clan members and elders alike, it didn't take a genius to realize this was the recitation of deeds that Snow-Falls had told me about.

When she was done, the crowd showed their approval, some stomping their feet, others saluting the way Aidan had the elders. As the sound died away, another nomad made their way through the throng and the cycle began again. Proud words, followed by applause, again and again. I let both wash over me, much like the sensations of the world itself… the nearby fire, the still-chilly breeze, the quiet murmur of whispering voices, and the distant neighs of the clan's horses, interspersed by at least few barks or howls by the dogs that made the camp their home.

If the cat in Moon-Over-the-Trees' lap was bothered by that last bit of noise, it didn't show it. Instead, it licked its paws clean and curled in upon itself to go to sleep. Clearly, it remained unimpressed by the night's festivities.

I'd never owned a pet in my life, a few of the more slavishly devoted townies I'd spent time with notwithstanding. Still, like I'd told Dorothea in Kansas City, it was hard to go wrong with a cat.

○○○

More than a dozen nomads came to take part in the recitation of deeds, the Titan Aidan had pointed out included. Meanwhile, Two-Feathers, who had traveled thousands of miles, faced down literal demons, survived one of the Terrors of Texas, and ultimately helped kill this era's answer to Napoleon, stayed quiet and still, a dark shadow flanked by the women of his family.

The world isn't fair. I'd known that since the Break—had been born knowing it, even. The world would *never* be fair, because life itself wasn't fair, and anyone who believed differently had either led an impossibly charmed life or spent all of it with their senses dulled by drugs a lot harder than stimweed.

But Two-Feathers wasn't alone, and his handicap in no way prevented me from speaking on his behalf. With a creak of leather, I stood and gave my own summary of the actions my nomad had taken over the long year away from his clan.

Most nomads spoke English as well as their own language, but even so, there was a long silence when I finally came to a stop. Two-Feathers' mom wasn't even looking in my direction, while his sister seemed… torn, somehow. As for my nomad, himself? I'd seen pre-Break statues that emoted better.

Another elder—one of the ones who had initially greeted me with a thinly veiled glare—rose to his feet. His voice was dry and thin as old newspaper, and the beaded necklaces around his neck clattered as he moved. "Our ceremonies are for the clan," he said in accented English. And then, before I could point out that Two-Feathers was *literally* part of their clan, he added, "and for deeds done in service of it."

"It was only after much debate that we chose to allow your presence tonight as an observer," added a second elder, her near-skeletal frame belying a voice that could drive spikes through solid stone. "*Participation* is a horse of a very different color."

Moon-Over-the-Trees looked up from the animal in her lap and barked a few words in the clan's native tongue, voice sharp as any spear. The other two elders replied in kind, and for the first time in almost an hour, the calico cat opened its different-colored eyes.

As if that was a signal, Snow-Falls finally stood, joints creaking as much as my leathers. He held his hands in front of him, palms forward as if to ward off a blow and turned to all three elders in turn.

"Peace," he told them, one after the next. "We should make allowances for those who do not know our ways, especially those who have been our ally in the past."

Ally was a bit strong, if I was being honest. I had better relations with the northern clans. My interactions with this one went back decades but had been barely worth mentioning until Eclipse's destruction.

Still, a peacemaker in the Badlands was a rare enough thing that I wasn't going to contradict this one.

"We thank the Storm Who Rides," continued Snow-Falls, speaking as much to his clan as to me, "for sharing the tale of our lost son's deeds beyond the clan. However, Smoke-on-the-Breeze speaks truth. This moment is for actions performed on behalf of the clan, not those taken in another's service."

For all that I'd just thought of some of my past lovers as pets a few hours earlier, I didn't much care for the way the elder described Two-Feathers' blood and sweat as *service*. Nor for the fact that even Snow-Falls was dismissing those efforts entirely. For the first time in a while, the rage inside of me ran hot instead of cold; the storm made its presence felt as metal leaked into my every word.

"Two years," I said, my voice carrying on the afternoon breeze. "Your clan would have had two years left. The Crimson Queen's spring campaign was mopping up the last shreds of resistance to her empire's southern expansion. The strongholds of the East Coast—New England, York, and Old Baltimore—are places she knew to leave alone. Atlanta remains a viper's den that consumes every warlord who tries to claim it, and as for Florida… the less said about that place, the better."

I let my visor's gaze sweep across the still-silent audience.

"She wasn't going east, and she had already taken the north and south. She was coming *west*," I said. "I've reviewed the plans myself. Kansas City was halfway hers already. Wichita hides behind its wall as the world outside falls deeper into chaos. The only obstacles to her claiming the Badlands were the clans, and she had plans for all of you. Children taken from their parents. Adults set to work in the mines or the fields. The Blessed pressed into service as newly minted Immortals. Elders buried in the earth along with the customs you hold so dear. Two years, and most of you would have been gone."

The storm was vibrating within my shell now, an audible roar even when I didn't speak. I turned to the elder that Snow-Falls had named Smoke-on-the-Breeze and the smile across my visor was cold and hard.

"You want *actions performed on behalf of the clan*? It was Two-Feathers who restored your clan's future. Without him, you would have become a broken people in a field of dust. It's time you pulled the spears out of your collective asses and acknowledged that reality."

Five hundred miles to my east, I was pretty sure my newly promoted Secretary of State had just broken out in a cold sweat, without the slightest clue why. In fairness, I *had* warned her that there was a high chance of this trip going pear-shaped. I just… hadn't expected it to happen with the nomads.

Smoke-on-the-Breeze had frozen, pinned like a butterfly in a scrapbook, but the elder by his side bristled, her pale eyes going hard. Before she could speak though, the clan's peacemaker spoke again.

"We thank you for elaborating," said Snow-Falls, his words loud enough for all to hear, and his gentle tone going a long way to defusing even my unexpected anger. "Questions of tradition and ceremony aside, you are correct in that the clan owes our wayward son for his contributions, just as he owes the clan for duties left unfulfilled during that time."

Two-Feathers might as well have been a tree for all the reaction he offered. A few of the nomads around him had made quiet signs of approval as I listed his accomplishments, but public sentiment still seemed mixed.

"It is our belief," added Snow-Falls, "that any remaining question of credit or debt can be dealt with while you meet with us to discuss what paths forward might exist between our peoples."

"Meaning?" Nobody could see my frown through the decal on my visor, but I was sure it resonated in my voice.

"This is the spring feast. With the recitation of deeds complete, we have only the tales of our ancestors to tell before the feast concludes. And tomorrow will bring the first hunt. Two-Feathers will lead that hunt." He turned from me to my nomad. "See that it is successful and that the younglings who depart with you return as hunters."

I'd picked up enough from Aidan to know that the first hunt was when kids like him would potentially earn their names, but the murmurs of the crowd suggested there was even more to it than that, and that Two-Feathers' assignment was a significant one.

Snow-Falls turned to the other elders. "Are there any who would object to this choice?"

Smoke-on-the-Breeze spoke for the first time since I'd stared him down, shaking his head. "It is fitting and just." Next to him, the hard-eyed woman agreed, and the other elders soon joined in.

Just to be certain, I glanced over at Moon-Over-the-Trees, who had so far seemed like the closest thing to an ally I had. The old lady patted my leg as I returned to my seat, her grin contagious for all that it was a small and secretive thing.

Her cat had gone back to sleep.

Snow-Falls nodded, and if there was an unmistakable hint of satisfaction to that nod, I couldn't blame him for it. The hunt would likely extend our stay, but if it fixed things between Two-Feathers and his clan, it was worth it. "Very well then," said the elder. "We will—"

"I call challenge for the role of First Huntsman." The voice was deep and rough, the kind best suited to be heard over pitched battle, and I knew even before I looked that it was Falling-Rock who had spoken. The man was on his feet, looming over the nomads around him as only a Titan could.

"You question the judgment of your elders?" asked Smoke-on-the-Breeze, presumably sticking to English for my benefit.

"Never. Instead, I speak on behalf of our younglings." Falling-Rock made his way through the crowd to stand across the fire from Two-Feathers and his family. "Their training has been *my* responsibility. There are none better suited than me to lead them on their hunt."

"A challenge is a right rarely invoked," warned Snow-Falls.

The Titan shrugged, spreading his massive arms wide. "Some of us work to safeguard the future of our clan from within rather than abandoning their responsibilities without warning." He turned to my nomad and rumbled something in the clan tongue. I didn't know the words, but his tone was clear, and it spoke of bad blood and ill-buried grievances.

Collectively, the nomads were a force in the Badlands, and I truly believed that my empire needed to forge *some* sort of peace with them. Still, I was starting to regret that we hadn't gone to a *different* clan to start that diplomatic process.

Two-Feathers said nothing, of course, but stepped forward into the clear space around the central fire, leaving his mother and sister behind. He saluted the elders and then turned to the Titan, his face an impassive mask.

"What exactly is this challenge?" I asked Snow-Falls, keeping my words low. "Because if it's a death match…"

"Not death," said the elder, voice equally soft. "All life is sacred, and those of the clan especially so. The two will fight, bare-handed, until one of them surrenders or the elders rule one incapable of continuing."

"Bare-handed?" My nomad was not a small man, but he was dwarfed by an opponent whose heavy slabs of muscle belied the agility with which I'd seen him move on the training fields. Getting in a wrestling match with a Titan was a lot like playing darts with a Wind Dancer; smart people made better choices, while dumb people got taken for a ride.

Still, this was Two-Feathers' decision and by the look of things, he'd already made it. A year of shared travel—not to mention decades of riding with men and their often-fragile egos—had taught me better than to get in the way of that.

But if Falling-Rock did any permanent damage?

The big man would be meat and his whole clan could go with him. There was business and there was personal, and the last person who'd dared confuse the two with me had died gasping for breath in her own throne room.

"One gold on Two-Feathers," I said coldly, raising my voice so the other elders could hear.

"I will take that bet," answered the hard-eyed skeleton of a female elder whose name I either hadn't been told or couldn't recall.

The circle of space by the fire had continued to widen, and the two men faced each other now, my nomad at least a foot shorter than his opponent. Falling-Rock spoke again, and though it was too quiet for anyone but Two-Feathers to hear, the long look the bigger man directed at my nomad's sister said absolutely everything.

Two-Feathers went still, the quiet before the storm and the emptiness of a moment soon to be filled with blood.

"Five gold," I told the elder, the smile across my visor widening to nightmarish proportions.

"You said one," she reminded me, examining the two opponents more closely.

"That was before he talked shit about Two-Feathers' sister."

Next to me, Snow-Falls started to speak, but if he'd wanted in on the bet, he had missed his opportunity.

The challenge was already underway.

15

Travel the Badlands long enough and you'll run across your fair share of duels. Some happen out in the streets, men or women staring each other down like pre-Break gunslingers. Others take place in cages or arenas for an audience's entertainment. The only real difference from your normal, everyday murder is whatever pomp and ceremony happens to be attached to the act.

But true one-on-one Power-vs.-Power showdowns? It's rare to find anything like that outside of the coastal cities, and even rarer for both combatants to walk away after. There are a lot of different kinds of Powers walking the earth, but the vast majority of them were made for killing.

As usual, you can thank my dad for that.

Maybe some Free States citizens see Powers differently. People who've only witnessed the violence and devastation through carefully edited vids or bloodless cinematic reenactments. Illusions are easy to cling to if nothing ever crawls through the window to tear them to shreds.

For the rest of us, violence is a neighbor, if not always a friend.

I watched raw emotions flit across the faces of Two-Feathers' family as the fight began. His mom had the expected mix of concern and fear, barely visible beneath the emotionless mask she shared with her son. His sister though? In addition to those first two, I was also getting something almost like pride and satisfaction from her.

They were closer to the action than me; maybe she'd heard whatever it was Falling-Rock said.

Along with Mineral Shifters, Titans are the bulwarks of the post-Break world: strong, durable, and a pain in the ass for anyone to fight in melee. Their weakness tends to be mobility. They can struggle against ranged Powers who safely evade wall-crumbling punches while returning fire from a safe distance. But against Stalwarts? In general, a Stalwart against a Titan is a bad matchup for the former, unless the rank discrepancy is significant, or the Stalwart is just so overwhelmingly skilled that rank didn't matter.

In the early days of the Break, I'd watched Wrecking Ball, one of Dominion's first recruits, wade through an army of mutants and monsters both, dealing death with every flick of her fists or feet. Decades later, I'd seen the original Paladin emerge unscathed from a warehouse battle that left his white costume painted red with blood from the chest down, the pieces of bodies left behind the only remnants of the Powers who had tried to challenge him.

But Two-Feathers wasn't anywhere close to Wrecking Ball or Paladin, and Falling-Rock had a significant advantage in reach, power, and durability, while being equally matched in skill and giving up only the slightest edge in speed.

By every measure but two, it was an unfair contest.

First, Two-Feathers *did* have the advantage in speed, and in a battle like this one, speed kills.

And second, Falling-Rock was a *hunter*, where Two-Feathers was a *warrior*. In the past year, Two-Feathers had battled more human opponents than Falling-Rock had probably ever even met. And while the Titan *might* be better suited to lead the clan hunt against buffalo and other four-legged beasts, there was no substitute for experience when it came to fighting fellow Powers.

I watched the first dozen exchanges in silence and then turned my attention to the crowd around me, cataloging the disparate looks of stoicism or focus on the elders' faces before identifying regular clan members who seemed overly invested in the fight taking place. When Two-Feathers won—and he *would* win, the storm and I both agreed on that—the challenge would be resolved, but nomads were humans, too, and humans were almost predictably unpredictable.

Anyone who chose to make an issue of the result wouldn't live to regret it, and if that cost my empire a treaty with one of the Badlands' clans, then so be it.

I sought out Two-Feathers' family again in the crowd. His mother's face had settled back into that too-familiar mask, but there was a grim sort of awareness in her dark eyes. The sister, again, was a mess of contradictions, eyes wide now and spine stiff as Two-Feathers flowed around another brutally fast punch to bury a fist in the Titan's side.

It was the seventh time he'd hit that spot, and though Falling-Rock's superhumanly tough body meant nothing had cracked, let alone broken, my nomad's pinpoint precision was already starting to take its toll on the other man. Titans are, by definition, enormous, and while their endurance is augmented just like their durability and strength, all that weight and muscle still comes with a cost.

Especially when your opponent keeps sneaking superpowered shots of his own right up under the ribs.

A minute later, the count had reached nine hits to the liver, and Falling-Rock was slowing, inhuman constitution fighting against all-too-human physical shock. He lunged forward, abandoning finesse for a bull rush that was still far faster than should have been possible for someone of his size.

Two-Feathers' sister sat up straight, her face pale, but if there was one thing you couldn't do against a Stalwart it was to telegraph your move. Two-Feathers was already out of the way, the whisper of fingers against fabric the only indication of how close the Titan had come. My nomad visibly passed up the kidney shots that might do permanent damage to even a Titan and instead backed away, a sheen of sweat on his bronze skin the only sign that the extended fight was starting to wear on him as well.

Falling-Rock spun, breathing like a horse on its last legs, and stalked his smaller opponent again.

Thirty seconds and three more exchanges later, I turned to Snow-Falls. "He could have crippled him again there. He chose not to."

"Yes," came the reply.

"Then why haven't you called the duel?"

The elder didn't reply, his eyes trained on the action in front of us. A tenth hit landed to Falling-Rock's liver and this time, his whole body seized up. The bigger man collapsed to the earth with a thud that sent sparks flying from the nearby fire. Still, the Titan tried to continue, crab walking back on one arm.

Instead of pursuing him, Two-Feathers straightened, folded his arms across his chest, and gave the other man a steady look.

The Titan met that look, started to reply, and then sighed, letting his head fall back against the dirt. For a long moment, his massive chest just heaved up and down, breaths audible even over the fire, and then he managed to speak a few words.

I looked to Snow-Falls for a translation, but the elder was already rising to his feet. "Having fought bravely and well, Falling-Rock has ceded the duel to the victor, Two-Feathers. Let any bad blood between the two men be buried with this challenge, and may their supporters follow suit."

For some reason, he gave me a look at the end there. As if I would want or need revenge after Two-Feathers had just kicked ass on his own behalf.

Instead, I eyed the people I'd picked out in the crowd earlier. To my surprise, the elder's words seemed to have reached them. Either that or nomads were a little bit less prone to stupidity than most people in the Badlands. Either way, those who had been rooting for Falling-Rock looked disappointed but far from violent.

It was a refreshing change from Kansas City, to be honest.

"We will now proceed with the—" Snow-Falls' sigh was barely audible as Two-Feathers stood and approached the elders. "Or perhaps not. What can your elders do for you, First Huntsman?"

Instead of answering the old man, Two-Feathers turned to me, his hands slowly moving through the signs we'd both been learning. It didn't escape me that, even back with his family and people, my nomad turned to *me* to be understood. Even his mother was looking my way, unable to make sense of her son's newly learned language.

Pride was an ugly thing that had brought more than one empire to ruin, but sometimes, it just felt *good*.

Of course, I technically still sucked at reading the signs, so it took three tries for Two-Feathers to convey exactly what he was trying to say. When I finally got the message, I just stared at him for a long moment, with no idea whatsoever what expression was scrawled across the true face of my visor.

There were times I worried that my nomad was unfit for the world, and other times, like this one, where I worried the world was, instead, unfit for my nomad.

"Two-Feathers," I said, all the iron gone from my voice, "says that Falling-Rock fought like a lion."

Honestly, it could have been any big cat; I wasn't sure what the appropriate signs were to distinguish them. Regardless, the Titan in question went still as my words reached him.

"He also says," I continued, "that the new hunters should be permitted to earn their names with the man who trained them, if that is their wish."

Smoke-on-the-Breeze scowled, directing his words as much to me as to Two-Feathers. "He won the challenge but is rejecting his role as First Huntsman?"

Two-Feathers shook his head, but I was already answering.

"No. He's suggesting there be *two* hunts. Two-Feathers will lead one tomorrow, and a few days from now, Falling-Rock can lead the second. The… younglings… can attend either hunt and claim their names in the process."

I guess I'd gotten it right, or at least right enough, because Two-Feathers nodded, walked over to his fallen opponent, and offered an arm. The bewildered Titan hesitated before allowing himself to be pulled to his feet. For the first time since I'd stood to speak of Two-Feathers' deeds, the crowd showed their support. Even the people I'd earmarked as die-hard Falling-Rock supporters seemed thoughtful or impressed.

"It would be… irregular," said the hard-eyed elder who owed me five gold coins.

"True," said Snow-Falls, "but there is wisdom in the idea."

"Our traditions…"

"Are what make us who we are, yes," interjected Smoke-on-the-Breeze. "However, Listens-to-Wind has long said the spirits want us to be firm yet not rigid in our beliefs. I have no issue with this lost… with *Two-Feathers'* request."

Snow-Falls scanned the other elders, receiving nods from each—some more grudging than others. "It is agreed then." He raised his voice. "Two hunts then. Two-Feathers leaves tomorrow for the west. Falling-Rock in three days' time for the north. We will ensure that each group has their complement of blooded hunters. The younglings will be permitted to choose which hunt they will join, with equal honor afforded to each. And now…" He waited, as if expecting someone to cut him off, and this time, his sigh had the sound of relief to it. "And now Moon-Over-the-Trees will share a tale from our clan's long history."

The elderly woman slowly climbed to her feet, cat still cuddled in her arms, and began to speak.

ooo

The elder's tale was long and once again told in a language I didn't understand. By the time she was done, the sun was setting over the western hills. Smoke-on-the-Breeze brought the ceremonies to a close and the crowd began to disperse, some families retreating to their own fires, while others retrieved the remaining plates or cups for cleaning or gathered plates of food for the scouts on duty. Most of the elders shuffled off without a word to me, but Moon-Over-the-Trees gave me a pat on the shoulder, and Snow-Falls leaned in to bid me goodnight.

"We thank you for your patience in waiting for our spring celebration to be completed," he said. "Tomorrow, we will begin our negotiations. If all goes well, you should be able to continue your journey by the week's end."

"How long do you expect Two-Feathers' hunt to take?" I asked.

He considered that for a moment. "Given the group's size and direction, no more than two or three weeks."

I met his contemplative look with the smile across my visor. "Then it looks like I'll be here at least until then." And then, because nobody likes a guest who extends their stay without asking, I added:

"Once the negotiations are complete, I'll be happy to help around the camp."

"I'm not sure that putting a visiting head of state to work is the most diplomatic of moves."

"It is if I'm the one offering." I shrugged. So far, the clan hadn't really treated me as a friend *or* as the queen of a neighboring empire, but as something in between. Why change that now?

"We will keep your offer in mind," he said, in a tone that suggested just the opposite. "For now, rest well."

I watched the elder disappear into the darkness and then turned to find the man of the hour. Two-Feathers was back with his family, his sister practically attached to his hip as if she feared he'd otherwise disappear, but he was looking my way. He slowly made a series of signs that I had no trouble interpreting.

We need to talk.

I nodded and headed his way, only to be intercepted by a young nomad I'd spent almost too much time with over the previous few days.

"I'm here to take you back to our fire," said Aidan.

"Good, but first, I need to talk to—" I trailed off. Two-Feathers had been met by two nomads his age, both chattering excitedly as they gestured to the spears in their hands and the bows on their backs. Hunters, presumably? At the same time, Two-Feathers' mother tugged on her son's arm, turning him around to begin the walk back to their family fire. I watched the five of them go—two hunters, my nomad, and his family—and swallowed my sigh.

Apparently, I'd be talking to him tomorrow instead.

Except when I reformed my shell and returned to camp the next morning, Two-Feathers and his hunt had already left.

16

Two-Feathers' departure shouldn't have been a surprise. I never really slept yet somehow the nomad was active before me most mornings. It stood to reason a group of experienced hunters and over-excited teenagers would share in that malady and want to be on their way even before the sun had crested the horizon. Nor was it a surprise that I'd missed them on their way out… I'd chosen my location for setting the storm loose precisely *because* it was out of the way.

What *was* a surprise was who hadn't gone with them.

"Aidan?" I asked, surprised to return to camp to find the young nomad waiting outside my tent. "You didn't join the hunt?"

He looked away, avoiding my unseen gaze. "It's nothing against Two-Feathers, but… he was already one of our perimeter scouts before I left my mother's tent. I barely know him. Meanwhile, Falling-Rock has been like an older brother to me. Elder Snow-Falls *did* say we had a choice."

"Fair enough." I ducked inside my tent, verified that my saddlebags remained undisturbed, and rejoined my guide. "Last night's challenge must have been tough on you."

"They both fought brilliantly," said Aidan, slightly overstating the case in my opinion. "Falling Rock lost but he kept his honor, and even in victory, Two-Feathers acknowledged his skill."

That… was one way to look at it, sure. And while it was slightly divorced from reality, I could live with that if it led to the unruffling of previously ruffled feathers in the clan. We wouldn't be staying here long, but the clan *was* Two-Feathers' home and extended family. It was a good idea to mend any broken fences before our departure.

Not that the nomads believed in literal fences, but still.

"Have you already eaten?" I asked him.

He nodded.

"Then I guess it's time to give peace a chance."

Aidan gave me a confused look, prompting another barely swallowed sigh.

"I'm ready to sit with the elders," I clarified. "Assuming you know where you're supposed to take me?"

"Oh! Of course!"

The clan was already active, men, women, and children doing all the things it took to keep an encampment of this size clean and functional. When the spring rains finished in a month or two, the clan would move elsewhere again, following the animals their livelihoods depended upon. But for now, there were hides, rugs, and clothes to be beaten free of dust and dirt. There was water to be retrieved from the nearby stream and rugged dishware to be cleaned. There were wooden staves to be hardened in a designated firepit, moving one step closer to becoming spears like the one Two-Feathers had lost, and there was animal sinew to be made into bow strings. There was cooking and cleaning and crafting and yes, I realized as the sound of clashing weapons reached me, even training still to be done.

In short, the twin hunts and my diplomatic summit notwithstanding, it was just another day in the clan's life. This early in the morning, there was no time yet for anyone involved to slack. All the activity wasn't *that* different from what you'd find in towns or even cities like mine. Without automation and technology, most people's days started early, with relaxation something pushed off until after the sun had set. But in the absence of homes, places of business, and warehouses, all that activity was front and center with the clan in a way that it rarely was for other settlements.

I had no interest in doing that work—even if I had needed things like food, clothing, or shelter—but damn if it didn't make me feel just a tiny bit lazy, following Aidan through the organized chaos. I'd been born to the road; this level of focused industry was foreign to the lifestyle I'd both been given and chosen.

"Were you able to find any solar charging?" I asked.

"There is one station, yes, but… you'll have to get permission from the elders to use it."

"It's a good thing we're headed that way then." If I was going to be stuck with the clan for multiple weeks, I might as well use that time to top off my batteries… both the one I'd removed from my bike upon arrival and the spares I kept in my saddlebags.

I didn't know what the clan needed solar panels for, but the Mission and their Free States donors had worked to spread the devices throughout the Badlands. Electricity was far more readily available than gas, even if that was a relatively low bar to clear. Considering my mount ran on the stuff instead of grass or hay, I took advantage of whatever solar charging I could find.

Mexico was going to be a problem, unless Bakersfield had become a captain of industry in his off hours. Considering that we had no idea where in the former country he had holed up, I would need to hit the border with as much charge as I could carry.

Aidan eventually led me to a larger tent, one that could have held the elders and at least a dozen of their closest friends had the weather turned during the feast. The warrior posted at the front held a flap open for me, and I ducked inside to find six wizened faces gazing in my direction.

Snow-Falls sat just to the right of center, but it was Smoke-on-the-Breeze who rose to address me.

"We greet the Queen of Smiles," he said in his accented English. "Ruler from the East and heir to the many misfortunes her predecessor visited upon this land."

The change in title from *The Storm Who Rides* made it clear I was being treated now as a visiting monarch, not an erstwhile ally, while the rest of his so-called greeting established the initial dynamic of our diplomatic relationship. And it wasn't good.

This was going to be fun.

ooo

By all rights, the summit should have been a cake walk. Unlike in Kansas City, I wasn't trying to re-establish order; the clan already had that. I wasn't trying to work out a full treaty either… the diplomats that would follow in my footsteps would handle that. All I was meant to do was finalize a framework *for* diplomacy. We had unilaterally made Two-Feathers the nomad ambassador to New Memphis, but international relations were a two-way street. I needed the clan to accept an ambassador from New Memphis, and to agree to at least nominally serve as our sponsor to the rest of the clans.

The rationale, as it had been explained to me, was that one clan would work better as a gateway to the others than having us try to reach each clan individually. And if it kind of reeked of the same tactics the Crimson Queen had used with Kansas City's Dead Rabbits… well, at least here, it was all out in the open.

And it wasn't costing me one of my empire's very few vehicles either.

Unfortunately, the geniuses who had put together the plan had failed to account for the fact that I'd be dealing with six cantankerous old goats, each with tongues as sharp as a younger person's eyes, and literal decades of bad blood, worse history, and tightly gripped grudges. Where the cartels had settled into an almost disappointingly business-like approach, and I'd been naïve enough to bemoan that fact, meetings with the clan elders too often devolved into bitter arguments that had one or more blanket-wrapped fogeys stalking out of the tent in mid-session.

It took three goddamn days before we even had a semblance of an agreement, and judging by the way things had gone so far, it would be *at least* another five before that semblance could be transformed into anything solid.

After the first day, I remembered to send the message about the Weaver back to New Memphis, using up another precious piece of Legion tech in the process. After the second day, I got permission to top off my bike's batteries. But when the third day of negotiations ended with yet another bitter argument and the request for a recess, I found myself with nothing to do to distract me from the succession of painfully slow debates.

Even the storm was tired of raging on the hill.

I sat in my tent for a few overly long minutes, looking at nothing and thinking of even less, and then forced myself to my feet again. Aidan had left on Falling-Rock's hunt that morning, but a new guide had been assigned to me, this one a young woman with strawberry blonde hair for all that it was woven in a nomad's braids. Maybe *she* would have a suggestion on what to do?

Except, when I emerged from my tent, I found my guide on the other side, a step away from knocking. She stumbled back with a strangled gasp and then brought her fist to her chest in a salute.

"Can I help you?" I asked. So far, she'd been a lot more skittish than Aidan. I hadn't even gotten a name out of her yet, which made her proximity to my tent all the more unusual.

"You have…" She cleared her throat and tried again. "You have been invited to visit another family's fires tonight. If you choose to accept, I will take you to Deep-Water's tent."

"Who is Deep-Water?" I was *reasonably* sure that wasn't one of the elders, but to be honest, half of them hadn't even spoken English so far, and I'd focused on the ones who did.

"She is Two-Feathers' mother."

I was glad my true face hid whatever expressions the half-formed face beneath might have made. I'd avoided Two-Feathers' family so far, first to give them time with their son and brother, and then, after his departure, because I was waiting for my nomad to handle our introduction.

Apparently, introductions were going to happen without him.

"I accept the invitation," I said, giving my shell a once-over to make sure it was free of dust and dirt. "But first, could I have your name?"

"My name? Why?"

"It would be a lot easier to have something to refer to you by when conversing with the voices in my head."

That joke landed with a thud in the slowly widening space between us. I sighed.

"You can call me The Storm Who Rides, if you must, or Your Majesty, if you'd rather. Anything else probably wouldn't be a good idea."

Jules had *earned* the right to call me Queenie, after all. Or at least we both pretended he had.

"I'm Stephanie, Your Majesty."

"It's nice to meet you, Stephanie. I don't know if Aidan spoke to you before he left, but this escort duty is going to be the easiest one you've ever had."

"He did say you didn't need to take your meals, sleep, or…" Her tanned face colored. "…visit the outhouse."

"That's right. Nothing goes in and nothing goes out." Which was *technically* not true, even if I'd been waiting *months* for Two-Feathers to prove it. Still, I doubted Stephanie wanted to hear about that sort of thing. "One more question then."

"Yes?"

"What sort of guest gift should I bring to another family's fire?"

"Flowers, feathers, or beads, if you're courting." She stopped and coughed. "Which you obviously are not. Blankets, pipe-weed, or food and drink would be appropriate."

None of which I had. I bit back a sigh. Family was still largely a foreign concept to me, and seeking the approval of someone's parents even more so, but hell if I wanted Two-Feathers to come back from his hunt to find his mother and me locked into some sort of blood feud either.

Hopefully, I'd already made a good enough impression by defending her son. If not? Maybe gold would suffice.

Which reminded me… I hadn't received my winnings from the one elder who'd bet on Falling-Rock.

One more thing for tomorrow's agenda.

I reached into my tent, slung my saddlebags onto one shoulder, and turned back to Stephanie. "Lead on."

However bad things went, I was confident it would *still* be better than twelve hours in a tent with old humans complaining about things done by the warlord who I'd literally already killed and deposed.

○○○

We traveled to a fire on the far side of camp, one that had three tents surrounding it. Over the fire, a dented teapot had been hung, the water inside starting to simmer. With his horse, gear, and the man himself all missing, there was nothing to tell me which tent was Two-Feathers, but my nomad's sister waited outside the middle tent.

It was the second time I'd seen her, and she was even prettier up close. Her long black hair had been freed from its braids and hung like a curtain of silk, cascading over her shoulders and down her back. She was maybe a year or two younger than Two-Feathers, and far shorter, but glowed with life and vitality.

I had yet to see any sign of their father, which probably meant he was out of the picture. It also left Two-Feathers the job of guarding his sister from single nomads. I wasn't sure how the clan handled such things, but it seemed like a minor miracle we hadn't arrived at the clan after a year away to find her married and pregnant.

"I greet the Storm Who Rides," she said. Her voice was melodic, her words only lightly accented, and a part of me couldn't help but wonder if that was how her brother would sound if he was able to speak. "My name is Bright-Meadows. I will be helping to translate for Deep-Water."

I nodded, looking for some sign of Two-Feathers in the young woman's features, but finding nothing beyond maybe the cut of her cheekbones. "She doesn't speak English?"

"She chooses not to."

There was clearly a story there, but it was far from the strangest thing I'd encountered in the Badlands, so I let it go. Whatever I was to Two-Feathers, whatever we were to each other, his family would almost inevitably be at least some small piece of that. In the absence of traumatic dysfunction or just plain assholery, that was how human relations seemed to work. Family mattered.

Be nice to them both, I reminded myself. *You've made it through three days without losing your shit with the clan elders. You can sweet-talk two humans who should already be predisposed to like you.*

Bright-Meadows pulled the tent flap aside, and I ducked inside. A regular human might have had to wait for their eyes to adjust to the interior's dim lighting, but I located Deep-Water immediately, seated on a blanket in the tent's center. As I walked forward, other details filtered in. Two additional blankets had been laid several feet away on either side of her, forming a triangle of sorts, and each had a woven and embroidered pillow on top. A simple set of clay cups on equally simply saucers sat at the center of the triangle and directly in front of the older woman.

There were three cups. Which meant I was going to have to explain, again, that I didn't eat or drink. I swallowed a sigh. Hell if I was going to apologize for who and what I was, but it would have been nice to leave some of my… oddities… unmentioned until later.

Deep-Water didn't stand or salute but gestured to one of the free blankets. I took my seat, leather creaking as I lowered myself to the ground. With Two-Feathers' mother on my left, his sister gracefully took the final blanket, directly across from me.

For what felt like an inordinately long time, the older human simply looked at me, her face a mask to rival that of her son's. When she spoke, her voice was stronger than I'd expected. Which… just went to show that I'd been spending too much time with the clan elders. Deep-Water was likely only a few years older than Jules, no longer in the prime of her life, perhaps, but still a long way from infirmity. She'd kept the weight off better than my old bandit friend… and retained more of her hair as well.

I filed that observation away for our return to New Memphis. Jules' ego was forever in need of deflation.

Anyway, Deep-Water was speaking. Naturally, her words were in the clan's tongue, but Bright-Meadows translated as soon as the other woman came to a stop.

"She thanks you for attending her fire," she said. "And wishes to speak with you about her son."

"Of course," I said. "I meant what I said at the feast. Two-Feathers was instrumental in helping me stop the Crimson Queen last year. He's been a credit to your clan."

Deep-Water didn't look for Bright-Meadows to translate what I was saying, making it clear that she knew English as well as the rest of us. Still, she continued to respond in her own language.

"Your words at the fire made a difference," Bright-Meadows said, "and she thanks you for that. However, her questions have less to do with her son's actions and more to do with Two-Feathers himself."

I looked from young woman to middle-aged woman and let the confusion show in my voice. "How so?"

"He is not the same as when he left," said Deep-Water through her daughter. "He returns to the clan a different person."

"The road will do that to you." I said, a lifetime of experience in my voice.

"Still, his silence is different now. Even here with the clan, even at his family's fire, he moves as one apart and alone."

I took that in, unsure what I was supposed to say or do. Part of me was cursing Two-Feathers for running off to hunt buffalo or whatever while he left me to deal with his family.

"I'm not sure what to tell you. He's seen a lot and done a lot, and that can change a person. Even so, spear or no spear, he's still Two-Feathers."

Deep-Water accepted my words in contemplative silence, but Bright-Meadows had a question of her own. "The two of you have ridden together for months. Has he shared his thoughts and feelings on returning to the clan?"

Her voice was still soft, but the intent look on her face and the way she leaned forward as she asked the question told me she was asking about something more permanent than the next few weeks.

Which meant Two-Feathers hadn't broken it to them that we were headed south as soon as the hunt and meetings were done.

Hell if I was going to get in the middle of *that*.

"You know your brother," I answered instead. "There's a lot he says and a lot more that he doesn't."

Outside, the tea kettle started to whistle.

Bright-Meadows tilted her head, wrinkling her cute little nose. "What does my brother have to do with this?"

Apparently, Two-Feathers' sister wasn't all there. Maybe *that's* why she was still single? I'd run across plenty of men and almost as many women who didn't care what was between the ears as long as the packaging was pretty enough, but still, there *were* limits.

"We're literally talking about him," I said, keeping my voice as gentle as possible. The metal in my soul and the screeching of the kettle outside made it an effort in futility.

The two nomads exchanged glances and then words. After a few short exchanges, Bright-Meadows' pretty mouth dropped open.

"You think *Two-Feathers* is my brother?"

Okay… maybe *I* was the one missing a screw.

"Isn't he?"

"No! Falling-Rock is my brother."

"The Titan? Then… why are you here with us?"

"It is my right and duty as Two-Feathers' promised."

"His what?"

"His…" Bright-Meadows stopped for a second, clearly searching for the right word. "Fiancée," she finally said. "The woman he is set to marry."

The storm went utterly still.

17

As I sat there saying nothing, the scream of the tea kettle continued to pierce the air, oddly similar to the tortured scrape of metal on metal when the storm was at its most bloody. Finally, Deep-Water gestured to Bright-Meadows and the younger woman stood and left the tent. Moments later, there was silence, broken only by the sound of Deep-Water's breathing in the tent and the movements of Two-Feathers' fiancée outside.

His fucking *fiancée*.

A lot of things had become clear with that word and a lot of other misconceptions had been laid bare, misconceptions I'd had not just since our arrival at camp, but all the way back to our time on the road, before and after the culmination of my final job.

No wonder I hadn't known what our relationship meant.

No wonder he'd rejected me that one night by the fire.

No wonder he hadn't touched me in the many months since.

And yet… for each truth made blindingly apparent, there were new questions forming almost as quickly.

Why had Two-Feathers joined me on my mission at all?

Why had he stayed so long in New Memphis, with both his mother and future bride waiting at home?

And most importantly of all: why had he not told me a single fucking word of this?

The storm started up inside of me again, chaos married to motion like dawn to the dew. As the screeching tea kettle finally went mercifully silent, the grind and scrape of metal against metal filled the tent instead. Deep-Water turned to me with eyes older than her face, and I'd spent enough time around Two-Feathers to pick up on at least a few of the emotions lurking behind her mask.

Curiosity.

Concern.

And… maybe… pity?

Still, she said nothing.

A splash of light heralded Bright-Meadows' return to the tent. She carried the teapot in with her and knelt gracefully to pour a small measure of dark orange liquid into each of the three cups. When she was done, the teapot was set in the middle, within reach of any of us, and she sat again on her own pillow.

In unison, Deep-Water and Bright-Meadows picked up their cups, breathed in the vapor wafting up, and took long sips. The clinks as those cups returned to their respective saucers were the loudest sounds in the tent.

I shrugged as both women looked toward me. "I don't eat or drink."

"Ever?" asked Two-Feathers' fiancée.

"Ever."

Deep-Water said something and the younger woman nodded in response. "Can you smell?"

"I can do a lot of things. Smelling is one of them, yes."

"Then Deep-Water suggests you experience the tea that way instead. The plant that it comes from is not native to the region, but there are a few Growers spread out through the various clans who can make do."

I nodded and took up my tea. Simple as it was, the cup looked delicate in my gloved hand, not so much overly small as simply out of place. The liquid inside swirled about, giving off steam, and if there were leaves still mixed within, I couldn't see them.

I didn't raise my visor but instead continued to show my true face to True-Feathers' mother and would-be bride. As much as my false face, my half-formed face, had features, they were largely vestigial. I didn't see through those eyes any more than I smelled through the cavernous wreckage that might have been a nose. Instead, I sensed things through my shell and translated those impressions into shapes or colors or even odors.

I didn't know if it was better or worse than the way humans did it, and I didn't really care either. It was probably a little bit of both, but that line of questioning, much like this tea ceremony itself, was just a distraction from the matter at hand.

The tea smelled… fresh, like green grass. And maybe sweet with a hint of vanilla, not that I'd ever had the latter. Despite the unrest swirling in my soul, both companion and counterpoint to the uncaring storm, I gave Deep-Water a nod and returned my cup to its plate.

"Thank you for the tea," I said.

The older woman simply waved to Bright-Meadows, who offered a slight bow, dark eyes never quite leaving my true face.

"Two-Feathers never told me about you," I told her.

I hadn't meant it as an attack—at least, I didn't think I had—but it landed anyway, her eyes dropping for just a moment as if to acknowledge the blow.

"As you said," she replied, speaking for herself and not the older woman between us, "there is a lot he does not say."

Clearly. And *annoyingly* too. But that was a discussion to be had with the man himself, not his fiancée. She wasn't responsible for Two-Feathers' actions any more than I was.

She might, however, have some insight to offer.

"You're right," I admitted, "and only he knows why. I've found he can communicate well enough when he wants to."

Deep-Water muttered something, and Bright-Meadows responded with a lilting laugh that filled the tent more the storm's noise ever could.

"She says her son is both a man of few words and far too many, and often the first is preferable to the second." The young woman's smile was just as brilliant as her laugh. "Even when we played as children, he was like that."

I didn't know if *she* had meant her casual reference to their lengthy shared history as an attack, but my true face didn't change a bit when it landed.

"Why did Two-Feathers leave the clan?" I asked instead. "Why would he choose to leave both his mother and his fiancée to follow me across the Badlands for an entire year?"

It was Deep-Water who answered, although Bright-Meadows once again served as translator.

"My son owed a debt," said the older woman through her translating future daughter-in-law. "We both did."

"To whom?"

"To you," said Bright-Meadows, brow cutely furrowed. "For saving their lives."

For the first time in minutes, the storm began to spin. I didn't have any clue what they were talking about.

"What?" I turned to Two-Feathers' mother and asked the question directly to her. "When? And how?"

The older woman, who was herself, at best, half my age, stared at me for a long while, perhaps searching for the hint of human features behind the opaque glass of my visor and the smiling decal atop. Finding nothing, because there was nothing to be found, she finally began to speak, her words again conveyed by the woman at her side.

"My partner—Two-Feathers' father—was an advocate for change within the clan. As much as we had already grown and changed since the Renewal, since we opened our clans to other people and cultures, he thought there was more that could be done. That there were ways to both teach and learn from those who continue to dwell behind village walls. He sought and received the elders' permission to visit those villages."

"He was… what, some kind of missionary? Or diplomat?" If so, Two-Feathers' role as ambassador was more fitting than I'd realized.

"Part ambassador, part teacher, part merchant," she replied. "Not every trip was a success, but enough were that the elders agreed to commit more resources to his dream. A wagon where he'd previously had only his horse. A handful of warriors to assist and learn from him in the process. A greater number of goods for trade with a growing list of items the clan wished to trade for."

"And you and Two-Feathers?"

"At first, we stayed with the clan. As his trips grew in frequency and duration, we began to journey with him. He wished for Two-Feathers to see the world outside our clan so that he might better shepherd that clan when he became an adult and I, blinded by love and ignorant of the potential costs, agreed."

"How did it happen?" My voice was soft and absent of metal. How, not what. I could guess *what* had happened. Hell, I'd rubbed elbows with enough crews that *made* that sort of thing happen. Still, I didn't understand how I fit into things, and thus I had to ask.

Deep-Water paused, pain lurking within the dark eyes that were so like her son's, and for just a moment in the quiet tent, there was a connection between us, ephemeral as the wind and fleeting as the dawn. She'd grasped the distinction in my question. She knew I already understood where the story was headed and why, in a way that her younger self never had, that the woman at her side would hopefully never have to understand.

The world is a toilet. It's always been that way, even before my creation, even before Dad doomed us all with his dreams. The world is a toilet, but some people get shit on more than others.

"We were traveling back to the clan," she said, and while it was Bright-Meadows speaking the language I understood, I could hear the jagged, unhealed edges of the other woman's words. "A day out from our lands, wagon full of a mix of pretty and useful things. My partner was pointing out trail sign of some creature that rarely made its way across the plains and Two-Feathers was comparing the size of its print with his own hand. We had hunters with us in addition to my partner's assistants, four of them, but we were almost home, and they had let the softness of the villages seep into their bones. Two fell before we even knew we had been stalked, the third even as the sound of the first shots were beginning to echo."

"Bandits?"

Deep-Water's face was stone but I could hear the snarl in her voice, an odd counter to the melody of Bright-Meadows' translation. "Monsters. Twisted beasts in human flesh. We fought. We lost. The few who survived were taken and put in chains."

Not bandits then, but slavers. There wasn't always a difference between the two, in action at least, but bandits tended to travel lightly, whereas slavers never left behind the tools of their trade.

"And Two-Feathers' father?"

"Left for the crows."

There was more than just pain lurking beneath her mask. There was anger too, and I wasn't sure if it was meant for the slavers, her dead husband, or even herself.

Bright-Meadows squeezed Deep-Water's shoulder, but I don't think the older woman even noticed, staring into a past the rest of us couldn't see.

When she spoke again, her voice was so hollow that that the words I couldn't understand seemed to echo as she spoke them.

"They took us east," translated Bright-Meadows. "Marching in chains and trailing our clan's own wagon, still full of all the pretty things we had traded for. The hunters they killed, but the rest of us were to be sold. It was…" The younger woman trailed off, her voice breaking. "She will not speak on it further, save to say that their only protection was that they were worth more alive."

"And Two-Feathers?" I asked, not sure which of the two women I was directing the question to.

"He would not be silent, no matter what I tried," answered Deep-Water through her intermediary. "The monsters beat him, which worked for a brief time, but my son…" The smile that made its way onto the woman's face was cold and sharp and as frightening as any that had ever graced my helmet. "He has always had too much strength in his convictions. When he raised his voice again, they took his tongue."

Somewhere in this story, I'd forgotten exactly how we'd gotten onto the subject. My mind was full of the images Bright-Meadows had painted with her future mother-in-law's words and the storm in my chest was gnashing its metal teeth like a thousand hungry predators. If Two-Feathers had been five when this happened, it must have been somewhere around twenty years ago. That was a long time for any slavers to stay in business out in the Badlands. Assuming they had survived, they had likely left the road entirely to retire with their wealth. Still, we were headed to Lawton soon, and even with the Old Man dead, that place would be a wellspring of information.

"I need names," I said. "Names, faces, and any distinguishing characteristics you can recall. Muscle turns to fat, and hair fades in color or goes away entirely, but scars and birthmarks can identify old men as easily as their younger versions."

The two nomads exchanged glances.

"What?" asked Bright-Meadows, speaking on her own.

"If any of them are still alive," I said, letting the storm fill my voice, "I will find them. I will hunt them down and I will kill them."

"You already did!" said Bright-Meadows.

"I… what?"

Again, they looked at each other. This time, Deep-Water resumed her story, words translated by her future daughter.

"We had been traveling for almost a day when the wagons stopped, and men began to scream. I thought they had come across a howler or something worse and felt nothing but joy in my heart for their deaths, even knowing that we would be next." The older woman shook her head. "But I had traveled our lands with the clan, and traveled outside those lands with my partner, and I had never heard a predator that sounded quite like that. Metal upon metal. Not a roar or a howl but an unending snarl. There was gunfire and more screams and then silence. Even the inhuman snarl disappeared, and then the quiet was broken by footsteps. Hard-soled boots against dry earth. A woman made her way past the final wagon, all in black, with a helmet unlike any we had seen atop her head and a face that was as yellow as a songbird's, its smile even wider than my own mad grin."

Deep-Water fell silent, her eyes going distant, and Bright-Meadows took up the story in her own words.

"She had heard of the Storm Who Rides but thought you to be only a legend among the clans, more story than person. Until you saved them. Until you killed seventeen slavers and freed four nomads and another half-dozen prisoners that had been taken on a raid."

I wracked my brain for the memory and came up empty. Maybe... *maybe* I remembered killing slavers, but I'd killed more than a few in my very long life and the event in question was two decades old. Nomad involvement should have made it stand out more, but...

More words from Deep-Water.

"She says you took the slavers' bodies, wagons, and gear as your price," continued Bright-Meadows, "but set the survivors free with their original wagon and the pretty things that had cost her partner his life and her son his voice."

That *did* strike a chord, a buried memory surfacing from the distant past of me burning one wagon and driving another to a nearby town where I had traded its bloody contents for more portable currency. But when I tried to grasp for more, for faces or even figures, the memory fled before me.

I met Deep-Water's dark gaze. "I'm sorry. I don't remember you or him."

"We remember you," said the older woman through her translator, "and the debt that was owed."

"I wouldn't have walked away if there was anything owed." That part I felt comfortable saying. Dr. Nowhere had still been alive and that meant I'd been subject to the rules that guided my existence, the laws that bound the chaos of my soul. Balance in all things, in the giving and the taking. "I *couldn't* have walked away if there was anything owed."

Bright-Meadows looked to the older woman for a response, but instead, Deep-Water leaned forward on her pillow, eyes intent on my true face. For the first and only time that I knew her, she spoke in a language I could understand, her voice a rasp of English and pain.

"You are mighty, but not all-powerful. You do not decide our obligation for us. Two-Feathers grew up knowing that debt."

An awful lot of things fell into place, just like that, and I can't say I enjoyed the sudden enlightenment.

"When I showed up looking for information rather than trade or passage, he decided this was his opportunity."

Something twisted inside of me at my own words.

"Yes. Blood for blood. Life for life. Death for death."

I thought of the past year with Two-Feathers. Demons. The Terrorbirds. A howler. His brief imprisonment and abuse at the hands of my enemy's army. More blood than any purely human person should ever have to wade through.

"By any standards," I forced myself to say, "he has paid his debt. And yours."

And now, with that debt paid, he'd returned to his clan, to his mother and his pretty future wife, and whatever life the three would be able to forge together.

It was a perfect story, and I had no part left to play in it.

○○○

Stephanie found me again, not long after, and escorted me back to the larger tent where the elders were once again sitting in wait. Negotiations resumed and metaphorical wheels were spun in the air as absolutely nothing of fucking value got accomplished, yet again.

All the while, I sat in silence, mind curiously empty, listening to the storm inside me, senses straining to extend past the camp's perimeter, to the road I knew was waiting.

18

I don't know how long I could have lasted, day after day in that tent with its elders and their laundry list of grievances both petty and not so much. I wasn't a diplomat, but I did have responsibilities, and those responsibilities kept me in my seat when I would rather have been anywhere else.

Part of me wanted to find Two-Feathers to ask some hard questions. Not so much about what I had been told, but why *he* hadn't been the one to tell me. Part of me wanted to just be gone again, on to Wichita and Lawton, then into the depths of Texas, and finally to the land of the dead where a very different young man waited with his own set of answers.

I didn't do either of those things, because I wasn't a teenager, had never been a teenager, and storming off in a fit of pique was a pretty fucking bad way of accomplishing anything at all, let alone establishing my authority as the newly crowned warlord and queen of the former Crimson-fucking-empire.

Still, it was hard, and whatever progress we made was so glacially slow that it seemed the elders had forgotten time was a thing that passed. And so it was a relief when, on the second day after meeting with Deep-Water and Bright-Meadows, a nomad I didn't know ducked his head and hurried into the tent to confer with the elders.

I, per usual, wasn't privy to that conversation, but when it ended, the elders conferred amongst themselves and finally turned to me.

"There is a matter that you could help us resolve," said Snow-Falls, "if you are willing."

"A demon of the plains has come south in the shape of a bear," added Smoke-on-the-Breeze, "and taken up residence in a cave within our lands. With so many of our Blessed away on the two hunts Two-Feathers recommended, we ask, in the spirit of cooperation between our respective nations, for your aid in driving it from our territory."

I gave the request all the consideration it deserved from a visiting monarch to the council of elders she was meeting. And then I looked across the open space at the semi-circle of old men and women arrayed before me.

"No."

"Very good. We…" Smoke-on-the-Breeze trailed off. "No?"

"That's what I said."

"If you truly wish peace between our peoples—"

"I'm not your errand girl," I said, turning slowly to speak to all the elders instead of just one, "fulfilling duties upon request. I'm not your confessor, here to listen to decades of grievances or disputes, many of which you don't even fully remember, and almost all of which have little to nothing to do with me *or* my empire."

"That is not—" began Snow-Falls in a conciliatory tone, but I spoke right over him, giving voice to the storm's sharp edges and the rage of the stars I saw each night.

"I'm not a pawn or a fool or anything you have ever seen or will see again. I am a queen in name as well as title and I have had *enough*."

"You are here seeking *our* peace," snapped the sharp-voiced woman from the campfire, whose name I still didn't know.

"And offering my own," I told her. "Blood for blood. Balance in all things, remember? We're not allies yet. If you want my help with this demon, you can *pay* for it."

Predictably, that statement was met with a mix of emotions and muttered words, but I didn't care. My Secretary of State would probably lose her mind if she ever found out what I was doing, but I didn't care about that either. I had responsibilities, yes, but the first of those were to myself. And even if I was no longer controlled by the laws of my creation, it didn't mean I had to abandon them entirely. There was *acting freely* and there was *being used*, and neither the storm nor I were willing to accept the latter.

"What is it that you want in return?" said Snow-Falls. He and Moon-Over-the-Trees were the only two elders who didn't seem caught somewhere between anger and concern.

"An end to the bullshit. I don't know why you're all dragging out these negotiations, but either I walk away today with a deal, or I just plain walk away. There are other clans, some of whom I've known longer than yours, and I'm sure they'd be happy to be the ones to bring my offer to the nomad council. We only came to you because of Two-Feathers."

They all traded glances and Smoke-on-the-Breeze sat back with a phlegmy huff, fully ceding the floor to Snow-Falls.

"If we have not been as focused on completing the framework for this treaty as we could have, it is only because we believed there was no hurry," said the other elder. "Two-Feathers is still away on the hunt, after all. Would you leave without your ambassador?"

"I might be doing that anyway. Although not," I allowed, "without speaking to him first. But if I must, I'll go find the hunting party myself." I let the silence build for a moment, then dropped my next words like a challenge. "In or out, elders. The choice is yours."

Two hours later, I had my treaty.

Twenty minutes after that, I was following Stephanie back across the camp to the tent designated as mine. I had a demon to kill, a mute nomad to trade words with, and the road whispering sweet little nothings in my half-formed ears.

Except… when we reached the tent and the saddlebags I'd stashed inside, there was someone already there waiting for me.

"Bright-Meadows."

She gave me something halfway between a salute and a curtsy. I hadn't seen the young nomad since the day of her revelations about Two-Feathers and I'd honestly been okay with that.

"I wished to speak with you," she said. Her hair was back in braids, and she wore a long skirt and an open-necked top in earth tones. Next to her soft femininity, I felt almost ungainly, my over-tall, leather-clad form out of place.

I can't say I was used to that feeling.

Can't say I loved it either.

"I have to go," I said, my voice a scrape of metal.

"I promise this won't take long." Her gaze came up to fix upon my true face, and despite her demeanor, there was steel in her dark eyes.

While I *could* have still walked away, the truth was I would be stuck waiting on the scouts that the elders had assigned to take me to the demon's cave.

Hear her out, said the voice inside me that was half taskmistress and half unwelcome conscience. *All she has are words.*

And so, ignoring that I'd seen words draw blood and even tear open the very fabric of reality, I stood my ground.

"You have three minutes."

For a brief while, it seemed like she was going to spend those minutes in silence. That would have suited me and the storm just fine, but eventually, she found her nerve.

"Deep-Water believes you have feelings for her son."

"She should show greater respect by not speaking out of turn about her elder," I said, ignoring the fact that I'd never done the same, even in the day I'd *had* elders.

"Her... elder?"

"It doesn't matter." I shook my head, feeling the late sun reflect off the curved polycarbonate exterior of my helmet. "So you're here to what... warn me off? Because I have to tell you, that is a strategy that rarely works with me."

"A warning without leverage is like a wolf without teeth," she replied. "Frightening from a distance, but pitiable up close. With Listens-to-Wind up north, there are none in our clan who can so much as contain you, let alone control you. I know that as well as you do."

"Then why are we having this talk?"

"For two reasons. First, I wanted to ask if it was true."

It was my turn to pause. Since the reveal of Two-Feathers' past, his reasons for joining me on my quest, and his attachments here in the clan, I'd carefully packed away whatever I felt about the nomad. I'd compressed those feelings down into a handful of words meant for his ears only and suppressed the rest under the sound of the storm and the call of the road.

Still, that I'd had to do *any* of that made my answer clear.

"Yes."

She simply nodded, again showing a core of steel inside her soft form that I couldn't help but respect. "My promised joined you to pay his debt."

"I already told you that debt is paid."

"He will need to hear that from your mouth. And even then, he might not agree. Two-Feathers can be as stubborn as the hills."

"I'd say the hills wish they were even half as stubborn."

For a breath, we were two women just sharing time by a fire, shaking our heads almost fondly at the idiosyncrasies of a man we both knew well.

Like so many other things, that breath died quickly.

"I'll tell him," I said, a spark of defiance within causing me to add, "but like you said, he is stubborn. He might choose to stay with me anyway."

"And that is the second reason I came here: to ask for your help. If you truly care for him, you will convince him otherwise. Honor your feelings for Two-Feathers and persuade him to stay with the clan."

"You're… going to have to explain that to me."

"His home is here. With his mother. With me. Our clan needs Two-Feathers, and he needs us. We can give him a life that is more than just travel and death. Responsibility, yes, but also a path forward, as part of the next generation of elders, along with my brother and a few others. The clan can give him purpose, and I can give him…"

She trailed off, unable to keep meeting the cold yellow smile across my visor.

"Can give him what?" I prompted.

"Someone to grow old with should the sun smile upon us both. Someone to share in his day-to-day burdens. Most importantly, I can give him the family he desires. If you care for him, shouldn't you want him happy?"

Beneath my true face, the half-formed lines of my near-human features twitched. Bright-Meadows had come to the fire empty-handed, dressed for dance instead of battle, and yet somehow, she'd still landed a blow worthy of Two-Feathers' lost spear.

The shell I'd been given wasn't human. It had *never* been human, but there were still some aspects of humanity it could mimic. Talking. Walking. Waging wars with sharp-edged words as well as weapons. Even—and perhaps especially—fucking, because I'd ultimately been created by a man and that made for more than just mile-long legs and skintight leather.

But children had never been in the cards for me. Would never be in the cards. *Could* never be when only my shell was flesh and blood and my core was all metal and fury.

I'd never felt the lack, that strange yearning for offspring that seemed to afflict so many biologicals. I'd known good mothers and bad in my long existence, and yet that shared facet of their lives had remained uniformly alien, something to be examined from a distance and dismissed with a degree of healthy skepticism.

Bright-Meadows was right. There were things I couldn't give the nomad who'd spent over a year at my side. Unless someone snuffed out the storm, I was going to live forever. Every current member of this clan, even the babies screaming on their mothers' breasts, would be dust in less than a century where I would remain.

I wasn't human, would never be human, and while that gave me advantages the world lacked, it also shaped both what I had to offer that world and the context of those interactions.

The silence grew, not just lengthening but also thickening, drowning out the inevitable noise of the surrounding camp. Finally, the young nomad swallowed. "I'm not trying to cause offense…"

"I'm not sure I believe that," I said, shutting her up just as quickly. "Even so, you're right."

Her eyes flashed. "You'll let him go?"

"Two-Feathers is a man, not a dog on a leash. If you treat him otherwise, all those comforts you and your clan think you can offer won't be worth a damn. Trust me on that."

I moved on before she could reply. "But yes," I added reluctantly, "with his debt paid, I think you're right. His place is here. I'll speak to him when he returns and make sure he knows that."

The nomad woman spread her skirts and gracefully dropped into a much deeper curtsy, the kind that wouldn't be out of place among New Memphis' ruling elite. "This one gives thanks to the Storm Who Rides."

"Treat him well," I said. "Love him as he deserves to be loved." The snarl of metal filled my voice. "Or I'll come back and kill every fucking one of you."

○○○

The scouts who led me out into the plains had about as much personality as Two-Feathers' horse and seemed just as uncomfortable around me. Since I wasn't in the mood for conversation, that worked out perfectly. The bike between my legs, the hum of its electric motor, the sound of rubber on grass and dirt… that was all the companionship I needed.

We'd left in the late afternoon, and with the cave a day's ride away, that made for a night under the stars. Like me, the nomads didn't bother with tents, but the younger, smaller one did set up a fire. Both men huddled around it, enjoying its warmth.

I stayed with my bike. I'd left most of my earthly possessions behind at camp, but the saddlebags still held my batteries. I'd learned a long time ago never to travel anywhere without extras; there was riding through the wilderness and there was pushing a dead bike, and of the two, I vastly preferred the first.

I leaned back against a frame that had been rebuilt a dozen times over the decades and listened to the storm inside me. What information the nomads had gathered about this so-called demon bear was scanty. All I knew was it had killed a horse and almost carved up the nomad rider too. It had then shrugged off their counterattacks and set three veteran scouts to flight. My guides seemed convinced that we would find it at its cave, but I was living proof that a creature's form did not always dictate their behavior. Still, it would be a good place to start the hunt.

Demon meant a lot of things to a lot of people, from the biblical kind to simply creatures that bore no resemblance to anything naturally occurring in the post-Break world. I'd thought they were fairy tales until last year, and even now, a demon that could shift forms was a new twist. Still, this one had picked a really bad fucking time to come south.

I had a few days to kill before Two-Feathers' return. Might as well take the kill part literally.

We traveled for most of the next day, headed west toward low-slung hills that had been barely visible upon the horizon. As we neared our destination, the horses started to spook, requiring the attention of their riders more and more frequently. My bike didn't have that problem, of course, but I couldn't help but notice the lack of wildlife. No rabbits, no deer, and definitely no buffalo. Even the sky above us was empty of anything but clouds.

I wasn't a tracker, but I could read the sign saying *Predator Here* in bright flashing neon just as well as the next person. The difference was that to me it was a welcome mat rather than a warning to stay away.

The cave itself was harder to find, making the presence of the two nomad scouts welcome for the first time since our departure. They led the way into the foothills, now walking their mounts instead of riding them, and eventually came to a stop.

"Over that ridge," said the older one, in a voice as grizzled as he was, "is the entrance to the cave the demon has claimed as its own."

"Are you sure it's still there?"

An unearthly roar split the air. Made by something larger than any bear I'd ever encountered, it set the two trained horses into panic mode, each jumping about and pulling at their reins.

"Pretty sure," said the younger nomad.

"Insightful." I looked at the ridge I still had to climb, looked at my bike, and dismounted with a sigh. "Keep an eye on my bike until I'm back. I like it a lot more than either of you."

The younger one grinned for the first time since I'd met him, but the older nomad just nodded.

"Good luck," he said.

"I won't need it." I left the nomads behind and climbed the ridge. Beyond it, as promised, was the open mouth of a cave set about a quarter of the way up a sizable hill. The rock around the entrance showed signs of fresh excavation as if the creature now residing within had been forced to widen the passage, and that, more than even the earlier roar, told me the demon bear was damn near house-sized, with claws that could rend red stone with ease.

No wonder the nomads had sent me.

For the first time in days, the smile on my true face felt fitting.

This was going to be fun.

19

This is not *fun*, I thought to myself, hours later, as a clawed paw that was as much thought as flesh tore through my shell for the hundredth or even thousandth time. The storm surged outward and for the same hundredth or thousandth time, found nothing to retaliate against.

If the snake I'd faced down in Delia Laine's throne room had been smoke, this was like fighting air, air that savaged my shell with ease without giving me anything to fight back against. Even the shape of the thing, once a mammoth bear, was now closer to an amorphous cloud, filling the confines of the cave we were both trapped in.

Trapped because one of the early blows from the fucking demon had collapsed its own cave around us, cutting off any chance of retreat and leaving me stuck fighting a monster every bit as angry as the storm itself.

As one-sided as the fight had been so far, it was *still* a stalemate, and I was just waiting for the demon to recognize that fact. My shell had been destroyed innumerable times, but the storm remained inviolate, as impregnable to the demon as it was to the storm. It had only taken me an hour to acknowledge the pointlessness of a battle where no victor could ever be crowned. To my great dismay, I'd realized this was a situation I'd probably have to talk my way out of instead.

The demon, on the other hand, seemed far slower on the uptake, judging by the fact that it kept destroying my shell every time it reformed.

My true self was the storm, not the flesh that housed it, but that didn't make getting torn to pieces any less painful. But either I talked this psychotic thing off its metaphorical ledge, or I'd have to let it wear itself out… and knowing what little I did about spectral things, that second approach could take damn near forever.

I didn't have that kind of time *or* patience, so I reformed my shell yet again. "This isn't—"

An unseen paw shattered my helmet and caved in the upper half of my chest before I could get a third word out.

A new shell.

"—accomplishing—"

A second paw cut my freshly formed shell in half.

A new shell.

This time, I didn't even get a word out before I was ripped apart. The storm was quick to offer its own response, but shrapnel and steel wasn't the kind of reply that invited conversation.

Fuck.

It seemed *waiting things out* was back on the table.

○○○

Set free, the storm raged. I couldn't say how much time passed with demon and steel trading ineffectual blows, only that it was substantial, that anything mortal would have long since passed out from exhaustion or dehydration or both. If either the demon or I needed oxygen, we would have depleted that too, but here we were, so much later, still as inhumanly hale and hearty as we'd been at the start.

Eventually though, the demon bear's attacks slowed. With a huff, it turned from the storm, pulling itself back into the shape of a mammoth bear, so large its thickly furred flanks brushed the interior walls of a cave the size of an aircraft hangar. It snuffled about, like it was the animal whose form it had taken, and then curled in upon itself.

I reformed my shell near what would have been the mouth of the cave, and this time, the creature finally let me be, giving me the first breath to think in far too long.

In the remnants of Texas, a Summoner named Shabaa had amassed an army of demons, but those had been flesh and blood, mortal in form, if damn near infinite in number. I'd expected the nomad's predator to be more of the same. Instead, I was now stuck in a cave with Smokey the Angry Bear.

Smokey being a bear that had been famous pre-Break for reasons my creator hadn't thought to attach to the random piece of knowledge.

It was pitch-black inside, but that didn't mean a lot for vision that functioned without eyes. The form of the bear was clear to me. So too was the mountain of rubble that had collapsed my only exit. I was stronger than your average human, but I was a long way from strong enough to clear that entrance by hand, and the storm had just as little hope of tearing through all that solid stone.

Of course, even if escape had been possible, it wouldn't do a damn thing to address the real problem, the elephant-sized bear in the room. I'd already proven, at least to my satisfaction, that neither of us could kill the other. The nomads weren't so lucky, and I *had* already accepted payment for this job.

That left me back where I'd been hours earlier, trying to find some way to negotiate with a creature of anger and air.

It seemed like all I'd been doing lately *was* negotiating.

"So," I said, breaking the cave's silence, "I don't suppose you can talk or anything? Because if you actually think you *are* a bear, I think we're both screwed."

Technically, that wasn't true. The demon wasn't screwed because it had already shown an ability to go intangible, and that meant I was the only one trapped in the cave. And while neither of us could kill the other, it had also shown—to a seriously excessive degree—that it could destroy my shell and bring me pain.

I wasn't used to bargaining from a position of disadvantage.

On the one hand, it was behaving an awful lot like a bear, and bears weren't notorious for their savvy in business deals. On the other hand, it was because the only kind of bears who *made* business deals were Beast Shifters. And on the third hand, it had been at least twenty seconds since I spoke to the demon, and while it hadn't savaged my shell, it hadn't offered a reply either. Which meant it was either giving me the silent treatment for no good reason, or…

Or it really does *think it's a bear.*

I didn't have a contingency plan to fall back on; negotiation *was* the contingency plan. With that gone, the only thing left was trying to dig my way out of this stone tomb. Who knew? Maybe the rock wasn't going to be quite as immovable as it seemed. And once I was free, I'd try to figure out some way to banish an intangible demon who could kill with relative impunity.

If all else failed, I could reach out to New Memphis again. Maybe one of my Immortals had a powerset that would help. And if not, General Cyrus could send a flier up north to collect the clan's absent shaman. Listens-to-Wind's experience with the ancestor spirits could be useful.

Except, when I turned to the collapsed entrance, something shifted in the cave around me.

And it *wasn't* the demon bear.

Instead, it was everything else. I was still trying to pick out the changes when a light flared. Then another. And another. Soon, I was surrounded by lights, stacked atop each other and arranged in haphazard rows. And each one came from…

If I'd been using my half-formed eyes, I'd have blinked. The cave was still there, but it also kind of wasn't, replaced by a dark alleyway better suited for one of the old cities in the Free States, or even what was left of York. Somewhere, water was audibly dripping, and behind that was a noise I'd become familiar with in the early months after my birth. Sirens. Ambulances, police cars, and fire trucks, all giving voice to the cacophony of chaos.

But all of that was just a backdrop to the source of illumination I'd already noticed: stacks of bulky, boxy pre-Break televisions, some with dials to change the channel and volume, others with buttons instead. None had their antennae extended, and I didn't see any outlets for them to plug into, but every television's face was brightly lit up to show the cold snow of static.

"Well, *this* is new," I muttered.

Several screens flickered, images appearing in place of snow. There were people depicted, though I didn't recognize any of them, and most were dressed outlandishly even for pre-Break times.

"Howdy. Citizen. What. Are. You. Saying."

Each word came from a different television set and a different person's mouth, young, old, male, female. Some spoke quickly; others drew out their single word like they were chewing on it. All in all, it formed a strangely discordant sentence.

But it *was* a sentence.

I turned my true face to the bear seemingly slumbering behind the rows of incredibly outdated electronics.

"We've established that neither of us can kill each other, right?"

More static. A handful of different screens flipped through images. Some of the people on screen were seated behind desks like Free States vid anchors. Others were angled to focus on someone else just off-camera. Here and there, multiple people were together on a single screen, even if only one person was speaking.

"Yes. What. Are. You."

"A creation of the Break. Just like you, I'm guessing."

"And. Why. Are. You. Here."

"To pass on a message," I said, channeling Jules as I improvised. "This isn't a safe territory for you to settle in."

No words this time. Just two to three dozen televisions showing scenes of violence. Often *terribly choreographed* violence. Television had still been a thing for the first few weeks or even months of the Break, but I'd been too busy grappling with my sudden existence to pay much attention, and whatever fictional shows had existed back then had swiftly been supplanted by broadcasts from increasingly terrified news reporters anyway.

Most of what I saw in the demon bear's clips suggested pre-Break entertainment had been every bit as fucked up as what we had post-Break, paired with significantly worse special effects, and acting that seemed to lean heavily into melodrama. Still, I'd been with Two-Feathers long enough that interpreting pantomime was second nature. And this was a lot more eloquent than pantomime.

"Yeah," I admitted. "You can fight. And I'm sure you'll kill a lot of people in the process. But the nomads that dwell here have Blessed ones they call shamans."

It wasn't *technically* what they called them... most of the clans had words or even whole phrases in their own tongue. But I doubted the demon was any more interested in a language lesson than I was.

"Those people," I continued, "are particularly suited for dealing with your kind."

The screens showing combat flicked back to snow and a new set of televisions turned the channel or whatever it was that caused images to appear. Back to people again.

"Then. Why. Are. They. Not. Here."

That was a great question.

"They sent me as a show of respect," I lied. "One old horror to speak with another. They ask that you return in peace to where you came from."

Different televisions.

"There. Is. No. Going. Back."

Every television in sight lost its snowy static, depicting scenes of fire and devastation like something out of a Pyromancer's fantasy. There was no such thing as a literal biblical hell as far as I knew, so it seemed likely the demon was saying its home had been destroyed. The how and the why remained dangerously open questions.

Anything that could drive away a demon who had stymied the storm for untold hours was one more potential catastrophe lurking somewhere out in the wilds. I made a mental note to get better directions so Cyrus could send *someone else* to check it out.

At the moment, however, I had bigger concerns. Like where to send a demon ghost bear thing. Somewhere that wasn't here, wasn't its destroyed home, and wasn't anywhere that my empire's growing list of allies or vassals might be impacted.

The *obvious* answer was Texas. Already home to three horrors, the former state would barely even notice the bear's addition. And if the creature ran into the Hunger That Walks or the White Wail… well, with all respect to the demon, I knew who I'd be betting on to come out on top.

Unfortunately, my route would be taking us into Texas once I was done with Wichita and Lawton, and I didn't particularly feel like meeting the demon bear a second time. Even if I wouldn't have Two-Feathers with me to worry about.

Thankfully, I *did* have an alternate solution, otherwise known as the most haunted place in the continent. Or… maybe the second-most haunted, now that Bakersfield had formally set up shop in Mexico.

Las Vegas. Former jewel of the dustbowl of Nevada.

Reno, Nevada's other major pre-Break city, had survived the Break, survived all the way up until Crimson Death's attempt at sacrificing the whole city a decade or two back, but Las Vegas… Las Vegas was different. My patchwork of implanted bits of knowledge told me that even before the Break, Vegas had had as many ghosts as humans. And when dear old Dad had dreamed his little dream…

Well.

Nothing lived in the City of Sin, not anymore, but that didn't mean there weren't things that called the place home. And if anywhere could house a demon bear the size of a hill without the residents even batting an eye, it was Las Vegas.

I looked to the massive shape mostly hidden behind rows of vintage televisions and the illusion of a city's back streets.

"I've got the perfect place."

○○○

It wasn't that easy, of course. Nothing ever was when it came to negotiation, diplomacy, and all the other words that really *should* have been four letters long. The demon wanted more information. It wanted reassurances. It even seemed strangely concerned about who it might be sharing the city with, as if the caliber of its new neighbors was a potential dealbreaker. By the end, I was feeling more like a saleswoman than a mercenary or queen.

I *could* have pivoted and tried to convince the demon to be a good neighbor to the nomads instead, but the damn thing had spent countless hours trying to kill me. Whatever form it took, it remained a predator, through and through, and far too many of the nomads would register as prey.

Besides, *making nice* wasn't the job.

Getting rid of the thing was.

So instead, I sold the shit out of a city I'd only seen twice. And if the thing ended up not liking Vegas… if some of what I'd described ended up landing a hair too far on the side of hyperbole and other bits were revealed as outright fabrication? Well, it'd be months before it made it back to clan territory, assuming it returned at all, and by then Listens-to-Winds would presumably be present.

Maybe he'd have an easier time than I had.

Eventually, the demon ran out of questions and concerns, though it still seemed as nervous as a teenager talking to his first puppy-love crush. The banks of televisions faded away and the rest of the dark-alley illusion did too, revealing the cave in all its not-too-inconvenient darkness. With a loud snuffle, the bear climbed up onto its massive paws, and then, every step as light as a feather even though the ground shook with the impact, it walked toward me, then through me, then right through the rockfall that had buried the cave.

If the nomad scouts saw its emergence, I didn't hear their response. Couldn't hear much of anything at all, really, since the demon had left me behind in its cave, still buried behind multiple tons of earth and stone.

While negotiating the demon bear's departure, it hadn't for a moment occurred to me that it *wouldn't* clear the cave-in for me on its way out.

I offered up a few new four-letter words to go with the one called negotiation.

20

When I was done cursing at myself, the demon, the nomads, and anyone else I could think of, I got down to business. Namely, checking out the rest of the cave's interior. With the bear gone, the space was bigger than I had realized, large enough to fit at least a dozen nomad tents. If I'd been at all claustrophobic, that would have been the good news.

Since I wasn't, there *was* no good news. Fifty feet by fifty feet, the cave had three walls of solid stone and one newly formed from literal tons of collapsed debris. No secret escape tunnels. No unexplored passageways. Not even any cracks I might be able to squeeze the storm through, one shard at a time.

Just rock, darkness, and me.

It was a far better trap than the Crimson Queen had managed the prior year, because this time, there was no door I could just wait for someone else to open.

I sat for a while in the center of all that darkness, the storm a discordant clash of metal inside me. It wasn't a bad cave, all things considered. It was dry, it was empty, and it was clean. Ish. Given that I didn't need to eat or even breathe, being trapped there didn't pose any real threat to me and I'd gotten my revenge on Delia Laine the previous year. I'd delivered Two-Feathers back to his family. I'd even finished the nomads' job.

I'd also likely made a hash of my diplomats' plans along the way, first in Eastwood, then Kansas City, and now the clan territories, but that was neither here nor there. Truth was, I could stay here until the stars burned out, until the earth's crust cracked and freed me all on its own, and when I emerged, hundreds or thousands of years later, the storm and its shell would both remain.

But the only time I'd stayed *anywhere* longer than a few months had been Eclipse, and that town was ash on yesterday's wind, along with all its inhabitants. The Badlands hadn't been able to hold me. Nor had New Memphis, York, or Atlanta. A cave wasn't going to either. Not when there was road left to travel.

Also? Hell if I was letting the nomads keep my bike.

My sigh barely audible over the storm, I turned back to the multiple tons of rock and soil blocking the cave entrance.

ooo

Hours. A lot of hours.

My shell shifted what it could, the storm blunted itself tearing apart rocks the size of livestock, and slowly, so very slowly, I made progress. Maybe there was some way to tunnel out instead, to build walls inside the rubble, other stones serving as headers or trusses as I scooted along the floor like a lizard… but I wasn't an architect or an engineer or even a craftswoman. I was a mercenary turned revolutionary turned ruler, and the only tools I had were the ones I'd been created with.

So, I dug. And when even more rock fell in to choke the space I'd only just cleared, I dug some more

More hours.

I could feel fresh air now, even if I couldn't see the cracks it was seeping through. I reformed my shell, replacing muscles and tendons that had practically exploded under the most recent load, and looked for a chunk small enough to move.

Only… when I was still a few feet away, that chunk shifted on its own. And then another, this one bigger than I could have handled. More fresh air rushed in as a boulder was rolled aside, revealing not the night sky I'd expected but bright sunshine, haloing the silhouette of a man.

I couldn't see his face, not really, but I recognized the shoulders even before Two-Feathers reached in through the space we'd both created and hauled me out into open air.

It was like being born again: bright light and space. But instead of asphalt beneath my brand-new boots and an eighteen-wheeler three seconds from running me over, there was earth and vegetation and an unreachable horizon.

For a moment, that was the sum of things. Fresh air, the nomad, and me, under a skyful of stars hidden by their closer cousin. I looked over and found Two-Feathers' eyes sparkling, a grin barely hidden beneath his usual stoic mask and something inside of me settled, the spaces between the storm, the pockets of air that held focus even in the tornado of my soul.

And then I remembered.

I crushed those spaces down as the storm began to howl. I pulled away from the nomad, and watched his grin disappear, watched the sparkle in his dark, deep eyes turn to confusion, even as they scoured my true face for explanation.

I gave it to him, the words coming easily despite each one weighing more than the entire cave I'd just escaped.

"I don't even remember saving you as a child. I'm not saying it didn't happen, but any debt you might have had toward me for it is gone. In fact, it never existed in the first place. So, go and live your life. Bright-Meadows is waiting." And then, because a part of me just couldn't help it, the part that had never been a child, that had never gotten to grow up, I added, in a voice of metal. "You should have told me."

Maybe Two-Feathers had something to say to that, maybe he didn't. There wasn't anything I wanted to hear. Not then and not from him; I headed over the ridge, where that same afternoon sun showed my bike was still parked next to the horses and the scouts who'd accompanied me on our journey out.

◦◦◦

After I informed the other nomads that the job was done, the four of us headed out: straight east to loop around the northern end of another series of hills. In a few hours, we'd turn south again, following a stream that I was pretty sure hadn't even existed before the Break, and soon after that, we'd stop for the night. Sometime the next afternoon, we'd arrive back in camp and once I had said my goodbyes, I'd be on my way again.

I had enough diplomacy left in me to realize I couldn't just skip returning to the camp entirely. There were farewells to be said and treaties to celebrate. But hell if I was going to sit through another feast.

I was *done*. It was time to move on to Wichita.

We all rode in silence for those first few hours. Nothing unusual about that, given my one-time companion's disability and the scouts' general reticence. Still, there was a timber to that silence that felt new. Uneasy. Uncomfortable. Maybe it was Two-Feathers' gaze, heavy on my back, or maybe it was the way the younger of the two scouts kept turning around to look at us both.

I turned my senses inward instead of out, listening to the storm inside me, to the low clash of metal on metal that formed an accompaniment to the sound of dirt beneath my bike's tires.

Soon, I told the storm. *Soon we'll be riding away.*

Riding? Or running? Asked the voice in my head.

Fuck if I was going to reward *that* with a response.

Soon after, all three horses went skittish. Moments later, a terrible noise filled the air, drowning out both the storm and the voice in my head.

Despite the name they've been given, howlers don't really *howl.* The noise they make is more like a roar, spliced with a handful of screams all occurring at once. It's one of the more distinctive noises in the Badlands, and not *just* because it's made by one of the region's largest predators. This one sounded like it was practically upon us already, but the horses would have been a lot more scared if that was the case. Given the way sound carried out here, it could easily be as far as twenty or thirty minutes away.

Without even realizing it, I turned to Two-Feathers. Beneath his stoic mask, I saw the same realization. A howler this close was bad news. As bad as the demon maybe, because howlers—much like humans—killed for sport as much as food. They would track their prey for days just out of spite... and if this one went any further south, it would come across nomad scent. *That* would lead it all the way back to the main camp.

The clan could hold its own against a single howler, even without their shaman and with Falling Rocks' hunting party away, but there *would* be casualties.

Two-Feathers had made himself a new spear, nearly indistinguishable from the first, although the feathers tied to its shaft were large and blue instead of crimson. Trophies taken in the latest hunt, no doubt. The nomad pulled that spear free and turned his horse to the north, to where the howler's cry was only now starting to die out. He looked to me, the question obvious in his eyes.

I'd already done the job the elders had hired me for, and a howler hadn't been part of that job. But Dr. Nowhere's death had freed me from my mercenary constraints. I was a free woman, and in the absence of forced transactions, choice was all that remained.

And after the damn untouchable bear, the storm was as eager for bloodshed as I was.

I gave the nomad a nod and turned my bike.

We headed north, the two scouts trailing behind.

ooo

We'd been riding for less than a minute when we heard the scream. It didn't come from anything human, but I'd heard cries like that before. This time, the nomads' horses outright panicked. Of the three, only Two-Feathers' kept running forward, its eyes wide and nostrils flared. The other scouts quickly fell behind, their mounts frozen or even actively fighting against their riders' instructions.

They recognized the sound of another horse in pain, just like I did.

As soon as we reached halfway flat terrain, I pinned the throttle and pulled away from Two-Feathers and his galloping steed. It was possible the howler had come across a horse in the wild, but the only herds I'd ever encountered had been significantly west, not north. More likely, this was another of the clan's scouts.

I burned through at least twenty-five percent of my installed battery's charge in the next few minutes, but the terrain flew by. I guided the bike as much through reaction and hard-won experience as anything so prosaic as sight or judgment and by the time my target came into sight, the horse's most recent scream was still dying away.

Sadly, so was the horse itself, sprawled on its side, far too much of its innards now outside its body for the wound to be anything but fatal. The howler, a young version of its species that nevertheless outmassed the fallen horse by at least a few hundred pounds, was ignoring its dying prey, stalking towards a bloodied figure barely standing on two legs just a dozen feet away.

Despite what townsfolk liked to say, all nomads did *not* look alike, but the commonality of their style and demeanor did sometimes make it harder to identify one on sight. I didn't have that problem. Not this time, because the nomad in question was a full head shorter than most of the adults of the tribe. Also, he'd been guiding me around the camp for days before he left to join Falling-Rock's hunt.

Aidan was in bad shape, one of his legs twisted and doing a terrible job supporting him. He held a spear in his hands, but his arms shook, and he waved that spear around like he wasn't entirely sure where the attack was coming from.

Concussion or fear? Sometimes, it was hard to tell the difference, but even if he'd been healthy and confident, he'd have had no chance against the howler on his own.

Thankfully, he wasn't alone anymore.

I didn't slow the bike, but rode it forward, angling to point not at the stalking howler, but just to its side. Fifteen feet away, and the creature finally decided whatever was bearing down on it was a greater threat than the nomad and his trembling weapon. It spun, almost a ton of muscle and flesh turning on a dime and lunged for the bike.

Even with the distance I'd given myself, the thing might still have taken me out of the seat and crushed the bike in the process… except I wasn't there anymore. I'd launched myself toward the howler a moment earlier, dismissing my shell in mid-air and letting the storm free to rage.

My bike, free of both my weight and my control, spun out and fell, and I was grateful that the storm's noise masked the sound of the motorcycle's impact. The vehicle and I had been through a hell of a lot over the decades, including multiple complete rebuilds, and hell if I wanted to have to go through another.

But that thought, like so many others, was just extraneous in the moment, a vague concern formed into mental words that skated across the surface, lost under and ultimately subsumed by the call of the storm.

It had been almost a year since I'd fought a howler, but I remembered it well. Its red and white furless hide was pebbled and looked like something had turned the creature inside out. It had six eyes and just as many legs propelling it forward, and an open mouth that was filled with multiple rows of teeth, like a shark.

The hide, I knew from experience, could hold up to bullet fire. Even the storm struggled to penetrate it in a single pass, leaving its strange clusters of eyes as one of the only weak spots on the creature's gigantic form. Its eyes... and also its mouth, which was opened wide for a bite that would have torn me in two if I hadn't dismissed my shell.

Instead, the storm went right down that enormous gullet, like an 18-wheeler barreling down a five-lane highway. Steel spread as it traveled, wrecking the metaphor almost as much as it wrecked the howler's throat. Spread further to savage the beast's three lungs, each one rubbery and as large as a fifty-gallon trash bag. Shrapnel dug holes through tender internal flesh, and wire slithered into those holes to wrap and rend and tear.

Somewhere in the middle of all that, the howler's spine went, and the creature collapsed, still alive somehow, for all that it was vomiting blood. The storm kept on spinning, spreading its brand of chaos across the inner tapestry of the predator's body. Some organs ruptured, others practically liquefied, and then... impact, like hitting a solid wall at top speed.

I'd made it all the way through to the creature's hide.

Rather than try to reverse the storm's motion, to find a way back out through a mouth that had lost most of its teeth and was even now sagging shut, I pulled the shards of the storm in tight, packed in like a school of piranhas, and sent the whole teeming mass forward again.

Even from the inside, the howler's thick hide was damn near impenetrable, but *damn near* is a long way from an absolute. Unable to simply cut through, the shrapnel and wire and rebar that made up the storm gnawed instead, each rotation taking its piece of tribute, digging a little deeper, extending and widening the hole that was slowly beginning to form.

It had taken me a little less than a minute to savage the howler so thoroughly that even its peanut-sized brain realized it was dead. It took me five times as long to make a space large enough for the pieces of the storm to slip through, a few at a time, and out into the open air.

By the time enough of the storm was available for me to reform my shell into something even vaguely humanoid, Two-Feathers was seeing to an unconscious Aidan. I took a step toward them both, only to totter on legs still missing large chunks of flesh, bone, and leather.

Still too much of the storm was stuck in the howler's corpse. I turned back to the dead thing, calling to the dozens of pieces of scrap within in its form. Each shard emerged, one at a time, and flashed through open to be absorbed into my core. Each time, a few more holes in my shell solidified.

When the other scouts finally reached us, I was whole, Aidan was conscious again, if woozy, and the howler was in an advanced stage of decomposition, as if it had been rotting for a long time before it died. The creatures were one of the few species that not even scavengers would go near. Every time a howler died, it seemed to scar the very earth its corpse touched.

Dear old Dad had dreamt up far nastier things than me; howlers were just the tip of that nightmarish iceberg.

With the arrival of the other nomads, the focus shifted from the dead howler to the alive Aidan. Chatter went back and forth in the clan's native tongue, leaving me none the wiser, but eventually, the older of the two scouts turned to me.

"He says the hunting party came under attack. His horse panicked and broke free of his control. The rest of the party is still somewhere to the north."

"They didn't come to help Aidan?" I didn't think much of Falling-Rock after his little demonstration at the spring ceremony, but sacrificing one of the clan's own still seemed out of character.

"They couldn't. This howler belonged to a pack."

Against my own will, I traded glances again with Two-Feathers. For all their vaguely wolflike appearance, howlers only ran in packs when they were forced to, either by circumstances or a significantly stronger member of their own species. And while I'd bet on a nomad hunting party against a single howler—even as I acknowledged the casualties they *would* take—there wasn't much in the Badlands that could stand against a full pack.

Hell, I didn't know if *I* could.

Two-Feathers turned to me, long fingers flickering through an almost dizzying array of the signs he'd learned in New Memphis. It was way too fast for me to follow, even if I'd been half as good as he was at them, but I didn't need a translator to know what he was asking.

"They're probably already dead," I told him.

He shrugged and nodded, dark eyes never leaving my true face.

Throughout my long life, nobody had ever used silence as devastatingly as the nomad. I didn't owe anyone anything, including him. And yet...

For what I thought we could have been in another time and another life, for the appallingly human feelings that insisted on making a home in my inhuman wreckage of a soul, I found myself agreeing to help.

Three strides took me to a bike which had gained a few more significant dents but otherwise seemed in working order. I hot-swapped the battery, hissing as its overheated exterior charred right through my riding gloves and the flesh beneath. With a fresh battery in place, I reformed my shell to repair the damage.

"I'm going to need directions. I don't know this land as well as the rest of you."

Two-Feathers patted his chest.

"Just give them to me," I replied, shaking my head. "None of your horses will keep up. Not for long."

He patted his chest again, but this time handed the reins of his treasured horse over to Aidan. Spear in hand, he crossed the chasm of space between us to stand next to my bike.

That bike wasn't *designed* to carry two, especially when the second rider was as big as Two-Feathers… but it had managed in the past.

"Fine," I agreed. "But you're riding bitch."

21

There are worse things in life than riding with a strong man's arms around your waist. I should know; I've seen, experienced, or even perpetrated half of them. Still, I can't say I enjoyed the ride as much as I should have. Death behind us, death ahead, and a goodbye waiting somewhere on tomorrow's horizon.

You're being ridiculous.

That voice was right; I was. Riding around, talking myself up with nonsense like *I'm eager for bloodshed.* That was the storm. It had always been the storm. For myself, I could take or leave the ultra-violence. Some people needed killing, and I'd never shied away from that, but I wasn't some human child, slave to her emotions. Rage, lust, grief… they all had their place, and that place was riding bitch on my bike, not steering the path.

I was too old for this bullshit. Too old to pretend. When we returned to the camp, Two-Feathers' role in my life would be over, and if that thought stung, well, pain was just as temporary as everything else. I'd only just taken control of my life again… hell if I was going to let emotions, any emotions, take that control away from me again.

Stay cold. Stay calm. Let the storm speak for us both.

I let those words rattle around in my head as we retraced the path of Aidan's recent flight.

It had been years since I pushed my bike this hard and *that* had been back when I was on a road that was in halfway decent repair. Aidan's now-dead horse had found a trail to run along, but it was a long way from smooth asphalt or even carefully laid cobblestone, and we were traversing it at a speed no horse could hold for long.

One mistake and my bike would be toast, my passenger the rural equivalent of street pizza, but time mattered. If anyone was going to be alive at all, *speed* mattered.

So I hunched over my handlebars, the nomad practically welded to my back, and guided the bike as much from instinct as anything approaching vision, sensing obstructions and weaving past them with a hair's breadth of free space.

We'd gone for almost half an hour, depleting the new battery at an absolutely horrific pace, when something other than the bike's electric hum filled the air.

Gunshots. Yells. Screams. And above them all, the horrifying call that gave howlers their name.

Two-Feathers patted my left shoulder, his disability irrelevant when the wind whipping past us would have stolen his words anyway. I leaned left accordingly, taking us off the trail and into the woods that we'd been traversing.

It was an old forest, thankfully, so most of the trees stretched high above us, with only shrubs and the trunks of those trees to block our path, but even so, navigation became more about picking the least bad route than seeking a totally clear path forward. Branches scraped at my bike's frame, at me and Two-Feathers too, and I had no choice but to lower our speed even further or risk blowing out a tire on the massive root systems wrapping the ground in front of us.

On an open road, we'd have reached the battle in less than a minute. Cutting through the woods, it took us ten, and I had no doubt that the hunting party was paying in blood for every second's delay.

Still, the noises of combat continued.

Finally, we broke free of the forest and found ourselves at the mouth of a ravine. Two howlers prowled the high edges of the ravine, trying to find their way down walls as steep as any cliff and too dumb or bloodthirsty to come around to the mouth. A third was dead in the ravine, four of its six legs broken, and at least four spears sprouting from its face.

The rest were deeper in the gully. Four additional howlers, making for a pack that was bigger than any I'd encountered. Like the demon bear, that pack had to be new to the area, or the whole damn territory would have been emptied of life.

Smoke was rising from just past the mass of unfurred bodies as more guns sounded off to little effect. As far as I could tell, the terrain was the only reason the nomads hadn't already been overrun; the ravine narrowed precipitously, preventing more than a single howler from attacking at a time. Two of the other three howlers in the ravine danced back and forth, looking for their opportunity to strike, but the fourth, big enough to make the one we'd just killed look like a house cat, was calmer. It stalked slowly back and forth, six-eyed gaze examining the walls about it, as if trying to devise a new plan of attack.

Howlers *didn't* plan. Howlers hunted and killed and occasionally ate, and while they had a kind of malevolent cunning, they weren't tacticians, let alone strategists.

And yet...

I killed the bike's engine and turned to the nomad who was already dismounting.

"Leave the two up top for last?" I suggested. Two-Feathers and I had killed our first howler as a pair months earlier and it had been a struggle. The swiftness with which I'd dispatched this last one on my own spoke not to any particular growth in my strength but to an improvement in tactics. Familiarity bred contempt, sure, but it did so by making a thing's weak spots that much easier to exploit.

But still… *six* howlers were a problem. We were upwind, but they'd notice our presence soon enough, and we'd lose whatever advantage surprise gave us. If I hadn't already mistreated my bike enough for one day, I'd have ridden us straight down into the fray. As it was, we needed to run.

"Soft tissue," I reminded him, the storm filling my voice with metal. "Eyes if you can hit them. Mouth or joints, if you can't. And don't die. Hell if I'm going to explain your corpse to Bright-Meadows or your mother."

That last line wiped away the grin that had been threatening to spill onto his face. Two-Feathers started to sign something, looked down with frustration at the spear in his hands, and then shook his head. He started into the ravine.

I stopped him before he could take more than a few steps. I was looking again at the howlers up above.

"Actually… hold back a second. I have an idea."

Moments later, I was tearing across the ridge of the ravine on the bike I'd only just resolved to baby until we could find an engineer. Two-Feathers was back at the mouth of the gully, waiting on my signal, though I hadn't spent the time it would take to inform him what that signal would be.

He'd know it when it came. All that mattered was that he was ready and outside of the impact zone.

There were two howlers up top, as I'd already seen, one on each side of the ravine. The walls of the formation widened as they rose, leaving a good thirty feet of air between the two creatures. That was far from ideal, but the likelihood of catching both with my maneuver had always been low anyway.

I headed for the one on the right. Despite the noise rising from below, it heard me coming but seemed reluctant to leave its perch. Twenty feet away, I dismounted, set my bike down gently, and sprinted forward. Much like I'd done with the last howler, I was aiming not at the beast itself but off to the left, angling to come between it and the ravine.

Two-Feathers would have been faster—a lot faster—but there were some things only I could do.

It wasn't until I was within ten feet that the howler finally focused on me, instincts kicking in to center its malevolent regard on the prey willingly running to its own death. I dodged past one almost casual swipe of a paw and then leaped into the air, launching myself right in front of the monstrous head.

It couldn't help itself. It snapped at me, found my flailing shell just out of reach, and launched itself forward, a macro-sized version of a house pet trying to snatch a bird out of the air. That close and at that speed, there was no room to dodge.

I could have dismissed my shell and freed the storm, but the truth was I didn't have time to slowly tear my way through another howler's insides. Not with a full pack to kill. So I did the stupid thing my plan required, held my shell, and braced for impact.

Jagged rows of teeth tore through leather, flesh, and bone like a chainsaw through taut yarn, shredding everything in their path. It was beyond agonizing, and if I hadn't just spent a full day being torn to pieces by a demon bear, I might have lost my head entirely.

Metaphorically… I was well on my way to losing it literally.

Regardless, I still had enough presence of mind to wrap the rest of my body around the creature's maw. It took another half second to crunch and grind before two facts sank into its peanut-sized brain.

First, the path I'd taken and its lunge to snare me had left it with four of its six legs out in the open air over the ravine's edge.

And second, the two-hundred-plus pound weight of a woman who carried a storm inside of her made for one hell of an anchor when wrapped around its outstretched head.

Its final, rear set of legs scrabbled in the hard-packed dirt, but the outcome was already decided: the two of us fell into space, plummeting towards the other members of its pack a good fifty feet below.

Now, I dismissed my broken and savaged shell.

Gravity's a bigger bitch than I could ever be, and it pulled both storm and howler straight down into the ravine. But where the storm was disparate pieces, all spinning at their own revolutions, the howler was a single, enormous mass. It hit the ground like a cannonball, blasting right into one of the prowling howlers below. Armored hide met armored hide and while neither one so much as tore or split, the blunt force impact was devastating. Bones broke and organs ruptured, and it was anyone's guess which of the two howlers got it worse.

If Two-Feathers couldn't recognize *that* sign, he and Bright-Meadows would have a hell of a time ahead of them.

I reformed my shell atop the broken, if still squirming, remnants of the howler who'd mistaken me for lunch and the howler we'd effectively bombed from above. Broken and maddened by pain, they turned on each other, doing just as much damage to themselves as their opponent. There were three others still standing in the gully… the one attacking the nomads, the remaining one still looking for a way to join in that assault, and the huge, grizzled bastard in back that almost had to be the reason there was a pack at all.

I left the first for Falling-Rock's hunting party, ignored the second, and focused on the third. *Cut off the head* was a saying about snakes or bandits or both, but I was betting it would hold true for howler packs as well.

And with Two-Feathers streaking towards the grizzled alpha's back with only a spear in his hands, I had to do *something* to keep its attention. I launched off the shifting landscape that was two broken howlers at war with each other and dismissed my shell in mid-leap, once again summoning the storm.

Howlers lived lives of violence, and this one had lived a longer life than most. It was slower than its pack members, but wily enough to turn into the avalanche of steel that hit it, ducking its head and protecting its weak points. A thousand shards fell upon it, but left only superficial cuts.

It *is* possible to bleed a howler to death, but it takes hours, not minutes, and if there's anyone even vaguely mortal on the battlefield with you, you can kiss them goodbye. I'd never kissed Two-Feathers— I'd never so much as seen him naked—but I wasn't saying goodbye either. Not yet.

And that meant *death by twenty million cuts* wasn't an option.

I pulled the storm together and reformed my shell atop the swaying head of the beast. It bucked, as if to throw me off, and I dropped down to lay supine on its oversized snout, legs dangling and squeezing like I was on a horse's back. My true face was level with the howler's eye clusters. I saw cunning somewhere deep in those alien eyes, almost lost beneath a fury the storm recognized. I didn't speak howler, but I knew its next move would be to toss me into the air or swipe me off its own face with one of its six oversized paws.

Before it could do either, I squeezed my legs even tighter. I wasn't anywhere near strong enough to crush its jaws, even if I'd been able to get my legs entirely around them. I wasn't even strong enough to keep those jaws closed. But doing so secured my position for a few seconds longer, and *that* let me rear back and drive a leather-clad fist straight through the largest of the howler's six eyes.

If these things had been created with helmets like I had, they'd have been an absolute scourge instead of just a serious problem.

My fingers roamed deep into an eye socket the size of a large squash and I dared to try something else: I dismissed my shell and then reforming it again just as quickly. That was something I usually did just as a sort of personal cleanse—healing any wounds taken or even just replacing my riding leathers—but I'd always had to be mindful of my personal space when doing so. Even if freed for just a second, the storm could do some damage.

And when a portion of the storm formed in the eye socket I'd just scooped out? Damage was exactly what I hoped for.

Something blurred past me and only the spear in his hand told me that Two-Feathers had skipped right over my duel to attack the third howler in the melee. Typical. You do all the work setting shit up for someone, and they go find a totally different way to get into trouble. Still, he *was* a Stalwart and a killer in his own right. I had to trust he knew what he was doing.

And if he doesn't?

I crushed the thought like it was another of the howler's eyeballs. There was no time for thought or second-guessing. There was only time for carnage.

My reformed right hand gripped the inside of the eye socket the storm had hollowed out even further, and I swung forward to drive my left hand into the next eyeball over.

Two down. Four to go. The only question was whether I'd find a route to the thing's brain before I blinded it entirely.

The howler wasn't eager to let me answer that question. It shook its head violently, and only the fact that I now had two handholds kept me from being thrown against the ravine wall. I *still* tore something in one of my shoulders, but as I moved to eye number three and repeated my micro-shift, that limb was as good as new again.

The creature's next gambit was to charge the ravine wall head-on, in an impact that sounded like cannon fire. It did more damage to that wall—and the howler's own skull—than it did to me; I'd hollowed out enough space in the monster's head to fit the lion's share of the storm. A few fragments of steel went flying, but the rest made a home in a skull that was starting to resemble a cave system rather than anything living.

Somewhere in there, I found something good. A twist of barbed wire followed the winding path of a too-long optic nerve and hit paydirt. Contrary to my assumptions, a howler's brain *wasn't* a peanut in size or shape. Instead, it was oversized, oddly shaped, and softer than I thought it should have been. That twist of wire burrowed its way in like a hot spoon into half-melted cream and then spun, laying waste to the flesh around it.

If anything was going to keep fighting even after it had lost its brain, it would be a howler, but as that organ turned to paste, life went out of the beast I was buried inside.

This is a much better way to kill the damn things, I decided. When I'd gone down its throat, I'd had to dig my way back out. Going from eye to brain ensured I already had an exit route.

I pulled the storm back out into the open air and took hold of the pieces the charge against the wall had scattered. And then, as the alpha's corpse sagged to the earth, I reformed my shell upon it, like a queen upon her throne.

The ravine was a warzone. Neither the howler I'd lured into jumping off the cliff nor the howler we'd crashed into was quite dead yet, but the fluids spilling from both bodies suggested it was just a matter of time. The howler who'd been facing down the hunting party had pushed forward a half dozen paces. If the rest of its pack had been available, that would have created space for them to join in. Instead, the other nomads had taken the opportunity to surround the howler and were harrying it from all sides. Front and center was Falling-Rock, silhouetted against the smoke of way too many bullets fired in vain.

Two-Feathers, meanwhile, had taken his cue from my own tactics, and was riding the other howler like a pre-Break surfboard, the spear in his hand lashing out to strike at targets as they presented themselves. Soft tissue targets, just like we'd said.

I went to join him, but a loud crack heralded Falling-Rock finally managing to break something in his own opponent's body. As that howler stumbled on legs that suddenly failed to respond, the rest of the nomads surged forward to join Two-Feathers' fight. Most were bloodied, a few looked like they shouldn't even be walking, but they surrounded the beast and helped to bring it down.

That left only the howler above us. I scanned the ravine's ridge just in time to see the creature slink away. Which… was honestly a first, even for me. Howlers didn't run. They just killed and killed and sometimes ate what they killed, and heaven help anyone or anything whose scent they came across.

Unfortunately, I doubted whatever cowardice this one had caught would last long. And that meant we couldn't let it get away.

"Two-Feathers!" I called. "Going to need your help."

We left the other nomads to deal with their casualties. The battery on my bike had cooled enough to make swapping in a third one something even humans could handle; I tucked the depleted battery into my saddlebags with its companion and straddled the seat.

"Hop on," I told Two-Feathers. "We've got one howler left to kill. If I lose its trail, let me know."

I felt him nod, and then we were off.

22

In some other story or another world, that final hunt would have taken days. We'd have hacked our way up and down the countryside: chasing our prey, losing the trail, and having to pick it back up again. Nights would have been a few hours spent around the campfire, where words—mostly mine—could be shared. Maybe the nomad and I would have even hashed out our recent issues, reaching some sort of new equilibrium.

But in this story and this world, the howler forgot it was supposed to be the prey a few miles from the battle site and tried to ambush us. Two-Feathers saw the attack coming in time to save my bike from further damage, and not long after that, we left another toxic carcass behind to rot as we rejoined the rest of the hunting party.

Falling-Rock and the others were ready to go when we returned. We started the journey back to the clan, a journey hampered by the large number of wounded, the severely reduced number of horses, and the handful of dead bodies that had to be returned to their families for funeral ceremonies. Of those bodies, most were Falling-Rock's blooded hunters, older men and women who had given their lives in defense of the vastly less capable younglings out on their first hunt. They had all died at the mouths or claws of the howlers.

Either the howler pack had been following the same herd of deer the hunting party had initially brought down, or it had come across the hunter's tracks and treated the nomads like any other prey. Either way, the result had been devastating. What had begun as a rite of passage had devolved into outright calamity. If the nomads hadn't made it to the comparative safety of the ravine, if I hadn't been stuck in the demon cave far longer than expected, and if Aidan's horse hadn't spooked and fled directly into our path… Well, Two-Feathers' clan would have been down a lot more than just a bunch of horses and a few men and women.

I didn't believe in God. My creator had been the closest thing there was and even he had ultimately proven mortal. But maybe one of the clan's ancestor spirits had been looking out for them in the absence of Listens-To-Winds, because that number of coincidences lining up to save the lives of so many nomads didn't make sense otherwise. Not that I was going to try to tell any of the battle-worn survivors, all of whom had just lost friends, mentors, and sometimes even family, just how lucky they were.

I didn't have a heart, but I knew how to fake it.

Half a day into our return trip, we met up again with Aidan and the two nameless scouts who'd been originally assigned as my guides. Their horses helped to transport the wounded, but with the rest of us still stuck walking, our actual pace barely increased at all. I'd had plenty of time in my very long life to experience the fragility of humans, but traveling with a caravan of wounded really brought that point home.

Falling-Rock and Two-Feathers had a few conferences with the scouts—both the hunting party's and ours—but even though I was present, everyone spoke in the clan's tongue. The only person I could understand was Two-Feathers, and even that was iffy. Still, both Powers did twice the work of the rest of us, somehow always there to offer a helping hand, lift far more than their share, or steady someone about to tumble from the back of their borrowed mount. That first night, they gathered the able-bodied survivors together to help with the cooking. By the end of the meal, full bellies and the prospect of sleep had seemed to revitalize all but the most badly wounded.

I wasn't built to be a caretaker, but I pitched in where I could, stronger than any but those two Powers and impossible to wear down when I could reform my shell and instantly replace aching muscles with fresh copies. I gathered wood for the fire, helped put up tents and break them down again and basically did anything that wouldn't involve me dealing with the wounded or getting too close to the horses. Two-Feathers' mount had had some time to adjust to my presence, but the other hooved beasts pranced nervously about and rolled their eyes whenever I came within arm's reach.

They saw me as just another predator, and I couldn't blame them for that.

As we traveled, I set aside whatever frustration the over-long negotiations had caused. I didn't always understand the clans— sometimes, I didn't even like them much—but it was impossible not to respect them. To respect *anyone* who could impose their collective wills on the shitshow my absentee father had made of the world that was. Despite their wounds and their losses, there was no complaining, no obvious signs of despair, or defeat. Nomads were a resilient people, and with the clans being a melting pot of ethnicities and bloodlines, that wasn't something they were born with. Instead, it was just a collective mindset, the determination it took to survive and even flourish out in the Badlands, miles from the nearest walls.

And Two-Feathers, I was forced to finally admit, fit in really well with his people. In my eyes, he was at least Falling-Rock's equal when it came to natural leadership ability, with a combination of stoicism and personal warmth that simply couldn't be taught. I watched random heads turn to follow him as he ranged back and forth and felt an odd mix of emotions triggered by that sight.

He'll do well with Bright-Meadows, I realized. *Better than well. Even at this age, he's going to be a true force in the clan.*

And if the storm inside of me gnashed its metal teeth at the thought and raged on into the night? Well, I was the shell that contained the storm, and the consciousness that was in turn contained, but I wasn't the storm itself.

I could accept truths I didn't like.

I could convince myself that some things were for the best.

As that last howler had demonstrated, self-delusion wasn't somethings humans had a monopoly on.

○○○

On the second day, I found myself walking next to Aidan. He had bounced back quickly from his concussion and was deemed one of the few younglings healthy enough to walk on his own. Between that and his role in bringing help to the hunting party, he was walking proudly, with his narrow shoulders back and his chest puffed out. He traded words with the two teens slumped over the back of the horse we were guiding, and one of them mustered up the energy for a laugh.

Like I said... resilient.

"Are you a hunter of the clan now?" I asked after the riders had fallen silent, too tired to respond to the blond teen's endless stream of verbal support.

Aidan started, as if only now seeing the 6-foot-plus woman in black leather marching noisily beside him, motorcycle practically drowning in the supplies the horses would have been carrying. It was a reminder that, despite his endless chatter, he too was only half there.

"Yes! I mean... I think so?" He grinned, frowned, dismissed that frown, grinned, and then frowned again, in the sort of dizzying sequence of expressions neither my true face nor the one beneath could ever manage. "The hunt was successful well before the howlers came. But…" Here, that lingering frown deepened. "…we had to leave most of the meat behind when we were fleeing. Do you think the elders will penalize us for that?"

"Not unless they're idiots."

That won me a slow blink. "I know you're a guest of the clan and you and Two-Feathers just helped save us, but even so… you probably shouldn't let anyone hear you call any of the elders an idiot."

Clearly, he hadn't been listening in on the negotiations.

"If you finished your hunt," I said instead, "then I'd think you'd be rewarded for such, regardless of whether the meat and hides make it back to camp with you. Besides, Two-Feathers' hunting party already delivered their haul. The clan should be in good shape."

"Did… did *they* have any trouble?"

"Not from what I understand." I hadn't spoken with Two-Feathers at all outside of combat, not since the cave, but it was remarkably easy to eavesdrop on a man who spoke with his hands. "It seems they lucked out and came across buffalo earlier than expected. They returned to camp several days ago."

"Oh good." He blushed for some reason under my unblinking gaze. "I tried to talk Amal into coming with Falling-Rock's but she went with Two-Feathers' party instead. I'm just… glad she's safe."

His blush told me there was a lot more going on than just that, but I let it be. Adult relationships were exhausting enough; I had no interest in involving myself in teenage romance.

"If you need a break from walking, let me know," I told him. "I can clear some space on my bike for a few hours."

That got Aidan's attention in a way that almost made me feel bad for poor Amal, energy and enthusiasm suddenly suffusing his frame. "You'd let me ride it?"

"Only while I pushed it."

"Oh."

"Sorry, kid. It's not as easy to ride as it seems."

"I've been on horses since I was five."

"This thing's not a horse. It'll kill you just as quick as any howler."

The young nomad paled and nodded.

I probably should have picked a different predator, considering who I was talking to and what everyone had just gone through, but… to be fair, that was also why howlers were on my mind. Besides, instant torque and only two wheels really *could* be deadly.

Aidan lasted another hour or so after the riders we were guiding passed out on back of their borrowed horse. After that, I slung my saddlebags and a nomad rucksack over my shoulders and cleared some of the bike's seat for the teen. Can't say he weighed much more than what he was replacing, and if he drooled a bit on the bike's worn leather…

Well, it had dealt with far worse fluids in its life.

ooo

It took two days to make it back to camp, as the scouts had predicted. We were still an hour or two away when we ran across the first of the clan's many outriders. Word traveled a hell of a lot faster than we did, and soon we were met by dozens of nomads with twice as many horses, all there to help as needed.

Things went quickly after that, both the return and the reunions. Regardless of the often stone-faced demeanors the clans presented to outsiders, there was plenty of emotion voiced and expressed, from the survivors to their families to the handful of men and women whose loved ones had been brought home for burial.

Well, not *burial*, exactly. The clan didn't do that.

I kept myself separate. Human or not, I did feel—pain and emotion both. But these weren't my people, and I wasn't theirs, and a helmet with a smiley-face decal on its visor just wasn't appropriate for certain situations. So instead, I unloaded my bike and headed for my assigned tent, a single individual swimming against the tides of nomads headed the other way. I'd burned through two batteries in a matter of days, and I'd need every battery in my saddlebags to be fully charged for the trip down into Mexico. Better to get started on that now rather than later.

Although… I had some doubts over that one battery ever holding a full charge again. Technology could be temperamental, even stuff originally created by a Technomancer.

Whenever I returned to New Memphis, I'd have our engineering corps look both the bike and its batteries over. A queen needed her throne, after all, and even if mine had wheels, it suited me a lot more than the black stone monstrosity that Delia Laine had used.

I had about an hour of quiet before someone joined me at the fire. Not Aidan, who was still being seen to and fussed over by his parents. Not Stephanie, Aidan's replacement guide, who likely didn't even know where I was. Not even Two-Feathers, who was likely still working with Falling-Rock and had nothing of significance to say to me anyway.

No, this person made almost as much noise as I did walking, though her creaking came from old bones rather than heavy leather.

For all her evident age, Moon-Over-the-Trees took her seat beside me smoothly enough, dwarfed by both my form and my shadow in the late afternoon sun. We sat in silence, the sounds of the distant camp and the nearby fire washing over us.

For that moment, at least, we were a matched set. I didn't have anything to say, and she, as far as I knew, didn't even speak English.

Then, she put the lie to the illusion by speaking.

"We are grateful for your aid with the hunting party." Her English was surprisingly good, if strangely accented.

"You and your clan signed a treaty," I reminded her. "A preliminary one anyway. We're allies now. Part of that is non-aggression, but part of it is helping where necessary too."

"And this was necessary."

It was a statement, not a question, but I nodded anyway.

"Tonight, families will be preparing their fallen," she said. "You will be welcome at those fires should you wish to stand witness." After a pause, she continued. "Which I suspect you do not. In two days' time, we will hold a ceremony to welcome the new men and women of the clan, both those who proved themselves on the hunting trips and those who have chosen the path of the turtle or bird."

I didn't know what that last part meant, but I nodded anyway. Every clan had their own traditions. I'd gotten a more in-depth look at this one's already, but while I would recognize those traditions, they weren't mine, and I didn't need to understand them.

"You are welcome to attend that ceremony as well," Moon-Over-the-Trees continued, "but again, I suspect you will not."

"I'll be leaving at first light," I said.

"And what of Two-Feathers?"

"He'll be staying with Bright-Meadows and Deep-Water. As I'm guessing you elders were hoping all along."

"The Storm Who Rides rides alone," she said, voice quiet if not at all soft, "Is that the way of things?"

"Most of the time." I shifted about, the noise of the movement lost beneath the snap and crackle of our fire. "This is where Two-Feathers belongs. I didn't understand that I was delivering him home when we started the journey, but then, I didn't know what he had waiting for him here either."

"That will make some elders very happy, Snow-Falls and Smoke-on-the-Breeze among them."

"What about you?"

"I believe we each must find our path." She stared into the flames, beady eyes lost beneath a maze of sun-weathered wrinkles. "Before the trip that ended his father's life and brought the two of you together, long before he had earned the name Two-Feathers, he was a bright child, with a smile that could warm a tent, and a voice that rivaled a falcon's for its… piercing qualities."

She smiled for the first time that I could recall, exposing a mouth of brown teeth. "He was loud and boisterous and full of energy as many children are. It was his father, more than Deep-Water, who channeled that energy, who turned his gaze outward. To look, not at our traditional lands, but the greater world beyond."

"Until the greater world looked back."

"Yes. And so ended his father's dream. So ended Deep-Water's joy and the child's smiles and bright voice. The dead are set free as spirits, but we who remain must shoulder the burden of life still to come. And so they did, each in their own ways. The boy became a man. The man came into his powers and gained a name. His spear grew and he did too. And yet…"

I'd been around enough old humans to be wise to their conversational tricks, the pregnant pauses and the leading questions. Even so, I couldn't help myself.

"And yet what?"

She blessed me with another smile, this one a pale imitation of its predecessor. "The man you know as Two-Feathers will never be a merchant. What happened to him forever altered his path. His father's dream, as I said, ended on that trip. But there was a reason he served the clan as a scout on our southernmost borders. A reason that Falling-Rock has served as master of the hunt, though both are of an age and equally capable. The spark his father lit was not extinguished. It simply burned in another direction."

"With respect," I said, doing my best to keep the metal out of my voice, "I have no idea what you're trying to say."

"Have you asked him if he wishes to stay?"

"He has a *wife*. Or… a promised, or whatever."

"Have you asked him if he wants that either?"

"Two-Feathers isn't big on communicating. Or he'd have told me all of that sometime in the past year." Like when I was naked and throwing myself at him, I very carefully did not add.

"Maybe you are right." The smaller woman wrapped the dyed blanket more tightly about her body. "Maybe this is his place. Maybe his travels with you were sufficient to banish the wanderlust from his heart. Maybe he has at last come to see this clan as a home and not a cage. As I said, that will make my fellow elders happy. But I bounced him on my knee as a child, and his mother before him, and I know that there is steel in his veins to match that of your soul."

"Meaning?"

"Nobody chooses his fate for him."

That wasn't what I was doing, so I stayed quiet.

Moon-Over-the-Trees sighed. "There are none in our clan, nor any of the clans, who were alive when the Renewal gave us back our lands, yet some of us elders are but a few generations removed from those times. We remember the stories our parents' parents shared. Of the dark centuries before, of course, but also of the span of years after the Renewal, those years you outsiders call the Break, when the cities and nations that had been built tore themselves apart, replaced by smaller, weaker copies."

I kept quiet, though the storm rattled and raged inside of me. I'd lived through those times, been born from those times, from the dream their people called the Renewal.

"Most of the names and faces in those stories have faded into legend," she continued, "their spirits gone to whatever land their people's ancestors claim. Most, but not all. When I was young, we were told of the rider who followed the roads from coast to coast. There were those who called her death for the steel she carried within her, but the clans knew she was a storm, and that, as with every storm, her passage could bring both destruction and renewal. Until today, that is how I have always regarded you, as the force of nature described in the stories, something remote and unreachable."

"And now?"

"I bear witness to the person behind the power."

"They are one and the same," I said, as gently as I could with the metal of the storm filling my voice.

"Are they? You are older than me, of course, but I have been a mother to many of the children in our clan, in deed, if not blood. I have helped bring life into the world and I have bid spirits farewell as they began their journey west. While I have never been accused of true wisdom, I have experienced many of life's lessons, and there are occasions when I hear the whisper of truths I only ever halfway grasped. Because I am old—if not so old as you—I am afforded the grace to share those truths with those in need."

"Moon-Over-the-Trees… despite what the last few weeks may have made you think, I'm not a diplomat, let alone a poet. I've lived my life among the outcasts of society, and when they speak with words instead of weapons, they do so plainly."

"Forgive an old woman's ramblings then. I will come to the point, like an arrow to its target." She turned from the fire and looked up at my helmet, dark eyes fixed on the unseen space behind my visor. "You know what you are, better than anyone. And that has served you well for longer than any but a few in this world have been alive. Yet when I hear you speak, I find myself wondering if you truly know *who* you are."

"I am me," I told her. "I have always been me, and always will be, long after everyone in this land is gone."

"Again, that is what, not who. Existence is not experience. Longevity is not life. You are a queen, yes. You are a mercenary. You are the Storm Who Rides. But you are the person behind all those things as well. A woman. An individual. If I have any advice to give, it is this: learn what gives that woman joy and then fight for it like you would against a hundred howlers."

She rose then, knees popping as she stood. "I will inform my fellow elders of your plans. I ask only that you come tomorrow before your departure, that we might bid you farewell."

"I can do that."

"Then I will have Stephanie bring you to our tent when we are ready. There are words that must be said and things that must be witnessed."

It was uncomfortably close to how I'd once described my reasons for seeking out Bakersfield, but the old woman had no way of knowing that. So, I held my peace, and once she was gone, I turned back to the fire, staring into its light and paying no mind to the shadow it cast behind me.

While Two-Feathers' childhood was proof I couldn't remember everything, I was pretty sure this was the first time anyone had tried to mother me. It felt unnatural, and not just because Moon-Over-the-Trees was young enough to be the granddaughter I could never have.

Whatever the old woman thought, I knew who I was, and I knew what was next. I knew the road was waiting, always waiting. I knew Bakersfield stood at the end of one journey, and my role as an empire's queen waited at the end of another.

And even if the outcomes of those endpoints remained uncertain, I also knew that everything would either work itself out or not. The sun would rise and fall, the land would reshape itself, and fresh horrors would spawn to replace the last of the old monsters. Eventually, even the nomads would fade away, much like the words they spoke and the whispers they thought they heard. One day, it would all be gone, just another layer of dust and dirt beneath my wheels.

As for joy?

I would find it where I could, yes… but I would also let it go when its time was done.

All things had their end.

Even that.

Even me.

23

Stephanie came to fetch me a few hours after dawn. My batteries were charged and stowed away, my saddlebags were tied down on the bike, and I was ready to go.

Moon-Over-the-Trees would probably be frustrated to know I hadn't spent a single minute thinking about her parting words; instead, I'd waited for the camp to quiet, save for the few fires where funeral ceremonies were taking place, and then headed up to my hill to set the storm free.

Just before dawn, I came back down to find the bodies laid out on stone biers on the west side of camp, each wrapped in some sort of cloth shroud. A few family members stood watch over the dead, a vigil they had clearly already been keeping for hours. I nodded to a few, but no words were exchanged. Under the soft glow of a sun still threatening to rise above the horizon, I found my way back to my assigned tent.

There was nothing there but my bike and the possessions it carried. Even the fire had gone out, without Aidan or Stephanie to feed it, but I stirred through the wood ash to find a few glowing embers below. That was the way of things, people most of all. There was always more going on below the surface than it seemed.

Okay… so maybe I'd spent a *little* bit of time thinking about Moon-Over-the-Trees' words. Nobody had spoken to me like that in ages—Jules had probably come the closest, but the shadow of what we'd been colored our interactions—and I was left struggling to parse her words, looking for the meaning behind the meaning.

Thankfully, I'd have plenty of time for that on the road. The only stop left on this diplomacy tour nightmare was Wichita. Then, I'd be on to Lawton to get information and maybe even directions from Big Ed, the owner and proprietor of the Last Shot.

And then?

Mexico.

Mexico and Bakersfield.

I was several weeks behind schedule, but that was okay. All that really mattered was not getting stuck in the snow on the way back and it was still spring. In the short run, New Memphis could run itself without me… might even do a better job without me. I just needed to be there and visible before some overly ambitious idiot wrote me off for dead and attempted a coup or something.

Stephanie remained a marked contrast to Aidan's natural chattiness, the young blonde staying quiet as she led me to a destination where I'd already spent way too many hours. The elders' meeting tent hadn't changed in the few days I'd been away from camp either, and I resigned myself to the usual sight of a bunch of old humans seated in an open semicircle.

No shock that that's exactly what I got.

The surprise was that they weren't alone.

Bright-Meadows was there too, standing before the elders, and Deep-Water lurked with Falling-Rock out by the tent's darker fringe. The Titan looked like someone who'd only recently survived an assault from a pack of howlers, but he was dressed far more fancily than he had been at the spring festival fire, his dark hair braided and gleaming with some kind of oil. Deep-Water too, looked more put together than I remembered, but it was Bright-Meadows who stole the show, her hair loose and falling almost to her waist, the flowers in it bright against the curtain of darkness. The simple dress she wore was buttercup yellow, rather than white, and she wore a wreath on her brow rather than a veil, but even so…

I knew a wedding dress when I saw one.

I almost left, then and there, but for the first time, Stephanie had followed me in. She motioned me to the left, clearing the entrance.

"What is going on?" I hissed at her.

"I will be your translator for the ceremony," she said, not really answering the question.

I scanned the sitting elders. Smoke-on-the-Breeze looked pleased with himself and Snow-Falls looked carefully dignified, but Moon-Over-the-Trees…

She was looking right at me, expression unreadable.

Apparently, I'd really misjudged the old woman. In the time I'd spent parsing her words, it had never occurred to me to question her invitation. And now, here I was, standing witness to Two-Feathers' official vows.

The man himself, however, was missing, and as the minutes passed, the expressions on the elders' faces changed, one after the next, to consternation.

"Where is he?" snapped Smoke-on-the-Breeze, according to Stephanie's translation.

"Word was sent," said Snow-Falls, tone still soothing, if not quite as certain. "He was summoned and will be here."

"This was ill-planned," said Moon-Over-the-Trees. "I told you old goats as much. Better to let the young set their own pace than to force your schedule upon them."

"Time and the clan must move on," barked Smoke-on-the-Breeze. "This day has been delayed long enough."

Through it all, Bright-Meadows kept very still, her face composed, though I caught her darting a look toward her brother and mother-in-law from time to time.

"I will find him," said Falling-Rock finally, when the wait proved interminable. "Perhaps he misheard the—"

The big man's voice trailed off as the tent flap to my right opened, and the man of the hour appeared. Two-Feathers looked… normal. Almost offensively so, given the circumstances, but that was the nomad to a tee. He wore a simple shirt, open at the neck, and comfortable work pants. In one hand, he carried his new spear, but the other was extended behind him, holding…

I blinked as a horse trailed in after him, led by the reins in the nomad's hand. Not just *a* horse. I'd traveled with Two-Feathers long enough to recognize *his* horse. It cast a wary eye in my direction, but otherwise stayed placid enough, following its rider to the tent's center.

"What is this?" asked Snow-Falls, but I already knew. Outside of the clans, there was a thing called a bride price. A gift that the groom gave to their wife or her family as a sign of their commitment. Jules had stolen some dresses for just that reason. Apparently, Two-Feathers was going one step further and gifting the one thing he cared about more than anything in the world.

His horse.

I let the sound of the storm within me drown out the chatter and Stephanie's whispered translations of that chatter, but my sight remained fixed on the two people at the tent's center. Two-Feathers made his way over to his promised, his wife-to-be, and bowed as neatly as any courtier in New Memphis. I couldn't see the words his hands were forming, but I'd been to a few weddings in my time, and those words were easy enough to substitute.

Love. Commitment. Probably something about beauty or success or children or stability. The many things that differentiated a life in the clan from one on the road. Bright-Meadows' eyes glistened with unshed tears, overcome with the emotion of the moment, and I couldn't find it in myself to resent her for that. She whispered something back, and Two-Feathers nodded.

Outside of the clans, weddings were usually overseen—and performed—by a third party, a priest in those places where religion still held any weight, a trusted family member, town elder, or elected official everywhere else. But there was something kind of pure about the couple involved doing it themselves. Even if their elders had forced the time and the place, they were making it *their* ceremony and no one else's.

Finally, the quiet conversation—one half hushed, the other pantomimed—came to a close. Two-Feathers handed the reins of his horse, of his living bride price, over to Bright-Meadows and she threw herself forward, to wrap slender arms around the nomad.

Next to me, Stephanie sucked in a breath.

"What is it?"

"This is a very strange ceremony," she said, voice still hushed. "I don't know if—"

She cut off again. At the center of the tent, under the watchful eyes of a dozen people, the couple had separated. Two-Feathers turned to the semi-circle of elders and offered another bow, shallower than the one he'd given Bright-Meadows. Then a third and a fourth, to Deep-Water and Falling-Rock, respectively. When he was done, he found me in the darkness, but instead of a bow, I merited only a long look that I couldn't begin to interpret. He hefted his spear in his hand, left his horse with Bright-Meadows, and departed the tent.

"Oh no," said Stephanie in a voice of dawning horror, even as some elders surged to their feet, and Bright-Meadows' tears began to flow in earnest. "He broke their promise."

"He what?"

"He ended things. Their commitment. The horse is his apology and his farewell. Poor—"

I didn't hear anything more, because I was already past her and out the tent, chasing after the departed nomad.

ooo

I'd never been much of a tracker, but it wasn't difficult to follow Two-Feathers through the tents. I knew he could hear me—I was rarely silent and never subtle—so I let him lead me to the north edge of camp, not too far from where we'd returned with Falling Rocks' hunting party. There, he planted his spear in the earth and waited, looking anywhere but at me.

My lack of subtlety was a facet in more than just tailing someone. I stepped around the nomad and stared him dead in the face. Two-Feathers' usual mask was gone, the hard lines of his face softer, his eyes unhooded. He looked unbelievably young and almost as sad, yet there was determination mixed in there as well.

I honestly had no idea what the fuck was going on.

A diplomat, like the one I'd been roleplaying as, would have found a way to work the conversation around to the point eventually; I went straight for the jugular.

"What the fuck is going on?"

His hands moved slowly through the signs, and though I didn't know *all* of them, the context was clear.

"You ended things? Yeah, I kind of saw that. Why?" The storm filled my voice. "Tell me you didn't do that for me."

He didn't sign anything at all... just sent me a level look that was all the answer I needed.

"I already *told you* that you had paid your debt! Your place is here. With your people. With the woman who loves you and can give you what you want."

This triggered an actual scowl and a flurry of signs that had to be repeated three times before I had any idea what he was saying.

"*Who* doesn't know what you want? Bright-Meadows?"

He nodded, and then gestured again, this time pointing at me.

"*I* don't know what you want either?" I was pretty sure the smile on my true face had gone cold. "Well, of course I don't. How could I? How could I know anything about you? You didn't even tell me you had a fiancée! I had to find that out from Bright-Meadows herself. Her and your mom and me, sitting around having tea, while you were out leading the hunt!"

I was getting loud, loud enough to attract attention from some of the nearby tents and at least one scout, on his way back from his shift out in the countryside. I didn't care that much—I wasn't shy, and I wasn't embarrassed either—but still… this *was* a private matter. I dropped my voice and focused back in on the nomad.

"You had all the time in the world to talk when we were traveling and didn't," I said, my voice quiet but hard. "That was *your* choice, not mine. I'm still here, but I won't be for long. If you have something to say, this is the time."

For a long moment, Two-Feather stood there in silence, jaw clenched and eyes hard. He looked frustrated, more than a little bit angry, and still very, very young. He scanned my visor, as if trying to look past it, even though he knew that *it* was my true face and not what lay beneath. Finally, the nomad took a long breath and let it out again. His fingers began to dance.

It was way too fast for me to catch all of it, but I thought I translated enough. Something about the right time… which sounded like an excuse to me. A mention of our language barrier was another excuse… albeit a slightly more valid one. Before we'd found the book in New Memphis, communication had been done through pantomime and while this new sign language wasn't *that* much better yet, it at least offered the promise of more detailed conversation.

So. Two reasons offered for why he hadn't told me he was engaged, one of which was at least moderately valid on the surface, if no more satisfying. I'd have pressed him on both if he hadn't hit me with a whammy of a revelation, this one signed slowly so there could be no mistaking it.

"You came back to end things with Bright-Meadows?"

He nodded.

"Why?"

For some reason, that question frustrated him even more, so I gave him another one.

"And why wait until you were literally both standing before the elders, about to get married?" I didn't really care for Bright-Meadows, one way or the other, but it seemed cruel, and the Two-Feathers I knew wasn't cruel. Hell, sometimes, I *wished* he was cruel.

"He didn't wait," said a deep voice that I'd only recently come to know. "He tried to break things off with my sister the day you two returned to camp."

Falling-Rock moved quietly for a man of his size, but it was a sign of just how rattled Two-Feathers was that the Stalwart hadn't heard the other man coming. Still, he adjusted, turning to regard the bigger man.

I wasn't sure why we were suddenly a trio instead of a pair, but Falling-Rock had a voice and I wasn't going to let the delicacy of the situation keep me from leveraging that.

"He did what?"

"Marched to my sister's tent and tried to break their engagement." The Titan saw something in my true face and swallowed heavily. "She refused. And then I challenged him for the insult."

That… put a lot of what had happened at the Spring Ceremony into perspective. But it didn't explain everything.

"Why?"

"To which part?"

"I don't know." I shrugged. "Both. Either."

"I can't speak for Bright-Meadows, but she has wanted to marry Two-Feathers since we were all children. Like me, I think she thought he was being hasty." He turned to the other nomad. "You came back with the dust of the outside world upon you and inside you. We thought once you had washed that dust away, you would be reminded of your position in the clan. You would return to who you had always been."

Two-Feathers' signs were short and almost savage in their sharpness.

"He says this *is* who he always has been," I translated.

"Yes. I came to that realization when I was out in the field with my hunting party. I thought of the many hunts before that, and how he had not only rejected a leadership role but often chose scouting assignments on the fringes of our territories."

Two-Feathers had yet to rediscover his equilibrium, dark eyes fixed on the other man's face.

"My sister believed you left because of a debt," said Falling-Rock, in a rumble not unlike his name. "I think your mother prayed for the same. And maybe there was some truth to that, but it was never the whole truth, was it?"

Two-Feathers shook his head.

"I didn't understand that for far too long. Whatever it was that your father had, that wanderlust or curiosity, you have it too. Our clan was too small to ever keep you, when a larger world awaited. It's not about what *she* once did," added the Titan, nodding to me in a way that might have been insulting if it had carried any malice. "It isn't about her at all."

Two-Feathers had been nodding along during most of that conversation, but he stopped on that last line. He left his spear behind and took a step toward me and extended a hand in my direction, palm upward as if in supplication.

"Oh," said Falling-Rock, but his voice had become just background noise, much like the sound of the storm itself.

I stared at that outstretched hand, examining it with my senses and half-formed eyes both. I had reached out to Two-Feathers once, a year earlier, shortly after our first battle against a howler, and he had turned away. Part of me wanted to return the favor, especially since *he* hadn't stripped down like I had the first time, but...

He'd had his reasons at the time, and while the last *year* would have gone a lot better if he'd just *told me* those reasons, I wasn't going to argue that they were valid. He was a stubborn idiot, but he was at least an honorable one.

And honestly? Moon-Over-the-Trees' words from the previous night were still fresh in my head: *learn what gives that woman joy and then fight for it like you would against a hundred howlers.* I didn't know if this would give me joy or if it would blow up spectacularly in both of our faces, but there was only one way to find out.

I took his hand in mine and tugged him closer, staring into a face laid bare. There was uncertainty there. There was regret and grief, slowly fading. There was the stubbornness I'd smashed my helmet against time and time again, and there was even still a little bit of anger, smoldering like embers in a campfire, but below all of that was something else, something I'd never seen in any of my handful of partners' eyes over the years.

Something more.

I didn't need to breathe—didn't really have an esophagus at all—but I swallowed anyway.

"We need to talk," I told him in a soft voice absent of metal. "Really, truly talk."

A loud cough interrupted us, sounding even more like an avalanche than the man's speaking voice.

I turned the baleful eye of my true face on Falling-Rock and he took a step back, his words lost beneath the metal clash of the storm, raging just beneath my shell.

"As much as I appreciate your help, especially given the people involved, I think Two-Feathers and I can take it from here."

"Right. It's just that… there was another reason I came to find you both," said the Titan.

I eyed the bigger man up and down, then shook my head, adding a touch of reluctance to the gesture just to tweak Two-Feathers' nose.

"I'm sorry," I told Falling-Rock. "I've already got myself a nomad. I'm not looking for a second one."

The nomad in question—*my* nomad—gave me a look that communicated, without signs or words, exactly how funny I was not being, but he didn't let go of my hand. Instead, he turned to his former future brother-in-law and used his free hand to pantomime a question.

"Bright-Meadows? She is with Deep-Water, who as you know has been a mother to us both since the loss of our parents. Promise or no promise, marriage or no marriage, I am not giving that relationship up and neither is my sister." Falling-Rock let those words sink in before continuing. "But the reason I followed the two of you out here was to deliver a message. From the elders."

I'd heard all I ever wanted to hear from the elders over the past few weeks, but Two-Feathers came to attention.

"Actions have consequences," said the Titan, in a voice that made it clear he was repeating someone else's words. "A promise is a commitment, a bond between two people, built on honor and responsibility. To sever that bond is to inflict damage upon your own honor, and this clan is not a place for those whose honor is in question."

The storm began to rage again within me, steel and shrapnel orbiting the focal point that was my soul, but Two-Feathers' squeezed my hand. My nomad's face remained calm and resolute.

"You are banished from this clan," said Falling-Rock, "for a duration of no less than one year. Return when the wounds you have inflicted upon your own honor have healed and not before then." The Titan shed his assumed formality. "I'm pretty sure they all know you're leaving anyway, although I don't think they realized the true reason why any more than I did. Except for maybe Moon-Over-the-Trees…"

His eyes drifted down to our clasped hands.

"Anyway, I was also told to say: *while the Storm Who Rides, as an ally of our clan, remains welcome in our territories, the warrior known as Two-Feathers must be gone by nightfall.*" The Titan eyed the sun, now high in the sky above us. "That gives you an hour or so to make any goodbyes you might have. I don't know that my sister will want to see you, let alone speak with you, but I do know she'll remember whether you made the effort. And Deep-Water…"

Two-Feathers nodded in understanding. He squeezed my hand again and then let go to clasp the other man's arm in that vaguely macho way men seemed born knowing how to do. The two twenty-something-year-old Powers traded glances, communicating without words, and then my nomad turned back to me.

"I'll wait by my bike," I said. "Just come when you're done."

He nodded, pulled his spear from the earth, and was gone again, just like that.

"I hope your motorcycle can carry both of you at least as far as your next destination," said Falling-Rock, "because there's no way my sister is giving back that horse, and his banishment means he's not permitted to choose a new one from our herds. You *might* be able to claim one on his behalf, but I wouldn't bet on it."

"We'll make do." If we couldn't buy a horse in Wichita, we'd just steal one in Lawton. With the Old Man gone, I doubted anyone would make trouble for me if I did. It wouldn't be Two-Feathers' mount, of course, but other than temperament, I was pretty sure one horse was a lot like the next. Not like my motorcycle, which was truly one of a kind, as much because of the history we'd shared as its construction.

Falling-Rock nodded, but I couldn't help but notice that he still wasn't going on his way.

"Is there something else I can help you with?" I finally asked.

"Yeah. Even before we were marked to become brothers, I have always seen Two-Feathers as mine," said the Titan. "Neither his wanderlust nor his temporary exile nor his feelings for you change that. He is my brother in heart if not blood or marriage."

"You tried to beat each other senseless at the Spring Ceremony," I reminded him.

"Exactly."

I'd never had a family of my own, but I'd met my fair share of siblings, and half of them adored each other, while the other half seemed bent on mutual destruction. So, simply telling me they were brothers, fake or real, didn't clarify much.

"He's a good man and a stubborn ass both," said the Titan, "and from what I have heard of the outer world, those two qualities, whether taken individually or together, are often an invitation for trouble. Please: keep him safe."

As Bright-Meadows had recently discovered, the post-Break world wasn't a place for promises. Nevertheless, I offered mine.

After a fashion.

"Two-Feathers doesn't want to be safe. I didn't coddle him this past year and I'm not going to start. He's a grown adult and a warrior to the bone; he'll find his way into the action and emerge all the stronger for it." I paused. "But I can promise you this: I will be at his side through all of it. If anyone or anything kills him, it will be because the storm has already been scattered into a thousand pieces."

I could tell Falling-Rock didn't get what I was saying... *couldn't* really, without greater knowledge of the storm than he would ever have, but it was the only promise I could give. I would outlive Two-Feathers. That was unavoidable. But anyone who sought his life would have to go through me, shell and storm both.

I didn't know where the road would take us, or how the world might spin in the years to come. I didn't even know if that promise, as limited as it was, was a promise I could truly keep.

All I knew was that it was a promise I had to make.

24

It took Two-Feathers slightly more than the allotted hour, which gave me plenty of time to say goodbye to Aidan and Stephanie. Eventually, my nomad arrived at the south-end of the camp with spear in hand and bags slung over one shoulder and we spent another ten minutes figuring out how to accommodate not just his extra weight but that of his stuff. I didn't hate the idea of him riding bitch with me, but a tent, rations, clothes, canteens, and that spear made for a fair bit of mass, on top of a man who was all muscle and bone.

Considering that the elders hadn't given him any credit for the gift of his horse when it came to the whole broken promise and wounded honor thing, I kind of thought Two-Feathers should have just kept the beast. Not that I was going to say so.

Several hours later, we pulled up at what I had always thought of as the southern boundary of the clan's territories. There were no markers, and if we'd had a map, it wouldn't have shown any borders either, but it was where I'd come in the past, first to meet Two-Feathers' predecessor and then to meet the man himself.

I dropped the kickstand, swung around on my bike, and looked at my nomad.

"Are you sure about this?"

He gave me a look, motioned in the direction of the camp we'd long since left behind, and flashed a few signs.

"Yeah, I know you've been banished. Temporarily at least. But I also know they'd probably forget it ever happened if you turned around now and went back."

Instead of responding, he dismounted. A few steps took him past the bike's front wheel, and a few more took him to the beginning of the overgrown path that led south. He stopped and took a deep breath, broad chest expanding and then contracting again as he breathed back out. When he turned back to me, he looked… relaxed. Still young—that wasn't changing with anything but tragedy, time, or both—but unburdened in a way he hadn't been since we left New Memphis. He pointed at the sun, now low in the sky, at the bike, and then the road ahead of us, and gave me a look of mock impatience.

The road is waiting, he seemed to be saying. *Let's go.*

A man after my non-existent heart.

"Alright then. Get your sweet ass back on the bike and we'll be on our way. We've still got a few hours left to ride."

It ended up being closer to *one* hour, because I had plans for the night. As soon as it got halfway dark, I pulled off the pathway. Two-Feathers pitched his tent and started a fire. I watched and waited until he had eaten his meal, then I sat down, not across the fire from him, but next to him, invading his space like he was just another town for my armies to conquer.

"We need to talk," I said.

He finished wiping down his tin plate and set it aside.

"We're both adults. If only barely in your case," I added, prompting a grin from the nomad for my exaggeration. "We're going to have our secrets, and as far as I'm concerned, we've earned the right to keep those secrets. But if this… whatever this is that we have… if it has any chance of working, I'm going to need two things from you."

The campsite was quiet, save for the crackle of the fire and the hoot of a nearby owl who didn't give a damn about even *more* relationship drama. Two-Feathers simply nodded and waited.

"First, there are secrets and then there are *secrets*. If there's something in your past, present, or future that will impact not just you and not just me but *us*? You need to tell me. I'm going to keep learning sign language as best I can, but if you have to act it out like one of those traveling performer troupes we occasionally see in the Badlands, that's what you're going to do. Another Bright-Meadows type of surprise and we're done."

He tilted his head and raised his hands, but I cut him off before he could launch into a rebuttal.

"I get it. There were extenuating circumstances. Sort of. And you've already paid the price for that. I'm not here to restart this morning's argument. I'm just saying… this has to be a rule going forward, for you and me both. I don't know how to have a relationship that's more than just fucking and fighting, but I'm pretty sure trust is a part of it."

Two-Feathers settled again, his defensiveness fading as I continued speaking. As stubborn as he could be, the man knew how to listen too.

"What I'm saying is… speak now if there's another fiancée out there or some other deeply kept secret sure to rear its ugly head and fuck everything up," I told him.

I waited, just in case, because you never really know… but he stayed silent.

"Good. Second, I need you to understand something about me. I am not human. I will never be human. I can't give you children or family or someone to grow old with. I can't even give you someone to eat, drink, or sleep with… and while I wouldn't be entirely against learning to cook from time to time, I'm not going to mother you either." I waited for his acceptance and continued. "But I *am* still a woman. A woman with needs. A woman who's been waiting almost a year for you to make some sort of move. I get now why that never happened, but Bright-Meadows is gone. It's just the fire, your tent, and the two of us. So, if you—"

I trailed off as Two-Feathers stood. He pulled his shirt over his head and stood there in just pants and the dirt of the road, hard planes of bronze muscle glistening in the firelight. With one hand and a Stalwart's strength, he reached down and pulled me up and against him, his other hand tracing a line around my waist to take a firm grip on my leather-clad ass. And if that wasn't clear enough, he pressed my hips into his, erasing any remaining space between us, and giving me incontrovertible and extremely tangible proof of his interest.

Fucking *finally.*

Our first time was right there next to the fire. Our second and third times in the tent. The fourth came the next morning, shortly after my nomad walked to the nearby stream to wash the sweat from his naked body, the early sun highlighting the water's path down his sculpted form.

I kept my true face on the whole time—before, during, and after—and while there *was* a delightful amount of noise, I didn't hear a single complaint.

ooo

I wasn't sure how things would change after that. Created as I had been, dropped into the world full-grown and without parents, family, or an instruction manual, it had taken me decades before I understood, let alone indulged, my shell and its needs, but I'd had a number of lovers in the time since. Most had been one-night stands, sweaty townies all too happy to help me take off the edge. A scant few had been longer-term things like Jules or the Old Man before him. None had ever truly risen beyond the level of *allies-with-benefits*, but they'd been enough to tell me that every man was different. Some were effectively immune to attachment. Others thought a simple touch implied ownership. Throw *feelings* into the mix and hell if I knew what was going to happen.

The answer, to my deep and abiding relief, was: nothing. Not really, anyway. Two-Feathers remained Two-Feathers, and while we talked a bit more than usual, and *touched* a hell of a lot more than that, my nomad seemed as content as I was to let everything else develop on its own. I didn't know if we were feeling our way through the process or if this *was* the process, but the days were cozy, and the nights were even better. My shell got its needs met, and then I set the storm free to dance out in the open air while Two-Feathers slept the blissful sleep of the young and thoroughly satisfied in his tent.

The actual journey was more of a mixed bag. My bike wasn't built for two people *and* their bags, but the lack of a horse meant we could travel faster and longer each day, so the net result was less comfort but more distance. And I didn't hate having two strong arms wrapped around me as we rode. But the damn spear and all of Two-Feathers' bags? They got in the way a lot.

"We're getting you a new horse in Wichita," I told Two-Feathers when we stopped for the night. After several days of travel, we had reached the main throughfare between Kansas' two remaining cities. The road was in better repair than most, and I'd taken advantage of that by riding for an extra few hours. "We should arrive sometime late tomorrow. You can scope out the available inventory in the stables while I parlay with the ruling family."

He rubbed his thumb and index finger together in a gesture that needed no interpretation, but I shook my head.

"We've got the money, but don't buy anything until you've heard from me. Maybe I can work our expenses into the terms of the treaty. A horse for you and a hotel room for both of us. With a bath. A big one," I decided. I didn't need water to clean myself, not when I could simply reform my shell and return it to its pristine state, but Two-Feathers didn't have that luxury, and I'd already learned what a potent combination water and my nomad made. And if that water was warm and scented instead of so cold that it turned my shell's skin blue?

Well. I wasn't human, but I *was* a woman.

The possibilities were enticing.

If Raya had still been alive, she'd have had something sharply sarcastic to say to me, no doubt, but I'd been celibate for a damn year, and a gap like that required some serious makeup time. And makeup *sex*, to be blunt. Besides, I'd been around for *her* teenage years and early twenties, and the spymaster had absolutely no room to speak to anyone about *their* sexual proclivities.

It was a moot point, of course, because Raya *wasn't* alive. Not unless you counted whatever piece of her lived on in her daughter. Still, her memory was fresh enough that even the thought of what she would have said made the smile on my true face go wide and wild.

Sometimes, I felt closer to the woman in death than we'd ever been when she was breathing. Hell if I knew what that said about me.

The road to Wichita paralleled a stream for a good part of its length, so Two-Feathers went off to bathe while his dinner cooked over the fire. We had rations that we'd refill in Wichita and then again in Lawton, but the nomad was supplementing his travel diet with meat from the occasional rabbit or wild turkey.

I didn't know how he could always be so successful with his hunts, especially when it was usually dark before he even started, but I was guessing a lot of it had to do with him not wearing riding leathers that made sneaking anywhere damn near impossible.

Part of it was probably skill, training, and his powers too.

I was waiting for him when a voice came from the darkness.

"Hello to the fire! Might you have space for a weary traveler to warm his old bones? I can pay in shared stories and company, if not actual coin."

Whoever he was, he *did* sound old. On the other hand, he'd also crept up on the campsite without me hearing, and unless I was being paranoid, had made a special effort to circle around to approach from behind where I was sitting. Neither of those things was a great sign.

Still, the open terrain gave the storm free rein and by announcing himself, he'd given up the element of surprise. And there weren't many Powers in the country, let alone the Badlands, that I had cause to actually fear.

"I don't need companionship," I said, letting the metal of the storm fill my voice, "but I'll take any news of the road west. Assuming you came from that direction."

"That I did." He emerged from the treeline, every bit as old as he'd sounded, a bag of bones wrapped in a green camo poncho. "And I'm happy to share what I know. If you can also spare some of that meat I'm smelling, I would—"

He came to a stop as he finally saw me up close, the fire's light reflecting off my helmet and the bright yellow menace of my true face.

"Your Majesty?"

I cocked my head. Behind the old man, a half-clad shape, spear in hand, had detached itself from the woods to slip into the unsuspecting stranger's shadow. Maybe Two-Feathers' success on the hunt wasn't *entirely* down to his clothing choices.

"Do we know each other?" I asked the old man, keeping my attention off the nomad approaching in his wake.

"It's me! Tonek!"

"*Two-Tongue* Tonek?" I looked the man up and down. "I figured you'd be long dead by now."

"Not for lack of the world trying. I can tell you that much." He stepped forward, offering a vaguely familiar grin that was now missing quite a few teeth. Beady eyes looked from my face to the spit of meat still roasting over the fire. "When did you start eating like the rest of us dirtbags?"

"I didn't." I was pretty sure the smile across my visor widened as Two-Feathers' spear snaked out of the darkness to caress the throat of a suddenly stiff Tonek. "Two-Tongue, meet Two-Feathers. As you can tell from the introduction, you've both got something in common."

"It's just Tonek now," said the older man, Adam's apple bobbing as he held very, very still. "But any ally of Her Majesty's is an ally of mine. And only an idiot would start a fracas with the Queen of Smiles just a few feet away. I came in peace and aim to leave that way too."

It was anyone's guess whether the *idiot* he was talking about was himself or Two-Feathers, but that was Two-Tongue to a T. Tonek didn't *actually* have two tongues… he was as mundane as they came, after all. It was just that the one tongue he did have was so long and twisted it practically counted for two. Truth and Tonek had maintained an uneasy and often outright adversarial relationship.

Still, he'd always had a strong sense of self-preservation… and as someone I'd ridden with briefly *before* the Old Man, he had to be damn near pushing eighty. A man that age should've been sitting at home by the fire, not out traveling the Badlands at night

But then, criminals weren't the best at settling down.

I nodded to Two-Feathers. "It's okay. Tonek and I rode together a long time ago. Don't believe even half of what he says, and verify the rest with someone you can trust, but unless he has a whole band with him that somehow escaped your watchful eye, he's not going to be dumb enough to cause us trouble."

My nomad sent me one of his all-too expressive looks, which I took to mean both that Tonek was alone and that he didn't appreciate my suggesting he might have missed any intruders. Regardless, he withdrew his spear and went to go check on the progress of his dinner.

"I didn't know you were riding with nomads these days," said Tonek, eying the bigger, stronger, younger man with a strange mix of envy and greed on his face.

"Just the one. And he's a Power before you get any dumb ideas in your bald old head."

"With muscles like that? Well of course he is! Like I said, I came only for the fire and whatever food your man might be willing to spare. As for my head and its conspicuous lack of groundcover…" He rubbed a liver-spotted hand over the few wisps of hair left on his pate and sighed, eyes returning to the fire. "I avoid mirrors for a reason these days; I'll thank you for not providing me one with your words."

"Why are you on the road instead of swaddled in blankets, drinking one of your nasty concoctions, and being waited upon by someone too naïve to know any better?"

"Well, therein lies a bit of a story, I'll admit."

"Another con gone wrong? Or…" I gestured to the fire. "…did you feel the need to set something on fire?"

"I would say a little bit of both, perhaps, depending on where the story begins. It *has* been a lifetime since we saw each other, after all, and a man needs his hobbies."

"You might want to find some new ones. Just saying."

"Yes, well. Old dogs and all that, I suppose. May I sit?"

"You may."

The seat he took was closer to the fire than I'd have advised if he had more than a few strands of hair left to burn off. I dropped down next to him.

"If you're nice enough to Two-Feathers, he'll probably agree to give you some of what he's cooking. In the meantime, you said you had some stories?"

"That I do. Stories, the clothes on my back, what few possessions remain in my pack, and that's about it."

"I'm fine with just the stories. Start with what happened to you. It was damn near forty years ago that you disappeared. Where the hell have you been?"

"Forty-seven, actually, and *disappeared* is one way of putting it. I'd prefer to say *run out of town.*"

"By who? And why?" The *town* in question was a shithole named Gladstone, way up north in what had once been the great state of North Dakota. I couldn't remember what had taken our merry band of mercenaries and murderers up there. A job, almost certainly, but the exact nature of that job had been lost, like so many other things, to time.

"I may have gotten a little bit drunk—"

"You were never just a little bit drunk," I corrected him. "When you weren't sober, you were somewhere between falling-off-your-horse drunk or pick-a-fight-with-the-moon drunk."

He harumphed, sounding every bit as old as he looked. "Perhaps there's some truth to that. Still, I got drunk and said some true but ultimately unwise things to Bian. You remember her, right?"

I did, and not *just* because she had been Raya's mother. I'd known more dangerous people—and quite a few of them—but Bian might very well have been the meanest. And she had held onto a grudge like a python to its prey.

"True but ultimately unwise?"

"Yes, well. I may have commented on her ancestry and said that her daughter would be better off with Bian's ex given what a shitty mother she was. And then I might have made a pass at her too."

"You were *way* more than just a little bit drunk."

"They make some strong moonshine up north," he admitted.

"Frankly, I'm surprised you're alive."

"It's not through lack of Bian trying. She came at me with that knife of hers, the one as long as a decent person's forearm? You better believe I ran. Not just out of Gladstone but out of the Badlands entirely. Decided it was time to make a new life for myself as a law-abiding citizen in the land of milk and honey."

"Two-Tongue going straight? In the Free States, no less? That's hard to imagine."

Tonek nodded. "It didn't take for very long, admittedly, but at least my heart was in the right place."

"Meaning still in your chest and not roasting on a spit over Bian's campfire."

"Exactly." His eyes turned to our fire's spit as Two-Feathers removed the roast rabbit and started to cut the meat into long strips.

I didn't eat food, of course, and was more than happy with that arrangement, especially given the disaster of human waste and elimination, but the rabbit smelled pretty damn good, even to me.

"Anyway, I spent most of the past few decades there, making connections and living my life. When a few things went wrong all in a row, I decided it would be best to put the Free States behind me and come back home. I doubt Bian will let bygones be bygones, but at our respective ages, I can outrun her if I have to." He slapped his spindly legs, as if there was some kind of muscle to show off.

Unprompted, Two-Feathers moved some of his roast rabbit onto a second plate and passed that over to Tonek. The meat was still sizzling hot, but that didn't stop the old man from shoveling the first few scraps into his mouth.

"Bian died years ago," I told him.

"Really? I always figured she'd be like you. Too mean to let death have its say."

"You humans don't get to make that choice."

"And the others?"

"I went my own way, not long after that. Bian settled back in Kansas City, but the rest split up. Joined different bands and met their ends accordingly, as far as I know. You're almost definitely the last one left from that band. Which means there's nobody left who wants you dead."

"Not this far east anyway." Rabbit juice dripped down his chin. "That's good to hear. Not that they're dead, of course, although my opinion there varies depending upon the individual. Bian, at least, was a hell of a woman."

There wasn't much I could say to that. Or *wanted* to say to that, anyway. I waited in silence as he finished off his plate.

"My compliments on the meal, young fellow," he told Two-Feathers when he was done. "It almost makes up for Wichita."

That got my attention. "What happened in Wichita?"

"Nothing at all; that's the problem! I was supposed to meet a contact there, someone in the market for a steady hand and silver tongue. Only, when I arrived from Albuquerque, the gate was closed. Nobody without special permission was being allowed in or out."

I traded glances with Two-Feathers. Was it too much to ask for even *one* of our stops on this road trip to go smoothly?

"Did they say why?"

"Can't say they did. But the usual bribes didn't get me so much as the time of day, so I'm guessing the order came down from on high."

"Meaning the Millers," I said, citing the name of Wichita's ruling family.

"Ayup, that'd be them." He shrugged. "I had the choice of arguing my way into a press gang or giving up and moving on. I took the one that *didn't* involve hard labor. Now that I know for sure Bian's gone, I might give Kansas City a try instead. I assume that's where you two are coming from?"

"In a way." I had known Tonek for only a few months and it had been a very, very long time ago. I didn't trust him with even the simplest of truths. Still, I felt compelled to warn him. Or maybe to try to limit the damage he might do to the newly allied city. "There's been some upheaval there. Cartel wars, leadership changes, and…" Here I fixed the old man with a look. "…at least one big fire. If you've still got the pyromaniac bug in you, I'd suggest not letting it out."

"Arson is a young man's game, Your Majesty," he said, completely contradicting his earlier statement about hobbies. His gap-toothed smile was all the more unsettling for the bits of meat now wedged into it. "These days, I'm just what you see in front of you."

"Meaning a conman and a thief."

He glanced at Two-Feathers and shook his head. "You're going to ruin this fine young man's opinion of me."

"Are you saying your first thought when you saw a fire and only one person sitting beside it *wasn't* on how to rob that person blind?"

"It wasn't my *first* thought, no. Second or third, maybe. But even if you were mostly just along for those jobs of yours, I'm sure you remember how the game is played."

"Things change and times do too."

"And nations rise and fall, thrones changing hands with unexpected results. Yet the Queen of Smiles remains. Or so it seems." He waved his free, mostly clean hand at the campsite. "I'm not a fool. The last thing I'd do is piss off you or your man. Bian's reach was finite; I'm not sure yours is. And if you can see your way to sharing your campsite tonight, I promise I'll be off in the morning with nothing but good things to say about you and yours. Who knows? Maybe one old man's positive press will prove useful in the end."

To be entirely honest, I wasn't thrilled about Tonek staying with us, even for just the night. Even if he did play things safe, he'd almost certainly claim a share of the tent with Two-Feathers, depriving me of some enjoyable times. But I hadn't missed the comment about thrones changing hands either. He was playing it sly, but clearly, Two-Tongue knew about my changed circumstances. I wanted to find out how… and see exactly what kind of word had spread all the way to the Free States and Albuquerque.

I also wanted to make damn sure he didn't go anywhere near New Memphis. Very old acquaintance or not, his brand of chaos wasn't something my capital needed. Not when we were still rebuilding from the effects of my own little revolution.

"One night," I agreed. "Then we both go our separate ways provided you agree to operate *west* of the Mississippi. But the news about Wichita? That only paid for dinner."

"Then I suppose it's a good thing I've got so many more stories to tell." His grin stretched wide across his face, almost a mirror image to the yellow decal across my visor.

I didn't trust that grin. Not at all.

Not even forty-seven years later.

It was a good thing I didn't have to sleep, because I knew I'd be up and keeping watch the whole damn night.

25

Contrary to my expectations, Tonek didn't do anything that night. Not unless you count getting in the way of makeup sex and snoring loud enough to scare away any wildlife within a mile of our site anyway. The next morning, he hacked and coughed his way through a cold breakfast, slicked back his few remaining strands of hair with water from the stream, and hiked his worn canvas pack up onto one bony shoulder.

"Your Majesty," he said, licking lips that were cracked and a little bit chapped despite the warm spring morning.

"Tonek," I replied. "Always a pleasure."

"No doubt. I hope my stories last night were as educational as they were entertaining." He rolled his head around on a too-spindly neck, sending a chorus of snaps, crackles, and pops through the air. "Aren't many from our day still upright and walking anymore. Think you'll look me up next time you and your young fellow pass through Kansas City?"

"Stranger things have happened."

"Ain't that the truth." His smile *still* had pieces of food stuck in it, but the old man didn't seem to notice or care. He gave a jaunty gesture that couldn't seem to decide if it was a wave or a salute, turned about, and headed north.

He was a dozen feet out of our camp when Two-Feathers caught up with him. The two men exchanged a few words and gestures, respectively, and then my nomad passed over a small, hastily wrapped bundle. By the time Tonek had started moving again, Two-Feathers was back at my side, watching the old man march out of view.

"Food?" I asked him.

He nodded.

"I know it's part of who you are, and I don't want to change that, but… you can't believe everything you see. That man's been running cons longer than your mother's been alive. Two-Tongue Tonek doesn't need help or assistance. If you knew some of the things he had done…"

Two-Feathers' signs were short and to the point.

"That was then? Now, he's just old?"

My interpretation won me a nod and a smile; I fought off the warm glow engendered by the latter with a sigh.

"People don't change on their own, Two-Feathers. Not on the inside where it counts. All time does is add some weathering to their shells. The Old Man. Evan. Even Raya? They all stayed who they were. They just got *better* at it."

Another gesture. This one wasn't from the book of sign language but involved Two-Feathers combing back his hair and pantomiming a bowtie around his neck.

"Jules? He *really* proves my point. Man was a con artist, a thief, and a liar from the day I met him. Now, he's a politician. That's not *change*. That's *levelling up*. Or doubling down, as they'd say in the card games you both love to play."

Two-Feathers gave it some consideration but eventually conceded the point.

"Now, Tonek may be old as dirt and twice as slow, but if he can still talk, he's a long way from helpless. He's not dumb enough to start something here in camp with either of us, but if a certain nomad were to meet up with him and pass over some food… well, it wouldn't be a great shock if that nomad found he'd had the bracelets stolen right off his arm."

The nomad in question arched an eyebrow at me. He slowly peeled back his left sleeve, exposing the beaded bracelets still tightly wrapped around his wrist.

My unseen, half-formed lips beneath my true face twitched. "*Or* he's doing everything he can to reinforce that innocent old man image so he can better leverage it the next time you meet. Like I said, age doesn't change a person. It just makes them sneakier."

I wasn't entirely sure how to interpret the look Two-Feathers gave me before he started to break down the camp, but it didn't seem like he believed me. That's the problem with the young; they all feel compelled to walk the road themselves rather than learning from those who've already traveled it.

My nomad was an adult. He didn't need protection. Not from this kind of mistake, anyway. But I sure as fuck would be around to tell him *I told you so* when the time inevitably came.

○○○

There are some who claim the walls of Wichita are one of the great wonders of the post-Break world. Most of those people just happen to live *in* Wichita. Still, as one of the few cities in the Badlands that had survived first the Dream and then the Break that followed it, it's hard to deny that the city had been fully transformed. Urban sprawl disappeared, along with a vast swath of the pre-Break population, replaced with a walled fortress that housed tens of thousands. I didn't know why Kansas had managed to keep two cities whereas other states in the Badlands had lost all of theirs, and since dear old Dad had died and taken the story behind his dream with him, there was nobody to ask about it. Given that so many of the larger cities on the east and west coasts had persisted through the dream, I was assuming some sort of coastal bias, but as someone created at that same time, I had no way of knowing if the bias was warranted.

In the end, it hadn't really mattered all that much. If a city survived the Dream, it just meant it was fertile ground for the devastation and chaos that followed in the Break. Either way, people got screwed.

Wichita's walls had appeared at the beginning of it all, but it wasn't until the Millers seized control during the Break that those walls had started to grow. All these years later, they were visible from miles away, looming over the surrounding countryside much like the thick clouds emanating just to the northeast from one of the Badlands' only remaining oil refineries.

There was a saying in Wichita: *the only thing that grows faster than the city's walls is the wealth of the family that rules it.*

Change that to wealth *and* ego, and I'd happily cosign the saying. Multiple generations of Millers had ruled their city with an iron fist, and while they supposedly left Wichita's free market to develop on its own, everyone knew that any roads to lasting prosperity inevitably went through them.

All in all, I preferred the festering dung heap that was Kansas City. At least there, people *admitted* to being criminals. The hypocrisy of both Wichita and the so-called Free States further west was tougher to swallow, especially when it came hand in hand with smug elitism.

Although the walls could be seen from miles away, the crowds outside those walls only became apparent as we reached the city itself. Whatever edict had been issued to close Wichita's gate clearly remained in effect, and the result was a chaotic mass of humanity that called to mind the tent district outside Kansas' other city. Here and there, an enterprising merchant had circled their wagons, selling goods to the crowds as they themselves waited for admission. Elsewhere, some children ran back and forth, shrieking loudly as they played some incomprehensible variant of tag, and other children took advantage of that distraction to look for loose wallets or easily lifted goods.

Wichita's soldiers, smartly dressed in grey and burgundy uniforms, were out trying to keep the peace, their numbers small, but their authority strongly backed by both the rifles in their hands and the presence of more soldiers high atop the looming walls. Two-Feathers and I dismounted, and I pushed my bike through the crowd, falling in with one such platoon of soldiers as they headed for the gate. We got a few looks and a lot more murmured words from the crowd we cut through, those who recognized me from the stories more than happy to share their questionable knowledge with those who didn't.

Nobody got in our way, so I was okay with that. No angry relatives of people I'd killed showed up looking for payback either, which just proved how long it had been since I'd worked a real job. Two of the soldiers we were following noticed us, of course, and hurried on that much faster, but we reached the wall unmolested.

Wichita's gate was a bit of a misnomer, as there were actually two of them, one to the east and one to the west. Each led to wide tunnels that ran through the twenty or so feet of space that the walls' massive base occupied. Anyone who forced their way into those tunnels would find gates of equal strength on the far end, and a seemingly random scattering of small holes in the ceiling above. They might even get a brief few seconds to wonder what had made those holes and why before the boiling oil fell down upon them like a baptism of pain.

In short, trying to bust down the gates was a terrible idea that would lead to a very quick end. While the storm could survive boiling oil, Two-Feathers couldn't. And recent history had taught me it was a bad idea to let myself be trapped in tight spaces, regardless. There was no point giving potential enemies the luxury of time to figure out what *would* prove fatal.

Thankfully, I wasn't here as an invader. I had come, for the third and final time on this road trip, under the metaphorical flag of diplomacy.

The gate cracked open to let the patrol we'd been following squeeze through, while another squad kept the nearby crowd from pressing forward. Being a peaceful and law-abiding sort, I didn't try to follow the first squad in but instead left the crowd behind and went to address the squad guarding the gate.

"My adjutant and I are here to meet with the Millers," I told them. No idea how Two-Feathers felt about his newest job title, or if it was an upgrade or downgrade from both ambassador and 'my man,' but he would almost definitely tell me when we were alone again.

More important was the reaction of the soldier I spoke to, a kid barely old enough to shave, who seemed to be trying to mask that fact with the world's wispiest excuse for a moustache. He went pale, swallowed, swallowed again, and then called for his sergeant in a mild panic, wide blue eyes never leaving the smiley-face across my visor.

"What is it now, Rooks?" asked the unnamed sarge, differentiated from the rest of the soldiers only by the flak jacket worn over her uniform. The scowl on her weathered face dropped away as she turned and took me in. "The Queen of Smiles, I presume?"

"Got it in one. I'm here to meet the Millers," I said again. "They should be expecting me, unless Ambassador Diaz *really* dropped the ball."

That *was* possible… while I'd appointed Two-Feathers as ambassador to the nomads, the Council had chosen who to send to Wichita. Diaz had seemed a solid enough sort, if simultaneously a little bit young *and* stuffy, but I'd never seen his credentials. If he even had any. There was a very real possibility that he was simply the favored nephew of one of my capital's ruling elite or the son of someone rich enough to ask for the favor.

Nepotism was a style that never went out of fashion.

"I'm going to have to ask you to wait here," said the sergeant.

Here, not inside. Whatever was going on in Wichita was apparently big enough for the Millers to have a visiting queen cool her riding boots out with the riffraff. If I'd been an actual diplomat, I was pretty sure I'd have been floored by the breach of decorum.

As it was, I didn't much care. "Fine. Can you get some water for my adjutant while we wait then? I wouldn't want him to get weak with dehydration."

I felt as much as heard Two-Feathers shift behind me, my nomad no doubt doing his best to not roll his eyes.

"I'll see what I can do. If you'll excuse me?"

The sergeant didn't wait for permission, but turned and headed for the gate, her pace halfway between a forced march and an undignified retreat. She disappeared inside, leaving the rest of her squad out front with us.

"It doesn't *feel* like she went to get you water," I told Two-Feathers. "If you start feeling faint or anything, feel free to drape yourself over my bike as dramatically as possible."

My nomad grinned and shook his head, dark eyes studying the wall that rose into the air before us like it was a mountain waiting to be climbed.

About ten minutes later, the sergeant reappeared. She took up station again outside the gate, making no attempt to come fill us in on what was happening.

That wouldn't do. I headed her way, only to have Mr. Make-a-Moustache interpose himself.

"I'm... I'm going to have to ask you to stay outside the perimeter, ma'am."

"He called me ma'am," I told Two-Feathers. "You should try being that sweet sometime." And then, to the soldier. "I just want to chat with your sergeant, kid. See what's taking so long."

"The p-p-perimeter was established for a r-r-reason." I don't know if he was trying and failing to sound tough, but the teen's fingers tightened around the gun in his grasp.

The barrel wasn't pointing our way just yet, and frankly, we were close enough that I could shove the rifle up his ass before it did, but still, I held up my hands. "Then why don't you go get your *sarge* while we wait behind the perimeter? That way, everyone wins."

The sweat beading on Rooks' face had to be from more than the slightly warmer than usual temperature. I hadn't been to Wichita since before Eclipse's destruction, and I hadn't left any more chaos in my wake than usual, so I could only assume that sweat was a result of his brain churning away instead of the usual fear.

Thankfully, the sergeant had a heart buried somewhere beneath her flak jacket and fancy uniform. She made her way over while Rooks was still trying to formulate a response.

"Sergeant," I greeted her. "As a visiting *dignitary*, I was hoping to get some kind of update on what the fuck's going on?"

"I passed the word to my superior," she told me. "And Lieutenant Pina passed it to his. Beyond that, I don't know. It's all way above my pay grade."

"Can you at least tell me why the gate is closed? I know the Millers rule here, but I can't imagine their citizenry is thrilled with the loss of revenue." And then, in a further sign that this stupid diplomatic mission was leaving indelible scars on my soul, I found myself adding. "If there's some kind of crisis my adjutant and I can help with…"

"That won't be necessary," said a new man stepping out from the gate, his voice rich, and polished, like a Free States vid actor rehearsing his lines. In lieu of the sergeant's flak jacket, he had a minor explosion of ribbons across his chest and two loops of gold braided rope across his shoulders.

I wasn't up to date on military decorations, even for my own army, but something told me this *wasn't* Lieutenant Pina. His next words proved me correct.

"I am Ozias Miller, Lord High Defender of Wichita." He even posed like a vid actor, squaring his shoulders and puffing out his chest. The overall effect was slightly undercut by a weak chin and a noticeable paunch, but if New Memphis had taught me anything, it was that the rich needed their delusions.

"And I'm the Queen of Smiles," I told him, "but you already knew that."

"Yes. Baron Diaz told us you were coming."

"Baron Diaz?" I cocked my helmet. *Diaz* wasn't the rarest of last names, but it seemed odd that Wichita would have a noble with the same surname as our ambassador. And how would this baron have known about my visit?

"Your former ambassador," clarified Ozias.

"*Former?*"

"Yes." Now, he sounded almost smug. "He hadn't been in Wichita for more than a few months when he decided to defect. That tends to happen when someone escapes tyranny and oppression."

"But he's in Wichita."

"Yes, of course he is."

"Then how did he escape tyranny and…" I turned to Two-Feathers. "Oppression, right? That's what he said?"

My nomad considered the matter for a moment then nodded. The sergeant had already smartly beat a hasty retreat back to her position, but Rooks remained nearby, wide-eyed and swallowing like a man drinking water for the first time in days.

"Wichita is a *free* nation," hissed Ozias Miller, his soft face going pale except for bright spots of color blooming in his cheeks. "Nothing at all like your barbaric empire."

Like most of his family, he didn't appear to have a sense of humor. Or an off switch.

"Fair enough," I said. "That's what we're here to discuss anyway. While Diaz is free to live his life as he wishes, I will ask that he at least return his stipend. And at this point, I don't see any reason to involve him in the negotiations."

"Negotiations?" Ozias threw back his head and barked out a laugh, all the while continuing to pose like someone standing in front of a mirror. "There will not *be* any negotiations. You wanted to know why the city is closed? It is closed to *you*."

"You're going to have to explain that."

"As long as my family remains in charge of our city and country, we will safeguard it from your presence, from the shadow of a looming tyrant, the mother of abominations, and the whore of Babylon."

His words had the air of mangled pre-Break scripture, for all that he had clearly practiced their delivery, but *Babylon* wasn't a name Dr. Nowhere had included in my list of pre-Break trivia.

Whore, on the other hand, had kept its meaning just fine.

Two-Feathers shifted next to me, a subtle movement that Ozias didn't even notice, but which had the veterans in the guard squad reaching for their weapons. I stopped the nomad with an outstretched hand, a breath before the Lord High Defender of Wichita learned how well his ribbons would protect him from an eight-inch spearhead.

"Fancy uniform or not," I said, voice flat and full of metal, "I'm not sure that's your decision to make. You have a father and three older brothers after all."

He had a mother and four sisters too, but something told me they didn't get much of a say in politics.

"I speak with my father's voice," said Ozias. "We are one family and one nation, and we will never entertain the serpent at our gates. Now go. Scurry back east to your empire of sin and take your filthy savage with you."

This time, I was the one who moved, and only Two-Feathers' hand on my arm—and the knowledge of what would happen to that hand if I loosed the storm—stayed me. Which was probably good, because between the soldiers on the wall and those before the gate, there were dozens of guns pointed our way. None of them could stop me, but Two-Feathers was, in the end, only human.

"We'll leave," I said.

"See that you do. Your stench offends us all."

I wasn't sure that a nation who traded freely with Kansas City had any moral ground to stand upon, let alone a right to talk stench, but that was neither here nor there. I looked past Ozias to the soldiers behind and above him.

"Keep building that wall. You're going to need it."

Two-Feathers' hand still on my shoulder, I turned and pushed the bike back into the watching crowds.

Whatever pretty speech Ozias gave them upon our departure, I didn't want to hear it.

ooo

My fury held as we made our way out past the crowd surrounding Wichita's eastern gate. It held even as we left the city far behind in my bike's mirrors. I'd been called plenty of things by those too stupid to know they wouldn't live to regret it, but that had been different. That had been me as a lone rider, or a mercenary, or even one of a group of outlaws.

Ozias and the Millers had known I was the ruler of an empire, and they hadn't cared. They'd spat not just in my face but in the face of my people. People like Evan or the pompous windbag, Tiberius Becks, who'd died to help topple Delia Laine from her throne. People like Jules or his revolutionary girlfriend, Aaniyah.

I was a shit queen, as evidenced by this extended joyride thinly disguised as a diplomatic mission. I hadn't figured out yet what I was going to do with the empire I'd inherited, and I was sure my council talked shit behind my back, but that didn't give an inbred bunch of theocratic assholes like the Millers the right to talk shit to my face.

To say nothing of the slurs and threats directed at Two-Feathers.

Wichita's wall *was* a hell of a defense against someone like me. Too tall to scale, too thick for the storm to break or even burrow under. As much as I wanted to park Two-Feathers somewhere safe and head back for some justified homicide, I wasn't convinced I'd be able to finish the job.

But that's what armies were for, and thankfully, I had a massive one that desperately needed *something* to do. The Immortals who had ultimately proven ineffective against the storm in tight quarters would be damn near unstoppable on the battlefields they'd been trained for: heavy shock troops backed by ranged weapons and the post-Break world's version of mortar bombardment.

Show me a wall and I'll show you a cadre of Earthshakers just itching to bring that bitch down.

I would let Cyrus handle the particulars—troop movements, supply lines, and the overarching strategy—but Kansas City was just a few days' ride away, and thanks to my recent efforts there and the multiple cartels secretly under my thumb, it could serve as a staging ground for any military action further west.

Given what I'd seen of the Millers over the years, Wichita would even be better off once they were gone. Short-term pain for long-term gain, and both my generals and my councilors would be happy to rake in the rewards.

Those thoughts rolled around in my head for the next few hours: dark, bloody, and ultimately satisfying. By the time we stopped for the night, my fury had drained away, replaced with resolve and something oddly like relief.

Two-Feathers picked up on the last bit right away.

"We're done," I told him, feeling lighter than I had since leaving Eastwood. "Wichita was the last stop on this shitshow of a royal tour. As much as I'm going to make them regret turning us away like we were panhandlers begging for change, I could thank them too. Them and former-Ambassador Diaz both. Lord High Defender Miller just saved us from weeks of boring negotiations."

He gave me a questioning glance and motioned behind us in the general direction of the city we'd been denied entry to.

"Their time will come," I said. "It'll probably be winter by the time we're back from seeing Bakersfield, but that will just give Cyrus and the generals time to plan the spring campaign." I cut off what I knew would be his next objections. "We came to play nice and they made it clear exactly what they thought of that idea. I'm not giving a hostile military force time or space to grow into a real threat. Especially not one that's just a few days south of your clan's territories."

Two-Feathers looked conflicted. We'd been taught very different moralities, after all. For me, it had always been about the balance. For him, some nebulous idea of *good* and *right*.

Since our assassination of the Crimson Queen, he'd become my would-be conscience, the voice in my ear suggesting alternate, less bloody paths. I wasn't going to break him of that, not when it was a part of who he was. And not when time and too much experience would do it for me.

"If Cyrus thinks we can overthrow the Millers through something other than a full-scale attack on the city, I'll let him try it," I allowed. "God knows Raya's killer can't have been the only Immortal Delia had who was suited for infiltration and execution."

He gave a sharp nod at that, proving me right in thinking that it was the civilian casualties he'd been thinking of and not the sanctity of the Millers' own lives.

"Anyway," I said a few moments later, over the crackle of the campfire he'd just gotten started, "we did our part. We played the role of diplomats and now we can get on with our damn lives. We're a week out of Lawton. Their inventory's going to be a lot smaller, but hopefully we can get you a new horse there. And then it's nothing but you, me, and the remnants of Mexico. Not a concern to be had until we track down Bakersfield."

Two-Feathers considered my words for a long moment, then smiled. He leaned away from the fire, like a badly dehydrated man dramatically draping himself over a motorcycle, and extended his other hand toward me.

I took it and let him pull me down next to him. For a long while we just lay there, the fire at our feet and the stars above us the only lights in the world. Two people, one human, one not, sharing in each other's company, enjoying the fortune and the freedom of the road.

Wichita notwithstanding, I'd had worse times.

Six days later, we reached Lawton and found it leveled.

26

It was early evening when we started our approach to Lawton, and the first sign that something was wrong wasn't how dark it was, but how quiet. Light could be at least partially blocked by the town's walls and the trees that ringed its cleared-out fields, but sound had a way of carrying across open spaces, and Lawton was a place where the parties only got louder after the sun went down. If there weren't people fucking in the street, they were fighting instead. Hell, most of the time, it was a little bit of both.

I'd expected things to change a bit with the Old Man's death, but this was too much.

As we got closer, the reason became obvious.

Lawton… simply didn't exist anymore.

What had once been a defensible palisade was splinters and shrapnel. Where buildings had once stood, there was now only rubble. The watchtower that had given a view of the surrounding landscape had been reduced to a single jagged pole, protruding upwards from the wreckage like a middle finger to the world.

Two-Feathers was off the bike before it even stopped, spear in hands and stalking forward, but I could tell the time for stealth had passed. There was nobody left in Lawton. The carrion birds made that clear, crows as large as pre-break buzzards who ruffled their feathers at our approach but refused to give up their feast.

What had started as an aging bandit's dream and then slowly grown into a town was now just a graveyard.

I walked what remained of Lawton's streets. The devastation was shocking in its completion. Walls with more than two bricks stacked atop each other were the exception. The bodies I found were a mess, having suffered from both decomposition and the predation of the crows. Most people would have looked at that jigsaw puzzle of rubble and rotting flesh and given up any hope of putting it back together again, but I'd spent a lot of time in Lawton since the Old Man's retirement.

The scrapheap on the corner had started its life as a whorehouse, then transitioned into a trading post store, then finally settled into an uneasy blend of the two, where go-getters could get their socks on and their rocks off in the same visit. Down the way from it had been the small house where Timorous Tim lived, Lawton's resident philosopher and, when the need called for it, barber.

I picked my way through the wreckage to other familiar landmarks. The Old Man's house that had extended along much of Lawton's north wall was rubble like all the rest. The ruins of the Last Shot showed signs of fire damage, no doubt from the lantern Big Ed had kept lit by the door at night. What was left of the barkeep and tavern owner lay in what had been the building's doorway, his shotgun shattered into multiple pieces just like the door, the building, and the town itself. Big Ed's eyes were gone, along with his tongue and a good portion of his intestines, but all of that looked to be postmortem. The blow that had killed him had come from above, and while that didn't say much since the only thing big about Ed was his name, whoever or whatever had hit him had wielded some serious power; his collarbone, left shoulder, and ribcage were broken into so many parts that they must have been soup, even before the decomp started.

I spent a few long moments looking down on what was left of a generally despicable man who I had nonetheless known for almost as long as Two-Feathers had been alive. In the absence of gods to appease and with the scavengers having already taken their fill, there was little point in burying his remains. Instead, I laid the bent barrel of his shotgun across the wreckage of his chest.

The storm gnashed its metal teeth and I let its rage fill me, spinning on one heel to stalk back through the graveyard of a town. Where at first I'd been wandering almost aimlessly, now every step had purpose. I went from body to body, from wreckage to rubble, focusing not on what they might have been, but on what it was that had happened.

There had been multiple attackers. That much was obvious. Lawton wasn't New Memphis or Wichita. It wasn't even Kansas City, but it had had its share of Powers here at any given time, from Kyros, the Old Man's chief enforcer, all the way down. They would have put up a fight and at least some of the people in town would have taken that as an opportunity to run. Given the bodies in the streets, there hadn't been time for that, which suggested both that the assault had come by surprise and that all escape routes had been cut off.

The pattern repeated itself everywhere I looked. Whoever the attackers had been, they were large enough to be Titans or to give one pause, and strong enough to tear buildings down to their formation, even those built from brick or stone instead of wood. I found deep, jagged furrows in a few bodies, suggesting claws, and other corpses that had literally been torn in half.

It was the kind of scene the storm often left in its wake, only with multiple days of decay heaped on top. The problem was, I'd never been much of an investigator, let alone a trained tracker, and if the puzzle of Lawton's streets had been easy enough to put back together, the mystery of the town's fate was a significantly harder nut to crack.

Thankfully, I wasn't alone.

I found Two-Feathers looking through the wreckage down the street from the Old Man's former house.

"Any idea who or what attacked?" I asked. "All I've put together is that there were a lot of them, and they were all big and strong, possibly with claws or some sort of primitive bladed weapons. But I haven't seen a single body. Did they take their dead with them?"

Two-Feathers nodded and led me down one of the many streets I had yet to explore. Next to a fallen beam, somewhat sheltered from sun, wind, and rain, there was a mostly intact footprint, as large as my helmet and as deep as my fist. Indentations showed where claws had dug even further into Lawton's dirt road.

I stated the obvious. "Big. And heavy too. And there are the claws. Beast Shifter *maybe*, but that much mass? I'm guessing it wasn't human. Have you been able to tell if they walked on two legs or four?"

He held up two fingers.

"Two legs, massive size, claws, swift or stealthy enough to surround and surprise Lawton, and social enough to work in sizable groups *and* remove their dead after. Whatever they are, I don't like them."

Two-Feathers nodded again, dark eyes scanning the dead town around us. Here and there, an enormous crow ascended into the sky, its appetite temporarily sated. He sent me a questioning look.

"You're the tracker," I reminded him. "You've got a better chance of finding something than me."

With a grim expression on his face, he took the lead. I followed my nomad through the wreckage of the town as he examined bodies and their surroundings, looking for clues.

Finally, we stopped again, back near what had passed for Lawton's main square. There, a half-dozen bodies had fallen together. The biggest lay at the bottom of the pile, a man with heavily scarred olive skin, the remnants of a tattooed eagle across one overmuscled shoulder, and a face not even his mother had loved.

"Kyros Shah," I told Two-Feathers. "The Old Man's head enforcer. Tough bastard too. I assume he inherited control of the town after we came through last year."

The nomad said nothing, per usual, but used the butt of his spear to separate the pile of bodies. All showed similar causes of death to the people we'd found so far… either massive blunt-force trauma or evisceration by sharp claws. Sometimes, it was a mix of the two. But as Two-Feathers uncovered Kyros' corpse, we found out first fresh oddity.

"Is that… a horn?"

It sure as hell looked like one. Jet-black, curved, and shiny even in the last vestiges of the day's light, this horn had been driven *through* Kyros' chest. The Power had managed to separate it from his attacker but given the puncture hole in both sides of his body, he would have bled out soon after, even if the creature *hadn't* ripped out his spine.

I frowned down at the horn. Something about it was familiar, a piece that somehow fit with all the other clues we'd gathered so far, but *what?* There were a few beasts with horns roaming the Badlands and the northern stretches of Texas, but none of them traveled in packs or walked upright. If this was something new—

Wait. Texas.

I reached down to remove the horn from Kyros' corpse. It had been wedged against the ribs and didn't come clear until I caused some additional damage, but shortly after, I had the horn in hand. It was more than a foot long and tapered to a sharp point on one end. The other end was broken and jagged, but there were bits of flesh still attached. I'd first taken that flesh to be Kyros', stained red with the blood that had no doubt gushed out of him like a fountain, but what if that wasn't the case?

I reversed my grip on the horn and held it up to my forehead, so that it curved over my helmet like I was a minotaur from legend.

Or something even worse.

"Remind you of anything?" I asked Two-Feathers.

He planted his spear and made the sign for wings with both hands, then pointed south. Not to Lawton's gate, but past it. Way past it, all the way into Texas, where we'd once run afoul of a certain Summoner with a penchant for demons.

"Fucking Shabaa," I said.

○○○

Now that we knew what we were looking for, the signs became increasingly obvious. By the time we'd completed our investigation, suspicion had become certainty. A cadre of demons had descended upon the town, likely dropping right out of the sky to take the defenders unaware. Not that I would have given Lawton's blend of outlaws and down-on-their-luck sad sacks much of a chance against enemies that outmassed them by thousands of pounds.

Not with the Old Man dead anyway.

"I don't know if this was just a raid or a precursor to something bigger," I said later that night as we camped a good two or three hundred yards away from what had been a town for free-minded people. "Either way, it deserves a response. Tomorrow, we're going back through Lawton to find any supplies we can salvage, and then we're heading south."

We'd avoided a fire, so Two-Feathers was little more than a shadow against the star-filled sky. Thankfully, the gestures he made were less than subtle: a finger pointing at me, then a finger pointing at himself, then two hands up in the air like a question waiting to be answered.

I shook my head. "Not just us. We saw it when we rescued Jules and his crew last year. There's no telling how many demons Shabaa can summon. And he has an entire city of cultists too. Taken together, that's an army. So, it only seems fair," I added, patting my saddlebags and the thick leather-like strips that were stacked at the bottom, "that we bring ours too."

There were no fun times that night, not with demons potentially on the wing and a town of the dead waiting just over the hill. Two-Feathers slept alone in his tent and I gave the storm full rein to vent some of its rage on the world around us, a furious assault on opponents too distant to feel it. When I reformed my shell, the world was still, silent in that way that only exists a little bit before dawn, and even then, only rarely.

Two-Feathers had pitched his tent beneath two entwined trees, taking advantage of the cover they provided. Even a handful of feet away, I couldn't see it, but I knew it was there. Part of me wanted to join him within, not for sex, not even for comfort, but simply to share the space. To see and hear the breath slowly moving in and out from his lungs.

I didn't know where that impulse came from, but for all its unexpected allure, it felt borderline stalker-ish too. Creepy in a not-so-great way. So, I turned and made my way back to Lawton instead. As I made my way through what was left of its streets, the sun started to peek over the eastern horizon. Combined with eyesight that didn't rely on eyes, it was enough to do something I'd only just recently told myself I wouldn't do.

By the time Two-Feathers joined me, two holes had been dug in the field outside Lawton. I'd found a shovel, used it until it had broken, and then leveraged the storm instead, and neither hole was particularly rectangular in shape. Still, they were both deep and large enough and that was what mattered. Big Ed was already at the bottom of one hole, his rotted and crow-pecked remnants wrapped in the blanket I'd used to transport his remains. I'd laid Kyros out on the ground next to the makeshift graves and my nomad helped roll the body into its intended space. Helped again as we refilled both graves and then stamped down the dirt above.

When we were done, we just stood there for a bit, two living people standing in acknowledgement of the dead.

"Big Ed was a bastard," I finally said. "Literally and figuratively. And Kyros Shah was as mean as a mutated rattlesnake, liable to kill you as soon as look at you until the Old Man taught him patience. There weren't a lot of *good* people in Lawton, and neither of these two qualified. But this town was never about good or bad. It was about freedom. A place for the outcasts of society to gather, to fight and to feast. That was the Old Man's dream, and these two were among the first to step up and help him make it a reality."

I looked from the graves to the dead town behind them. It wasn't the first such sight I'd seen. Even Eclipse had just been another in a long line of such vistas. Anyone who survived the Break had watched cities tear themselves apart, sometimes literally, and while the scale of that destruction had diminished along with the continent's human populations, it was still something I stumbled across every decade or so; another outpost wiped clean off the map by its own inhabitants or the monsters, man and beast alike, that stalked the night.

The only difference was that this town, like Eclipse, had meant something to me. In its fucked-up way, Lawton had been the sole legacy of one of the few people I respected.

And now… this.

Beneath my true face, half-formed lips twitched in a scowl. "The Old Man's dream didn't survive for even a single fucking year after his death. It'd be funny if it wasn't sad. It'd be sad if it wasn't so damn predictable. Almost a century later, there's still only one dream that matters. And the rest of us are stuck living in it."

Two-Feathers took a step closer to me and rested a hand on my shoulder. I didn't shake it off, but I didn't let myself draw comfort from it either. This wasn't a time for comfort. Comfort could wait until justice was served. Justice or vengeance or simple punishment, whatever you wanted to call it. I was no longer bound by my creator's precepts, but there were still some laws that remained universal. Blood for blood. Carnage for carnage. Balance in all things, *especially* when it comes to the dying and the dead.

"Gather any supplies you can find that will fit on the bike," I told Two-Feathers, metal thick in my voice. "I'll have Cyrus send more along with the troops, but it's a long road to what's left of Dallas, and we were supposed to restock back in Wichita."

The nomad's hand, warm even through my riding jacket, fell away. I watched him disappear into the ruined town and then turned to my saddlebags. I removed one of Legion's creations from the bottom of the left pocket, leaving two of the devices still tucked away.

After sending messages from Eastwood and then the nomad camp, I was already running low on stolen Legion tech. Too low, with Fallen Mexico still so distant. Still, I didn't see any alternative. New Memphis was many weeks away, even by bike, and we didn't have that kind of time. The mundane army would take twice as long to reach Lawton, let alone Dallas where Shabaa was headquartered, but a fair number of the Immortals who had survived my coup in New Memphis were fliers. They could transport a hundred or so of their more offensively inclined brothers and sisters to our destination in a matter of days. They might even be waiting for us by the time we arrived.

But only if we got word to them as quickly as possible.

I placed the strip of leather that wasn't leather on the dirt at my feet, pulled the riding glove off my right hand and made a deep incision with the same knife I'd used back in Eastwood. After the debacle that had been the demon bear cave, the pain of that cut barely even registered, thick blood rising to the surface in a crimson tide. I squeezed my hand, let the blood splash down onto the strip, and waited.

And then… kept waiting.

Some of my blood seeped into the leather, but the rest splashed off its surface and onto the ground. There was none of the greedy guzzling I'd come to expect, and the technorganic creature wrapped in its wings of human skin and other things didn't stir.

I frowned, gave it a few more minutes, and then tried with the second device instead. Then the third and the last, until all three devices lay inert at my feet.

I'd traveled the continent with a bag full of the varied creations I'd stolen from Old Baltimore, payment for a job the city's Technomancer lord had reneged upon, and while each of those devices had been unique in its own disturbing way, there had never been a time or a place when one failed to activate.

Not until now.

I scowled again. There was nothing special about Lawton or its surrounding terrain. Nothing that had ever kept a Technomancer's creations from functioning in all my previous visits. And if it wasn't the location, then it could only mean one thing.

Legion, Lord of Old Baltimore, sick-minded sociopath, and younger brother to one of the two scariest people I had ever met, was dead.

Technomancers were an odd breed. Like most Powers, their abilities manifested in different ways, but even so, most built things that would outlast them. Gage's training and testing tools. The solar generators manufactured within my own empire, created by one of the long-dead founders of New Memphis. Even the self-replicating repair bots designed by the ostentatiously anonymous CEO of Things, Inc., a company that had sprouted up in the Pacific Northwest and gone under again almost as fast.

Legion was different. Obsessed with control, he had linked himself to his creations. Maybe that was where the idea of using organic material had come from, or maybe he really had just been hunting greater efficiency like he claimed, but every invention the man ever made—every disgusting automaton, every weapon, every messenger bug—had been powered by a fragment of Legion's energy.

Given the sheer scope and scale of creations involved, that kind of mental drain would have been enough to drive anyone insane, but I was pretty sure Legion had been mad to begin with.

And now, he was dead.

Dr. Nowhere. Dominion. Amos the Undying. Tyrant. Tezcatlipoca. Legion.

The old names—the great Powers—were dropping like flies. Many of those deaths left the world safer, but *all* of them left it smaller. I could count on one hand the Full-Fives who remained and still have a finger left over:

The Weaver, apparently on the last of her too-many legs, being assisted by the nomads' shamans, of all people.

Grannypocalypse, no doubt parked in her rocking chair in West Virginia, drinking a bottomless mug of tea and gazing through cloudy cataracts at the irradiated wasteland around her.

The Voidsinger, Legion's brother, who walked the land like a wraith in human form, listening to the inaudible music of the distant stars.

And Bakersfield, known to the rest of the world as Damian or Walker or even the Lord of the Dead, somewhere down in Fallen Mexico, waiting with answers.

Things fall apart; the centre cannot hold.

They were words that had been in my brain when I was first created, along with so many other snippets and half-formed fragments of thoughts or memories or images. I didn't know their origin, but they fit the moment. The world was changing, always changing. The Break was far behind us, but the reality it had left continued to shift and crumble.

I didn't know if something new would rise to replace what was being lost, what was being swallowed by the years and the seasons, or if this slow crumbling simply *was* our new reality; if the world would simply continue to shrink in upon itself, one name, one Power, one town at a time, until what was left was not just mundane but infinitesimally small.

I just knew I'd be around to see it happen.

And that nobody else I knew would.

When Two-Feathers emerged from Lawton, his pack stuffed so full I had to question how he'd ever balance it on my bike, I was already mounted.

"New plan," I told him. "We're going by ourselves."

Surprise flashed across his handsome face, and he shifted the pack on his shoulders so that he could make a handful of signs.

"As advance scouts?" I translated. "Something like that."

27

We'd been riding south for an hour or so when Two-Feathers tapped my arm. The bike's electric motor was quiet enough to talk over, but of course that didn't help him at all, so I pulled over to the side of the path we'd been following.

"What is it?"

He gestured to the sky. A cloud of birds was circling in the air over a spot somewhere deeper in the woods. They were crows again, by the looks of them, if smaller than the ones that had taken over Lawton.

"More of the town's dead?" I asked, not expecting an answer. We were far enough south already that it seemed unlikely. "Or some other battle?"

The nomad shrugged, but his gaze kept returning to the birds in the sky. Whatever it was, he clearly wanted to check it out.

And honestly? After burying two more old acquaintances and having a minor existential meltdown, I was ready for some violence.

"Fine," I said, "but I'm not risking the bike this time. We'll hide it off the trail and go on foot."

It was no sooner said than done. Once again, I let Two-Feathers take the lead. I did my best to mimic his grace and stealth, coming up woefully short on both fronts. Frankly, if stealth was my goal, I'd have been better served sneaking through the woods in only my boots, but I resisted that temptation. I'd suffered enough pain over the decades to completely recalibrate my scale of suffering, but *naked in the woods, being scratched by shrubs and prickle bushes* still sounded awful.

I intentionally lagged behind as we went, giving Two-Feathers a few extra feet of space and hopefully just as many seconds of surprise before my storm-in-a-china-shop routine would give us both away. I had been made for the road, but those roads were slowly disappearing, and I was a fish out of water in the wilderness replacing them.

We walked for about twenty minutes, and Two-Feathers never once stopped to reassess our direction. The woods were thicker the deeper we went, and the canopy of branches and fresh green leaves meant we couldn't see the circling crows anymore. Still, I was happy to follow in his footsteps. The nomad had better senses than I did, if more limited in a few distinct ways, and he moved like a man who knew where he was going.

Finally, he pulled to a halt, flashing a sign that predated the book we'd found in New Memphis and which anyone would recognize to mean *stop*. I came up beside him and peeked through the foliage.

We'd found a clearing of sorts, created by two trees that had fallen at some point in the past. A murder of crows sat in the clearing, one occasionally flapping back into the sky only to be replaced by another. Their numbers were so thick that it was hard to see what they were feasting on. I did at least get the impression of size; bodies bigger than a human's, if not quite as large as one of Shabaa's demons.

"What did they find?" I asked, helmet to Two-Feathers' ear as I did my best to whisper. "Can you tell?"

In answer, he pointed past the swirling cloud of feathers and beaks to the far side of the clearing.

If I'd had fully formed eyes, I would have blinked. Instead, I just dumbly stared for a moment.

A horse stood there, mere feet away from the winged scavengers. It had a saddle on its back but no bridle and appeared to be calmly chewing its way through the grass around it, unmindful of the death so nearby.

I refocused on the crows and was able to pick out some additional details under the shifting mass of black feathers and sharp beaks: a hoof there, hair from a mane or tail there. At least two other horses—likely three, given the number of birds—lay sprawled out in the clearing, though it wasn't clear what had killed them. Or why the fourth horse was so unmoved by their deaths.

Two-Feathers pointed to himself then the horse.

"Be careful," I told him, still watching the beast in question. "I think it might be a sociopath."

I stayed behind, just in case my presence would spook the beast where the death and slow desecration of three of its kind had not. Two-Feathers didn't head through the clearing, but circled around instead, leaving the crows to their feast. I lost track of him almost immediately, but a few minutes later, he appeared near the horse.

It lashed its tail, side to side, but a few pats on its long neck and a handful of what looked like dried fruit from the rations soon had it turning into Two-Feathers instead, butting its head against his broad chest like it was a cat. When the nomad made his way back around to me, the horse followed placidly after.

Not a sociopath then. Just really, really dumb.

Or maybe Two-Feathers was part Druid. Some of them were good with animals instead of plants.

My presence didn't seem to set off any red flags for the horse, which lowered my estimation of its intelligence even further. But at least that meant we wouldn't have a breaking-in period as we traveled, assuming my nomad could get the beast to let him ride it.

Another dried fruit had the horse following us all the way back to the road, where Two-Feathers fished a bridle out of his pack. *His* bridle, in fact; I recognized the rope of braided hair.

"You kept your bridle?"

He nodded and went to put it on. The new horse accepted it without any sort of fuss, but then that seemed to be its general reaction to the world at large. I'd known a few people like that. They tended to end up dead or fabulously rich.

"I'm guessing it and the others escaped Lawton's stables. But any idea what killed the rest?"

It took a few signs, and then more pantomiming when I didn't recognize some of those signs, but eventually I got the picture.

Assassin mosquitoes. They weren't usually a concern this far west. I scanned the road, looking for any indication of the foot-long monsters, but found nothing. They must have drunk their fill and returned to their nest. It was pure luck that three horses had been enough for them when there were four available.

Either that or the new horse is some sort of double agent, working for the mosquitoes…

I shook my head. Even if the giant insects had been known to have any shred of intelligence at all, one look at the utter blankness in the horse's big brown eyes told me it did not.

Dumb *and* lucky.

I helped Two-Feathers transfer his packs from my bike to his new steed. The nomad tightened the saddle, then sprang up into that saddle, and the horse did little more than prance slightly to the side, tail swishing now like it wanted to show off.

"Huh," I said. "That was easy."

Two-Feathers' smile came and went, but I could practically feel the smugness radiating off him.

○○○

All the good-weather luck we'd had so far on the road finally ran out. It rained for four straight days, turning what was already the mere suggestion of a road into a muddy quagmire. Impromptu ponds formed in our path as the rain continued and streams and rivers already full to bursting with runoff from the mountains further north overran their banks and flooded the surrounding lands.

My bike was as weather proofed as an early Technomancer and a succession of mundane mechanics could make it, but that didn't help much when the water was waist high. Multiple times a day, we had to make our way forward on foot, Two-Feathers leading his mount and me literally carrying the bike over my head to keep it out of the drink.

Can't say I loved any of it. Can't say I didn't blame the horse either. After all, the weather had been just fine until *it* showed up.

The beast in question didn't have a name. I just called it *horse* and Two-Feathers obviously didn't call it anything at all. The two of them were already practically inseparable though, even after only a few days. Whenever the horse managed to rub its two brain cells together and muster up some sort of spark of a thought, it would follow the nomad around like a puppy or small child. The rest of the time, it just did its own thing, untroubled by the water falling from the sky, the water pooling around its legs, or even the foul-tempered woman in black cursing up a blue streak as she reformed her shell for the twentieth time.

Every new shell came with a fresh set of dry riding clothes, after all. For about fifteen seconds. Then, I was just damp and cold all over again.

It was *still* raining when we crossed into Texas. There were no signposts—not anymore, not after so long—but I knew it. There was something in the dirt or the air that had always made Texas different. Even *during* the Break, it had been its own place—sometimes better, often worse, always itself—and that feeling persisted all these years later.

Texas was Texas. The Badlands were the Badlands. And no matter how similar the two might look at first glance, only a fool believed it.

"Keep your eyes on the skies, boys," I told Two-Feathers and his idiot horse. "We're in it now. Any birds you see won't be crows."

Two-Feathers got a little pinched around the eyes, no doubt remembering our encounter with the Terrorbirds, the steel-winged and steel-beaked birds of prey that owned Texas' skies. We'd lost one man and most of our horses in that encounter and were beyond lucky to have come away so easy.

There were three great horrors that made Texas their home, and I prayed my nomad would never meet the other two. Because if he did, I didn't think I'd be able to protect him from them. The Terrorbirds were a nightmare. The Hunger that Walks was worse. And the White Wail…

I shivered and reformed my shell again.

Goddamn rain made everything cold.

ooo

The rain followed us into Texas like a bad habit, only slowing us down further. Still, we fell back into a rhythm. The horse added a new wrinkle, but it was one we were familiar with, and if the beast wasn't as well-trained or half as smart as Two-Feathers' last one, well, it was at least less likely to wander off and get into mischief too.

As for my nomad and me, it took us most of that time before I found my way back into his tent. It wasn't just the rain, or what we'd seen in Lawton, or even the very real threats that Texas presented, but instead a combination of the three. Thankfully, the physical side of our relationship was new enough and fresh enough to eventually overcome those concerns. No fire, because the rain didn't allow for that. Just rations for the nomad, grass and a bit of grain for the horse, and two sweaty bodies finding each other in the darkness.

I'd have wondered what the horse thought of all that if I'd truly believed the creature thought at all.

Finally, the rain stopped. Blue sky broke out from behind its steel-grey curtain, followed soon by the early-summer sun. The land around us took longer to dry out, for new streams to turn back into the trailways they'd begun at and for lakes to revert to rivers instead, but by the second day, travel was close to what it had been before the rains began. Never easy, not in the post-Break world, and not when what had been a nation of roads had become a continent of trails… but easier, at the very least.

On the third day, we reached Dallas.

Like many of the cities in the country and continent, Dallas had been changed by the Dream and the Break that followed. I'd never seen the original version, but the collection of useless trivia in my head said that the city had once had three professional sports teams and that somehow meant it had been important. *Why* was a detail dear old Dad apparently hadn't deemed necessary to include.

Regardless, I was pretty sure Dallas had fallen as far as any municipality in the country. *Including* Kansas City. What had once perhaps been urban sprawl was now almost entirely ruins, decrepit shells of former buildings overgrown and reclaimed by the surrounding wilderness. It was only as you followed the river south, past the rubble of long-broken dams and eroded levees, that you found buildings still standing. Even those were little to write home about… multiple stories, yes, the last vestiges of the city's downtown, but if they'd ever had glass in their windows, that glass was long-since gone. Empty holes in weathered and worn concrete stared back at us like eyes that had seen too much.

There were people living there. We knew that much. This was where Shabaa had established his cult. The Summoner had arrived from elsewhere, years back, and encountered the city's surviving population, slowly starving to death as people fought each other for scraps in the ruins of their once-great city. Food had been his initial currency for conquest, and I wasn't sure if it was that food being literal demon meat that had driven his followers mad or if the madness had come separately, but mad they were. Mad and numerous. Our best estimates were that there were still *at least* several thousand people in Dallas, without even counting the demons.

That's why I'd wanted to call in my army. Without military support, I was pretty sure even the storm would get tired before the killing was done.

But thanks to Legion getting his ass killed, we didn't have that army. We were going to have to make do. And if we *were* going to attack a force that didn't just have vastly superior numbers but also a bunch of Powers in its ranks, we needed more than just the storm and Two-Feathers' spear. We needed a plan. We needed information.

I hadn't lied to Two-Feathers… we *were* here as advance scouts.

I just didn't plan to stop there.

Justice required blood. Vengeance required a city's worth of it.

If the woman we'd known as Selene had been with us, and not a fugitive I very badly wanted dead, we might have been able to ask her ghosts for more information. That was how she'd helped Jules originally, after all. With just the two of us, that wasn't an option. Nor were we going to hatch a plan of any substance here, where we couldn't see much of anything. We needed to get closer and we needed to find the high ground… somewhere that gave us a view of more than just ruins and the hint of buildings.

I scanned the area ahead of us for a raised position. The region that had once been Dallas was predominantly flat, river cutting through a carpet of grey and green. Sunlight reflected off a lake to the far east and while I could just make out the shape of a single low hill to the city's south, it was far too short to offer much of a view. To the west, however, was a stone ridge that might offer a better vantage point. It wasn't as high as I would have preferred, nor as close to downtown, but we weren't particularly spoiled for choice.

I pointed it out to Two-Feathers, who nodded. My nomad wasn't a professional in these matters, not in the way some people I'd ridden with had been, and there were times I wondered if he was too soft for my kind of work. And yet he'd still managed to grasp exactly what I was looking for and why without me even saying a word.

Hell if I was letting him go now that he'd chosen me.

It took several hours to circle around to the back of the ridge, and by the time we did, the sun was starting to set behind us. I parked my bike, Two-Feathers dismounted, and the two of us made our way up the steep incline. This side of the ridge was lusher than the sheer cliff facing Dallas, and the wind out of the west a near constant presence. I did my best to follow my nomad's footsteps and minimize all the noise I was making.

It took a good minute or so—maybe a hundred steps, all-in— before I realized *I* wasn't the one making the noise. I came to a stop and Two-Feathers' horse brushed right past me, intent on following its friend, or owner, or the random two-legged person it had imprinted on as the giver of apples.

My sigh brought Two-Feathers up short in a way the noise of the horse hadn't. Part of me knew he was probably just accustomed to the racket I made, but a greater part thought the man should have been able to tell the difference between the woman he slept with and a seven-hundred-pound, four-hooved animal.

Then again, *I* hadn't realized it was the horse making all that noise at first either.

"I think you're going to have to tie that thing up," I told the nomad. "At least until you've had more time to train it."

Two-Feathers looked about for a suitable hitching post. As much vegetation as there was on our side of the hill, the nearby trees were small and thin, unlikely candidates for restraining anything larger than a non-mutated bunny. Above us, two earthen mounds formed an unlikely passageway between them, but beyond that passageway, I could see a tree that looked like it might fit the bill.

Two-Feathers spotted it too. He took hold of his horse's bridle, lest it wander off and somehow bring all three of the great horrors of Texas down upon us and headed up.

The passage we'd seen stretched for almost thirty feet, and I spent the first ten of those feet trying to figure out how the hell it had been formed. Wind seemed to fall equally on the western side of the ridge making the cause more likely to be rain, but while I knew well the destructive nature of water, the placement here was odd. Maybe there'd been a lightning strike in a recent storm, burning off the vegetation and leaving this small stretch of terrain that much more susceptible to erosion?

Hell if I knew. I did my best to put it out of mind.

We were twenty feet in when the dirt walls on either side of us fell away, like snow melting in the sun. Two-Feathers reacted just as quickly as I did, but before we could take a step, we were surrounded, a dozen rifles pointed at us from behind dirt bulwarks. At the same time, the earth beneath our feet liquefied. The three of us—me, Two-Feathers, and his horse—all sank into the ground before that same dirt solidified again around us.

Just like that, we were trapped.

28

All I had to do to free myself was dismiss my shell. I could reform it above the earth or just let the storm have its way with what appeared to be gun-wielding humans. The problem was, Two-Feathers and his mount were both at least temporarily caught, sitting ducks if bullets started flying. I wasn't going to take that risk unless I had to.

"You can shoot the horse," I told our ambushers and the unseen Earthshaker who was definitely with them, if somewhere further back in one of the two tunnels. "But if you touch the nomad, we're going to have ourselves a problem."

Two-Feathers couldn't quite turn all the way about, but he still sent me a look over one shoulder.

The horse in question was currently stretching its long neck out to one side at an awkward angle, doing its best to get at one of the nearby shrubs. It was a solid two feet short of reaching it, but didn't seem to realize that. Nor had it even penetrated its pea-sized brain that it was stuck in the dirt with the rest of us.

Even so, I found myself clarifying.

"Actually, don't shoot the horse either. It's too dumb to die."

"Nobody's going to die," said a woman's voice, deep with more than a hint of Texas drawl in it. "At least not until I learn why a motorcycle mama and a nomad are trying to climb my little hill."

I'd left my bike back at the base of the ridge, so either the speaker had eyes down there or she knew who I was. And I was betting on the latter, because her voice was oddly familiar. It made me think of New Mexico, of the town where dear old Dad had met his end, and of the young woman I'd last seen standing alone in the middle of a field of dead.

But... what had her name been?

"Is that you, short stack?"

"Like I told you back then," said the woman in question, stepping out from behind the armed men and women, "size isn't everything."

"If that were true, you wouldn't have dropped the three of us down to *your* height." I knew the smile across my visor had gone wild and manic. "It was Silt, right?"

"Yeah. Yeah, it was. At the time at least. These days, I go by my given name, Sofia. And here you are, exactly as I remember."

That made one of us, because Sofia had changed. Still squat, strong, and dressed in earthen shades that almost matched her skin and thick brown hair, yeah, but that hair spilled past her shoulders now and had been pulled back from a face with a few more lines and a hell of a lot less softness. The biggest change was in her brown eyes. There was a weight that hadn't been there when we'd met. A weight that came only through age and responsibility and more than a few deaths.

I knew where and when at least some of those deaths had happened. I'd been there, after all, for Bakersfield's official unveiling to the world as a Full-Five, as the Lord of Death, as the killer of Dr. Nowhere and a whole lot of others besides. But as for the rest?

Again, hell if I knew.

But the young woman had become an adult.

It had been years, so I guess that should've gone without saying, but it was still a shock. I was pretty sure she was Two-Feathers' age now. Maybe even older.

"Aren't you supposed to be east of the Mississippi, ruling an empire or something?" Silt asked me.

After Two-Tongue Tonek, I was no longer surprised to find that word had spread. "I've got advisors for that kind of stuff. The three of us? We're headed south."

She waved a muscled arm in a direction perpendicular to the path we'd been hiking. "South is that way."

"Yeah, well… we figured we'd stop, see the sights, and maybe do some pest control along the way." I didn't know why someone from the Free States—let alone one of their vaunted Capes—was all the way out in Texas, but she and the men and women surrounding us seemed way too sane—and fully clothed—to be part of the Summoner's cult.

Sofia's eyes flicked to the east, as if she could see through the ridge we were standing on, and then back to me.

"Shabaa."

It wasn't a question, but I answered anyway.

"Wiped out a town a week or so north of here. Little place called Lawton."

"I've never heard of it."

"That makes one of us." I shrugged, my arms the only thing not currently pinned by the earth. "We went there for information, but it was in short supply, seeing as how everyone in the town had been killed by demons."

Two-Feathers gave a not-at-all-authentic-sounding cough, and sent me another look, patting the earth that imprisoned him.

"Oh, right." I turned back to Sofia. "Mind letting him out? I can't vouch for the actions of his horse, but Two-Feathers, at least, is good people."

"I'm not sure you get to make that judgment."

"Huh. You were more fun the first time we met."

The Earthshaker sighed. "A whole lot of things were different then. But if even half of what I've heard about you is true, this trap of mine isn't any more effective against you than my people's guns."

"I figured I'd let you have your moment," I agreed, "but they're both equally useless, yeah."

"Fair enough." With one hand, she ordered her companions to lower their weapons. With the other, the ground beneath our feet firmed back up, pushing us to the surface. I reformed my shell, just to clean it, Two-Feathers squatted down to brush the dust from his pants, and the horse finally got up close and personal with that shrub it had been eyeing.

Basically, everyone won.

"Introductions first," said the woman I now towered over. "I'm Sofia Black, one-time Cape of the Free States and current Lady Protector of the Brownsville territory way down on the south edge of Texas. These are some of my troops. The grey-haired man to my right who looks like he's sucking on a lemon is Rocco. He's my second on this little excursion and a whole lot nicer than he looks. When we're done, the others can give you their names or not, as they like."

I turned my true face to sweep across the people standing with Silt, still conscious of those at our back. The sour-faced Rocco got a nod, the rest just the smile I carried with me. Most looked petrified to meet me. That wasn't as satisfying as it should have been; scared people did dumb things, and my nomad was only mortal.

I stepped forward to keep all eyes fixed on me. "And as I guess most of you have already gathered, I'm the Queen of Smiles, the new ruler of the Crimson Empire after my predecessor choked on a whole lot of nothing and died." I waved to Two-Feathers. "That's Two-Feathers. Yes, he's a nomad. No, he doesn't talk. And hell no, he's not half as funny as he thinks he is. As for the horse? The less said, the better, to be honest."

I ignored whatever new look the nomad was sending my way and focused on Silt.

"The southern end of Texas is almost as distant as my empire. What are you all doing this far north?"

"Same thing as you, it turns out."

"Shabaa?"

"He's been hitting merchant caravans. About a week ago, he took down an entire wagon train of settlers."

"Dead?"

"Only some of them. The rest—women and children mostly— got taken back to Dallas. We're here to get them back."

"All…" I did a quick headcount. "…twelve of you?"

"There are a few more on the way." Her smile was as cold as mine, for all that there was a humanity to it that my true face would never have. "In the meantime, we've set up here to do some recon."

"Because it's the only high ground overlooking Dallas."

"Got it in one." She tapped the side of her nose. "I don't suppose you brought your army with you?"

"For just one city? Please. That's way too much paperwork." I ignored another cough from Two-Feathers, this one sounding vaguely strangled. "Still, it sounds like we've got common cause."

"Boneboy trusted you," said Sofia, using a nickname that I could only assume was for Bakersfield. "Can't say I know why, not really, but can I do the same?"

"It depends on the terms, to be honest." I listened to the words I'd just said and sighed internally. I'd spent *way* too much time at the negotiating table lately.

She grunted and gave it a moment's thought. "We work together—you, your man, and my forces—then we all go our own ways in peace. You leave me and mine alone and we do the same. Does that work for you?"

"Maybe." I had to ask. "How do you feel about Wichita?"

"I do my best not to, if I'm being honest. Only been there twice and the whole place was a little uptight for my tastes. Any trade outside my territory involves heading west. Why?"

"Just making sure." I stuck out my hand, waited for hers, and then we shook on it. "You've got a deal."

And that was that. Just two women coming to a decision like rational, fair-minded people, without endless days of deliberation or painstakingly crafted legal documents. The world was a toilet and that was never changing, but even so… it would be a hell of a lot better if more deals could be struck that way.

ooo

Sofia led us into what she called her office, even though it was really just a large cave at the very end of the tunnel. An empty section of the space had been segmented off for some reason, its floor slightly raised and smooth as glass. The rest of the cave held a few beds, a table, and multiple chairs.

All the furniture was made of dirt, which was a new experience, even for me. I took my seat gingerly, while giving the walls around us an appraising glance. Those at least were stone.

"You can work with both rock and earth?" I asked, impressed despite myself. A lot of Earthshakers only did one or the other. Some were even more specialized than that.

The other woman shook her head. "Just good old-fashioned dirt. But this whole ridge here is limestone. The caves and crevasses already existed when we arrived… I just had to reach them and make them livable." She walked over to the table that I was seated next to. "Have you gotten a look at what's left of Dallas yet?"

"From the north and only at a distance."

"I'm guessing you'll be wanting to see it with your own eyes too, but in the meantime, I can fill you in on what we've discovered in the last couple of weeks."

"You've been here *weeks*?"

She scowled. "We don't all have an empire to do our bidding. The people with me were the only ones I could spare from guarding my towns. That means we had to seek outside help and that sort of thing takes time."

As she spoke, the thick surface of the table shifted. Hard-packed dirt rearranged itself into the shape of a half-dozen tall buildings, twenty or so smaller ones, and a wall that encircled the whole place.

"Downtown Dallas," she said. "Way I hear it, the wall showed up overnight. Apparently, there was some sort of fort in the area before then. Somehow, old Pete got the two mixed together in his dream, and just like that, downtown had itself some defenses."

Pete meaning *Dentist Pete*, the real name for the man the world called Dr. Nowhere and I called Daddy Dearest.

I stood from my chair again and leaned over the table, Two-Feathers a warm presence at my side. If this diorama was to scale, it meant the area we were looking at had to be several square miles. Even given the dilapidated state of the high-rises, that was significant for an urban center.

"How many people does Shabaa have living in there?"

"That's a bit harder to say. We think his cult tops out at around a thousand armed combatants, but then you have his High Council, the working class, and the serfs."

"Serfs?"

"People taken prisoner in raids or sometimes, local folk who fell out of favor with the ruling elite. Might be some captives from your town down there too."

I thought back to Lawton's utter destruction. "I don't think so. It was just demons and they don't seem interested in captives."

"True enough. Which brings me to the real reason it's hard to know their numbers: those demons. Near as we can tell, Shabaa can summon at least a dozen of them at a time."

"More than that," I said, remembering our last encounter with the man's troops here in Texas. "I've seen at least three dozen of the ones with wings… and that was after killing quite a few of the landbound variety."

"Well, shit. He keeps getting stronger."

I turned to face the other woman. "You've dealt with him before?"

"Yeah. Back when he was my uncle's drug-addicted lackey in Brownsville, he only ever managed one of the damn things at a time."

"You actually *know* him."

"Sort of. Used to go by Steve. Liked hallucinogenics, moonshine, and hurting women, not necessarily in that order."

"And your uncle kept him around?"

"They had that last bit in common." She kept her voice even, but those brown eyes were as hard as the stone she couldn't shape. "After I served my time in the Free States, I went back to Brownsville with some friends and freed the place. Uncle Manuel got what was coming to him, as did a few of my cousins, and a lot of other animals who thought themselves men. Steve was wounded but got away. We figured he'd bled out somewhere until word slowly trickled south about what was happening in Dallas. *Shabaa the Demon Summoner*, preaching his gospel. Even then, I figured he'd end up dead in a ditch once his cult got tired of him. Guy was never big on leadership. Or hygiene."

"Instead, he flourished," I finished for her. "And now he's a pain in all our asses."

"That's the short of it, yeah. Even when my extra help gets here, we can't take on Shabaa and his entire cult." She pointed at a small section of the city. There, the buildings were all squat, single-story things, far longer than they were tall. "My goal is to free the serfs and do whatever damage we can in the process. Set his progress back, maybe get some internal discord started too."

"They'll give chase," I said, speaking from experience. "Last time I dealt with Shabaa, it took the Terrorbirds to get his troops off my ass."

The Earthshaker twitched. "I heard the birds were roosting way the hell up northeast of here."

"They were. At the time anyway. The cult chased us for days."

"Well, that won't be a problem for us."

I waited, but that was all she was willing to say on the matter.

"Why not cut the head off the snake instead?" I suggested.

Two-Feathers stiffened next to me.

"Like you did with your predecessor, you mean?"

"Yeah, except the Crimson Queen had a personal forcefield that required some delicate planning." I let the storm rattle about inside of me, metal scraping on metal. "From your description, it sounds like Steve is just flesh and blood."

"With a dozen or more Powers defending him and all those demons besides," she reminded me, tapping the center high-rise. "Besides, getting to his headquarters means getting past the rest of his cult. I saw a little of what you could do outside the City of the Sun, but unless your nomad is the Singer in disguise or Dominion's second coming, I don't see it happening. Now, if you want to come back here with your army *after* we've evacuated the city of innocents…"

It was my turn to shake my head. "It'll be a while before I make it back to New Memphis. Months, most likely."

"You sure must trust those advisors of yours a whole heap to leave them the keys of the kingdom so soon after taking your throne."

"One of them, yeah. As for the rest… they'll keep in line if they know what's good for them."

"Got to be honest, I got a little chill up and down my spine when you said that just now, so maybe there's something to it. But where the hell are you heading that's going to keep you away that long."

As a former Cape, I didn't trust Sofia any further than Two-Feathers could throw her, but she *had* been Bakersfield's friend. And that meant meeting her was an unexpected opportunity, especially with Lawton's destruction.

"Like I told you before," I replied. "We're headed south. As far as we have to go."

She caught her breath. "You're looking for him. For Damian."

"Damian. Walker. Bakersfield." After a moment, I added the nickname she'd given him outside. "Or Boneboy. Whatever name you want to give him."

"Can I ask why?"

I showed her the smile across my true face. "We never got a chance to talk after the City of the Sun."

Her broad face clouded. "He's not—"

Motion came from the back of the room, from the raised platform clear of any furniture. A swirling spiral of shadow had appeared there with a core of darkness at the center.

I tried not to sigh. *What fresh hell was this?*

29

Unsurprisingly, Two-Feathers had been the quickest of all of us to react. He was already crouched, spear in hands, awaiting whatever might emerge from the portal. I stepped up beside him, the storm roaring within my shell. Together, we watched as that portal collapsed again, depositing two people in the cave.

One was a woman about Sofia's age. She was a head shorter than the Earthshaker but twice as wide—big enough to make Dorothea back in Kansas City seem almost svelte. If I'd ever seen her before, I didn't remember it, but the way the collapsed portal sank back into her chest told me she was its owner.

Which was interesting, because the other person was *also* a Teleporter. And him I actually knew.

A face that was already heavily lined under the worn fedora went pale as the man the Free States called Door spotted me. I held my ground, putting a hand on Two-Feathers' shoulder.

"Long time, Door."

"And yet you look the same as ever." His voice had changed in the last few decades, trading some of its depth for a scratchy quality almost as thin as the brim of his treasured hat. "First, I heard you were dead, then I heard you were royalty."

"I've *always* been royalty," I reminded him.

The other Teleporter was a lot slower on the uptake, but when she finally responded, it was to whirl on Sofia.

"Silt, that woman is the Queen of Smiles!"

"No codenames here, Evie," said Sofia, her voice gentle. "You're not doing this as Capes, remember?"

"That's not the point! Why is someone on the Security Council's Most Wanted list *here*?"

"She kind of wandered in all on her own," admitted the Earthshaker. "Turns out she's here for the same reason we are."

"*She* wants to rescue some prisoners?"

"*She* can speak for herself," I said. "And not particularly, no. But Shabaa needs to be put down. I guess I'm willing to take a chance on people with questionable moral character if it means ending his threat."

That reduced the oversized woman to splutters of indignation, which suited me just fine. In the meantime, Sofia turned to Door.

"Thanks for coming. Given how tight the timing is for everyone, we wouldn't have been able to do this without you."

"Not everything that needs to be done can be done as Capes. My team thinks I'm taking a spa week," he told her, before hefting the bulky bag he held in one hand. "If you don't mind, I'm going to get started? I'll have to prepare the space before I can open any doors here."

"Please, go ahead. The others are already waiting. Right, Evie?"

The other Teleporter nodded. "Yes. I contacted them just before we came. They're gathering at the two locations Door—*Francis* specified."

Kneeling on the platform, looking at who knows what, Door winced. "Just call me Door," he said. "There's not much point in hiding my codename when my power gives it away at a glance. If word gets back to my team or the government, well, I'll deal with it then."

I gave Silt a look. "You're bringing in Capes from the Free States?"

"Friends and allies, yes. Part of our deal needs to be you keeping their involvement quiet. The new administration is prickly about Capes operating outside their borders."

"I have no interest in talking to the Free States' government, now or ever."

Of course, once I took Wichita, I'd probably *have to*, as we'd practically be neighbors at that point, but I had people for that sort of thing. I'd just have to make sure whoever we sent *wasn't* going to defect within days of arrival.

Regardless, tattling on Capes wasn't how I got my kicks.

"Sofia," said the Teleporter called Evie, "can I talk to you for a second? Alone?"

"Don't mind us," I said. "Two-Feathers and I will just wander over to the far side of the cave."

While the other two women huddled up a good distance away for what was no doubt a discussion that had nothing to do with my presence, I headed over to Door. Two-Feathers followed.

The older man was on one knee. He'd dumped out the contents of his bag: a bunch of slats of polished wood, all loosely joined together by pieces of wire. Off to the side was more wood, this time in square panels.

"I'm going to have to ask you to keep your distance," he said, not even looking up. "This will go a lot faster without having to adjust for footprints or shifting dirt."

"What are you doing?" As I watched, he took two of the pieces of wood and twisted them together, a counterclockwise motion causing the piece of wire extending from each end to disappear into the upper portion's wooden core.

"What does it look like I'm doing?"

"Playing in the dirt?"

"My power lets me connect any two doors I've used with a portal," he said. "But sometimes, you find yourself out in hellholes like this one and doors are in short supply." He attached another piece of wood to the growing frame, and I finally got it.

"So, you bring your own?"

"Yeah. I've got an automated version that assembles itself, but it's checked into the team armory. I remove that, people would have some questions about what kind of spa weekend I'm taking. This is an older model. It's a pain in the ass to put together, but nobody even remembers I have it. Now if you don't mind, I'm going to need some space and quiet. There's more to making this all work than just the door itself."

The two women were still having their face-to-face, so Two-Feathers and I found a different stretch of wall to hang out by. I lowered my voice.

"Are you okay? Seemed to be a lot of coughing and choking going on."

My nomad gave me a look that needed no translation, then followed it up with an array of signs that did.

"I wasn't planning on assaulting the city by ourselves," I told him. "And a handful of people with guns doesn't change that equation. But if everyone Door brings through is a Power, things might change."

More signs.

"I don't know Evie, but Sofia was one of Bakersfield's classmates and friends back at the Academy of Heroes. A good enough one that he left her alive even when he lost his shit and killed everyone else. Given their similar ages, I'm guessing the Teleporter is from that same class, which raises the possibility that *everyone* Door will be bringing in is. Maybe the lot of them can get something done against Shabaa, maybe they can't. Worst comes to worst, we'll at least have a better idea of how to assault Dallas with the army next spring."

I couldn't tell what he thought of that, and his fingers weren't flashing to show me either. But after a moment, he sighed and signed his acceptance.

It wasn't enthusiastic, but he didn't seem nearly as annoyed with me about my ever-changing definition of *scouting out the city*, so I'd take it.

"In the meantime," I added, "I'm guessing at least one of them will be able to give us better directions to Bakersfield than the *somewhere in Fallen Mexico* shit we're going off now. And we'll probably be able to replenish our supplies again too."

More signs. It was my turn to sigh.

"Yeah, I'll see if they have any fresh fruit for your horse."

Two-Feathers grinned, just enough to leave me questioning whether he'd been fucking with me the whole time… if the whole point of the conversation had been to get his idiot horse an apple. Still, my true face didn't do suspicious all that well and I'd gotten what I wanted too, so I just let it go.

"Watch your back," I said instead. "I don't know how many Powers will be coming, but I have to imagine this Evie won't be the only one less than enthused to see us."

He didn't reply, but his eyes strayed over to the two women. The Teleporter was still gesturing wildly as she spoke, while Sofia seemed prepared to ride out the tempest with a noncommittal look on her broad face.

More signs from Two-Feathers and I took another look at Evie.

"You're right. She *has* changed." I couldn't explain it, but the Teleporter looked *smaller* than when she'd first arrived, the grey jacket and black pants no longer quite so tight on her frame. If I didn't know better, I'd have thought she'd lost five to ten pounds, just by standing there.

Maybe she was a Body Shifter as well as a Teleporter? But if that was the case, why would—

A dozen feet away, Door heaved himself back up to his feet, knees cracking and popping like one of the breakfast cereals that hadn't survived the Break. His project was fully assembled now and standing upright from a small base, the frame holding a simple two-panel door within. The knob was brass, old, and heavily tarnished; it looked small in Door's stubby fingers.

The older Teleporter turned the knob and pulled, opening the doorway onto another place entirely. I had a brief view of what appeared to be a lushly appointed apartment before several people came through in single file.

The first was tall and all in white, from her long hair down to low heels better suited for a boardroom than a battlefield. As she stepped through the doorway, she was swiftly followed by another woman, fit and lovely, with dirty-blonde hair in braids and eyes the color of the sea. I didn't have to see more than those first two steps to know that the second woman was a Stalwart, like Two-Feathers.

Next came a smaller man with a round face, close-cropped dark hair, and a mustache and goatee like an early vid star villain. The fourth and final person through the gateway was twice the size of the third, so big he had to be a Titan or Shifter, deeply tanned, and bare-chested except for pants in a virulent shade of yellow.

All four spotted Sofia and Evia and made their way over to the other two women, who had stopped their argument when the portal first opened and now turned to give welcome.

Behind them, Door closed his portal, took a long, deep breath, and then opened it again. This time, it showed a warehouse of some kind, shelves stocked with unknown supplies. And then, the parade of strangers continued.

The first one through the door this go-around could have stepped right out of a recruitment poster. Hell, I'd have hired him to pose for one of mine. Blond hair, blue eyes, and chiseled features, he moved with some of the same grace as the earlier Stalwart, strong, fit, and always in control.

Unlike the others, who had all almost definitely been part of the infamous Class of 76 along with Bakersfield, I could identify this one. Mainly because the resemblance to his father was undeniable. The original Paladin, the leader of the Defenders all the way back before this whelp had even been born, was a monster of the old-school variety, his all-white costume regularly drenched in red blood.

I'd heard conflicting rumors about how well the son who'd inherited his Cape name filled his old man's shoes, and seeing him now, I had to side with the naysayers. There was a certain look to hardened killers, and for all his handsomeness, this man didn't have it. He might as well have been wearing his costume, along with a sign saying *Hero* in flashing neon.

After the younger Paladin came someone almost as pretty, a woman with blonde hair and silver eyes that glowed with their own light. *Literally* glowed… they lit up the shallow confines of the increasingly full cave in a way the lanterns hadn't.

A Lightbringer then. If she was strong enough, she would definitely come in handy. And if things went bad, I'd have to kill her first.

Third was an enormous black man with a beard best described as bushy. Another Titan? Hell if I knew. His smile would have been lost within that beard if his white teeth didn't shine so brightly against the darkness of both skin and facial hair.

The first portal had discharged four people. Knowing how much Capes like fairness and equality, I waited for the second to do the same, but after a long pause, Door closed the portal again, severing the pathway back to the Free States.

Seven Capes. Nine if you included Door and Evie. Ten, with Sofia, even if, by her own admission, she wasn't a Cape anymore. Put together, it was a full team. Two Teleporters for some semblance of mobility. A Lightbringer and an Earthshaker. Two Stalwarts and two heavy hitters. And then whatever the woman in white and the man with the moustache brought to the table.

Add Two-Feathers and me to the mix and it was a potent combo, but unless some of these people were what the Free States called Category Four Powers—a single but vast step below the true world-shapers known as Full-Fives—ten people wasn't anywhere near enough to take on an entire city. *A thousand armed combatants*, the Earthshaker had said, not to mention whatever Powers Shabaa had on his inner council, and, of course, the demons that made this whole mission necessary.

Any sort of direct assault would be suicide. I was starting to understand why Sofia was focused on rescue rather than destruction, and even *that* would take some doing.

"Kayleigh sends her regards and her apologies that she couldn't make it," said the younger Paladin. Matthew Strich, if I remembered his name correctly.

"Nobody expected her to come." That was the smaller man with a moustache. His voice was smooth as silk and dripping with a mix of sensuality and power. A Siren, maybe? "How's she holding up? One more month to go, right?"

Matthew's smile lit up his face, bringing warmth to rigid lines, and transforming him from merely good-looking to something damn near swoon-worthy.

"She's hanging in there, Johannes. Her mom's with us helping out, and we've got the whole house set up to be as cozy as possible. The doctors say the baby's healthy, and Kayleigh swears she can already feel his emotions. Most days, she just sits in her little nest and glows like Olympia here."

"I'm so happy for you both," said the silver-eyed woman in question, smiling as she said it. She turned back to Sofia. "Unfortunately, Tessa couldn't make it either."

"Trouble?" asked the Earthshaker.

"The usual," answered the large black man, his voice a low rumble. "After that last interview she did, the government's got their eye on her. There's even whispers that they might strip her of her leadership role with Stormwatch."

"They can't do that," said the woman in white, whose nose had either been broken multiple times or simply been created as crooked as a politician's tongue. "The teams elect our own leaders, and she was hand-picked by Dominion besides."

The other man shrugged heavy shoulders. "I'm just saying what I heard, Penelope. There's talk of some sort of public confidence act."

"Can you blame them?" asked the Titan in harem pants. "She's on record supporting a mass murdering asshole. That's the sort of thing that makes us all look bad."

"You know there was more to it than that—" began Matthew.

"Just because your wife had a crush on the guy," replied the bigger man, "doesn't mean you need to roll over and show your belly too."

"Enough!" Sofia stomped her way between the two men. "We're not here to argue about Damian. We're here to save a fuck-ton of people, including some of your country's citizens. But we're only going to be able to do that if you knuckleheads work together. Erik, if that sounds like too much of a task for your peanut of a brain, Door can send you right back."

"I'm here to help," said the man, his outfit a direct contradiction to that statement. "We can agree to disagree on the rest."

"Deal," said Matthew, his voice controlled, despite the bright spots of color flaring in his sculpted cheeks.

"Santiago couldn't come either," said the bearded black man. "Aspen has half the Society out in the field, and he was tapped to head up the reserves."

"What about Alan Jackson?" asked the Lightbringer. "Any word from him?"

"Every time someone says his name, I *still* hear *Alan-Fucking-Jackson* in my head," muttered the bearded black man, prompting a few scattered laughs.

"No," said the woman in white. Penelope, if I was following this dizzying series of non-introductions correctly. "His team hasn't seem him in months. All I got from Ripcord was that he was on *special assignment.*"

"Guess we'll be doing this without any Fours then," said Sofia. "This is going to take some planning. Before we get to it, I just want to say: *thank you.* Seriously. None of you had to come, but you did. It means everything."

"We're Capes," said Erik. "It's what we do, knucklehead or not." And if he flexed just a bit while he said it, sending his pecs bouncing up and down, well, it didn't *totally* undercut his words.

"*We're* Capes," agreed the ultra-fit female Stalwart whose name I still didn't know. "But those two are definitely not. What's a known Black Hat doing here, Sofia?"

I didn't particularly love the label. If we were being literal, it was a black *helmet*, not a hat, and if we were being figurative, I had been a mercenary, not an outright villain. Still, I knew the gym bunny was talking about me and Two-Feathers. As the rest of the Capes spun to face me, I stepped forward, only to have Sofia steal my thunder.

"She's here to help," said the Earthshaker.

"She's on the Security Council's Most Wanted list!" said Penelope, her already nasally voice reaching new heights.

"What number am I?" I asked.

"Sixty-seven," came the reply.

"That's it?" I'd been up in the thirties before my self-imposed exile to Eclipse.

"Your new status as a foreign head of state makes it all a bit fuzzy," said Door, the only person other than Sofia who didn't look prepared for bloodshed. Of course, he *was* standing right next to one of his own doors.

"I have history with Shabaa," I told the cave full of Capes. "Even before he wiped out a town of people I know. I came to see justice done. You lot should love that shit."

Nobody so much as cracked a smile. Tough crowd.

"You've heard the stories," said Sofia. "We could use her help."

"Right," said Penelope. "And the man with her? I'm guessing he's some sort of walking horror show too?"

"His name's Two-Feathers, apparently."

There was a long pause.

"That's it?" asked Matthew.

"That's all I've got. He doesn't talk and she says he's not funny."

"I said he's not as funny as he thinks he is," I clarified. "That doesn't mean he's not funny at all."

That won me a pat on the shoulder from Two-Feathers' free hand. In the dual interests of decorum and public image, I refrained from squeezing his ass in response… but the impulse was there.

"And what does he do?" asked Matthew, stepping forward and sizing Two-Feathers up like a gunslinger in one of Kansas City's ridiculous honor duels.

Two-Feathers didn't move, but I could practically sense the violence brewing inside of him. As regularly as I worried that my nomad was too soft for the world he'd invited himself into, he was young too and had plenty of pride and aggression lurking just under the surface.

"Same as you," I said. "Probably not as prettily, but I'm guessing at least as effectively."

"He's another Stalwart," said the third of their kind in the small cave, the woman whose name I still didn't know. She moved to join Matthew and even those few steps had me reassessing her. She didn't look like much—unless you were into gorgeous, ultra-fit, gym bunny-types, maybe—but there was something to the way she moved, like every step she took was practically predestined.

She wasn't a patch on Matthew's father, the original Paladin, not if she was only a Three like the others had said, but I wasn't positive Two-Feathers could take her. And if it was two on one…

Within my shell, the storm began to rage. Hell if I was going to stand by and let anyone touch a hair on—

"It's good to have you aboard," Matthew told Two-Feathers, breaking out into another warm smile. The nomad matched his grin and slapped the other man on the arm in reply.

I traded glances with the killer gym bunny. She seemed as confused as I was. Men were an alien species sometimes. You'd have better luck trying to understand a horse.

"Now that that's settled," I began, fighting back a sigh as the tension immediately ramped back up in the room, "I'd like to hear what the plan is."

30

T he *plan* was to wait until morning. That part I could get
behind. Stealth was all well and good, but trying to evacuate
a bunch of prisoners, or serfs, or whatever you wanted to call
them, in the middle of the night was a disaster waiting to happen.
Especially when they didn't know we were coming.

The rest of the plan… well, it was kind of a disaster. Part of
that was that Sofia had expected to have three of the four missing
Powers at her disposal—a Druid, a Telekinetic, and a Beast Shifter, by
the sounds of it. A bigger part was that there *was* no perfect plan for
trying to free several hundred people with as small a group as ours. And
the biggest part was that everyone there except Killer Gym Bunny and
the big guy in the harem pants had wildly different ideas on how it
should be done.

If nothing else, I got some actual introductions. The big black
guy was Jeremiah, a Mineral Shifter. Penelope, the white-haired
woman with the crooked nose, was a Weather Witch. And Killer Gym
Bunny was Nadia. And obviously a Stalwart. The others I had mostly
figured out… Matthew aka Baby Paladin, another Stalwart; Olympia
the Lightbringer, Johannes the Siren, and Erik the Titan.

It wasn't a bad mix of Powers, but I wasn't sure it was going to be enough either.

An hour into the ensuing discussion, I wandered back to the far side of the cave, away from the table with its map of Dallas and the too-many people trying to cluster around it. Door had left a while back, walking with Sofia's second-in-command to the top of the ridge to scout for an appropriate spot to set up his portable portal. His part in the plan was decided, if not at all simple: he was the escape man, the reason they wouldn't have to worry for long about any pursuit.

It was just *everything else* that remained up in the air.

I wasn't typically a wallflower, but everyone in this room had history except me. Well, me and Two-Feathers, and he seemed to be getting along just fine. Clustered around the table with the others, he somehow both stood out and fit in. I could envision a world in which, if he'd been born in the Free States instead of the Badlands, he would have ended up at the Academy of Heroes with the rest of them and spent his life as a professional Cape instead of roaming the world with me.

I listened to the storm rattle and rage. Two-Feathers and I were fundamentally different. I'd known that from the start, from watching him interact with Evan. He *cared*, and not just about what he could see and touch, but about abstract things, values that had lost their shine around the same time the world lost its mind.

Honor. Compassion. Respect.

I'd spent a lot of nights wondering how to break him of those attachments, how to rid him of what the world would see as weakness and attempt to exploit. But watching him there, rubbing elbows with people who at least professed to believe in the same thing, I wondered if I had gotten it all wrong. I wondered if—

"We haven't properly met," said Nadia, aka Killer Gym Bunny. She'd appeared at my side like the last step of a magic trick. "I'm Nadia. My Cape name is Orca."

"What can I do for you?" I shook the metal out of my voice. Truth was, I wasn't mad at having my train of thought interrupted. There was a time and a place for deep thoughts, and this wasn't it. Two-Feathers was mine, by choice and nonverbal decree, and hell if I was going to let the differences between us change that.

"You look as bored as I am." Nadia made a show of rolling her shoulders and then stretching. "Want to get some sparring in while they hash things out?"

That got my attention. I looked over—and down—at her. She moved like she was part dancer and part force of nature, her strength, stamina, and agility clearly far beyond human norms. On the other hand, she *was* only mortal, and Stalwarts were incredibly poorly suited for facing the storm.

"I don't think you could survive it," I told her honestly.

Her eyes brightened. "That's what makes it interesting."

I'd known more than a few combat junkies in my life. A lot of them ended up on the wrong side of the law, after all. Even the best tended to die young, because there is only so long anyone can ride the razor's edge. Still, I knew it wouldn't do any good to tell her that. Either she'd learn the lesson for herself after barely surviving someone and something that put her down hard… or she'd join the rest of her peers in the no-doubt expensive cemetery the Free States had created for the young and the aggressively justice-minded.

Either way, it was none of my business.

"Another time," I lied, turning back to watch Two-Feathers some more. Moon-Over-the-Trees had told me to find what made me happy, and while watching my nomad probably *wasn't* what she'd meant, it qualified.

Given how tight the quarters were here, and how late this planning meeting would go, *watching* was all I'd be doing. I had to get my joy where I could.

I could tell Nadia didn't like my refusal, but she didn't stalk off in a huff either. Instead, she just stretched some more before leaning back against the wall I was already propping up.

"What do you think of the plan so far?" she asked.

"Why do you care what I think?"

"Am I supposed to answer that with another question, or do you really want to know?"

"Somewhere in the middle, I think."

"Fair enough." Nadia twisted her left wrist until it popped. Then her right one. I'd never been happier I could just reform my shell to rid myself of aches and pains. "The stories say you've been around forever. The reports I've read—"

I stopped her there. "You've read *reports*? On me?"

"I've researched everyone on the Most Wanted list."

She said it like it was the most obvious thing ever. And hell, maybe it was, but I had a hard time seeing the bare-chested Titan at the table doing the same.

"Anyway, the reports said you've attacked a few fortified locations over the years, even before you went into the Crimson Queen's capital city, fought off her Powers, and executed her in her own throne room. I figured if anyone in this cave would have an opinion on the plan, it would be you."

"And the rest of the stuff in those reports didn't bother you?"

"I didn't say that. I didn't say that at all. But I'm not with my team, and I'm not here as Orca. I'm just Nadia Kahale, off having a mini reunion with my old classmates in the fanciest of places. And if there's a way to ensure they all make it back to *their* day jobs, I'm going to take it."

My eyes strayed to Two-Feathers. *That* was hard to argue with.

"The plan sucks," I finally said. "And most of them know it. That's why they're all arguing… they're trying to figure out how to make it work. Problem is, I don't think that's possible. Even if you could reach the prisoners unseen *and* get them to both listen to you and leave in an orderly fashion, there's no way the guards or Shabaa's demons wouldn't respond as soon as they did. And because Door can only make portals with doors he has personally used before, you either have to risk your escape man or have him set the exit way the hell outside downtown using his portable device. The old, the sick, the weak, and the way-too-young… none of them are fast. Not fast enough to stay ahead of armed cultists and not fast enough to stay ahead of demons either."

"I think that's why *we're* here."

"And how long do you think the twelve of us will be able to stem the tide?"

She gave that some serious thought, immediately raising my opinion of her. "If it was just the cultists, I imagine we could hold them for hours. Maybe even days. The enemy Powers are a bigger problem, but we're all used to fighting their types and we've got a good mix of combatants with us."

I waited for her to keep working the problem.

"The demons, especially the winged variety… they're a problem," she admitted. "Penelope's the only one of us who can fly, and she's not what I'd call graceful or swift in the air. Johannes is solid at crowd control, but his range is limited." Another moment's thought, and she frowned. "They could just overrun us and cut off our retreat."

"Exactly. Powers are force multipliers, but there are limits. As soon as anyone on Shabaa's side realizes something is up, the clock starts ticking, and I don't see how you can rescue the prisoners in whatever time you'll have left at that point."

"So, what *do* you suggest?"

"I have no idea. I have generals to do this shit for me." But even as I said it, my mind was wrestling with the problem. I hadn't always had armies at my beck and call, and I hadn't always been able to brute force my way through everything either. The closest I'd come to a rescue op recently was freeing Two-Feathers and Evan from the Crimson Queen's processing camp, and that had gone sideways in a hurry. But... "It's like you said. The demons are the real problem, especially when Shabaa can just keep them coming."

Which... left only one resort, really.

Funnily enough, it was the plan I'd suggested at the start.

Wordlessly, I left Nadia behind and made my way to the table. Two-Feathers slid to the side to make me space, but it was a few moments before the rest of the table realized I was there. Silence spread like cancer from my intrusion.

"Yes?" said Sofia.

"I have an idea."

"I was hoping you might." The Earthshaker made eye contact with Nadia as the other woman joined us at the table, and I had the sinking suspicion I'd just been played.

Still, we were all on the same side... and judging by the look on Two-Feathers' face, there was no way I was talking him out of helping free the prisoners.

"Kill Shabaa," I said.

The cautious optimism fled Sofia's face. "I understand the impulse, but there's no way we can get to him."

"Not we. Me." I scanned the collection of Capes, not a damn one of them even close to thirty yet. "I go after Shabaa, you go after the prisoners."

"I've seen your profile," sniped the white-haired Penelope. "You're not Dominion or Grannypocalypse. Throne or no throne, you're basically a thug who sells—"

"Penelope!" Matthew cut the woman off a fraction of a second before Two-Feathers could do something wonderfully imprudent. "Can you dial it down to like a *seven*? Please?"

"This *is* me at a seven, *Paladin*. Anything higher and I would have already dropped a lightning bolt right through that helmet."

Weather Witches. Always so emotional.

"A five then," sighed Matthew. At the other woman's sharp, vicious nod, he turned back to me and gestured to Sofia's dirt map. "Insults aside, she has a point. How are you going to make it through all those defenses to even reach Shabaa?"

"I'll go over them." I turned toward Penelope, who unwittingly took a half step back. "You can fly right? So, fly me up over the city, high enough that they won't see us."

"And then?" asked Nadia.

"She drops me." I tapped the roof of the building they had identified as Shabaa's sanctum. "I land here and fight my way down. Not only will it keep Shabaa, his Powers, *and* his summons busy, it will distract the regular cultists in the rest of the area. You all work on freeing the prisoners, I'll cut the head off the snake that would otherwise swallow you whole. No Shabaa, no more demons. That makes everything else feasible."

"It... not the worst idea I've heard," said the round little Siren, Johannes. "Of course, that bar's been set pretty low over the last hour or two."

"It *could* work." Matthew frowned down at the map. "You'd survive the drop?"

I showed the room the smile across my true face, and was gratified to see *Penelope* take another step back. "I can survive damn near everything."

"What if you miss?"

"Then I land outside and fight my way up from the ground floor. It'll be more difficult, but still doable. Having White Hair get me to the target saves me a mountain of time and reduces the chances of me getting bogged down before I truly get Shabaa's attention."

"There's one problem with all that," said Silt, her voice slow and considering. "We need Penelope with the prisoner team. She's going to be creating fog as a cover for the jail break."

"Two problems, actually," said the Weather Witch in question. "Unless this criminal weighs less than she looks, I'm not going to be able to fly fast *or* high with her in tow. We'll be spotted long before we reach the building."

"You could bring in some cloud cover," suggested Jeremiah.

"You want me to create rolling fog on the western edge of the city, bring in cloud cover over the entirety of downtown Dallas, *and* fly a dangerous fugitive to the heart of the enemy's base? Are you sure you wouldn't rather I just blow the city walls down, scoop up the prisoners, and level the whole place with a million lightning bolts?"

"*This* is her at a five?" I asked Nadia in a quiet voice.

"Penelope is… yeah."

"I'm *good*," said the Weather Witch in question, continuing her rant. "I'm *very, very* good. But there are limits. And we're hitting mine. There's only so much multi-tasking I can do, especially when my powers aren't well suited for troop transport."

The word *transport* rang a bell with at least a half-dozen of the people around the table. Door was gone and wouldn't be useful anyway, due to his power's limitations, but we *did* have another

Teleporter with us. More than a few eyes turned to the shortest woman in the room.

"How about you, Evie?" asked Sofia. "Do you think you could take her there? You don't have to have been there before if it's in your line of sight, right?"

"If I can see it and there are no obstructions, I can teleport to it," agreed the woman in question. She was now noticeably slimmer than when we'd first met and had even swapped out her previous set of clothes for something befitting her diminished stature. "But I can only take one person at a time, and it'll take me a few seconds to re-orient and teleport back. That's eons in a fight. If anyone's waiting on the roof, I'm dead."

"Can't you just check beforehand?" That was the Titan, Erik.

Matthew was already shaking his head. "At this distance, even from the top of the ridge, it'd be far too easy to miss them."

"Not to mention the whole place could be booby trapped," I added. "Explosives *are* still a thing, even outside your precious borders."

"So we're back to not having a plan." Johannes' voice, for all its suave richness, carried an undercurrent of tiredness.

"Not quite." I didn't care anymore that Sofia had clearly sent Nadia over to engage me and get me talking. In fact, I'd have to remember that tactic for the future. Good leaders leveraged the skills of the people they had available. And now that I *was* part of the planning, I was anxious to get things finalized. I turned to the steadily shrinking Teleporter. "You said it takes you a few seconds to teleport again?"

"Yes...?"

"Then we can go with my original plan. We'll just swap you in for White Hair."

"You want me to teleport the two of us into mid-air?"

"It takes around ten seconds to fall a thousand feet. That's plenty of time for me to disengage and for you to teleport back to safety."

"I really want to know how you know that," murmured Nadia.

"Live long enough and lots of weird shit happens to you. Be me and you'll survive it."

I wasn't sure if Evie would go for the plan. Bakersfield had been tough as nails and more than a little bit crazy even… *before*… but that didn't mean his former classmates were. Still, the little Teleporter didn't leave us waiting.

"I'll need to check things out from the ridge above, and it'll have to be light enough for me to see, but…" She squared up and sent me a challenging look, even as her cheekbones continued to emerge from under the disappearing layers of fat. "I can do it."

○○○

In a perfect world, that would have been the end of things. In *our* reality, it was just the beginning. This time, I stayed for the rest of the planning. At one point, Two-Feathers gave me a look that said we were going to be having our own discussion before dawn came. I could tell he wasn't happy with me taking on Shabaa and his so-called High Council on my own. Or about the whole plummeting down out of the sky thing either.

Truth was, I'd have welcomed Two-Feathers as backup, but there was no way he could survive the kind of drop we'd planned for. Not in any kind of shape where he'd be useful afterward. And as skilled a killer as he could be, being part of the rescue team was a better fit for him, personally and emotionally.

He would always do what needed to be done, yeah. He'd proven that and more. But he was also young and human and soft-hearted. Meanwhile, any shreds of conscience I'd been created with had long since been washed away by the rising tide of blood.

And the storm? It basically *existed* for this kind of action.

I didn't contribute much to the rest of the planning session, which only made sense since it didn't involve me. I did translate a bit for Two-Feathers until we discovered that Matthew knew sign language himself. The more the young man spoke, the less of a resemblance I saw between him and his father.

When they'd finally put together a plan everyone could accept, people bunked down for the rest of the night, some in our cave, others in the cave at the end of the second tunnel with Sofia's militia.

Meanwhile, I wandered back out into the night air. I didn't need sleep, but I did need space. I went down the hill to check on my bike, then back up it again, bypassing the tunnel entrances to climb all the way to the ridge above. Dallas spread out below, dark except for a few fires here and there, the shapes huddled around them far too distant to distinguish between guards or cultists, prisoners or prostitutes. Every now and then, a much larger shadow or two could be seen, evidence that Shabaa's demons walked the city streets.

Doing what, exactly? I couldn't tell. Any screams were unlikely to carry this far, but if they *were* out looking for a late-night snack, I couldn't find any evidence of it. Frankly, I wasn't even sure if summoned demons *did* eat. All I knew for sure was that they killed easily and died a whole lot harder.

I didn't free the storm, not with one of Sofia's soldiers nearby doing a piss-poor job of stealthily keeping tabs on me. Last thing I needed was to spook our temporary allies or—even worse—accidentally cut some overly curious Normal to pieces.

It was already going to be tricky enough making sure Evie the size-changing Teleporter survived. I'd have to make sure we got some separation from each other *before* I dismissed my shell and that wouldn't leave me a whole lot of time, especially considering I'd also have to aim for the rooftop I'd be plummeting toward.

This is a really stupid plan.

Still, I'd survived worse, and thinking of popping in unannounced on the asshole who'd hunted us across Texas and then laid waste to Lawton put a smile on my face.

Or it would have, if one wasn't there already.

Sometime before dawn, I felt Two-Feathers come up beside me. If my nomad felt tired after the long night, he didn't show it. He was his usual stoic self, features set in the pre-dawn light.

I waited for him to sign something, but this once, he kept his peace. Together, we maintained our vigil, looking eastward, looking toward the sun set to rise above what promised to be a very bloody day.

Silence with Two-Feathers was rarely uncomfortable, and despite the weight of what awaited us, this was no exception. We stood side by side, one of us breathing, the other not, and said nothing at all.

Naturally, it couldn't last.

This time, I was the one who broke the moment.

"When things go wrong today," I said, "and they *will*, keep your head on a swivel. Watch your back and get the hell out of the city as fast as you can. No heroics. Not this time. Capes look after their own before they spare a moment to care about anyone else."

He patted me on the shoulder, which could have meant absolutely anything, but most likely meant my advice had been heard and would not be followed. That was how it went. If Two-Feathers had been a weak person, I'd never have been interested in him. As a strong one, he was going to inevitably do what he deemed best. And if that put his life at risk and annoyed the living shit out of me in the process? Well, there wasn't a damn thing I could do about it, was there?

Sofia showed up a few minutes later to collect him.

"The team's gathering down below." We both watched the nomad head down the hill before she turned back to me. "It'll take a while for us to get into position and set up outside the city. Evie will join you in a second, but I wanted to check in with you before we left."

I was still looking after the departed Two-Feathers. I didn't believe in fate or superstition, but I had the strange feeling I might never see the man again. Given the careful step Sofia took back, I guess some of that sentiment made its way onto my true face.

That was a hell of a trick for a smiley-face decal on a visor, but dear old Dad hadn't been the closest thing to God for nothing.

"Is this where you tell me you want the nomad cut out of the action?" she asked. "Because unlike Matthew, I *don't* speak sign language, but I've known some stubborn men in my life, and I can't see him taking that too well."

"Two-Feathers is an adult. He can make his own choices and live with the consequences."

That surprised her, I think. "Well… good. Because we need every Power we can get if we're going to pull this off."

"You know *something's* going to go wrong, don't you?"

She shrugged shoulders that were almost as broad as Two-Feathers' despite their different heights. "Something always does. I learned that as a Cape and then again as the head of my own territory. We'll adapt and overcome. And you'll just… do what you do."

With those words, she gave one last look to the city of Dallas, slowly being revealed by the dawn's light, and turned to go.

My reply caught her before she could take a step.

"If anything happens to Two-Feathers, you're all going to see *exactly* what I do."

Sofia went still. "I thought he was an adult who could make his own choices?"

"He is, he can, and he will. But we're *all* adults and we've all got choices. This one is mine: if he doesn't get to live with the consequences, nobody else will either."

It wasn't fair, it wasn't right, and it definitely wasn't helpful…
and yet I couldn't find it in me to care. *Find what makes you happy*,
Moon-Over-the-Trees had said. *Find it and fight for it.*

I wouldn't just fight. I'd kill.

It was what I'd been created for, after all.

A strange look came across Sofia's brown face. "Fuck the world
if he's not in it, huh?"

"One day he won't be." Try as I might, I couldn't keep the
metal out of my voice. "None of you will. But that day's not here yet."

"Message received."

"Good. Then I'll see you when the bleeding's done."

31

By the time Evie showed up—real name *Evelyn*, I'd learned, after the Weather Witch had dared to call her by Sofia's nickname—the sun had just crested the eastern horizon. It bounced off the few intact windows in downtown Dallas, adding a glow that poorly matched the scene. It was kind of like when lantern light refracted through a glass of the worst moonshine you'd ever seen; the effect was pretty, even if the cause was anything but.

Beneath us, fog crept its way down from the ridge to enshroud the western edges of the city. How well that fog would serve its purpose depended a lot on whether it was the sort of thing that Dallas saw regularly. If not, someone would know something was up. Even then, it would at least make the rescue team harder to locate.

And once I got within striking distance of Shabaa, those in charge would have bigger things to worry about.

I gave the Teleporter a once-over as she went to stand at the very edge of the cliff-like eastern side. She had stopped shrinking finally, which was good, because by that point, she was practically pocket-sized, topping out at about five feet. If she weighed more than a hundred pounds, I'd eat Two-Feathers' horse.

Even her current set of clothes hung on her, just a bit, a long-sleeved, padded jacket, pants, and boots that were a more fashionable take on what I was wearing.

"You're not going to bust out of that outfit when we teleport or anything, are you?" I asked.

She shook her head. "This short a hop won't gain me much mass at all. Going all the way back to the Free States is another thing entirely."

"I figured it was something like that." All Powers were different, but physical growth being a consequence of distance traveled was a wrinkle I hadn't encountered before. "I bet that made your teenage years hell."

"*Everyone's* teenage years are hell."

"I wouldn't know."

She sighed, still not looking in my direction. "I'm not going to talk shit like Penelope and risk you snapping and killing me, but could you just wait for Olympia's signal in silence and *not* bother me for a bit? This isn't as easy as it looks."

A little bit of the storm's natural defiance forced me to ask. "What isn't?"

"Figuring out where to teleport. It's a big sky and while you should have some ability to direct your descent, that won't matter if we end up over an entirely different building because I didn't account for the haze from the city generators, the curvature of the earth, or a dozen other things."

Again, I felt that childlike urge to ask her to list all those other things, because frankly, I was betting it was a whole lot less than a dozen. But I'd never been a child, and I wasn't going to start now. This wasn't my usual sort of job but that didn't mean I couldn't be a professional.

So, I swallowed my questions, honest and otherwise, and watched the fog below us. There had been a lot of discussion given to the idea of sneaking Door all the way into the city so he could use one of *its* doors rather than the one he'd brought with him. The problem was, we hadn't been able to spot many intact doors in the western slums. Even the prison halls had portcullis-like gates instead. Not to mention that Door was literally the most important component of the plan, myself included. Keeping him safe was paramount, and that meant keeping him out of the action.

They'd be looking for a spot somewhere in the happy middle area to set up his portable door. Not so close to the city as to risk losing the Teleporter to a lucky bullet from a trigger-happy guard, and not so far as to make reaching the portal an impossibility, even with the fog *and* my distraction. By now, he was probably setting the thing back up again. After that, the rescue team would move forward, pushing toward the city, but before they reached the wall, we'd get a—

There. A soft glow flickered somewhere within the fog. Once, twice, then it was gone. I'd been looking for it and had almost missed it. The likelihood of one of Dallas' defenders seeing it was practically nil.

Of course, the space between practically nil and *actually* nil was large enough to swallow a county, but that was how plans went. You did what you could to prepare and then everything else was a matter of hoping, praying, and killing.

"That was the signal," I said, in case *Evelyn* hadn't seen it. "We're up."

The Teleporter nodded, swallowed, and took my gloved fingers in her much smaller hand, eyes still fixed on whatever specific spot in the sky she'd selected. "Hold on until we're there, but make sure you let go of me before you shift. In fact, I'd suggest staying in your human form for as long as you can so you can better direct your fall."

I didn't *shift* and I didn't have a human form either, but some Cape from the Free States didn't need to know the ins and outs of what I was. "Let's make it happen," I said instead.

"This is going to suck."

From this side of things, I didn't see that void of darkness appear. Instead, reality simply warped around us. The sun was gone. The sky was gone. There was only shadow and cold, a lack of oxygen and a surplus of strangeness.

A human would have probably found it uncomfortable to be stuck in that moment, unable to breathe, their limbs utterly unresponsive. To me, it felt kind of like home, like peace, like the mother's womb I'd never known.

The problem was… only my *shell* was frozen.

The storm inside? *It* began to rage.

My shell is just that. A shell. A container. Order imposed on chaos. Function given form. But in that endless space, that singular moment, both form and function fell short. I could feel the storm cutting its way out, breaking free of my shell rather than being loosed from it, tearing through the semblance of organs, then bone, as it squirmed to the surface.

I didn't want to know what would happen if the woman holding my hand, the woman controlling this teleport, died in transit.

My shell was faltering, might have already faltered in this strange, endless moment, so I turned to the only thing I had left: my will. The storm had always been with me. It possessed none of the humanity or identity I attributed to my shell, but it was still a part of what I was, chaos married to order. With flesh failing, I imposed that order with my mind instead, the way I had outside the processing plant in Tillatoba, the way I had in a bloody hallway in Mobile, Alabama.

I didn't know how long I could pin the storm within its faltering shell, particularly in this place where no other motion existed, but I would—

Light hit me like a freight train, blinding though I didn't *really* use eyes to see. My shell was a bloody mess internally, but what remained now held its shape without effort. The woman holding me breathed in air with a sudden gasp, and then yanked her hand free from mine, her body tumbling in the opposite direction.

We were falling.

It took a precious second to orient myself, high in the sky. The remnants of downtown Dallas spread out below me: the handful of still-intact skyscrapers, the squat complexes that had been converted to barracks for less privileged cultists, and the fog creeping in from the west to swallow the slums and the prisons within. To the south of the city were two hills now, instead of the one I'd seen on our initial approach, each so alike as to almost be twins, and directly below me was the building Sofia had identified as Shabaa's lair.

Okay… *below* me, at least, if not directly below.

It took me another of my all-too-few seconds to figure out how to use my shell to steer, and then I directed myself toward the building I'd already drifted away from. Evelyn disappeared again and it was just me in the sky, hurtling toward my target, the air whipping past my helmet and blood-soaked form.

I'd had worse times. That much I knew.

The roof of the building was guarded, as we had suspected it might be. A couple men in robes with rifles sat near the stairwell access. As the distance between us rapidly disappeared, I could see that one was asleep, while the other was chewing on what I could only hope was a chicken leg.

If the halfway-alert guard heard me coming, he didn't have time to react accordingly. Fifteen feet from impact, I dismissed my savaged shell. The storm took all my momentum and paid it forward, tearing through clothing and flesh with abandon. When I reformed my shell amid what had been two people, I had to pull some pieces of the storm out of the roof they had embedded themselves into.

I toed through the remnants strewn around me to make sure there weren't any keys I'd be smart to take and then headed for the door.

The stairs were dark and not particularly clean. I could hear sounds echoing up from the floors below, roars, screams, and even the occasional low murmur of distant conversation. Some of those noises were muffled, while others were not, suggesting that not every floor still had its door.

We didn't know where Shabaa was located. The pre-Break world had had something called *penthouses* at the top of buildings like this, so the richest people could literally look down upon everyone else. In a world with flying things—Powers and monsters both—that was less advisable, so I was guessing the Summoner would be somewhere in the middle instead, sandwiched in between layers of protection.

There was only one way to find out.

I'd made it down to the first landing when a hum, then a crackle filled the air. I looked above me and found a speaker mounted high in the corner even as it blared to life.

"And there I was so gently napping, when there came a tip-tip-tapping, creeping down from high above."

"Shabaa, I presume?" If he was one of those assholes who had to rhyme everything, I might just have to kill him twice.

"I saw you in my dreams, you know." Even over the cheap speakers, the words were audibly slurred, Shabaa's pitch rising and falling with every syllable. It was a distinctly unpleasant voice to listen to, and I struggled to imagine anyone *willingly* subjecting themselves to an entire sermon, let alone sticking around for an endless succession of them.

Maybe the members of his cult had been crazy even before he fed them demon flesh?

"Saw you, saw you, saw you!" continued Shabaa. "And lo, you have descended from on high! Angel of wrath, creature of sin! But there is a price that must be paid to enter Heaven's Tower, and we who are pure stand ready to collect!"

Bodies flooded into the stairwell. Some were human and armed. Some were demons and *more* than armed. Some were no doubt Powers, itching to prove themselves to their crazed boss.

They were all dead: chunks of flesh and bone, bags of blood spattered across the walls.

They just didn't know it yet.

I dismissed my shell, and the ever-eager storm went to work.

○○○

There were good and bad things about being stuck in a tight, enclosed space. Often, the lack of mobility was firmly entrenched in the bad category, like in the cave with the demon bear or when I'd been trapped in my first meeting with Delia Laine. Here, that same situation worked *for* me instead; a mass of enemies rushing into a blender that never slowed, a hunger that would never be sated. A small army of blood sacrifices with nowhere to go but the storm's embrace.

The first wave came from the level I was already on, cultists armed with swords and clubs. They fell in scraps of flesh and cloth and sometimes wood, their blood pooling on our landing until it overran the lip of that first stair and became a gruesome waterfall.

The second wave was a blend of caution and ferocity, mortals mixed in with a couple of Shabaa's demons. I reformed my shell and followed the waterfall's path, leaping down onto their waiting weapons and dismissing my shell again only heartbeats before contact.

Demon hides were tougher than human flesh, even when that flesh wore leather armor beneath stained cultist robes, but all that did was slow the storm's forward progress, forcing a death of ten thousand cuts into whatever space we had been temporarily arrested. Scaled limbs fell, twitching. People died, screaming.

When I reached the second landing, it was already flooded with blood from above. There, I was met by massed gunfire. Bullets tore through the shell I'd only just reformed and unleashed jagged hell once more. Lead streaked through the air only to be subsumed by the whirling mass of steel and shrapnel, the storm momentarily growing with the enemy's offerings.

I hit the third landing moments later. If there were people still above me, they were hiding, forsaking the gospel of their would-be god in favor of a more ancient and primal calling: survival.

Another speaker crackled to life.

"In my dream," said Shabaa, "you had wings of black oil, dripping across the painted sky. A smile on your face and malice in your heart."

Huh. Maybe he *had* dreamed of me, after all.

I met the first of Shabaa's Powers. Fire billowed forth from the hands of a shaky teen who needed a bath and a shave. An older woman with a pot belly and a scowl attacked with a battle axe stained and crusted with the blood of its victims. A Shifter who gleamed like fine crystal charged through the open door.

They all fell, one by one. Crystal shattered. An axe tumbled to the ground, along with the dirt-stained hand that clutched it. Fire guttered out as a teenager gaped down at the lengths of rebar driven through his chest.

These were barely tougher than Normals. Not a one would have been tapped to join my Immortals, let alone the Free States' Academy of Heroes. Twos at best, Ones at their swiftly dying worst.

Was *this* all that Shabaa had to offer?

Things changed on the fifth landing, where instead of meeting me *en masse*, the defenders tried to employ some semblance of tactics. Demons up front to slow me, Powers and riflemen behind to attack from a distance. A few people even emerged from the floors above, their patience giving them the first opportunity to surround me.

None of it made a difference. The storm didn't have a vulnerable side. It couldn't be crept up on or flanked. It was a seething mass of sharp edges and anything that entered its radius died in pieces. The demons up front, a heavier, more armored variant that barely fit in the stairwell at all, slowed me some, but their forms also made for great shields from the few Powers whose ranged abilities could touch the storm. I burrowed my way into them, then through, and fell upon the ranged attackers like a blizzard, like an avalanche, gore-soaked pieces of the storm baptizing them in blood before their demise.

Nothing about what I did was pretty, but war's never been pretty. Anyone who says otherwise is lying or a recruiter.

By the time I reached the seventh landing, there was nothing left to stand against me. Not in the stairwell anyway. Far below, I heard a few doors slam shut again.

"The price has been paid!" said Shabaa, voice issuing from yet another speaker. "And thus is admission granted. Come to me, angel of putrescence. Step into the light of Shabaa and be anointed with his blessing!"

I was genuinely starting to think less of Sofia for having let this nutcase escape.

The next two landings were quiet and empty. The doors leading into their respective floors were open, nothing but quiet darkness and empty hallways lurking within. I pressed onward, more cautious now. If there was going to be a trap, it would almost definitely come with the stairway cleared and after Shabaa had given me his blessing to enter.

Every landing had a speaker. Trust a cult leader to wire the whole damn building so you couldn't escape his voice. With every floor I descended past, Shabaa piped up with more slurred inanities, until the thought of shutting him up held even more appeal than ridding Dallas of his demon hordes.

Thankfully, I'd be doing both at the same time.

Twelve floors down, I found Shabaa's lair.

                                32

Light streamed into the stairwell through the open door. Inside,
what had once been a hallway had been mostly demoed,
leaving a series of open archways all leading into the same
massive room. Here and there, columns stretched from floor to ceiling
in seemingly random fashion, propping up a ceiling in place of the
missing walls.

I stepped through the central archway. The space was as big as
my throne room back in New Memphis, if lacking the fancy balconies
where spectators could come and witness a monarchy in action. Shabaa
and his council waited within.

Six demons flanked a pathway leading to the much smaller
figures waiting at the far wall. These demons had serpentine lower
bodies instead of legs, their torsos masses of armored flesh topped by
shrunken heads.

"Step forth and be saved!"

We were far enough apart, the space vast enough, that Shabaa's
voice likely wouldn't have carried to me if he hadn't installed even *more*
speakers in his throne room. His voice boomed around me like he was
some sort of god in truth and not just a weirdo who'd found religion in
the desert.

Still, it would be rude to ignore his invitation.

I closed in on the man and his council. The snake demons let me pass without issue, crimson eyes winking in their chests like rubies, even as their eyeless heads barely twitched.

Five humans waited at the far side of the place, standing a good fifteen feet in front of what had once been floor to ceiling windows and now simply opened onto the city skyline. Four of those humans were standing, their brown robes halfway clean and bulging over armor a cut above anything I'd seen in the stairwell. The fifth sat cross-legged on a filthy pillow, eyes wide and bloodshot. He was naked except for a surplus of hair on his head, his face, and his body, and at his side was...

Well, I wasn't entirely sure *what* it was. It didn't have legs or even a tail like the demons I'd seen but settled directly on the floor like a pot, for all that it was clearly organic. It didn't have arms either, but a spattering of nipples and at least three eyes could be spotted on its torso. It had two necks, one short and seemingly vestigial, the other long, narrow, and corded, like a firehose or a Titan's straw. It ended, not in a head, but a fleshy nozzle.

As I approached, Shabaa reached a dirt-stained hand over and pulled that nozzle to his lips, taking a deep breath in. When he released it again, smoke the color of spoiled milk issued from his flared nostrils.

"I saw you in a dream," Shabaa slurred, for at least the seventh time since I'd entered this godforsaken building. "Your eyes wept blood and your legs ended in cloven hooves."

I looked down at my riding boots, then at the Summoner and his council. They were still a good fifty feet away, but the distance closed with every step. None of the standing humans seemed to be stoned out of their mind, yet none had the grace to be ashamed of the utter disaster that was their leader either. One was a Titan by size and shape, but the others could be damn near anything. Or even nothing at all.

No, that last thought didn't hold water. As presumed members of Shabaa's council, they *had* to be tougher than what I'd faced already. Demons alone weren't sufficient reason for Shabaa to have survived this long.

"It is good that you have come," said Shabaa, still breathing nastiness out of his nose. "There is much to teach you before you are permitted to join the faithful."

"Didn't I just... *kill* the faithful?"

"Those who are pure need not fear death, for they are loved."

I took a few more steps while pretending to consider his words. I'd seen a lot of things since entering the building—at least half of those things highly infectious—but love wasn't one of them.

"So, what then?" I asked. "You're just going to let bygones be bygones and give me a seat at your table?"

I was being metaphorical, obviously, given the absence of both seats and tables.

"Call it instead a helping hand," he said, taking another puff from his demon drug hookah. "Angel though you are, you swim in the muck with the lesser beings. It is my sacred duty to lift you into enlightenment."

Fifteen feet now.

"And you think that's going to happen?"

"Why else would the universe have brought you to me?" He hacked up something foul and green and spat to the side, narrowly missing the bare feet of one of his councilors. "I saw you in a dream, you know."

Eight times that I'd had to hear that nonsense, and honestly? It was enough.

Ten feet from the would-be prophet, I loosed the storm.

A cloud of sharp-edged steel and jagged iron surged forward, feeding off the momentum my shell had given it, feeding off the anger that had been building within me.

Shabaa didn't react, didn't even flinch. He just sat there in the handful of heartbeats he had left.

A bare foot from the man, the storm and I found out why.

Shrapnel and rusted wire, rebar and razor-sharp edges, every piece of the storm came to a sudden stop, a swarm of savage violence straining toward expression.

I'd restrained the many pieces of the storm in the past, with sometimes mixed results, but this was different. This was all-encompassing. Worse, this was not my doing.

"In my dream, you had teeth of steel," continued Shabaa, the storm so still that I could hear him even without ears, "shoved into a mouth that bled for all the world's trespasses. And I knew then—I knew!—that it would be a struggle for you to find your place. I knew you would require great encouragement."

The storm didn't have eyes, but then, neither did my shell. I did my best to sense the Powers flanking Shabaa, to see which of them could be doing this. Delia Laine had possessed a telekinetic shield that the storm couldn't penetrate, but this was different. This was someone actively controlling the storm, not by air or invisible fields of force, but by the very material it was made from.

Some Earthshakers had an affinity for dirt. Others stone.

And apparently, there was at least one who could control metal.

I willed the storm to split and separate, to spread the focus of whoever was doing this to a thousand different pieces.

Nothing. Their control was overwhelming.

"I knew," said Shabaa, still ignoring the death hovering only inches away, "I knew that you would have to be taught your place. And in my dream, you were made to kneel."

The storm's mass began to descend, forced down piece by piece despite my best efforts to stop it, and still I couldn't tell who was responsible.

"To kneel and be taught," continued the madman. "Humbled by holiness. Sanctified through suffering. Purified in pain."

Three of the four humans standing by Shabaa moved forward to surround the storm, elements gathering about them: light and fire and another that the storm wouldn't know until it struck.

But the fourth stayed where he was and though the storm couldn't make out the beads of sweat gathering on his face, that stillness said enough.

I did the only thing I could.

I reformed my shell.

Flesh and blood replaced the repressed chaos of steel. I wasn't kneeling, but crouched, a hand's breadth from Shabaa, from the naked filthy man whose bloodshot eyes even now were barely widening at my reappearance—but I ignored the Summoner and lunged at the man standing by himself, the man whose Earthshaker powers gave him no control of my shell.

A wave of green darts took me in the back, searing through leather and flesh like the acid they'd been formed from. A cloud of light filled the space where I had been, motes striking empty air like cannibalistic fireflies. A whip of fire cut clean through my right leg, removing the limb from the knee down.

Still, I reached my target, taking him to the ground.

My shell is many things. A container. A mask. Flesh, blood, bone, and the occasional hint of an organ. It's the shape that hides the storm, and the true face I show the world.

But it's also ultimately a body. The body created for me. Shaped to draw the eye. Too tall for many men's comfort. And *strong*. Not Stalwart-strong, let alone Titan-strong, yet still strong enough to hoist an electric motorcycle in the air. Strong enough to remove one-hundred-pound boulders from a cave-in.

And *more* than strong enough to twist the head right off the Power who'd dared shackle the storm.

Still on my hands and knees, I spun and threw that head and its dripping broken fragment of a spinal column at one of the other members of Shabaa's council. Then, I dismissed the broken shell that had served its purpose.

The storm surged forth again and this time, there was nothing to stop it.

○○○

Whether it was through luck, planning, or the magic or his stupid dream, Shabaa had surrounded himself with Powers who could damage the storm. Fire, light, and acid to melt its shrapnel to scrap.

It didn't save them. Not when they'd let me come so close already. Pieces of the storm burned and fell away, a thousand teeth becoming hundreds instead, but what remained was ample to swarm the gathered Powers, to find exposed flesh, and to rend physical bodies into their component parts.

The snake demons fared even worse, particularly as the parts of the storm that had been struck down regained their shape and rejoined the melee. Thick scales were less a defense and more a momentary impediment. The storm left the demons' tail-like lower portions flopping on the floor like landed fish, then struck down the new demon the Summoner tried to summon from their remains.

I reformed my shell again, flesh and bone unharmed under leather both shiny and new. Three steps took me to Shabaa, where I kicked him onto his back, pinning his naked form to the floor with my boot.

"I saw you in a dream," he gasped up at me, smoke still leaking from his nostrils, eyes struggling to focus on my form.

"There's only one dream that matters," I told him. "And it sure as hell isn't yours."

I pressed down with the boot that had him pinned. Filth-covered limbs and a shrunken penis flopped about like the severed tails of his fallen snake demons, and my boot slowly, tortuously, made a new road into his chest. Ribs cracked under the pressure, then broke entirely. The organs those ribs were meant to protect gave way like rotting fruits, and just like that, it was done.

Shabaa, once known as Steve, cult leader, would-be oracle, and well-known hurter of women, died in his throne room, an ant beneath my literal boot.

And then, just because I could, I punted his strange demon hookah right out the open window.

I left the dead Summoner and his equally dead councilors behind as I returned to the stairwell. I made my way up through all those flights of blood and gore, headed for the rooftop again. With Shabaa dead and any resistance in his tower crushed, there would be nothing to prevent Evelyn from teleporting directly to that roof. Then, she would take us both west again, down to wherever the others were completing their prisoner evacuation.

That was the plan, at least.

One step outside told me the plan had gone to shit.

To the west, the fog cover was *gone*. A white-haired Weather Witch soared high in the sky, doing battle with another flyer in cultist brown. Below them, there was no sign of Door or his portal, just a stream of people fleeing the city, while another bare handful held off a tide of cult members. Even with my vantage point, I couldn't pick out Two-Feathers in the mess.

That was bad.

Worse was on its way.

Demons were flooding the streets beneath me. Not a dozen, like Sofia had expected, or even the multiple dozens I'd warned her about, but hundreds. Literally hundreds. All the demons were *supposed* to have gone away with Shabaa. Instead, it looked like we'd just unleashed them instead.

I should have realized it when Shabaa's hookah hadn't disappeared.

It took me a precious moment to do the necessary math. Most of the demons below seemed to be of the landbound variety, but even with that and the head start that both distance and the fog had given, they'd be able to run down the fleeing prisoners—and overrun their protectors—within the next twenty minutes. With Door's exit gone and the demons still very much alive, the outcome was inevitable.

Unless…

I looked to the south of the city, to the twin hills just a mile or two away. Identical hills, down to the copse of trees that circled their rounded tops like nature-given crowns. The ground between them was flat and even, maybe a few dozen feet wide at the narrowest point.

It would be close, but I was reasonably sure the fleeing people could reach those hills before the demons caught them.

But only if they changed direction.

I stepped into the open, looking toward the distant ridge to the west and waving my arms. It was anyone's guess if Evelyn was even up there now that shit had gone to hell, but I didn't have any choice in the matter. The storm could kill and kill and kill for days, but it couldn't prevent the army of demons from simply bypassing it to fall on easier prey. And even if I jumped down to the streets, there was no way to catch up to the demonic vanguard, let alone reach the fleeing humans before they did.

So instead, I had to hope that Sofia's friend and former classmate would stick to the plan.

A few seconds later, the woman in question appeared next to me. She was heavier than she'd been this morning, but still a far cry from the woman who had brought Door all the way from the Free States.

"What's going on?" she demanded. "Why haven't you killed Shabaa?"

Before I could answer, a crack of lightning split the sky. The brown-robed figure high above the western slums faltered and fell, dropping to the earth. More lightning descended, this time among the charging cultists. Wherever it struck, bodies were left behind, but it was like emptying an ocean with a teacup; more simply piled in after.

"I *did* kill him," I told the Teleporter. "And his council. But apparently, his summons stuck around anyway. What happened to Door?"

"He's down there somewhere. I think. But when the fog was dispersed, someone destroyed the frame he was using for his portal." She scowled. "Maybe a hundred prisoners made it out. The rest are running for their lives… as if there's anywhere *to* run."

"There is," I said, hoping I was right, "but it's south, not west. Get me to Sofia or whoever's still in charge. We need to redirect traffic, and we need to do it now." I eyed the distant white-haired Weather Witch, now fighting off the few demons who had taken to the air, aided by pulses of silvered light that shredded the sky from the ground. "Before those two run out of juice."

Whatever you might say about Capes—and there were a lot of things to say—Evelyn didn't flinch any more than Evan had back in New Memphis. She didn't ask any more questions either. She just took my hand and then we were teleporting.

33

This time, I was prepared, and the storm only chewed a little of its way through the shell around it. I coughed blood, released Evelyn's hand, and reformed my shell, now a handful of feet from a mass of people I mostly recognized.

"What went wrong?" asked Sofia, her voice barely audible over the cracks of gunfire, the hum of another blast of light, and the screams of both the fleeing and the dying. The Earthshaker had formed a wall to blunt the advance of the enemy cultists, but her eyes were fixed on the demons emerging from the distant city streets.

"Shabaa's death didn't dispel his summons," snapped Evelyn. "But *she* says she has a plan."

I'd finally spotted Two-Feathers. He was in the thick of the action, just like I knew he'd be, fighting in strange synchronicity with Matthew and Nadia, three dancers instinctively knowing the others' steps. Where they moved, brown-robed figures died, but that wouldn't be enough. Nor would than the massed fire from Sofia's militia, the bulky shapes of the Titan and Mineral Shifter, or even the area effect abilities of the Weather Witch, Lightbringer, and Siren.

Capes were ultimately only human, and numbers possessed a power all their own.

"We go south," I said. "Cut between those two hills. Stick to the left one as closely as possible."

"I'm not leaving these people."

"Then get them moving in the right direction! And figure out some way to speed them the fuck up while you're at it."

Sofia cursed and spun to eye the hills I had mentioned. "Those hills?"

"The path between them. Stick to the left as close as you can. The *left* one."

I saw the moment the realization hit her, saw her eyes go wide and her brown skin go ashen. A moment later, she was back in control. "Evie! Get me to the front of the mob. We need to redirect them. I'll carry as many as I can."

"What about the others?" asked the Teleporter.

"Rearguard action for as long as they can. Then, they need to follow." Her eyes scanned my visor, looking for the face beneath. "What about you?"

"My place is with him," I said, gesturing to my nomad.

I could tell it wasn't the answer she was looking for, but it was the only one she was getting.

The two women disappeared. I didn't spare a glance for the crowd of former prisoners but headed instead for the Capes—and one nomad—who were trying to hold back a horde.

I reached Nadia first and took a titanium fighting stick right through the visor for my trouble. A step away and a careful reformation of my shell and I was speaking again.

"Sofia's turning the prisoners south. We need a fighting retreat to cover their six."

Killer Gym Bunny was dripping with sweat, her cheekbones prominent in her face, but she moved as easily as when I'd first met her, and her eyes were bright and full of life.

"Shabaa?"

"Dead."

"Shit." We were well out of the city, but behind the cultist horde, we could all see the approach of the even larger army of demons. "Maybe you should try killing him again? Or better even?"

"I'd love to. In the meantime, you're minutes from being overrun. Unless you get moving."

"South it is."

She spun past a salvo of bullets and fell onto the gunmen responsible, picking them apart with blows that were no less deadly for their blunt-force nature. And then, she was next to Baby Paladin, spreading the word.

Slowly, too slowly, under the pressure of far too many assailants with far too little concern for their own lives, the cluster of defenders got moving, retreating step by step, fighting for every one of those steps, unable to gain the space to turn and run without inviting a weapon in their backs.

The Titan was a boulder in a sea of chaotic melee, the Shifter a more literal version of that same boulder, flesh exchanged for stone as weapons struck with minimal damage only to be answered by great fists that broke bone with every strike. The Stalwarts danced their dance, Sofia's militia fired scattered shots, finding easy targets in the seething mass of humanity, and the three ranged Powers brought attackers down by the dozen.

Still, it wasn't enough.

I had yet to join the fight, partly because the quarters were too tight to avoid friendly casualties, and partly because I needed to see and despite my shell's lack of eyes, its senses were stronger than the storm's. I turned and saw that Sofia had gotten the remaining prisoners traveling in the right direction now. The old, the very young, and the infirm rode on a shifting carpet of earth with the Earthshaker herself.

Most importantly, to the Capes I stood with at least, a gap had opened between our small force and theirs, and they were now at least a quarter mile ahead of our rearguard action.

Paladin saw it almost the same time I did. He cut a cultist in half, for the first time showing a true resemblance to his father, and then waved his arms at the Weather Witch now hovering above us.

Sheet lightning flashed down and the world turned white. An entire rank of cultists fell, and before those behind them could fill the gap, the blonde Lightbringer stepped forward instead of back. Instead of fading, the afterimages of the lightning strengthened, then redoubled. Silver light cut cultists down like wheat in a field, leveling a swath of dead humanity several dozen people wide and almost as many rows deep.

Then it was the Siren's turn, his song somehow carrying above the din of battle. The cultists still standing, those nearby but outside the range of Penelope and Olympia's blasts, stumbled to a halt, then collapsed to their knees, grief-stricken wailing creating a harmony to the sporadic gunfire.

It wasn't enough to stem the tide of cultists, let alone the demons now on those cultists' heels, but it *did* create the space we'd been lacking. Nadia tossed the Siren over one shoulder and sprinted for the fleeing prisoners, as Matthew did the same with a barely conscious Olympia. Sofia's men were already in motion, followed by the lumbering forms of the Titan and Mineral Shifter.

But Two-Feathers…

My nomad was still staring down the horde, a horde rapidly becoming a mix of cultists and demons with every passing moment. I reached him and pulled him away, only to be met by a snarl and wide-eyed gaze, the nomad's habitual mask replaced by a strange blend of adrenaline and battle madness.

Two-Feathers was a killer, yeah, but *this* was battle on a scale beyond what he'd ever had to deal with. The Capes had their training and their years in the field to fall back on. My nomad… didn't.

"We have to go!" I yelled at him. "Now!"

It only took a few seconds, but every second was an eternity in that situation. Finally, he blinked and truly *saw* me, eyes widening as he also took in the already-distant backs of the fleeing Capes. With a nod, he hoisted his spear and turned from the certainty of oncoming death.

As a Stalwart, Two-Feathers was faster than I was, but we ran in unison for several minutes, his strides matching mine. We weren't making up any ground on the rest of the rearguard, but we *were* staying ahead of the renewed pursuit, and that was what mattered. Far ahead, the vanguard of Sofia's mob was nearing the base of the twin hills, the rest stretched out behind them like the tail on a snake.

I dared to think, for just a moment, that we might make it.

Another dream, in so many words.

I didn't hear the gunshot, couldn't separate it from all the other noise behind us, but Two-Feathers went down hard. He was up again a heartbeat later, but blood was streaming from a hole in his leg, and this time, *I* was the one slowing down to match his pace.

Lightning flashed from above, the obnoxious Weather Witch doing what she could to provide a shield, but she was clearly just as tapped out as the Siren and Lightbringer. What landed struck only single cultists and even then, wasn't always enough to bring them down.

The distance to the Capes ahead of us widened.

Our lead over the cultists behind us narrowed.

Another handful of shots. These, I heard. Two caught my shell in the back, center-mass, and tore straight through, but the third took

Two-Feathers in the shoulder and spun him about, tossing him to the ground again.

He tried to rise, stubborn to the last, and I stepped over him, turning to face the last vestiges of Shabaa's vengeance.

"Stay down, you stupid idiot," I raged at the nomad beneath me. "Stay down and *dig.*"

I gave him all the time I could, as more bullets tore through my shell, one shattering my true face and the false face beneath. I stood while cultists and demons alike crossed the bloody fields south of Dallas.

And then, when I could see the red of their eyes, bloodshot or infernal, I dismissed what was left of my shell.

An army fell upon us and the storm was there to greet it.

ooo

I don't know how long it lasted.

I know blood soaked the earth and filled the air.

I know the press of bodies at one point became as strong as the grasp of Shabaa's Earthshaker, that only the storm's constant motion allowed it to hold, steel tearing through what might have been a wall of flesh, then bone, then hides.

I know that the storm maintained its position, like a tombstone standing over its grave, and that anything that entered a five-by-five area about twenty-five minutes outside downtown Dallas met its end.

And I know that, as I'd predicted all along, the rest of the army simply overran us. The storm left a swath of death, of bodies, of carnage. It parted the sea, but the waters on either side swept by.

More death. More killing. More blood.

The storm was chaos given motion, hunger given motivation. It didn't stop and it didn't slow… not until its teeth found nothing but air, until gravity took hold once more and the blood that had encircled it like an angel's halo began to drip to earth.

I reformed my shell in a field of the dead. The backs of Shabaa's army were already a hundred-plus feet away, chasing the fleeing Capes and the prisoners before them, and for all the corpses around me, it was hard to see that army having lessened in size at all. But the truth was, I didn't care about that army or even the people they were chasing.

I cared about what I would find beneath me.

Two-Feathers had dug down like I'd told him to, Stalwart strength limited by the wound to his shoulder and the scant few seconds he'd had. Here and there, a tear in what was left of his shirt showed where the storm had come too close, but despite the rain of blood that had showered down upon him, I didn't see any fresh wounds. His bronze skin remained intact except for the damage he'd already taken, first in melee, and then when we tried to flee.

Yet he wasn't breathing.

Heedless of what was going on to the south, I pulled my nomad out of the earth and rolled him over. There was dirt clogging his mouth and nostrils, but I brushed it free. A quick check showed he hadn't choked on anything, but still… he wasn't breathing.

Heart attack? I didn't know.

I wasn't a healer, even one of the mundane variety, but I had a head full of often useless pre-Break trivia and one of those snippets involved the kind of first aid I'd never had cause, let alone motivation, to provide.

They called it CPR before the world fell. I wasn't sure what any of those letters stood for, but still, I knew the basics.

I knelt at my nomad's side, gloved hands together, and started chest compressions. Stalwarts were tougher than your average human, and Two-Feathers tougher than most, and that was probably the only thing that kept those compressions from cracking his ribs. I pushed a dozen times, then two-dozen, finally stopping at thirty.

I didn't know how this next part would work, but I wasn't spoiled for choice. I dismissed my true face, my helmet and the smiling decal across its visor, to expose my false face, the half-formed bits of flesh that Dr. Nowhere had gifted me with. I tilted my nomad's head back, opened his mouth again, pinched his nose shut, and blew a slow and steady breath inside.

I didn't *have* lungs, but I could speak. I could sigh. I could even, on rare occasions, moan, and on far less rare occasions, curse. I didn't know how it worked, but I knew all those things required air flow. And that meant *maybe* this would help.

Two breaths, each slow and steady, though I wanted to rage instead, and then I went back to chest compressions. Another dozen down and nothing. Eighteen more to go before another two breaths and then—

Someone landed next to me, someone clothed all in white that matched her waist-length hair. I heard a choked gasp as she took in the ruin of my face, and then she was kneeling on Two-Feathers' other side.

"That won't restart his heart if it's stopped," said Penelope, the Weather Witch. She recoiled from whatever she saw in my false face and hurried on. "I can help. I think."

"How?"

"I'm not a Spark, but I can summon lightning."

"You want to *electrocute* him?"

"That's how the heart works! And I barely have enough energy to fry an egg right now. It will either save him or he'll be no worse off."

It wasn't trust that had me stopping my compressions, leaning back to give her space to call whatever last shreds of lightning she had left in her. It was the realization that it was my only chance. Two-Feathers' only chance.

My nomad's body spasmed with the electrical charge, though it was so weak I could barely see the air ionize between us.

"I'm sorry," said Penelope. "That's all—"

Two-Feathers coughed. Color slowly seeped back into his face. I dismissed a glove from my hand and checked his vitals. It was thin and it was reedy, but my nomad had a pulse. Even better, he was breathing again.

I took a careful step back and reformed my shell, turning to the Weather Witch.

"Thank you. Of all people, I would never have expected you to help me."

"Maybe I'm just a sucker for doomed romances," she said wearily. "Or maybe I realized I had about ten seconds of flight left in me and decided that, if I couldn't catch up with the others, you were the safest destination." Tired eyes looked from the still-unconscious nomad at our feet to me. "Of course that means you owe me now. Figure out a way to keep me alive when that army turns back around, and we'll call it even."

It felt like it had been hours since I started treating Two-Feathers, but the army in question had only traveled another quarter mile or so. Here and there, cultists had fallen, some simply from exhaustion, others to their own allies, the demons who increasingly made up the bulk of the army's ranks.

The fleeing Capes remained ahead of the pursuing army, but the distance between them had shrunk considerably, largely because Nadia and the others had reached the vastly slower column of freed prisoners. As I watched, they finally entered the passageway between hills. I didn't have a whole lot of use for the Free States or its people, but damn if their Capes couldn't follow orders: the whole column, Capes and prisoners alike, stuck close to the left-hand hill as they ran.

I didn't *have* to breathe, but I gave air to my relief anyway as nothing catastrophic happened. It had ultimately been a coin flip, but it looked like I'd gotten it right.

"I don't know why they went south," said Penelope. "There's no protection for dozens of miles. If they went east, they could have at least used the ridge as a defense."

"They went south because I told them to," I said, metal absent from my voice as even the storm seemed to still in anticipation. The vanguard of the pursuing army had reached the two hills, maybe half a minute behind the rest. They swarmed forward, as mobs so often do, some of them flooding into the narrow passageway, others ascending the hills themselves to find higher ground.

"And why—"

Penelope's voice cut off in a choked gasp, her second since she'd landed next to us.

A vast swath of Shabaa's army had simply ceased to exist. From where we sat or stood, it was impossible to see more, but if Penelope had been able to fly, if the Weather Witch had been high in the air above, I knew that space suddenly absent of life would look kind of like a semicircle.

Or maybe even a bite.

One bite followed the next as the right hill, the hill that hadn't been there the previous day when Two-Feathers and I approached Dallas, simply faded away. Anyone climbing that hill fell into open air, yet none survived to hit the ground, vanishing into the unseen maw of something whose appetite outstripped even the storm's.

"What the hell is happening?" asked the woman at my side.

"There are three great horrors in Texas," I told her. "The Terrorbirds, who fill the sky. The White Wail, preceded by a child's final cry. And last but never least, the Hunger that Walks. Congratulations. You've just met one of them."

A hundred demons disappeared in another monstrous bite.

I bent to tear shreds of cloth from Two-Feathers' pants, binding gunshot wounds that had already begun to clot, but for all my careful nonchalance, I couldn't resist the occasional glance south as Shabaa's army was consumed. There was a chance the horror would turn on Sofia's group once it was done, but an even greater chance that it would instead go back to sleep, borrowing from the surrounding landscape in its slumber.

Of course, it might also head north, directly toward us. I wasn't some kind of apocalypse-beast whisperer or anything.

"We should head for the ridge," I decided. "Get my bike and Two-Feathers' idiot horse, so we can circle around and meet up with the others."

Penelope groaned as she climbed back to her feet, but for all her attitude, she wasn't dumb. She wasn't dumb and I *did* owe her. Respect, if nothing else.

"Better there than out in the open here," she agreed.

I scooped Two-Feathers up in my arms, the man a feather compared to my bike, and found the nomad's eyes open, pain-filled but alert. With a visible effort, he made a few short signs.

"Yes, I *know* you like your horse," I replied. "It's *still* an idiot."

He managed a grin.

Walking next to us, Penelope gave a suspiciously wistful sigh.

34

It took us forty minutes to make it back to the far base of the ridge, but my motorcycle was where I'd parked it. The bigger surprise was that Two-Feathers' horse hadn't wandered off either. It *had* chewed through its rope, but only so it could get at a cluster of now decapitated dandelions a few feet further away.

Having spent her whole life in the Free States, Penelope's sole experience with horses had been in a very short-lived petting zoo, and while Two-Feathers insisted he was up for riding, I didn't want her making that process any more difficult for him. That meant the Weather Witch rode on the bike with me, her hair flapping behind us like a flag of surrender because she ignored my suggestion to put it up in a braid or tail.

To be fair, she *had* requested a helmet. And then seemed pretty put out that I didn't have an extra and wasn't going to offer her mine. No part of my shell persisted after it was removed, but I didn't share that bit of information, and I doubted she'd have been satisfied with the explanation even if I had.

I rode slowly and kept an eye on Two-Feathers, but despite the *two* gunshot wounds he'd taken *and* the cardiac arrest he'd suffered as an immediate consequence, he didn't have any trouble staying in the saddle. He didn't look all that great, but I figured that was par for the course for everyone who'd been there down in the melee. Those who couldn't reform their shells at a moment's notice anyway.

Even Penelope, who'd been airborne for the whole battle, was tired and sweaty, her white not-a-costume scorched here and there from near misses.

We took a very wide circle around where the Hunger That Walks had last been. There was only one hill there now instead of two, but the problem with a horror that can't be seen except when it's sleeping is pretty damn obvious. After such a big meal, it would be primed for another nap, and then there would be a mirror image of a forest, mountain, or even a town somewhere, but for now, we were playing it as safe as we could.

I guess Sofia felt the same, as she'd kept the prisoners and her former classmates headed south until they'd crossed the river on a bridge the Earthshaker had formed out of packed earth. That bridge was functional rather than pretty, but it was also way too narrow for the Hunger That Walks. If the creature came south, there'd at least be some warning when it displaced the river's water.

Penelope shrieked a little bit when I took the bridge at half-throttle, which did a better job of announcing our arrival than the hum of the bike's motor or the clip-clop of the horse's hooves. By the time we reached the others, Sofia was out front.

The Earthshaker's face, set in a mask that couldn't quite hide her worry, eased when she caught sight of Two-Feathers behind us. Even so, she stepped forward to meet my bike.

"The longer it went without any of y'all showing up, the more worried I got." She turned to me. "On my mother's grave, I swear that they didn't realize Two-Feathers had stayed behind until after they reached the canyon. By then, there was no going back."

"He's alive," I said, the storm an audible murmur within me, "but it was a very close thing."

"I saved the day, as usual," said Penelope, awkwardly dismounting from my bike. She went to pull the hair out of her face and quickly discovered just how many knots had been formed by the wind. "Ugh. Just tell me that *someone* has a brush."

Two-Feathers hopped down from his horse with a wince that made me want to punch him for not getting help. The nomad dug into his saddlebags and passed the Cape a brush.

She graced him with a smile that looked strange on her too-narrow face. "Apparently, you have to go all the way to Texas to find a real gentleman." She turned to Sofia. "I'm going to get something to drink, something to eat, and a bath, in that order."

The three of us watched her go with varying levels of disbelief.

"She does understand we're miles away from the nearest restaurant or hotel, right?" asked Sofia.

"I'm more curious if she realizes that's the brush Two-Feathers uses on his horse."

"I won't tell her if you don't." The Earthshaker managed a shaky grin. "How did you meet up with her?"

"She ran out of flying juice right around the time Two-Feathers got shot—twice—and had his heart stop."

Just like that, the tension was back, silence undercut by the growing sound of the storm. I'd *warned* them what I would do if something happened to Two-Feathers… and then they'd gone and left him behind anyway.

The nomad's hand squeezed my shoulder gently, and against my better judgment, I found myself backing down. *Some* of them had left him behind, yes, but part of that was on Two-Feathers himself for getting lost in his battle rage. And *one* of them had then saved his life.

"He's alive," I finally said, "thanks to Penelope, like she said. And in the end, that's what matters. If anyone in this group can clean and redress his wounds, we'll call it even."

"That we can do." Sofia turned and pointed to where several members of her militia were walking through the crowd. "Cory and James are trained medics, or at least the closest we have out here. Supplies are limited, but they'll get you taken care of," she told Two-Feathers.

My nomad headed off, his horse once again following behind him like a puppy of the non-feral variety.

"What a mess," said the Earthshaker with a sigh. "The plan fell apart almost as fast as we put it into play. I lost two of my men, every single Cape that came to help is either injured or exhausted, and only a hundred prisoners got through Door's portal before it was destroyed. If it hadn't been for the Hunger That Walks, we'd all be dead."

"Look on the bright side," I said. "Shabaa is dead, his army has been annihilated, and most of his demons are dead."

"Most?"

"I can't imagine they *all* left Dallas to chase you, not when there were plenty of people still to kill within the city limits."

That prompted a scowl. "Steve's going to be a pain in my ass even after he's dead, isn't he?"

"Without someone giving them orders, I think the problem will take care of itself eventually. If not, I might have my troops swing through and clean Dallas out sometime next spring."

"*Just* Dallas?"

"I'm not looking to conquer Texas. Now or ever. Whoever's crazy enough to live here is welcome to it."

"I'd be offended by that if I wasn't so damn tired. Thankfully, Jeremiah's working with Door to find wood for a new temporary frame. Once that's built, these people will be the Free States' problem."

"You're not taking them down to your territory?"

"Most are injured, malnourished and riding the edge of dehydration. We don't have the facilities in Brownsville to treat them. Besides, Matthew's wife, Kayleigh, just paid a small fortune to have a warehouse retrofitted into an emergency clinic in northern Los Angeles. After the refugees get the medical attention they need, I'm sure they'll decide to stay or go on a family-by-family basis. Anyone who wants to come back to Texas is welcome, but I'm guessing most will be ready for a fresh start."

"My empire is always in search of fresh citizens, but truthfully, we've got a lot on our plate right now."

"I'm not convinced they'd see the appeal anyway."

I shrugged. "We've got roads. And a kick-ass ruler."

"Fair enough." She glanced past me, at the bridge, and with a wave her of her hand, sent it crashing back into the river. "How did you know? About the Hunger, I mean."

"When we came out of the north, there was only one hill to the south. I remembered because I had briefly thought about using it to scout out the city before settling on the ridge instead. This morning, there were two hills instead."

"Shit. Somehow, I missed that."

"You're only human."

"Most days, I barely even feel that. Still, even if I *had* noticed a second hill appearing out of nowhere, I don't think I'd have trusted my memory well enough to know which was the original and which was the eldritch horror that could consume an army in a handful of bites." She sighed for at least the fifth time in as many minutes. "Thankfully, *I* didn't have to."

I didn't have much to say to that, because the truth was, I hadn't known which hill was which either. Not with any real degree of certainty. It had a coin flip and for once in my life, that coin had come up heads.

Not that I was going to tell Sofia that.

Besides, everything had worked out just fine. And since *that* rationale had served well enough when it came to all those Capes abandoning Two-Feathers, it would serve in this case too.

Balance in all things.

I didn't hate that ideology, so long as it was mine.

ooo

It took two days for everything to get sorted and to everyone's relief, the Hunger That Walks never came for our camp. Evelyn made a trip to the Free States for supplies, each jump separated by the hours it took for her to lose the extra mass, and by the end of the first afternoon, Door's portal was up and operational. Soon after, medical professionals were streaming through, first to provide immediate aid, and then to assist people back through to the warehouse the door opened onto.

Even that warehouse was too small to house all the people saved from Dallas, so there was a lot of organizational wizardry being performed to swap people in and out, move healthy survivors elsewhere at a steady clip, and, above all, reunite families who had been separated in flight.

I got involved in precisely none of that. Instead, I spent most of my time watching over Two-Feathers, keeping him from doing anything that would reopen his wounds. The rest was spent on a brief foray back to Dallas, looking for any remnants of Shabaa's army that might have reorganized in our absence.

I didn't enter the city itself, nor did I need to. The bodies of all those who had been slain in that short, desperate flight were gone, leaving the land behind free of even the blood that had stained the earth. Grass that had been trampled remained so, trees that had been torn from the earth still lay strewn across the fields, but anything human, demon, or animal was simply no longer there.

To the west, the limestone ridge still stood, looming over the city, but to the east, there was now a matching ridge, identical in all ways to the first. It left downtown Dallas, all that remained of a once-great city, shrouded in darkness for most of the day.

The city itself was as quiet as one of the mice that must have once crept through its alleyways and midnight streets. Whoever was still among the living knew their survival depended upon stealth, for however long it took the Hunger to move on.

Maybe someone else would have felt something for the surviving inhabitants. But I'd seen a lot of cities rise and fall. I knew justice was rarely served and that karma was a poor person's lie, invented to make something good of the awful. All *I* felt was grim satisfaction. The Capes had saved the people who were imprisoned in Dallas. Everyone else had chosen to join Shabaa's cult. They'd been complicit in that cult's actions. Justice or karma or pure unlucky chance, they deserved what was coming.

Dallas hadn't been torn to the ground, like Lawton, but it was a dead place all the same, and I could live with that.

On the second day, all but one of the remaining Capes disappeared through the teleportation gate, followed by Door himself. Sofia and Evelyn dismantled the man's portable—and now makeshift—door back into its component pieces. They dumped those pieces into the bag Door had left for them, Evie slung the bag over a shoulder that was once again a shade too skinny, and then the little Teleporter vanished.

Just like that, there were only twelve of us: Sofia, her remaining nine militia members, Two-Feathers, and me, standing several miles south of another fallen city.

The Earthshaker took a long breath and then let it out again. "At least that's done. Now, all that's left is to get back to Brownsville and break the news."

"I wish we could have recovered the bodies," said the man I vaguely recalled as Sofia's second-in-command.

"You and me both, Rocco."

"Neither Tom nor John had families," said another of the militia. "That's why they volunteered to come. Just like the rest of us."

"They still deserve funerals," retorted the older man.

"Body or no body, they'll get them." Sofia's words put an end to the discussion. She turned to the two of us. The three of us, if you counted the horse. "You're welcome to come with us to Brownsville."

"How are you even getting there?"

"Land carpet," said the stocky Power, as if that explained anything. "It's not as fast as a horse, but it's a whole lot more comfortable, it doesn't require food or water, and the only person who gets tired is me."

I *still* didn't get it, but that didn't matter.

"Sorry. We've got places to be."

"You're really looking for Damian? Down in Mexico?"

"Yeah. I don't suppose you have a suggestion on where exactly we should go? Last I heard, it was a big place."

She paused, studying first the nomad at my side and then me. I let her have that time, knowing my true face wasn't giving away a thing.

"Why do you want to find him?" she finally asked.

"It's like I told you the other day. I want to talk."

"And that's all?" She spread her hands. "I'm just asking. I can't imagine you were particularly thrilled at what he did to Dr. Nowhere. *Or* Mammoth."

"I need closure. I need *answers*. My life's quest ended there under Bakersfield's hand, and I was too busy being scattered across the field by a Weather Witch's tornado to see it happen. To know what it meant. I have to close that chapter before I can move on again."

"So, you're *not* going to kill him if you find him?"

"I'm not sure I even could. Why do you care?"

"Damian Banach is my friend. Despite what happened."

"He's a Full-Five. The Lord of the Dead."

"You say that like it changes a damn thing."

I… wasn't sure how to take that.

"I just want to talk to him," I said, not sure if I was lying.

"Good. But I can't give you directions to where he is—"

"Fair enough." I turned to go, only to be stopped by the Earthshaker's next words.

"—I can only give you directions to where he was."

"Was?"

"We lost contact. Little more than a year ago. A friend of his— and mine—secured some devices that allowed long-distance communication. They didn't work great, and what we got wasn't real-time communication either, but it was enough to pass word back and forth. Kind of like the Pony Express without the ponies, maybe. Only, he stopped replying."

"And you don't know why?"

"We're pretty sure someone took a swing at him. Our friend thinks it was the Free States, but given that the country still exists, I'm guessing it must have been someone or something else. Problem is, none of the drones we've sent down since have been able to find him. If he's still there, I'm guessing he's moved further south, out of their travel range. Either that or…"

"He's not dead."

"Of course not," she agreed, as if she hadn't been raising that very possibility. "Boneboy's too stubborn to die. He'd just stand back up, swear a bit, and get on with his business."

That fit. Hell, *Sally* had done the same thing, and she'd never been a Five.

"Maybe you'll be able to find him where we couldn't," continued Sofia. "If so, you can tell his skinny ass to drop his friends a line or something while you're down there."

"It would help to have a place to start," I reminded her.

"Head to the City of the Sun, then go south."

I *really* hoped that wasn't the sum of her directions.

Thankfully, it wasn't.

"Go far enough, and you'll eventually come across it."

"It?"

"Damian waged war against Tezcatlipoca for almost two years. Nature's reclaimed some of that space, but not nearly enough. You'll find a line of destruction a mile or two wide that leads east. Follow that to its endpoint, to Tezcatlipoca's temple, and then go south again. Maybe two to three days travel on horseback? That's where the drone found him a few Christmases back. That's where we he was holed up when we lost touch."

I didn't know the heavyset Texan well, but it was painfully obvious how she felt about the missing Crow. Love took a lot of different forms, from familial to romantic to just plain sexual. I was pretty sure hers was the first, but that didn't matter. There weren't many flavors that could survive a gap of years and events like hers had.

"You could come with us," I found myself suggesting.

That surprised her, but she shook her head. "I wish I could. I've got responsibilities though. People who need me. And you're already bringing one living body with you. Another might be too many."

"I don't follow."

"You saw him in New Mexico when he lost it. The reason Boneboy stayed down in Mexico after killing Tezcatlipoca, rather than coming to live in a cute little hacienda in Brownsville where I could bust his balls on a daily basis, is because he can't be around the living. Not for long anyway. He gets… itchy, I guess, and I don't know about you, but I don't want to be the trigger for—or the victim of—another undead apocalypse."

"Pardon the interruption, Lady Governor," said Rocco, "but if we're going to leave today, it should be soon."

"Miles to go before you sleep," I said.

"Too many." He clearly didn't get the reference.

"Sorry," said Sofia. "Should've had had this talk earlier, I guess, but things were a mite busy."

"It's fine. That was the agreement anyway: when the killing was done, we'd all go our own separate ways."

"Yup. Guess I'll see you around." She started to walk away, then stopped and turned back. "If you find him… if he's still himself… tell him I say hi. Tell him Tessa, Kayleigh, Lynn, and Paco all do too. Ask him to get word to us somehow. I don't know what he's doing or why, but I hope… I hope he's at peace."

"Peace is a dream, you know."

She chewed on that for a bit, running a hand through thick hair only vaguely cleansed of dirt and blood. Finally, she sighed. "Most good things are."

The three of us watched Sofia and her remaining militia members float away on a conveyor belt of dirt—the land carpet, as she had described it. I waited until they had departed and then turned to Two-Feathers.

"We need to talk."

The nomad, his shoulder and leg both bandaged, flashed a smile that made him look twelve. He pointed a finger at his mouth and made an exaggerated face.

"Yeah, you're hilarious. Even before you learned sign language, you know I couldn't get you to shut up." The laughter drained from my voice. I hadn't planned on having this conversation... ever. But the last few days had changed that, changed me. "I think I should head on alone."

Just like that, the mask fell back over Two-Feathers' face. He didn't say anything, not with his expression or his fingers, but simply stood there, waiting.

"You almost died two days ago," I reminded him.

That won me a distinctly untroubled shrug.

"I know. You think it was worth it. We saved some people, stopped an asshole, avenged a town, right?" I didn't wait for the nod I knew was coming. "And I'm not going to argue with that. You've got to make your own decisions and live with the consequences."

More silence. Of course.

"But Moon-Over-the-Trees said something to me before we left the clan and somehow, it's gotten stuck in my mind. She said I should find what makes me happy and fight for it." The storm shifted inside of me, as if to echo my uncertainty. "I don't know if someone— something—like me deserves happiness, and even if I did, I don't know what form it would take. But I think you're a part of it."

A second smile, though I could read the confusion in it.

"You're going to die," I told him. "That's the price of being human and there's not a damn thing I can do about that, but I want it to be years from now, not days or weeks. Bakersfield is *my* mission. You should head back and wait for me in New Memphis. Hell, by now, Jules has either married Aaniyah or lost her, and either way, he's in need of a shoulder to cry on."

For the first time since we started the conversation, Two-Feathers looked away.

"I can't protect you from everything," I told him. "I don't want to either. It would rob you of who you are. But Bakersfield's *best friend*, the one and only person he left alive in an entire town after he lost his shit, is worried about what we'll find if we reach him. I don't want that for you. Go back to New Memphis. Please."

My nomad sighed and patted my shoulder in the way he so often did, then turned to his horse. His namesake spear went into the loop he'd added to the saddle and then he was up in the saddle.

That was… a little faster than I'd expected. If I'd had a heart, it might have twinged, just a bit, to not even get a real goodbye, but at least he had *finally* listened to me.

Only… ten, fifteen seconds passed, and nothing changed. The nomad just continued to wait, sitting astride his horse.

"New Memphis is *that* way," I finally said, pointing back across the river.

Two-Feathers nodded.

"Are you just waiting for *me* to leave then? Because we could make more of a thing of it. We do still have the tent."

That prompted his third grin of the conversation, this one the most unexpected. He tapped his broad chest, pointed at me, and then wiggled the fingers on his hand in one direction.

West, toward New Mexico and the City of the Sun.

Still grinning, he then pantomimed a yawn and tapped the pommel of his saddle impatiently, like he was waiting.

What was it Sofia had said about *Bakersfield* being stubborn?

"You're the absolute worst," I told him.

His grin slowly grew, transforming into a smile to match the one across my visor.

I guess he could tell I didn't mean it.

35

I t took us more than three weeks to make it to the City of the Sun, thanks to roads that went further to shit with every passing year, and streams and rivers still swollen from the late spring rains and runoff from mountains further north.

I'd had worse months, to be honest. The former state of New Mexico was a sort of no-man's land between the Badlands, Texas, and the Free States, with elements of all three intermingling within its uncertain borders. A lot of times, that spelled trouble, but the worst we ran into was a nest of dog-sized scorpions and a rattlesnake as big as Two-Feathers' horse.

The first, we had to kill, but the snake seemed at *least* as intelligent as the horse; we watched each other warily and then all went on our ways. I don't know about *fences*, but good manners certainly make good neighbors.

We stopped off in civilization twice along the way. The first was a walled fort in the western portion of Texas, with a name I forgot almost the moment I read the sign. The townsfolk there had had their own small problems with Shabaa and the news that he was gone prompted one hell of a party. That celebration mostly seemed to center on moonshine, peaches, and smoked pig, and while I didn't partake,

Two-Feathers seemed happy enough. The feast was still going on when we left the next morning.

The second town barely qualified as such, a small selection of huts that had sprung up around a ferry across the Rio Grande. While neither the people nor the place was much to remark upon, it saved us the difficulty of finding a bridge still in working order or a shallow enough space to ford.

At both towns, I paid a pretty penny to make use of their solar generators, topping up the batteries in my saddlebags for the long journey we still had ahead of us.

Hell, we were still headed to the *starting point* of that journey, according to Sofia.

I wasn't sure what to say as we rode up on the remnants of the City of the Sun, so I didn't say anything at all. The past few years hadn't been kind, but then, the battle that had taken place there hadn't been either. A few of the houses near the remnants of the northern wall still had evidence of their former brightly painted exteriors, but more than a few roofs had fallen in, and nature was already starting to reclaim the place.

It wasn't much to look at. Just the place where Dentist Pete, aka Dr. Nowhere, the most powerful man in the world, had once dreamed a dream that broke the world.

And brought me into existence.

I stopped for a moment in the field to the north, where dear old Dad had died, but there was nothing to see. There hadn't even been a body for Bakersfield to raise as a walker. Just a handful of dust quickly lost to the wind.

I'd thought I would feel something—anything—to be back there for the first time, but the storm inside of me kept spinning, and not even the half-formed lips on my false face twitched. Creator and absentee father, Dr. Nowhere had died as he'd lived… a stranger with no answers.

It would have been infuriating if it wasn't so disappointing.

Two-Feathers sent me a look. I gave him a shrug back and turned my bike away, riding through what had once been a gate into what had once been a town. We made our way through the empty streets and back out again in a matter of minutes. The graveyard to the south was as empty as the town itself, and that was ultimately all there was to say about the City of the Sun.

That night, I set the storm loose under a star-filled sky and thought of nothing at all.

○○○

The next day, Two-Feathers gave his horse a thorough grooming with a brush that still had more than a few white hairs wedged between its bristles. I swapped in a fresh battery from my pack, and we continued south.

At some point, we had crossed the border into what had once been Tezcatlipoca's domain, and the fact that both Two-Feathers and I kept our minds finally drove home the reality that the lava god was dead. Tezcatlipoca had been one of the continent's few Full-Fives that I'd never met, and I'd never regretted that omission.

Whether Bakersfield would prove to be an even greater terror was still to be determined.

A few days later, after a driving rainfall that temporarily relieved the growing summer heat, we came across the first of Sofia's waypoints. It was pretty damn hard to miss.

I'd seen my share of battlefields, large and small, but this was something different, a stretch of land where even years later, nothing grew. It called to mind the fields of West Virginia, the dead space that surrounded the single rickety cottage with a blind and ageless black woman seated on its front porch, drinking from her never-ending cup of tea. There was nothing but dirt in front of us—black like it had been forever stained—interspersed with the occasional chunks of bone. That devastation stretched south for at least a mile, and east all the way to the horizon.

For a moment, the storm went still. Two-Feathers took a deep breath, let it out again, and said nothing, but not even his habitual stoicism could mask the shock in his eyes.

Of us all, only the horse took it in stride.

When my nomad was feeling himself again, we went east.

ooo

We spent weeks on the road of devastation, and though the journey was easy enough—the terrain mostly flat, the weather mostly mild—the unrelenting sameness wore on both of us. The only breaks in scenery we got came from the remnants of specific battles: artillery positions that had been overrun, patches of ash or even fused glass among the dirt.

There were no bodies, not because it had been years since those battles, but because anything that wasn't shattered into fragments had picked itself back up and rejoined the march east.

The further we went, the more frequently I had us leave the road entirely. Just a few miles north, nature reasserted itself, giving Two-Feathers and his horse the opportunity to forage without depleting our supplies. Almost as importantly, it gave us all a break from the persistent morbidity.

Strangely, one day the devastation began to peter out, death replaced by green and growing things. I traded confused glances with Two-Feathers. The Earthshaker, Sofia, had said to follow the road east until we found Tezcatlipoca's temple. Had we somehow missed it already?

After some silent debate, we opted to press onward.

What else could we do?

Three days later, we crested a hill that was strangely flat at its apex and found the dead god's temple sprawled out below us, surrounded by evidence of a battle that put those we'd already passed to shame. There were massive craters where Powers and maybe cannons had traded fire. Fragments of enough human skeletons to fill a large city, mingled in with the shattered bones of vastly larger beasts and even a few carapaces. Most of all, there was irrefutable evidence of the lava god's power, finally brought to bear on his opponent.

The temple's wall was still intact in places. Inside, the crests of a few buildings poked upward like the masts of sunken ships, but the rest of that space had been filled by rough black stone that caught the light of the summer sun. Here and there, that stone was smooth and rippled instead, glassy like the surface of a mountain lake.

There weren't any active volcanoes on the continent that I knew of, but somehow, I recognized what must have once been lava.

"This is where he fell," I said, the first words I might have spoken aloud in hours or even days. "Tezcatlipoca."

It was hard to imagine anyone surviving a fight like that, let alone the too-skinny Crow I'd once known, the broken boy with a mountain-sized chip on his shoulder and a world's worth of anger in his heart.

But Sofia hadn't led us wrong so far. And we hadn't come all this way to stop now.

We went south this time.

ooo

Without a string of battlefields, there was no trail to follow. Just rolling hills, shrubs, and the occasional cactus with needles a foot long that shone like silver. I don't think we cared much. It was just a relief to leave behind the scars of a war between two Full-Fives.

I was the nominal ruler of an empire that had claimed a good sixth of the country formerly known as the United States. I'd been a mercenary for longer than anyone mortal had been alive. I'd seen a lot and done a lot and killed a lot, but there was still a scale and a scope to the destruction a Full-Five could wreak singlehandedly that overshadowed anything I could take responsibility or blame for.

Maybe it wasn't such a bad thing that all the old monsters were dying. Maybe a smaller, less colorful world was the price that had to be paid for safety.

Sofia had said it would take us two to three days to find the final waypoint, but it ended up being four instead. Even then, we nearly missed it. I don't know how, given that there wasn't much in the way of scenery, with the first forests we'd glimpsed still distant on the southern horizon. Still, we were riding along, making our way down a game trail that wove between hills, when Two-Feathers veered off.

I didn't know what he'd seen, smelled, or heard. Still, he was the tracker, not me, and even if we hadn't really had anything *to* track other than the occasional rabbit or tortoise, I trusted his instincts. I turned my bike and followed him off the trail.

I never did find out how he knew it was there, but about three minutes later, we came across a crater. This one was far wider than even the largest of those that had ringed Tezcatlipoca's temple. What had caused it was well beyond my ability to even guess, but the destruction was significant.

Significant and *old*, if the plant life in the area was any indication. Sofia had said they'd lost contact with Damian well over a year earlier, and Two-Feathers seemed to think that fit the timeline we were seeing here.

"If Bakersfield was here when that hit, he *died*," I said. "He was tough in his own way, but not *survive a massive explosion dropped on his head* tough. And if he *wasn't* here… where did he go once he realized someone was trying to bomb him out of existence?"

Once again, time worked against us. Any tracks Bakersfield might have left—presuming he'd been alive to leave any—had long since disappeared, and Two-Feathers couldn't find signs that anyone other than us had been there recently. Well, us, the horse, and a nest of regular-sized rattlesnakes that had apparently seen a big hole and thought *hey... home!*

We'd found all our waypoints and hit a dead end.

Two-Feathers fed his horse some water and then set the thing free to graze on scrub grass while I walked the perimeter of the blast site. Not sure what I was looking for, since this was way outside my wheelhouse. Maybe Cyrus would have had more of a clue about military armament and been able to tell me whether someone had fired a missile at Bakersfield or just dropped something heavy from way up high.

More likely, he'd have dodged the question entirely and wondered loudly what the hell we were doing wasting our time down in Fallen Mexico when there was an empire to run.

All these months later, I was starting to think he was right. I was starting to wonder what could possibly make this expenditure of time and energy and effort worth it, when there was so much else to be done. What questions could Bakersfield really answer, even if he *was* still alive? Dr. Nowhere had been the most powerful man in the world and *his* answers had been next to worthless. I'd looked for meaning, method, and a plan and instead gotten a scared dentist hiding from what he'd done.

The storm was chaos, wrapped in order, and maybe that was as good an example to follow as any. Maybe it was time to stop trying to make sense of the chaotic past, to instead impose my own order onto the future.

Maybe *this* was closure?

There was something deeply sick about traveling halfway across two countries to have the epiphany that I shouldn't have gone at all, but—

I stopped. Ahead of me was a black-winged bird, perched atop a scraggly sapling that might one day, with time, effort, and more water than I saw it ever getting, become a tree.

It was a crow.

That wasn't what stopped me, although I was sure if I asked Two-Feathers, he'd somehow know that crows weren't indigenous to this part of Mexico. No, what stopped me was that the crow was missing at least half of its chest feathers and a good portion of the flesh beneath, exposing the white bone of its ribcage.

The crow was dead, yet still upright and watchful.

"I'm not one to tell you how to live your life," I told it, though I wasn't sure if Bakersfield could hear through his undead minions. "But a human Crow raising a bird of the same name? It feels a little bit on the nose."

It tilted its head, revealing more exposed bone, and then made a noise, something closer to a strangled screech than a caw. It hopped off the shrub and flapped its way to another one, ten to twenty feet to the south.

Two-Feathers made his way over. He gave me a questioning look and a handful of signs.

"Yeah, I don't know how it's flying either. But I think we've found ourselves a guide."

ooo

We followed the dead bird for multiple days, as arid grassland gave way to forest and then something akin to jungle. More than anything else, that told me just how much Bakersfield's range had grown. For the most part, the bird left us alone, content to find a perch whenever we stopped for the night, but there were too many times I caught it watching Two-Feathers. Not me or the horse… just Two-Feathers. The only one of us both alive and human.

I didn't like that—I didn't like that at all—but we were in too deep to send Two-Feathers back, even if he would have bothered to listen to me at all. Instead, I tried to stay between the crow and the nomad, as if blocking its line of sight was some kind of ultimate solution.

I was down to half my charged batteries by that point, even after topping them up back in New Mexico. Much further, and Two-Feathers' horse would have to carry both of us—and my bike—all the way back to civilization.

It was late evening, the sun barely more than a discontented glow on the western horizon, when we finally emerged from the jungle to find a swath of land that had been cleared ahead of us. The crow continued forward, flying on wings more bone than feather at this point, and we followed behind. We crossed a hundred feet of open space, then two hundred, before I spotted a figure waiting next to a small fire. I dismounted and pushed my bike, Two-Feathers following my lead.

As we approached, more details became clear. He was tall, taller than I remembered, and skinnier too. He had his right arm tucked behind him, like a New Memphis gentleman waiting at a dance, but was dressed in worn grey sweats instead of a fancy suit. His hair was too long, long enough to fall in front of his face. It almost hid the hole where his left eye had been. The other eye was tombstone grey and depthless, the eye of something wholly inhuman, something that had transcended life and mastered death, something that looked out on a world the rest of us would never see.

"That is close enough." His voice reverberated with the same power that flooded out of him like a dark ocean, soaking the soil and saturating the air.

Two-Feathers stiffened even as my own senses told me we'd been surrounded, that *things* had risen from the earth and dropped out of the sky. Things that had never been human, things that did not breathe but still stood or flew or crawled, waiting to do their master's bidding.

I didn't know if I could kill the once-baby Crow. I didn't know if he could kill me either. But Two-Feathers? His life rested on a razor's edge, a heartbeat from death despite all his skill and significance.

The storm rattled in my core, but it was a small noise, dying in the stillness of the moment.

"Hi, Damian," I said, filling that silence. "It's been a while."

He said nothing, lone eye looking through me, looking past me, to the nomad behind.

"We've come a long way to find you," I finally added. "The least you could do is invite us in."

"Is it really *you* this time?"

"This time?" Shit. Dangerous was one thing. Even *evil* was something I could deal with. But my time with Selene had taught me that insanity was something entirely different. "There's only one me, Bakersfield. You should have realized that years ago when I picked your sweet ass up from the testing facility."

For the first time, that terrible eye focused back on me, and something vaguely human swam in its depths. I didn't know what was going on, but recognized progress when I saw it. I just needed to keep going, to talk one of the most dangerous people I'd ever met off whatever psychotic ledge he'd somehow found himself on, and maybe, just maybe everything would—

A shape brushed past me from behind, heedless of the undead walkers surrounding us or the true monster standing ahead. It had four legs, a mane in need of brushing, and absolutely no brains in its head, and it brushed past Bakersfield too, bumping the Crow with its shoulder before it lowered its head and started to snack on what appeared to be some kind of flower.

I didn't have to breathe, but I held my breath anyway. If that goddamn horse got us all killed…

Damian looked at the creature whose tail was still thwapping against his hip and then back to the rest of us. "Should I ask?" Just like that, the undercurrents of power and menace were gone, leaving his voice hoarse and worn and thin.

"I'd prefer you didn't. That thing right there might be the dumbest creature in existence."

"I don't know," he said, as something like a smile found an uneasy home in his face, "It might face stiff competition from your average teenager."

"See if you still feel that way by the time we're done." My nomad stepped up beside me, immediately getting Bakersfield's attention, and I hurried to introduce them.

"This is Two-Feathers, my ambassador and…"

"And more." It was almost odd to hear humanity in his voice where there'd been nothing at all earlier. He didn't sound like the man I remembered, but now, there was at least a resemblance. "I figured that out from the way he was preparing to defend you."

"Well, he's not always much smarter than the horse. Or teenagers. But he's got his good points too," I admitted. "And I'm not sure I'd have found you at all without him."

"Why try to find me at all? It's a long fucking trip just to say hi, Your Majesty. Or are you here on a job? Did someone in the Free States hire you to kill me when their first attempt failed?"

That answered the question of who had bombed him.

"I don't take jobs anymore. Not unless I want to. That all changed with Dr. Nowhere's death. Which is what I—"

I trailed off. He wasn't paying attention to me anymore, not really, eyes distant.

"Fuck," he said, almost to himself. "They're a day early. *Again.* The timetable keeps moving up."

"They?"

He blinked, as if only now remembering we were there. "Come and see for yourself. We can talk when the killing's done."

"*What* killing?"

He didn't answer, already headed south towards what appeared to be buildings in the grainy twilight, though who and what had built them remained in question. The dead that had encircled us followed with him, a menagerie of monsters that didn't bear any resemblance to anything I'd seen before.

I turned to Two-Feathers. "Stay with the horse and my bike." And then, when he got that look on his face I was starting to recognize and even anticipate, "Please? I don't think you want to be standing anywhere near him during a battle."

My nomad scowled but relented. I hurried after Damian and his squad of the dead.

The buildings, I quickly realized, weren't buildings at all. They were massive battlements, stretching east and west through acres of cleared jungle. Great stone walls that must have been built by undead hands and were now manned by an army of the same.

Which raised the question: why would a Full-Five Crow, who could raise—and likely had—anything he killed need *walls?*

I had a feeling I was about to find out.

I climbed one of about ten staircases on this side of the wall and found Bakersfield above. His menagerie still surrounded him, like a shield of rotted flesh, but there were vastly more troops already positioned. Some were human. Others were unrecognizable.

"Here they come." He pointed toward the jungle that began again almost a mile to our south. I could only vaguely make out shapes spilling forth, some on two-legs and some on four, none of them moving like anything natural. They flooded the open field in seconds, crossing the space to fall upon the army of dead that awaited them.

"Looks like they prioritized speed this time," muttered the Crow at my side, single eye effortlessly piercing the gloom. "We'll see how that works out for them."

"Where do you want me?" I asked.

"Up here on the wall. I'm not sure you'd enjoy fighting them. If they're anything like the last generation, they've got acid for blood."

If I had eyes, I would have blinked. *Generation? Acid* for blood? "What the hell are they?"

"What Tezcatlipoca warned me about, right before he died." This time, the smile on Bakersfield's face was cold and hard, a snarl of bared teeth. Still, as pandemonium erupted beneath us, as the dead and the monstrous crashed against one another like two opposing tides, he spared me a single glance.

"Welcome to the war."

AUTHOR'S NOTE

Well, *that* was an ending, wasn't it? Rest assured; I will *not* leave this particular plot thread dangling. There's a lot of ground to cover in the trilogy's final book, *The Queen of Everything*, and it will start right around where this one left off: The Queen of Smiles, the Lord of the Dead, two armies, a nomad, an electric motorcycle, and one very dumb horse.

This was very much a bridge novel: the middle book in a trilogy and a road trip that ultimately ended as soon as the destination was reached. Even so, it had a lot of important stuff to cover. Her Majesty has taken further steps to re-evaluate her place in the world but remains oblivious to just how human she truly is. She's taken on the mantle of leadership but then left her empire to its own devices to embark on a months-long trip in pursuit of answers she might not actually want or need. She's suborned Kansas City, allied with the nomad clans, and eliminated a major threat in Dallas. Those are actions that other kingdoms and countries are going to take notice of. A big rule of thumb for this world is that every choice should have consequences, and we're going to see those consequences in the next book.

And then there's Two-Feathers, who has never spoken but seems to always have a lot to say. We spent a lot of time in this book on the nomad, on the past that motivated him to join Her Majesty's quest of revenge and the growing feelings that led him to stick around. There was more romance than I initially anticipated, but their relationship is a core piece of the narrative. And given their often-unusual dynamic, they still have a very long way to go as a couple.

Because nothing's ever easy, is it?

I hope you enjoyed the ride! As always, if you enjoyed *The Queen of the Road*, please consider spreading the word and leaving a review. As an indie author, my books depend almost entirely on word of mouth and the feedback and support of readers like you.

Thank you!

ABOUT THE AUTHOR

Chris began life as a gleam in someone's eye, but birth and childhood were quick to follow. He's been fortunate enough to live in Spain, Germany, and all over the United States of America, and is busy planning a tour of the distilleries of Scotland.

A graduate of the Johns Hopkins University's Writing Seminars program, he put that degree to ill use for twenty years as a software engineer but has finally circled back around to the idea of writing for a living.

Chris currently lives in Nevada with his angelic wife and ever-expanding whisky collection and occasionally ventures outside to peer upwards, mutter to himself about 'day stars', and then scurry back into the house.

The Queen of the Road is his eleventh novel, the fifth set in the post-Break world, and the second in *The Storm Who Rides*. Chris frequently shares updates on his author website at https://christullbane.com.

www.ingramcontent.com/pod-product-compliance
Lightning Source LLC
Chambersburg PA
CBHW021226190726
48289CB00005B/1193